OBSESSIVELY YOURS

A STANDALONE FANTASY ROMANCE

JAMIE APPLEGATE HUNTER

FAE KINGS OF EDEN BOOK II

Obsessively Yours

An Unhinged Standalone Fantasy Romance

Fae Kings of Eden Book Two

Obsessively Yours is a work of fiction.

DEDICATION

To everyone who hates the word cunt—

Cunt is the oldest known word in the English language used to
describe female genitalia.
It even predates vagina.

Respect your elders.

WORLD GUIDE

Please note: *this is a guide to use as reference if needed. It does not have to be read before the story.*

HUMANS

- No magic
- Not immortal
- Do not have fated mates

NON-ROYAL FAE

- Stronger and faster than humans
- They can glamour small areas around themselves.
- Their glamour works on humans and animals.
- It takes their magic thirteen years to fully manifest.
- They do not have fated mates unless mated to a royal fae.
- Not immortal

ROYAL FAE

- Stronger and faster than non-royal fae
- Their glamour works on every living creature, including non-royal fae.
- Their glamour is stronger than non-royal fae (they can glamour entire kingdoms at one time).
- They have fated mates.
- Royals traditionally only have one child.
- It takes twenty-five years for their magic to fully manifest.
- They cannot leave their kingdoms until their magic fully manifests at twenty-five years of age.
- Royal fae heirs take over the throne at twenty-five years of age.
- Royal-born fae receive a *familiar* and *familiar* mark on their fifteenth birthday.
- Not immortal

MATES

- Only royal fae have fated mates (their mate can be a non-royal fae).
- On a royal fae's thirteenth birthday, the name of their fated mate is whispered into their minds by the gods.
- Fated mates can feel each other's stronger emotions.
- A mate bond can be broken if one of the mates marries another person before the two fated mates marry.
- A mate bond does not make them love each other.

- Mate bonds are the strongest form of pure magic from the gods and were created to ensure the strongest royal fae heirs.

FAMILIARS

- An animal bonded to a royal-born fae on their fifteenth birthday.
- The "bonded" (royal fae) can see and hear through their *familiar*.
- The bonded receives a tattoo of their *familiar* on their upper left chest at midnight on their fifteenth birthday, and their *familiar* finds them within a few days.
- *Familiars* and their bonded can communicate telepathically.
- *Familiars* have immortal healing to ensure they live as long as their bonded. When their bonded dies, so do they.

KINGDOMS

- Mountain Kingdom (fae—cold, snowy, mountainous)
- Desert Kingdom (fae—desert land with mountains and plateaus, hot days with cold nights)
- Tropical Kingdom (fae—thick canopy of tropical trees, humid, mild temperatures, borders the ocean)
- Garden Kingdom (fae—lush flowery greenery with comfortably mild temperatures all year)

- Human Kingdom (human—surrounded by the four fae kingdoms. Made up of all four habitats, depending on which fae kingdom the human regions border).

Note: Fae kingdoms possess magic that the Human Kingdom does not. Their vegetation, animals, bodies of water, etc. are different and can be dangerous to humans.

THE BARRIER

- A magical wall that protects the humans from the dangerous fae lands
- Fae can pass through the barrier freely, but humans require a fae escort in order for the magic to allow them through.
- The five kingdoms agreed to erect a wall along the barrier with only one gate to each fae kingdom.
- Any fae or human who passes through the barrier must have a legal permit to do so.

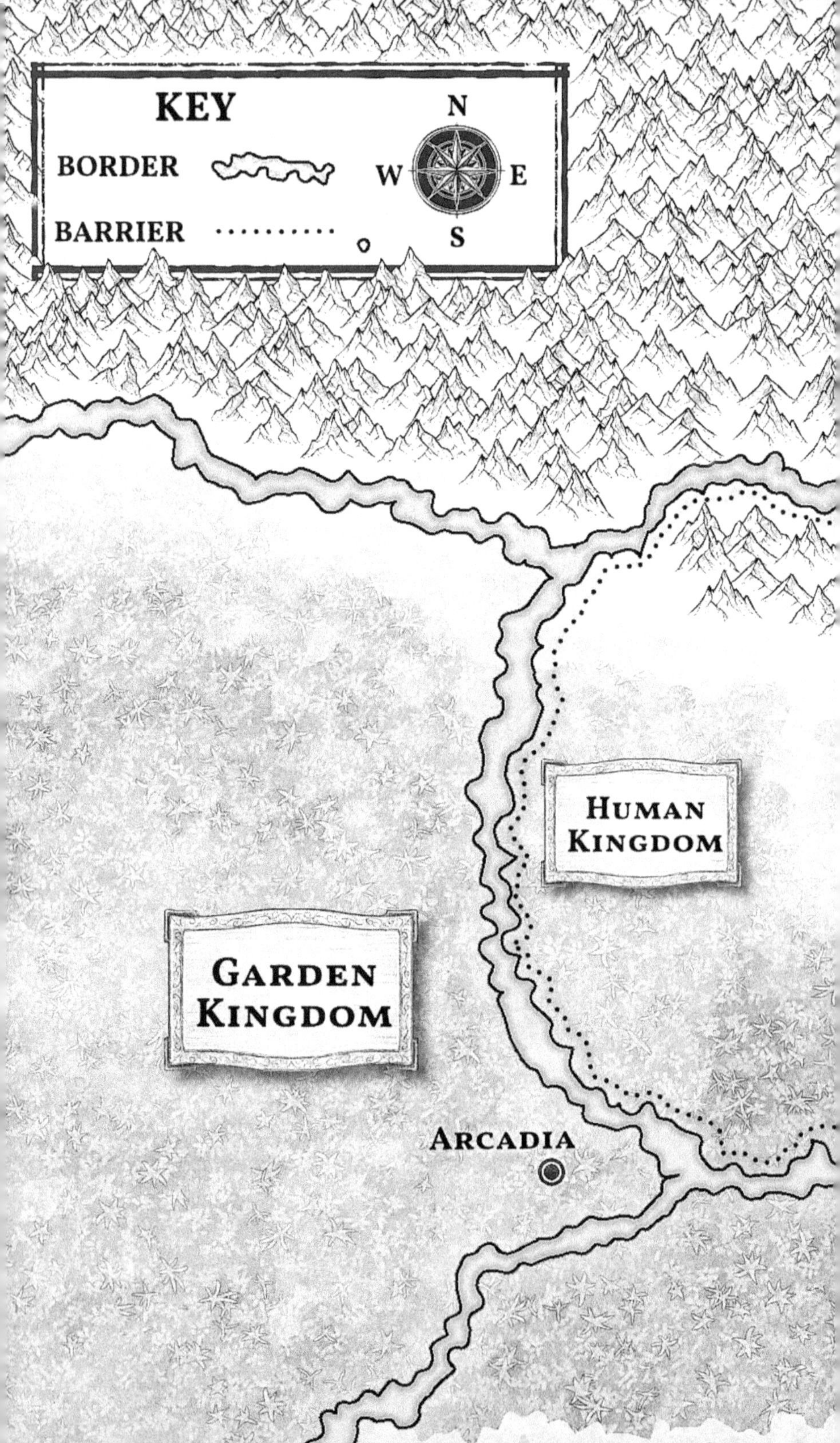

KEY
BORDER
BARRIER
N
W
E
S
HUMAN KINGDOM
GARDEN KINGDOM
ARCADIA

EDEN
MOUNTAIN KINGDOM
VALE
FRIYA
DESERT KINGDOM
LUNARI
TROPICAL KINGDOM
SALTU

SPOTIFY PLAYLIST

SCAN THE QR CODE BELOW TO START LISTENING.

PLEASE NOTE

Content warnings can be found on the last page or on the author's website at www.authorjah.com/content-warnings

THIS IS NOT A LITERARY MASTERPIECE. IT'S NOT EVEN LITERARY MASTERPIECE ADJACENT.

This is an unhinged "fantasy" romance.
It's not your typical romantasy. There's minimal world building, no overarching background plot, and no big villain. The plot focuses **solely on the romance** between the two main characters.

For those of you thinking, *"There's no way someone could write a fantasy romance without a fantasy plot."*
I love your enthusiasm—but you need to lower your expectations.
And then lower them again.

The hero makes a few morally black choices in the name of protecting the heroine, and at some point, you might think, *"That might be too far."*
"Might," as in, you most definitely will think that.
Do not take this book too seriously. It was written to be a fun read with a bit of *"that's fucked up"* thrown into the mix.
You might have a good time. You might not.
Good luck.

YOUNG OBSESSION

1

TEN YEARS OLD

There is nothing worse than being forced to participate in physical activity, Violet thought sullenly as Vivian, her identical twin sister, stared at her with a twinge of annoyance.

Violet tried to push her dark auburn hair away from her face, but the sweat made it stick to her light tan skin. She hated sweating almost as much as she hated sparring.

Vivian wanted to become a warrior in the Tropical Kingdom battalion someday, and unlike Violet, she loved training with their father. They were close, closer than she and Violet. Vivian thrived under their father's approval, like she needed it to be happy.

Violet preferred to wander through the cool, shaded jungle looking for pretty flowers to make into crowns. Yet here she stood, trying to catch her breath, wondering if someone could die from too much exercise.

"Raise your sword," Vivian instructed. Violet raised her wooden weapon and considered whacking it against the ground until it broke. She only subjected herself to Vivian's lessons to spend more time with her sister.

"You're not standing right," her sister said patiently. "Position your legs like this." For the twentieth time that day, she demonstrated the correct form. It wasn't that Violet didn't know it; it was that she'd been trying to catch her breath between rounds, but Vivian thought they needed to start again immediately.

Violet begrudgingly mirrored her sister's stance, arms shaking from the weight of the sword. Even though fae were faster and stronger than humans, they still had to work out their muscles to build their strength. Vivian always teased Violet that she was weaker than a human.

"Ready?" her sister asked.

No. Violet nodded.

Vivian rushed forward, slicing her sword through the air with deadly precision. Violet didn't move fast enough and screamed when her sister's sword connected with her temple. She stumbled and fell flat on her back, the impact knocking the breath out of her.

Vivian screamed, too, and dropped to the ground. Violet's sword had flown from her hand and hit her sister in the face.

I knew sparring would kill me one day, Violet thought as she stared at the blinding sun, unable to breathe.

A boy about their age with blondish-brown hair and a slight sunburn tinting his cheeks ran over and crouched next to Violet on the ground. "Are you okay?" he asked, cautiously touching her forehead.

Behind them, Vivian cried and held a hand over her eye. "Viv," Violet mumbled with spots dancing in her vision. *Is she okay?* "Viv?"

"Shh," the boy soothed. "Don't talk." His eyes were kind and concerned as they gazed down at her, but they hardened as he swung around to glare at Vivian. "What is wrong with you?"

"I didn't mean to," Vivian insisted through her sobs. "She was supposed to duck."

"You told me she's a lost cause at fighting," the boy snapped. "I saw you swing as hard as you could."

Violet struggled to sit up and saw Vivian's face fill with hurt. *They know each other?* Vivian had never mentioned a boy, and he didn't go to their school.

"It's not my fault she's slow," Vivian retorted, her cries softening into sniffles.

Violet frowned. She wasn't *that* slow.

Their parents, who'd been speaking with a friend of theirs on the other side of the small park, heard the commotion and rushed over. Their mother gasped when she saw the three children on the ground; Vivian with a small cut on her cheek and a red eye that would likely bruise, and Violet with blood coating the side of her head and face.

The boy stood and moved out of the way so their father could scoop Violet into his arms to carry her toward the house while their mother assisted Vivian inside. Violet tried to look over her shoulder at the boy to thank him.

He stared after her with an unreadable expression on his face, and she gave him an appreciative smile. His eyes lit up, and he waved before turning to leave. She'd have to ask Vivian his name and how they knew each other.

Once they arrived home and both girls were cleaned up, their father tore into Vivian, scolding her for being too rough with her sister. Violet tried to interject on her sister's behalf, to explain that it was an accident, but their father wouldn't hear it.

Vivian's face fell, her chin wobbling. Violet didn't blame her. If anyone understood that accidents could happen in sparring, it was their father, but he'd berated her anyway.

Violet tried to comfort her twin later, but Vivian wouldn't

speak to her for an entire week, and once she did, things were never the same. Something changed within Vivian that day. She trained harder, played with Violet less and less, and wore cruel sarcasm like armor.

2

TWELVE YEARS OLD

Violet rushed through the halls of the palace toward the school rooms, furious with herself for losing track of time. She loved collecting shells and pebbles on the shore to make jewelry or sew onto her clothes. She'd risen early that morning and ventured through the jungle to the beach since morning low tide provided a better selection of treasures than any other time of day.

As the daughter of a general in the Tropical Kingdom's battalion, her family lived on the warrior compound located within the palace walls. The children in the compound attended a school located inside of the palace, which was both a blessing and a curse. A blessing because it was close to Violet's home, but a curse because her mother worked as a cook in the palace kitchens and knew before the end of the day if one of her daughters misbehaved.

Violet glanced at a large golden clock hanging in the palace hallway and groaned. Ms. Bonner, their teacher with the personality of an ornery stable cat, would scold her in front of the entire class if she arrived late. Violet could see it now. Her permanent scowl would deepen as she shook her head, the dangling earrings adorning her pointed ears clanging against themselves.

Running around the next corner toward the school rooms, Violet collided with someone and bounced backward. The momentum sent her sprawling across the floor, and her treasures scattered everywhere.

"I'm sorry," she apologized and pushed to an upright position. "I shouldn't have been running." She tilted her head up and froze. Roman Covington, heir to the Tropical throne and the cutest boy in all of Saltu, stood over her with a startled expression. She couldn't help but admire how his short sandy blond hair looked nice against his slightly sun-tanned skin. The lightest brown eyes she'd ever seen stared back at her, and to her utter mortification, she realized she'd stared too long. *Great, he probably thinks I'm strange.* "I'm sorry," she said again.

He lowered his already muscular body to her level, his focus still on her. "No, I'm sorry. I was trying to get to class and wasn't watching where I was going."

Violet dared to look at him again. "You were going the wrong way." She pointed behind him. "The school rooms are still upstairs. They keep us in the same room every year."

The prince hadn't joined their school until last year. Before that, he took private lessons with the royal tutors. He always had a serious expression on his face and seemed mature for his twelve years of age. Violet thought he acted *at least* sixteen.

The points of his ears turned pink. "I wasn't paying attention," he mumbled and gathered her books while she scooped up her shells and pebbles.

Most of the shells had broken in the fall, and she groaned. Roman shoved the books into her bag and glanced down at the shards in her hands. "What are those?"

She dumped the broken pieces into her satchel. "Shells I collected this morning."

"You were at the shore this morning?" He scooped up more of the broken pieces and studied them before dropping them into her bag. "Are they important?"

She shrugged. "It doesn't matter. I'll find more tomorrow."

"I can help you look," he offered.

Violet lifted her gaze to his, her lips parting in surprise. "You don't have to do that. Thank you, though."

After scooping up the rest of the broken shards, Roman helped her stand. "You're Viv's twin sister. Violet, right?"

Roman and Violet had never interacted until now, but it didn't surprise her that he knew Vivian. Everyone did, and Violet was simply known as "Vivian Maekin's twin sister."

Where Violet was quiet until she knew someone better, Vivian was loud; Violet liked clothes, jewelry, and decorating things, while Vivian liked fighting and strategy games. Vivian and Roman trained as junior warriors together, but Violet only saw him in passing.

At least he hadn't mistaken her for Vivian and actually knew her name. Since Violet and Vivian were identical, people sometimes got them confused. Violet never understood how. Their clothes, personalities, and hobbies screamed *complete opposites*. The day Vivian walked around in flowery dresses and beaded jewelry would be the day horses walked on water.

"That's me." Adjusting her book bag on her shoulder, she motioned toward the stairs. "We should get to class."

Roman fell in step beside her and tapped the satchel draped across her torso. "What do you do with the shells?"

She pulled back the flowy sleeve of her dress to reveal a row of bracelets. "I like making jewelry and other things."

He reached out and twirled one around her wrist. His

fingers brushed against her skin, sending tingles up her arm. "I like them. Maybe you can make me one someday."

Violet forced herself not to giggle like a little girl. "I don't know if they'd look good on you," she teased, hoping she sounded nonchalant.

His crooked smile made her insides flutter, and she blushed harder. At this rate, her face would stay permanently red. When they reached the classroom door, he held it open for her and followed her inside. "See you around, Violet."

The prince lifted his chin to another boy in the back and wove his way through the desks while Violet stood at the front of the class, searching for an empty seat. She felt eyes on her and fought the need to flee.

She noted the full desks around her best friend, Griff, who lifted his shoulder apologetically.

"Find a seat, Miss Maekin," Ms. Bonner clipped, the older woman's sharp voice making Violet jump.

Roman waved to get her attention, and her heart skipped a beat when he pointed to the empty desk next to him. With hot cheeks that would never cool, Violet hurried down the aisle and sat down. "Thanks."

"Look around at your neighbors," Ms. Bonner told the class. Violet's desk backed into a wall. Roman sat to her right, a girl named Millie sat in front of her, and a boy named Theo sat on her left.

"These are your assigned seats for the rest of the year."

Griff turned to look at Violet across the room and mouthed, *"Sorry."* He'd promised to save her a seat.

She lifted her hand and sliced her finger across her throat, making Griff laugh. They'd met two years ago when she was running back from the forest and twisted her ankle. He'd stood over her, pushed his black hair behind his ear, and said, "You're supposed to stay upright when you run."

She'd told him to buzz off as he'd helped her up, and they'd been friends ever since, but junior warrior training started last year, and he'd been spending more time with the other trainees and less time with her. Violet understood, but it made the fact that she only had one close friend glaringly obvious.

As class droned on, Violet kept her eyes straight ahead and furiously took notes, struggling to keep up with the teacher's rapid explanation of the Human Kingdom's wildlife compared to the fae kingdoms'. The four fae kingdoms—Mountain, Desert, Tropical, and Garden—surrounded the Human King-dom. A magic barrier erected by the gods thousands of years ago prevented humans from crossing into fae lands without a fae escort. No one knew for sure why the humans couldn't pass through the barrier on their own, but scholars theorized it was because they had no protection against the fae beasts. According to Ms. Bonner, anyway.

Not only were fae faster and stronger than humans, but they also had glamour—magic that allowed them to make humans and animals see whatever they wanted them to. It also helped protect them against the animals in the fae lands, which were infinitely more dangerous than those in the human lands. Some animals were the same, but most weren't.

Violet covertly glanced at Roman. As a royal fae, he and his parents were stronger and faster than non-royal fae, and their glamour worked on other fae as well, whereas non-royal fae could only glamour humans and animals, but not each other.

Roman could make the entire class see a giant wulfer waltz through the door if he wanted. She smiled faintly at the image of Ms. Bonner screeching at the sight.

Other than stronger magic, royal fae had two things non-royal fae didn't: *familiars* and mates.

Familiars were animals royals bonded to on their fifteenth birthday, and a mate was the only person a royal could marry.

Royals and their mates were born on the same day. Violet wondered if she and the prince had the same birthday. Roman caught her staring and lifted a brow with a knowing smirk.

She jolted out of her ridiculous thoughts as mortification shot through her. Next time she came across a beast in the forest, she'd forego glamour and let it eat her.

Violet resumed taking notes and prayed Roman would never look at her again. Better yet, maybe she could transfer to the other school in Saltu. Despite being the capital, Saltu was fairly small, and the walk wouldn't be too far.

A few minutes later, a folded piece of paper landed on Violet's desk, and she froze. It came from Roman's direction, but she refused to look at him.

With a steadying breath, she unfolded the paper.

Is sitting next to me that bad?

What? Violet peeked at Roman, who watched her, that same smirk still in place. She bit her lip and hurriedly wrote back.

Why do you say that?

After checking to ensure Ms. Bonner wasn't looking, she tossed the paper on his desk and turned her attention back to their teacher. Tried to, at least. *Roman Covington wrote me a note.*

Her stomach flipped when the paper landed on her desk again, and she tried to look aloof as she opened it.

· · ·

You threatened to kill your friend.

Violet's eyes slid to the prince. His body faced forward as he wrote in his notebook, but she could see him fighting a smile. Had he been watching her, or did he happen to look over at the right time? Violet scribbled her reply and discreetly tossed it back.

A threat means it might not happen. I'm actually going to kill him.

Roman laughed out loud, and the sound bounced off the stone walls. Violet sank down in her chair when everyone, including Ms. Bonner, swiveled their gazes to the back of the room.

Violet glared at Roman, and he clamped his mouth closed, puffing out his cheeks to hold in his laughter. When everyone turned back around, she looked him dead in the eye and slid her finger across her throat.

He drew everyone's attention again with his uncontrollable laughter, only this time, Violet laughed too.

The next morning, Violet hurried into the classroom and slid into her seat at the back of the class. Thoughts of seeing Roman again had kept her awake all night. *Will he write another note?*

When the prince waltzed in, she held her breath and pretended to read over her work from yesterday. A small canvas sack plunked down on her desk, and she pulled back with a start. Roman sat down without looking her way.

She turned her attention back to the bag and noticed a piece of paper attached to the twine holding the sack closed. Violet ate up the words, and she bit her cheek to keep from squealing.

Sorry about yesterday. My mother helped me pick these out. I hope you like them.

Violet's hands trembled as she untied the string and opened the bag.

Pretty shells of all shapes, sizes, and colors stared back at her. Violet worried her heart would tire of beating furiously and stop entirely. Folding up the note, she stuck it inside of the bag and carefully placed them in her satchel.

She dug out a charcoal pencil and a piece of paper, scribbled her reply, and tossed it across the aisle.

I guess I won't kill you after all.

Ms. Bonner scowled in their direction when Roman's laughter filled the room.

Violet decided it was her favorite sound in all of Eden.

3

THIRTEEN YEARS OLD

"You look sick," Ares, Roman's best friend, remarked as they walked through the palace toward the prince's rooms.

He wasn't wrong; Roman *did* feel like puking. Tomorrow, at midnight on his thirteenth birthday, the gods would whisper the name of his fated mate into his mind for only him to hear. It happened to all royal fae on their thirteenth birthday, and the thought of a random voice in his mind freaked him out.

Very few people knew when Roman's birthday was in order to keep parents of children born on the same day as him from bombarding the capital, and he'd made a point to not know the birthdays of any girls his age. What if he met someone who shared his birthday and liked them, only for the gods to mate him with someone else?

His mother said he was too young to worry about things like that, but what did she expect? He hadn't grown up around other children. Other than his parents and a few select warriors, guards, and palace staff, he rarely interacted with anyone else. He'd endured a ruthless training regime from the time he could walk, and when he wasn't training, they forced him to study.

He didn't know how to act his age.

And he hated it.

Thanks to his tutors and parents, he knew the importance of mates, and that royal fae *had* to marry their mate or it could mean the downfall of their kingdom. A mate bond contained the strongest magic in existence and kept the royal bloodlines strong, allowing them to protect their kingdoms in ways non-royal fae could not.

Roman thought, like many other things in their history, it was ridiculous. Ruling based on bloodlines had the potential to end horribly. What if the heir was a terrible person?

Ares jostled Roman's shoulder, shaking him from his thoughts. "You'd be sick too if you had to meet your future wife at thirteen," Roman told him. He reached into his pocket and pulled out a small shape-shifting puzzle. They were small puzzles that were a jumbled mess with all different colored pieces, and when twisted correctly, they made a certain shape.

His father once took him to a shape-shifting puzzle competition, and he'd been enamored ever since. He'd hoped his father would let him compete someday.

He twisted the pieces into place, easily seeing the connections in his mind.

Ares tapped the top of the puzzle, stopping Roman's progress. "Viv's birthday is tomorrow too," he informed the prince with a sly smile.

Roman said nothing as they rounded the corner toward his rooms. He'd heard her mention it earlier that day to a group of junior warriors. This past week made him grateful his parents had insisted on keeping his birthday a secret all his life. A week ago, invitations to his thirteenth birthday ball went out. Since he'd know who his mate was tomorrow, there was no longer a reason to keep it a secret.

Barely two days after the invitations went out, three different girls he'd never met approached him, claiming their birthday was tomorrow too. The rest of the week had held more of the same.

Vivian was less conspicuous about it. Instead of telling him outright, she'd announced it to others loud enough for Roman to hear.

Vivian Maekin. She was okay, he guessed, but she annoyed him with her constant bragging and need for attention. All the junior warriors liked her, but something about her didn't sit right with him.

That means Violet's birthday is tomorrow too. The thought made his lips curl into a small smile. *Being mated to her would be fun.*

He and Violet had formed a friendship last year, but during the long break between school years, they rarely saw each other. It didn't stop him from thinking about her, though.

This year they sat on opposite sides of the room, and their friendship had dwindled to greetings in the hallways and the occasional quick conversation.

"You're smiling," Ares accused smugly.

Roman's smile dropped. "This past week proved a lot of girls share my birthday," he reminded him. "Not just Vivian." *Or Violet.*

"You two like a lot of the same stuff," his friend pointed out. "Sparring, boring strategy gam—oof!"

Roman cut him off with an elbow to the gut and reached out to keep him from falling down the stairs. "I don't want to talk about it anymore." He steadied his friend and went back to his puzzle.

Ares rubbed his stomach and wisely changed the subject. "I'm going to have a bruise."

He held up the now star-shaped puzzle with a face splitting grin and tossed it to his best friend. "Good."

Later that night, Roman stared at his reflection in the mirror and adjusted his green royal coat. Every kingdom had a royal color, and he'd always liked the vibrant green of the Tropical Kingdom.

Facing away from the mirror, he scanned the room. Hanging clothes, two mirrors, and multiple cabinets housing his various shoes and accessories lined two of the walls. He plopped down on one of the plush benches in the middle of the room and stared glumly at the other two empty walls where his mate's things would one day go.

He grabbed the collar of his coat and tugged. When he inherited the throne, his first order of business would be a new style of coat because these itched like crazy.

Roman added "wearing uncomfortable clothing" to the growing list of reasons he hated formal events.

No amount of begging would get him out of this one, though. Tropical Kingdom tradition dictated that royals host a ball on the heir's milestone years: finding their mate at thirteen, gaining their *familiar* at fifteen, marrying their mate at twenty-two, and ascending the throne at twenty-five. To his detriment, his mother loved parties and said she would start throwing him one every year.

His mother, Sarah, walked into his dressing room in a long green dress to match his and his father's coats. "Are you ready, honey?" Her blonde hair, the same color as Roman's, resembled a weird ball on the side of her head, and it poked him in the face when she hugged him.

Roman pulled out of her grasp and tried not to look sullen. "I'm ready."

After being announced and led into the ballroom by the king and queen's royal guard, Roman's mother kissed the top of his head. "Go tell your friends hello and meet us on the dais."

If Roman tried to find Ares in the crowd, dozens of people he barely knew would stop him for a chat. Hiding seemed like a better option. Nodding to his mother, he turned on his heel and strode toward the nondescript side door leading to the smaller balcony.

Guests seldom used the small balcony because it had no view other than the tropical trees beyond the palace walls. The main balcony overlooked the gardens and was a party favorite.

He closed the door behind him, crossed to the railing, and stared out into the colorful trees. Roman had never traveled to the Human Kingdom because magic bound him to the Tropical Kingdom until he was twenty-five, but he'd seen pictures. Their trees and plants were dull compared to the rainbow foliage in the fae lands.

An amused voice interrupted his thoughts. "Are you hiding too?"

I know that voice. Roman pushed back from the railing and turned toward the shadows on the far end of the balcony. He stepped closer and made out the faint outline of a person perched on the railing. "Violet?"

Fabric rustled and shoes slapped softly against the ground as the shadowy figure jumped down. "Were you expecting someone else?"

Roman's retort died on his tongue when Violet stepped into the light. Her reddish-dark hair, normally twisted back, hung in loose waves around her face with a small crown of light purple flowers resting on top. Had she put something on her eyelashes, or were they always that dark? He didn't know, but they looked nice against her blue eyes.

Her lips looked more pink than usual, and instead of the loose dresses she wore to school, the dark purple gown she wore hugged her upper body tightly. She reminded him of a faerietale princess.

Roman swallowed hard and pulled at his collar, unable to form words. *Gods, she's pretty.*

Violet adjusted the flowers in her hair. "Why are you staring at me like that?"

No excuse came to him, leaving only the truth at his disposal. "You look pretty." His shoulders eased, and he tried not to grin when her cheeks flamed in response. She blushed a lot. "Why are you hiding?"

The pink receded and she lifted a brow defiantly. "I asked you first." Her shoes whispered against the ground as she stepped closer. "Are you nervous about tonight?"

He ran a hand through his hair and winced. His mother would kill him for messing it up. "I hate big celebrations."

Violet's head tilted to the side. "Really? You seem like someone who would enjoy the attention."

He frowned at her. "Why would you think that?"

"You're always surrounded by a group of people." She hung her hands on her hips, daring him to argue.

Stepping closer, he leaned forward and stage whispered, "Are you stalking me?"

Violet dropped her arms and fluffed her skirt without meeting his gaze. "It's hard to miss large groups of people."

Is she nervous?

Roman wanted to smile like an idiot. "I don't think my friends count." He used the word *friends* loosely. Most people around him were only there because of his title. Leaning back against the railing, he sighed dramatically. "I have to stand on the dais with my parents and shake hands all night. It's boring."

Violet lifted herself onto the railing beside Roman. He started to steady her but yanked his hand back at her amused expression. "Sorry," he muttered. "I thought you might fall." His coat felt tighter around his neck, and he pulled at the stiff fabric. "Why are *you* hiding?"

The insects of the forest chirped through the quiet. She blew out a loud breath. "I don't like parties either."

She seemed embarrassed, but he didn't know why. "Is Griff not here?"

Griff was the only person he'd seen her with regularly. Not that he watched her all the time or anything.

"He's with the other junior warriors, and I didn't want to tag along and listen to them talk about stabbing things." Roman laughed, and she smirked in response. "I would've stayed home if my mother had let me."

"Me too," he mumbled under his breath. "What about Vivian?" As one of the top junior warriors in their class, Vivian had a ton of friends. Surely Violet knew them too.

Violet shifted uncomfortably on the railing, and Roman knew he'd assumed incorrectly. "We see each other enough at home."

He almost asked why that mattered—they were sisters, after all—but the look on her face told him to drop it. "We can hide out here together," he offered instead and climbed up beside her.

The balcony door opened, and Roman's mother stepped outside. "I've been looking everywhere for you." She glanced at Violet and smiled warmly. "Hello, Violet. You'll have to excuse Roman." She looked back at him, her face hardening. "To the dais, *now*." With a final warning glare, she disappeared inside.

Roman groaned and jumped down, reluctant to go. "I guess I'll see you later."

"Wait." Violet slid off the railing, and Roman fought the urge to pick her up and set her down safely. She dug into a secret pocket in her dress, and he homed in on the movement, wondering how many pockets that thing had. She produced an envelope and held it out. "Happy Birthday."

Roman stared at the envelope, shocked anyone other than his parents had gotten him something.

Violet withdrew her arm. "Never mind. It's stupid. Happy birthday, Roman." She tried to hurry past him, but he reached out and snagged the gift from her grasp.

"Hey!" She swiped at the paper, but he held it out of her reach.

"You said this is mine."

"Actually, I didn't." Every inch of her exposed skin glowed bright red. He liked it. A lot. "Give it back."

Roman's face split into a wide grin. He felt genuinely happy for the first time all week. "No. It's my present, and I want it."

Violet stomped her foot with a small *harrumph*. "You don't have to pretend to want it. It's just a stupid card."

The lumpy envelope rattled when he shook it. "It sounds like more than a card. No one gives me gifts, and I want it."

After an intense stare off, she rolled her eyes. "Fine. Goodbye."

Roman stared after her as she spun around and marched toward the ballroom door. "Thank you, princess," he called after her, earning himself a glare before she slipped inside.

Later that night, Roman stared at the bracelet of green pebbles in his hand, then read the note again.

. . .

Roman,

You may not remember, but last year you said you liked my bracelets and maybe you'd want one someday. I know you think you were kidding, but I saw the way your eyes watered because you didn't have one. (You didn't have to cry, I would have made you one if you'd asked nicely).

I decided to forgo shells since they break easily with your nasty habit of running into things. I don't know your favorite color and decided on green stones to match your royal coat.

It's a terrible color, really. A shame they make you wear something the color of human grass. It would be better if it were a prettier color, like purple. Maybe even a nice shade of violet. *I bet you can change it when you're king. (hint hint)*

Anyway, happy birthday, Roman.

Violet

P.S. Don't be nervous about tonight. I'm sure whoever your mate is will look very nice in human-grass-green too.

Roman's laugh bounced around his bedroom, and he held up the green stone bracelet to inspect it closer. *Violet Maekin.*

"What are you smiling at, honey?" his mother asked as she and his father walked into the room.

Roman stashed the letter and bracelet in his side table and stood. "Nothing." Upon his parents' arrival, Roman's nerves returned full force.

One look at his face, and his mother wrapped him in a tight hug. "There's nothing to be nervous about. When I heard your father's name, it was the best night of my life."

She smiled at Roman's father, Felix, and patted his arm. "From the time I met your mother at eight years old, I knew she would be mine, and I told her so."

"It's true." His mother sighed dreamily. "The day before

our thirteenth birthday, he said the gods would say his name." She pecked her husband on the cheek. "He was right."

Roman's mind flashed to Ares' comment about Vivian. "What if I don't like my mate?"

His father patted him on the back. "You'll make it work. You have to."

"I know." Roman sighed and raked a hand through his already disheveled hair. "I have to keep the bloodline strong." He was sick of having the sentiment shoved down his throat.

If a kingdom suffered an attack, a royal could glamour their citizens to be invisible to the attacking forces. Other than that, why did they need to be stronger? There hadn't been an attack of that magnitude since before the gods placed the barrier.

Supposedly, having children with a fated mate was the only way to keep the bloodline strong, but no royal had ever married anyone other than their fated mate to test the theory.

"What if my mate lives in another kingdom?"

His mother patted his arm. "Don't worry, honey. Your father or I would travel to each kingdom to check the birth records."

Without me, Roman thought bitterly. Royal fae only had one child and the heir's magic didn't manifest fully until they turned twenty-five. Fae drew their magic from the fae lands, and if a royal heir left before their magic fully developed, it could weaken them. To prevent this, the gods used magic to bind royal fae to their kingdoms until their twenty-fifth birthdays.

A stupid rule, in Roman's opinion. Why couldn't the royal heirs go to other fae kingdoms? He understood why they couldn't go into the Human Kingdom. No magic filled their lands, but other fae kingdoms had just as much magic as the next.

Stupid.

His mother clapped excitedly, breaking him from his disgruntled thoughts, and ushered everyone into Roman's sitting room to have a seat. "It's almost time."

Roman sat in one of the large wing-backed chairs and feigned nonchalance, though his knuckles turned white from their harrowing grip on the chair's arms. The golden clock's second hand ticked at a snail's pace. His palms slicked with nerves.

When the clock struck midnight, he closed his eyes, and a voice not of this world resounded through his mind.

Vivian.

Acid churned in his stomach and crawled up his throat. Vivian? Disappointment tunneled through him, followed by dread.

Maybe the voice didn't mean Vivian Maekin. He once asked his mother why the gods didn't give the mate's surname. She said it was because in the early days, surnames didn't exist.

But they're gods, he'd thought at the time. *Can't they update their ways?* At this point, he thought the gods were dead or liked to screw with the people of Eden with one ridiculous rule after the other.

However, the knowledge that it might not be Vivian Maekin didn't make him feel any better.

Roman opened his eyes and looked at his parents. "Her name is Vivian."

His mother's smile faltered, but she recovered with ease. "The Maekin twins share the same birthday as you." She reached forward and clasped his hand. "We'll go to her tomorrow to confirm." She turned her brilliant smile to his father. "Isn't this wonderful? She comes from a family we've known for years." His mother gave him a watery smile. "I'm happy for you, honey. You two have a lot in common, and I know you'll be happy together."

Why does everyone keep saying that?

He looked away, hoping she wouldn't see the disappointment on his face. "We do."

But would that be enough?

Violet paced the length of her room, too nervous to eat lunch with the rest of her family. What had she been thinking giving Roman that stupid bracelet? She'd meant it to be funny, but in hindsight, it was dumb.

Anxiety crept over her skin thanks to something she dared not utter aloud. She wanted to be Roman's mate. She'd harbored a crush on the prince since last year, and something inside of her *knew* they were meant to be together. Would he be upset if the gods bonded him to her?

Violet flopped down on her bed and stared at the ceiling. Last night, she'd prayed to the gods to make them mates. *Pathetic.*

Mates could feel each other's emotions, and that morning, Vivian had claimed she'd felt someone else's emotions. Violet's stomach soured. She and Roman belonged together, she could feel it, but a small seed of doubt bloomed in her gut. Even if Viv had lied about feeling something in her chest, Violet didn't feel anything.

After her declaration, Vivian had looked at Violet with triumph, as if she'd won a game Violet didn't know they were playing. Vivian treated everything between them as a competition, and Violet hated it. It had never been that way until the day she'd accidentally hurt Violet, trying to teach her to sword fight. If Violet could go back, she'd have never agreed to train with Vivian that day. Or ever.

Since then, there'd been a rift between them, one that hurt

deeply. She didn't understand why her sister blamed her for their father's reaction; Violet hadn't asked their father to yell at Viv. But since that day, Vivian had tried her hardest to make her look bad. Not just in front of their parents; in front of everyone.

A commanding knock on their front door startled Violet from the memory, and she sprang off the bed. Everything in her buzzed with excitement. *Oh my gods.*

She tried to act unaffected as she walked into the family room and watched her father cross to the door. Her father, Edgar, was tall and broad like most fae, with dark golden-tan skin, black hair, and dark brown eyes that creased at the corners from laughing. He had a proud, prominent nose and heavy brows. He was an unshakeable force. *Usually.*

Today, Violet noted the way he wiped his palms on his pants and took a deep breath before reaching for the door handle. No one in their household voiced it, but they'd all been anxious for today, as had every family with a child who shared a birthday with the prince.

Her father opened the door to reveal King Felix and Queen Sarah on the other side. Violet sucked in a sharp breath, and Vivian cut her eyes in her direction with a cruel smirk.

"Hello, Edgar," King Felix greeted politely. Felix was bigger than Violet's father, with light brown hair, medium-beige skin, and Roman's light brown eyes. He smiled politely at Violet's mother. "Meri, it's good to see you."

Her mother dipped into a slight curtsey. "Likewise, Your Grace. And you, Your Grace," she said to Queen Sarah, who had discreetly moved between Meri and her husband.

The queen possessed flawless skin the color of Roman's, dark sandy-blonde hair free of grey, and hazel eyes that always seemed to sparkle. Everyone's gazes moved to the door when Roman walked in, his hair styled neatly for once. His gaze collided with Violet's, and when his lips tipped into a small grin, she almost fainted. *I knew it.*

But when he turned and moved farther into the room toward Vivian, confusion, realization, and horror took turns assaulting her. Violet watched in slow motion as he bowed to her twin and said something, to which Vivian nodded. Violet would never know what he'd said because embarrassment and heartbreak blocked out her surroundings.

She approached the others with forced happiness. "This is exciting."

Vivian's condescending smile made Violet want to hit her, an urge she'd never had before. "I get to be queen, Vi. Can you believe it?"

The thought of being queen hadn't crossed Violet's mind. She'd been too focused on getting to spend forever with Roman. She begrudgingly admitted that Vivian would make a great warrior queen—someone who could fight alongside Roman to defend their kingdom. Violet could never have lived up to that role.

"It suits you," Violet forced out and faced Roman. "You two will chop people down together like the heroes in adventure books." She made a slashing motion in the air, and Roman twisted his lips to unsuccessfully suppress his laughter.

The adults joined in, and Vivian's eyes cut to Violet, her mouth curved down in a vicious frown. Before anyone else noticed, Vivian's smile slipped back into place.

"What happens now?" Vivian asked.

Their father gestured for everyone to have a seat, and their mother offered to make tea.

"It's tradition in the Tropical Kingdom to keep the identity of the heir's mate hidden from the public until after they graduate school," King Felix began. "Once we reveal Vivian as the future queen, all eyes will be on her, and we don't want that for any of the children." He patted Roman on the back. "It's bad enough my boy has to go through it."

The king spoke the truth. It was well known that royal mates were not announced until after they finished school. Their classmates were used to Roman by now, as were most of the warriors and palace staff, but that didn't stop them from falling over themselves to gain his attention. The townspeople gawked on the rare occasions they saw a royal in town.

Queen Sarah leaned forward conspiratorially. "Felix and I understand more than anyone how it can sometimes be hard to hide your affection for one another." King Felix's eyes shone with so much adoration that Violet had to focus on something else. The thought of Roman showing her sister affection made her heart twist.

"But we ask that you are discreet," the queen continued. "It's as much for Vivian's safety as it is for her privacy."

"Violet," her father reprimanded. "Are you paying attention?"

Dear gods, I know you didn't answer my prayer last night, but could you please *open the ground to swallow me whole?* She waited and sighed when the floor beneath her stayed intact. "Yes, sir. We can't tell anyone that Viv is Roman's mate." She lifted her hand in a small salute, and Roman coughed to cover a laugh.

Her father muttered something under his breath, and Queen Sarah looked as amused as her son. Violet ignored Vivian's glare, knowing her sister hated any positive attention Violet received.

The adults droned on while Violet lived through the biggest disappointment of her life. Eventually, the Covingtons left, leaving her with a sister who wouldn't stop yapping about being the future queen, digging the knife a little deeper each time.

4

FOURTEEN YEARS OLD

Roman and Violet sat with a game board between them in the Maekin's family room, arguing over the legality of Violet's move.

Once a week, Roman joined the Maekins for dinner. His parents insisted he, his mate, and his future in-laws get to know one another better. At first, he'd protested, claiming it would make people suspicious that one of the twins was his mate. His father pointed out he could glamour himself invisible when he slipped in and out of their home. Knowing he couldn't get out of it, Roman had decided to try.

Vivian's father insisted on giving her extra training now that she would have a target on her back as the future queen, and the two didn't return home until an hour before dinner. So every week, Roman would arrive an hour before dinner to spend time with his mate before they ate.

His mother and father assured him his affection for Viv would grow if they spent more time together. It hadn't.

What *had* developed was his eagerness to see Violet. She made him laugh; a stark contrast to her sister, who made him want to stuff his ears with sand to cut off her constant stream of self-importance.

Lately, he'd found himself arriving two or three hours early to hang out with Violet under the guise of getting to know his future family better. Meri gave him a curious look the first few times he'd showed up early. *"I don't want to cut into my time with Vivian,"* he'd lied. *"It's important I get to know all of you."*

"You can't move that piece," Roman insisted. "That piece has already moved ten spaces."

Violet looked indignant. "It has not. It moved three spaces on the first round." She pointed at the board. "Then four spaces on the second, and three on the third." She looked at him like he was dense. "That's only eight spaces."

He rolled his lips together and tried not to laugh. "That's ten, princess. Count them again."

Violet glared at the checkered board. "How are strategy games fun when you have to do homework to play them?"

Roman turned his head to compose himself. She might throw the board at him if she saw him smile. "A piece can only move ten spaces. That's hardly a full sheet of homework."

She reached across the board to thump his nose, but he grabbed her wrist and pulled her forward. "I'll write down every piece ten times, bind the pages with leather, and hit you with it," Violet threatened. "We'll see if it's enough to be considered homework then."

Their close proximity made Roman's body buzz, and he dropped her wrist to lean back. Drumming his fingers on the table, he debated asking the question that'd been bugging him all day. "Are you and Theo dating?" he blurted out. *Smooth.*

Violet's brows shot skyward. "Theo Bront? Why do you ask?"

Roman stared at the gameboard and grappled for an

answer he didn't know himself. *Why* do *I care?* "I noticed you sitting with him and his friends at lunch." *And laughing.*

Violet pinned him with a curious stare. "Griff sat there too. Who else would I sit with?"

Me.

Griff sat on the *other* side of the table, while Theo and Violet sat next to each other, but Roman decided not to point that out. "I'm trying to look out for you. I don't like Theo."

Violet bristled and sat taller. "I can look out for myself."

Roman leaned forward and moved Violet's piece back in place. "It's your move." He gave her a stern look. "No cheating this time."

Grumbling under her breath, Violet studied the board. "Why do you and Viv like these games? They're hard." She moved her piece in the worst position possible, and he dropped his head.

"My father said it helps to improve at guessing your opponent's next move." His father obsessed over strategies. In the history of Eden, no kingdom had battled another. They dealt with rebel attacks, but the rebels were hardly worthy opponents. Still, his father insisted they stay prepared. Roman suspected it had something to do with the Desert King. Rumors claimed the man to be cruel.

Roman's father had always treated him as an adult. As a small child, instead of playing with others his age, he read old war books and practiced how to deliver killing blows. Junior warrior training started at age eleven, but for Roman, he started at age five, training tirelessly with his parents or their top generals for hours every day. No breaks meant no friends. There'd always been a disconnect between him and his classmates, even now.

Except with Violet.

"If I'm to be king, I have to be ready long before I take the throne." He gestured to the board. "These games help."

"Do you do anything for fun?" She sounded concerned, her freckled nose scrunching a bit.

"I like training." He waved his hand over the board again. "I like strategy games and puzzles."

"But do those things make you laugh?" she pressed. "I can count on one hand the number of times I've seen you laugh."

He always wanted to laugh when they were together. "What does it matter if I laugh or not?"

A piece of hair hung limp in front of her face, and she blew it back. "Everyone should do things that make them laugh."

His tone turned defensive. "I laugh."

"Okay," she replied and pointed to the board. "Your turn."

Her tone suggested she didn't believe him. "What do you mean, '*okay*'?"

She sighed. "Everything you listed is to make you a better king, but have you ever done something just for the fun of it?"

He frowned. "I'm too old to do pointless things."

"You're only fourteen," she shot back. A mischievous smile spread across her face. "I bet I can change your mind." Leaning forward, her voice lowered to a whisper. "Do you think you could sneak out tonight?"

Roman stared at her, intrigued. "Why?"

She rubbed her hands together. "I've had an idea forever, but Griff refuses to help. You can help me instead."

"Why do we have to sneak out?" Her answer didn't matter. He'd do anything she asked.

She ignored his question. "How far can you glamour?"

He leaned forward too. His glamour wouldn't be at full power until he turned twenty-five, but at fourteen, he could already glamour farther than adult non-royal fae. "Farther than you."

She reached over and poked him in the shoulder. "Don't be a showoff. Meet me at our back door at midnight."

The front door opened, and Vivian waltzed inside. She looked at the two of them hovering over the game board and scowled. "What are you two doing?"

Roman sat back and pointed at himself. "I'm playing a game." He turned his accusing finger on Violet. "She's cheating."

Violet gasped. "I was not. He's making up rules as he goes."

Vivian rolled her eyes. "You've never understood strategy games." Roman didn't like the condescension she directed at her sister.

He opened his mouth to defend Violet, but she spoke before he could. "If I'm stuck with you two for the rest of my life, I'd rather learn to play these games than learn to whack at people with a sword."

"You wouldn't be able to do that, either," Vivian replied dismissively.

Roman started to object, but Violet stood abruptly with an air of indifference. "You're right. I'm going to the forest for a little while. Tell Mom I'll be back for dinner." Roman noticed the hurt she tried to hide, and it made him furious.

Vivian took Violet's seat across from him and rearranged the pieces on the board to start a new game. "I'm sorry about her. I know she's annoying, but thank you for entertaining her anyway."

Roman hated this side of Vivian. "I like hanging out with Violet," he bit out, trying to rein in his temper. "You shouldn't speak to her that way."

Vivian's fingers tightened around the game piece in her hand. "She does nothing but climb trees, pick through the sand, and worry about clothes." She looked pointedly at the board. "She can't even play a simple game."

That might be true, but it didn't make her less than. He knew fighting with this stubborn girl was a losing battle, but he couldn't stop the words from spilling out. "And yet people still love her." Vivian's body went rigid. "I don't like this side of *you*."

Vivian's icy eyes lifted to his. "What side of me?"

He met her glare with a stony expression of his own. "You act like you're better than everyone. It's a terrible trait to have. If you'll treat your own sister as if she's beneath you because she doesn't possess qualities you admire, then how will you treat my people if you're queen?"

Vivian's fist tightened even more, her knuckles turning white. "You don't know how insufferable she is behind closed doors, and my relationship with my sister is none of your business."

Roman forced himself to let it go, even if her comment about Violet being insufferable made him want to flip the table between them. He tapped the board. "You can have first move."

Violet stood in the darkness of their back porch with a hooded cloak pulled tightly around her. It wasn't frigid in the Tropical Kingdom at night, but it was cool enough to need the extra layer. She checked her pocket watch. *Five minutes past midnight.*

Disappointment doused her excitement. Roman had never agreed to meet her, but she'd hoped. Without his royal glamour, she'd never be able to pull this off because *her* glamour didn't work on other fae. Violet told herself the fact that her plans were foiled caused her disappointment, not the fact that she wouldn't get to see Roman outside of their weekly dinners. Yes, that must be it.

Violet thought back to her predicament. There had to be a way to make her plan work. She just needed to figure it out.

Roman materialized in front of her, and she jumped a foot in the air. His hand clamped over her mouth to muffle her scream. "It's just me."

The beating of her heart rivaled the speed of a humming-bird in flight. He dropped his hand and smirked. "You scared me half to death," she whisper-yelled and shooed him down the back porch stairs. "We need to be quick. Glamour us both."

He sighed and disappeared. "Done. Are you going to tell me what we're doing?" She'd forgotten that she wouldn't be able to see through his glamour even though it included her. Hearing empty air talk was strange.

"We're going to the chicken pen in the palace farm," she told him excitedly.

"Why are we going to the chicken pen?" Roman asked right as she bumped into the air in front of her.

Violet reached blindly until she felt a hard chest. *Oh my.* Quickly yanking her hand away, she tried not to look flustered. "We're borrowing a few chickens."

"*Borrowing* chickens?" His voice held an obvious note of skepticism.

"Yes." She held out her hand, refusing to accidentally hit something she shouldn't. "Take my hand so I know where you are." His warm fingers wrapped around hers, and she dragged him toward the palace gates, stopping far enough away so as not to be heard by the guards. "We're sneaking through the side gate."

There were two entrances into the palace grounds: two large gates in the front for large groups of people, horses, and carriages, and a smaller barred door on the side for individuals on foot.

"How are we supposed to do that?" Roman sounded incredulous, and she wished she could see his face.

"You're going to glamour the door to look closed while we walk through."

"They'll hear it," he argued. "I can't glamour sound."

Violet dug into her pocket and pulled out a bottle of oil. "I'll put this on the hinges, and we'll go slow."

He chuckled. "You've thought this through." She grinned and nodded. The prince sighed. "Alright. Lead the way."

At the gate, Violet carefully oiled the hinges, handle, and anything else she thought might make a sound, then glanced at the guard who stood sentry on the outside. As slowly as possible, Roman helped her open the gate and slip through. It was a miracle from the gods that her trick worked.

Their shoes made a slight noise as they tiptoed across the gravel and the guard looked around. Roman and Violet hurried down the path toward the palace farm, and once out of earshot, she squealed a little. "It worked!"

Roman appeared in front of her with a slight smile as he watched her hop up and down. "How are we going to *borrow* a few chickens? The guards will hear them when we take them through."

Did he think she'd come unprepared? Violet dug into her other pocket and pulled out a bottle of liquid. "Night drops."

He stared at her skirts with drawn brows before pointing at the bottle. "You're going to drug them with a sleeping elixir?"

Violet tucked the bottle back into her pocket. "I thought you were braver than this."

"This has nothing to do with bravery." He waved his hand toward the farm behind them. "You're drugging chickens and refuse to tell me why. This is *insanity*."

"We're going to leave four of them in our school room." She dug into another pocket and pulled out twine attached to a small potato sack. "I'm going to fill this with seed. We'll rig the door so when it opens, the bag will dump out and the chickens will rush toward our *lovely* teacher."

Roman stood, stunned, but before she could plead her case, he burst out laughing. It was her turn to cover his mouth. His body shook as she pressed harder to shut him up.

"You're going to get us caught," she hissed. Something wet and warm rubbed against her palm, and she yanked it back. "Did you lick me?"

His handsome smile lit up his entire face. "You're something else, Violet Maekin."

It sounded like a compliment, and she decided to take it as such. "We need to hurry, or we'll be out here all night."

Luckily, no one stood guard over the animals at night, and the farmhands didn't arrive until dawn. They snuck through the pasture gate and hurried toward the chicken area. "How are you going to keep the bag from falling when we leave?" Roman asked suddenly.

A devious grin spread across her face. "When I first had the idea, I hid a small shelf inside my desk. We'll hang it above the door and balance the open bag of feed on it with the twine hanging in the doorway. After we close the door, we'll cut the twine short and attach it to the top of the door, and when Miss Bonner opens it, the door will pull the twine and the bag will go with it." She stood tall, proud of herself.

Roman laughed again, the sound warming Violet from the inside out. When they reached the gate to the chicken pen, Roman glanced at her over his shoulder. "Have you ever caught a chicken before?"

No. "Yes."

He narrowed his eyes. "Liar."

"Just open the door," she snipped and playfully pushed him forward. The chicken enclosure consisted of a field of bright pink grass surrounded by a tall, netted fence with a large wooden coop at the very back.

The pink grass glowed brighter than the surrounding area thanks to the natural fertilizer. She could already imagine how pretty it would look in a flower crown.

She pushed the thought aside. They hadn't the time for that now.

Roman held the gate open until Violet hurried through. *He's a gentleman*, she thought. *Unlike the other boys in school. Not that many talked to her.*

They hurried toward the coop in the back, and Violet twisted her lips to the side at the sight of the wooden structure's tiny door, barely big enough for her to wiggle through. "I'll crawl in and chase them out one at a time," she told Roman. "You catch them and give them one drop of the elixir."

Roman crossed his arms and looked down at her. At fourteen years old, the prince already stood around six foot tall. "Why do I have to catch them?"

"Because you're too big to fit through there." Violet pointed at the chicken door. "Your shoulders would get stuck."

He opened his mouth to object, but she held up a hand. "No arguing." He held his hands up, but the smug look on his face raised her hackles. Deciding to ignore him, she shoved the elixir bottle into his hand. "Get the drops ready."

Violet removed her cloak, got on her hands and knees, and crawled through the hole. With her eyes trained straight ahead, she chose to ignore the questionable substances on the ground. If she looked down, she might puke. *It smells awful in here.*

She stood and wiped her hands on her dress with no idea how she'd explain the stains to her mother.

Chickens stirred at the sounds of her entrance, and the air stilled as the birds took stock of the new intruder. It didn't take long for them to erupt in a flurry of chaos. The chickens on the ground rushed at her, and those sitting in tiny hay-filled boxes ran down little ramps like soldiers on their way to war. She screamed and tried to evade them, but they were everywhere. *How are there* this *many chickens in here?*

There were a lot of ways to die, but death by pecks was not one Violet had ever considered. Would they eat her alive if she hit the ground to crawl out? She should have brought the night drops inside and dosed them all.

A large door on the side of the coop opened and Roman stood on the threshold, trying, and failing, to smother his laughter with his hand. She gasped and ran toward him. "Run! They've gone feral!"

He grabbed both of her shoulders, flipped her around, and held her against his chest. "They think you're going to feed them. Watch."

Roman reached into a sack beside the door and threw a handful of seed into the middle of the coop. The ruthless predators ran toward the food and stabbed mercilessly at the ground with their razor-sharp beaks. *That could have been me down there*, she thought with horror.

Her erratic breathing evened out, and Roman's body vibrated with laughter. Violet whirled around, wondering if pushing a prince on his butt was considered treason. "Why didn't you tell me there was a door? You left me to the mercy of those feathered beasts." She held up her hands and motioned to her dress. "And I'm covered in dirt."

Roman's laughter came harder, and she glared with all her might. The temptation to force the night drops down his throat and leave him with the chickens overwhelmed her.

"I promise I would never leave you in danger," he assured her, still laughing. "I tried to tell you about the door, but you cut me off." He plucked at her sleeve. "And I don't think that's dirt, princess." She didn't either.

"It's not funny." She tried to sound fierce, but his infectious joy had her joining in. Their laughter faded, and they stared at each other with goofy grins.

Roman rubbed the back of his neck and looked away. "Let's fill your bag with feed and round up your chickens."

Together, they chased four feathered demons outside, and when Violet tried to grab one, it launched an assault and pecked her arm. The thin sleeve of her dress ripped, and the bird's sharp beak drew blood.

The screech that exploded from her would have been embarrassing if she wasn't bleeding out.

"It got me!" she cried while Roman doubled over laughing. Gripping her arm, she backed away from the chicken who now strutted around like it hadn't torn a chunk of her flesh. She lifted her hand, surveyed the damage, and wailed, "Oh gods, I'm bleeding everywhere."

Roman's laughter died a quick death, and he was by her side in seconds, forcing the chickens between them to scurry out of the way. "Shh," he soothed her and turned a glare on the chicken clucking around their feet. Moving his attention back to her arm, he ripped open the fabric around her wound and, with gentle fingers, prodded the area.

Amused light brown eyes found hers, and her lips turned down. "This isn't a joke. What if it gets infected?"

He struggled to compose himself and ran his thumb soothingly around the wound. "It's barely a scratch."

That couldn't be right. Violet glanced down and her frown deepened at the thin line surrounded by a faint swipe of blood. She sniffed haughtily. "It hurt."

Still smiling, he placed the lightest kiss over the cut. "Better?"

Violet's mouth dried and tingles erupted where his lips touched her skin. "Yes," she somehow managed to say.

Bending over, he scooped up one of the closest chickens and petted its head. "Grab the drops."

The drops were made for fae children, and the concentrated formula knocked the small chickens out cold in no time. "You're sure this won't kill them?" Roman asked warily.

Violet stared down at the limp birds. "I asked the animal healer in town if the night drops were safe for animals. She said yes."

"I doubt she thought you meant chickens," Roman deadpanned.

Violet ignored him. "You take two, and I'll take two."

Once they had the chickens safely inside the palace walls, a feat in and of itself, they snuck upstairs to the school rooms. Roman tried the door handle. "It's locked. How do you plan to get us inside?"

Violet gently set her chickens on the ground and dug out small tools from one of her pockets. "I'm going to break in."

Roman muttered something under his breath about pockets and covered the keyhole with his hand. "How do you know how to pick locks?"

"There's a lot you don't know about me, Roman Covington." She popped his hand to move it out of the way. "They'll never know it was us."

He squatted down beside her. "I didn't take you for a criminal."

She went to work on the lock like her uncle had shown her. He was a locksmith in town and had taught her all sorts of tricks when she was younger. He'd thought it was hilarious when she'd showed her father the new tricks she'd learned. Her father had not. "If I'm a criminal, you're my accomplice."

When the door opened, the two gathered their hopefully-not-dead birds and snuck inside.

After setting everything up, Roman stared warily at the chickens. "Will they wake up by morning?"

Violet pushed her hair out of her face and threw the feathered beasts a worried look of her own. "I hope so."

The next morning, exhaustion plagued Roman's body, but he didn't care. He jumped out of bed and readied for school faster than he ever had before, wanting to arrive early to see the look on Ms. Bonner's face when she opened the door.

After scarfing down breakfast in his rooms, he hurried downstairs and careened around the corner to find Violet waiting on the second-floor landing. "Has Ms. Bonner arrived yet?" he whispered in her ear from behind.

Violet gasped and whirled around. "Don't do that! You're going to give me a heart attack. And no, she's not here yet."

"I'll glamour us, and we can wait by the door." He cloaked them both in magic and urged Violet forward.

She turned in his direction and visibly shivered. "I hate that I can't see you. It feels like I'm talking to myself."

When they stopped, he reached around her and tapped the back of her shoulder. She spun around with a choked gasp, and he had to muffle his laughter. "You're ridiculous," she hissed, swatting at the air but missing him completely.

Roman had never had fun like he had the night before, and seeing Violet in her dirty dress, screaming as chickens chased her, had made a fondness bloom within him. He absentmindedly wondered how she'd explain to her mother why her dress sported a hole in the arm and chicken droppings.

At the reminder of her arm, he glanced down and cupped it gently. "Is your near-fatal wound okay today?"

The scratch had been small, but seeing her blood had made his own run cold. He'd fought to keep his face light and teasing, but to his surprise, all Roman had wanted to do was snap the chicken's neck and carry her away from the others. The irrational urge should have worried him, but it didn't. Something deep inside him liked the idea of being her protector.

Violet pulled out of his hold and lifted her chin. "It still stings."

Roman considered her arm and tapped his finger against his pants leg. "I'll bring you a salve this afternoon."

"You don't have to do that. I'm sure my mother has something."

To be safe, he'd send her the biggest jar he could find, whether she wanted him to or not.

Ms. Bonner crested the top of the stares, and they both held their breath as the woman pulled out her keys to unlock the classroom door. Violet's eyes went comically wide when the bag of seed tumbled off the ledge, narrowly missing Ms. Bonner on the way down.

The older woman dropped her bag on the floor and screamed. The loud sound sent the four chickens fluttering like crazy. Feathers were everywhere, along with droppings, and Roman guessed the stench alone would shut down classes for an entire week.

"Good heavens!" their teacher shrieked and bolted back into the hallway, forcing Violet and Roman to jump out of the way.

When one chicken followed Ms. Bonner into the hall, Violet tried to flee, but Roman banded his arm around her waist to stop her, not wanting her to miss anything.

The chicken sped after the older woman, and Roman

leaned down close to Violet's ear. "Do you think he'll catch her?"

Violet snickered and whispered back, "I hope so. She could use a good peck or two."

Much to their dismay, two guards hurried down the hall to investigate the commotion and stepped in front of Ms. Bonner to save her from the impending assault.

One of the guards picked up the chicken, approached the school room, and cursed. "Send for a farmhand," he instructed the other guard as he deposited the runaway chicken inside the room and shut the door. "I'll alert a maid."

Once both guards and Ms. Bonner were out of hearing range, Roman and Violet burst out laughing.

"Did you see her face?" Violet wheezed, her nose crinkling as she laughed.

Roman's gaze snagged on a familiar figure over Violet's shoulder, and he nearly groaned out loud. His mother stood down the hall watching them, but instead of the anger he expected, she appeared curious.

The queen's eyes jumped from Violet to Roman, and when they met his, her curiosity morphed into something that looked a lot like sadness.

5

ELEVEN MONTHS LATER

Roman sat tucked away between the dark bookshelves in the palace library, studying the massive book on Eden's wars throughout the years. It was interesting, but not interesting enough to hold his attention for longer than half an hour.

His father expected excellence, and Roman spent most of his free time studying or fighting. Weekly dinners with the Maekins became his favorite pastime, and he often found himself counting down the days until he could disappear into their cozy cottage for a few hours.

When tucked away in the privacy of the Maekins' cottage, there was no one to observe him, waiting for him to screw up. Violet had become one of his best friends, and knowing she'd be in his life, despite the reason, made him happier than he'd like to admit. He smiled to himself.

Muttering laced with frustration caught his attention, and he looked around for the source. Something familiar nibbled at his mind. Curious, he stood and followed the grumblings around the impossibly tall bookshelf behind him. The very object of his thoughts sulked on the other side with a book and an array of papers scattered around her.

He grinned as she righted an overturned inkwell, spewing more curses that would scandalize his mother. "You're supposed to keep the ink inside the jar."

Violet's head snapped up with slitted eyes. "Hilarious." She stared helplessly at the mess in front of her and used extra papers to sop up the ever-spreading goo. Giving up, she dropped her head into her hands. "I'm never going to finish this in time."

Roman moved closer to the disaster and tried to make sense of the chaos smeared across the pages. "Finish what?"

Violet dropped her hands and said something, but he heard nothing when he took in her appearance. The laugh that exploded out of him couldn't be helped, and much as he tried, it couldn't be ebbed either.

"It's not funny," she snapped. "I don't understand the arithmetic." She pointed at the ink-soaked paper, "and now I can't read my notes."

Roman moved around the table, biting back his laughter the best he could. "You have ink all over your face."

Her eyes widened. "What?"

Roman picked up her arm. "Your hands."

She looked at the ink covering her hands. "Could today get any worse?" she wailed, eyeing the ink stains on her dress. "I just made this."

"Here." Roman stripped out of his shirt and tilted her chin to look at him. He ran the white cloth over her forehead and cheeks. The black liquid smeared, but after switching to clean areas of the shirt a dozen times, most of it came off, leaving only a dark tint on her tan skin. "That's as good as I can do without water."

Her chin still in his hand, Violet's eyes pierced his, and a quiet moment passed between them. Roman's breathing picked up, and he didn't understand the feeling in his chest, having only experienced one other time: the night of his thirteenth birthday, when he saw her on the balcony in her flower crown and purple dress.

Her gaze moved to his bare chest and a pink flush crept up her slender neck. Roman stepped away and donned his ruined shirt. "I can help you."

Her obvious hope sparked a pull he couldn't explain. *If she isn't my mate, why do I feel this way?*

Bonded mates typically had eyes for no one else, the mere *thought* of them considering another unfathomable. From the stories Roman's parents told him, they'd been that way from the day they met.

So how did the bond allow him to feel this way about Violet and have borderline disdain for Vivian? Everything he'd read about mates described the tug he felt now, and not for the first time, he wondered if the gods made a mistake.

He shook himself from his confusing thoughts and gestured to the scattered papers. "I'm good at arithmetic, and I've finished the assignments already."

She looked to be contemplating whether to rip her book in half or not. "I'm not sure I'll ever understand. We started learning arithmetic when we were nine, Rome, and I'm almost fifteen. Eight years, and I still don't understand it." She leaned back in her chair, and Roman decided not to correct her.

Instead, he clucked his tongue and dragged one of the other chairs over to sit beside her. "Where do you want to start?"

A few hours later, Violet hurried across the palace grounds toward the warrior compound with her heart in her throat. *What happened in the library with Roman?* She'd thought the crush she'd formed when they were twelve disappeared not long after the gods bonded him to Vivian. She'd forced it away, refusing to betray her sister.

Not to mention, signing herself up for guaranteed heartbreak would be foolish.

You're being stupid, Violet scolded herself. In no part of their world would Roman feel that way about her, especially while bonded to someone else. The nervous energy buzzing through her had her hands shaking and her breaths ragged.

The moment in the library was a one off; a fleeting feeling. That's all.

Violet rushed up the porch steps and through the front door, kicked off her slippers, scooped the shoes into one hand, and rushed to her room.

Removing her ruined dress, she wrapped a robe around her body and carried her soiled clothes to the laundering room to treat the stains. Harsh whispers on the other side of the laundering room door brought her to an abrupt halt.

Violet shamelessly planted an ear against the door and strained to hear.

"Why do we have to hide our relationship?" a boy's voice demanded. "Are you ashamed of me?"

"No," Vivian's familiar voice insisted. Violet covered her mouth. "But no one can know about us."

Vivian has a secret boyfriend?

"Why not?" The boy sounded frustrated. "I love you, Viv."

Violet pulled back and gaped at the closed door.

A shuffling sound broke the silence, and Vivian's voice came out softer, with more emotion than Violet had known her sister possessed. "I love you too, but please, trust me. You know why we can't say anything. I don't know what would happen to you if anyone found out."

More silence. "I trust you, but I can't hide us forever. You swore when we explored our feelings that you would choose me."

"I know, but I need time to figure things out."

"I'll give you time for now," the boy murmured, followed by a faint smacking that sounded an awful lot like kissing. Violet's face screwed up. Why did it sound so slobbery?

"Go," Vivian said breathlessly. "My sister will be home soon. Check before going through the window."

Violet turned and ran on tip-toes back to her room, then closed the door loudly to alert them of her arrival with her heart beating erratically at what she'd overheard.

Vivian is cheating on Roman. Maybe not *cheating* because according to Viv they weren't dating yet, but they were mated. If Violet were mated to Roman, she couldn't imagine wanting anyone else.

She pressed her hand to her chest in a futile attempt to stop the anxious ache taking root. Should she betray her sister and tell Roman, or keep quiet and let them work it out on their own?

If she told no one and Vivian ran away with her boyfriend, would Roman choose a new mate? A wretched part of Violet wanted that more than anything, but it felt like a betrayal to her sister.

Sitting on her bed, Violet stared out the window. *But is it a betrayal if Vivian loves someone else?* She decided not to tell anyone, telling herself it was to protect Vivian, but deep down, Violet knew her motives contained a tinge of selfishness.

She wished she hadn't heard a thing.

6

FIFTEEN YEARS OLD

Violet screamed and scrambled up the nearest tree, breathing hard as she stared at the tigon below. She'd glamoured herself to be invisible, but the beast seemed to see her anyway. Animals shouldn't be able to see her.

Could fae lose their magic? *Have I upset the gods and they've decided to feed me to the wild?*

Tigons were large cats the size of a small horse. Black stripes lined their snow-white fur, and a large mane of pitch-black quill sheaths covered their head and neck. When a tigon felt threatened, sharp quills shot out of their skin into the sheaths, forming a razor-sharp barrier to protect their throat.

She'd seen sketches and paintings before, but neither did their bright orange eyes justice.

Tigons were larger and more dangerous than the jungle cats in the Human Kingdom, as were all animals in the fae lands, but they tended to dwell in the lesser populated areas of the dense jungle.

Apparently not this one.

Violet grasped a bright purple vine to steady herself and

looked up to see if she could swing to the next tree. The branches didn't line up, and to reach another, she'd have to either climb higher or slide lower.

"Please go away," she pleaded with the animal who seemed determined to wait her out. Did tigons eat people? Violet didn't know, but judging by the look in the tigon's eye, she would find out the hard way.

The sound of someone approaching caught her attention, and she breathed a sigh of relief. "Help!" The footsteps sped up, and she added, "Be careful. There's a tigon."

They ran faster, and when Roman materialized at the base of the tree, Violet's shoulders sagged. He wouldn't let anything happen to her. "Maybe your glamour will work on him," she said shakily. "Either mine isn't working or he can smell my fear."

Roman looked from the tigon to Violet and suppressed a smile.

"If you're going to laugh at me, then leave," she snapped.

Roman's lip trembled, and he lost the battle, doubling over in a fit of laughter. Maybe she could convince the tigon to eat him instead.

"He's my *familiar*, princess. He won't hurt you," the prince informed her once he'd regained control of himself.

Her attention involuntarily moved to Roman's chest. He wore a lightweight, white, long-sleeved shirt tucked into dark green trousers. The top buttons of his shirt were open, and she could see the black lines of his *familiar* mark.

Royal fae bonded with a *familiar* on their fifteenth birthday, and when the bond formed, the royal fae received a mark on their chest of the animal, like a tattoo. "Show me your mark."

He unbuttoned his shirt and proudly displayed an artistic version of a tigon. Lips parting with awe, she leaned forward a little to see it better. "It looks cool." Roman beamed with pride. Violet held onto the vine in her hand and jumped down. "What's your *familiar's* name?"

Roman jolted forward and caught her around the waist before she hit the ground. "I hate it when you do that," he grumbled. "I haven't named him yet."

"Why not?" she asked, staring at the tigon.

"He hates everything I suggest," Roman complained. "I told him to name himself, but he refuses."

Violet tentatively reached over and scratched the tigon's head. His mane slid through her fingers like silk. "How do you know he doesn't like the names? Does he bite you or something?"

Roman shook his head with a half-cocked grin. "He tells me." Her eyebrows shot to her hairline, and he added, "I can sense his thoughts." *Huh.* She hadn't known they could communicate that way.

Violet stared at the beast again. "His mane is glorious. You could call him Samyaza," she suggested, referencing a fictional angel warrior in an old faerietale. The tigon nudged Violet's hand and licked her fingers. "I think he likes it."

Roman took a step closer and observed the two, all humor dropping from his face. "Over my dead body."

Violet leaned over and cooed into the beast's fur, "That can be arranged, can't it?"

The tigon purred, earning a scowl from Roman. "Don't be childish."

Violet straightened and stared him down. "What twisted your undershorts?" Roman didn't look amused, and she knew him well enough to know something else bothered him. "Is everything alright?" His eyes flitted to hers, confirming her suspicions. "You can tell me. I'm a good listener and even better at revenge." She wiggled her eyebrows.

The boyish smile she knew well made an appearance, but it didn't last long. "I'm sorry," he muttered, rubbing a hand over his face. "I didn't sleep last night, and I took it out on you." She waited expectantly, and he cleared his throat. "Apparently, I can feel when Vivian has an, uh, orgasm."

Roman's face turned beet red, and Violet wished she'd never asked. As a matter of fact, she wished the tigon had eaten her when he'd had the chance. "I didn't know you two were having sex yet. Not that I need to know," she added.

Fifteen seemed a bit young, in her opinion, but plenty of her classmates were already doing it. If it was what they wanted and they were safe about it, that was their business.

Roman stiffened. "Gods, Vi, we're not having sex with each other. I can feel her with someone else." He paused and added, "Unless she's doing it herself, but there are other emotions when it happens that I don't think she'd feel on her own."

She remembered months ago when she'd overheard Viv and another boy. What did you say to someone who found out their mate cheated on them? "I'm sorry, Rome."

He scratched the back of his head. "I don't care if she does."

Well, I guess they aren't together after all.

Dropping his hand, Roman shrugged. "It feels great, actually." He chuckled when Violet's jaw fell open, "but I don't want to feel *her*." His emphasis on the last word struck Violet as a bit odd, but she brushed it aside.

"Are you two friends?" she asked. The prince and her sister got along well enough at their weekly dinners, but Violet rarely saw them speak otherwise.

A guilty look passed over his face. "Kind of."

"*Kind of?*" she parroted, planting her hands on her hips. "That means no. No wonder you two don't want to be together." She should have kept the last bit to herself, but it didn't take a genius to see they didn't like each other in *that* way.

They couldn't act on it in public if they did, but even at their weekly dinners they were cordial. Nothing more.

"That's your problem," she continued. "How do you expect to love each other if you're not friends first? Mom says the best friendships turn into the greatest loves."

His gaze bored into hers. "Meri is a smart woman."

"You both like doing sword stuff," Violet pointed out. "Maybe you could practice sword stuff together or punch each other."

Playful mischief laced his expression. "Sword stuff?"

"You know what I mean," she muttered.

Roman tilted his head with feigned interest. "I don't think I do." He leaned casually against the wide, blue, iridescent trunk of the tree. "Explain it to me."

Matching his stance, she smiled sweetly. "If you'll let me borrow your sword, I'll run it through your middle as a demonstration." She glanced at the short sword strapped to his hip.

His mouth curled with amusement. "The princess has claws."

If she had claws, she'd scratch his eyes out just to wipe that smug look off his face. *No, you wouldn't. You like it too much,* a small voice whispered in the back of her mind.

Violet bent down to gather her satchel and studiously ignored his teasing. She tried to straighten and nearly head-butted the giant tigon who'd moved closer. The big cat licked her cheek, and she swiped at it with a mock glare in its direction. "You need to name him so I can scold him properly for sneaking up on me."

Roman rolled his lips together and looked away. He hid his smiles a lot, but she didn't know why. Some were annoying, but most made him even more handsome. "He's been sitting there the entire time," Roman said, his amusement clear. "I wouldn't call that *sneaking up on you.*"

Violet looked the tigon over. "He looks ferocious enough to win a battle on his own, and clearly he has the stealth." She turned back to Roman. "You should name him War."

The cat purred. Roman stared at his *familiar* and his shoulders loosened. "Thank the gods. He likes it."

Violet clapped excitedly and leaned over to kiss the top of War's head, whispering, "Don't let him get too big of a head when he's king." The beast tried to lick her again, but she jumped back. War's tongue caught Violet's necklace instead, and she yelped, snatching the string to keep it from breaking.

Roman glanced at the jewelry clutched in her hand. "Did you make that?"

"Yes." She fiddled with the shells. "I think I look quite pretty with it on." Flipping her hair dramatically, she popped a hip and struck a pose.

An unreadable emotion shone in Roman's eyes, and his voice softened. "You're pretty without it. You don't need that stuff."

Violet did everything in her power to ignore the fact that he'd called her pretty and adjusted her satchel. "I never said I was ugly without it."

Roman stiffened, and she turned to War. "Remember what I told you." The beast nodded his head, and Violet turned back to Roman. Hopefully putting space between them would squash the furious fluttering in her stomach. "Be friends with my sister or you'll be miserable for the rest of your life."

Violet hurried off before she did something stupid, like tell him she thought he was handsome too.

"I like her," War told Roman as they trekked toward the palace. *"Are you two close?"*

Roman didn't respond at first. They were close, but the older they got, the more he wished they were mates with a ferocity unlike any other. "I like her, but I'm mated to her sister."

"Do you like her as more than a friend?"

"Yes," Roman answered without hesitation. He stopped abruptly when something occurred to him. It was a stupid thought, he knew that, but he needed to ask for peace of mind. The gods blessed *familiars*; maybe they knew things the fae didn't.

"Do you know a way to transfer a mate bond from one person to another? I know the bond can break if Vivian or I marry another, but is there a way to form a bond with someone else?"

"That is a fool's wish," War replied after a moment. *"The bond can break, but only the gods can grant a new one."*

Marrying Violet would break his bond with Vivian, but he didn't know if it would form a new bond because it'd never been done.

"If I married Violet and broke the bond with Vivian, it would force the gods to bond me to Violet, right?" His excitement grew the more he thought about it. It made sense. The royal bloodline must stay strong, and they'd have no choice but to bond them together.

War chuffed. *"You cannot force the gods to do anything. I like Violet, but do not play with fate. It will not end well."*

Only silence followed, and a darkness blanketed Roman as his *familiar's* words settled in his soul.

7

SIXTEEN YEARS OLD

Vivian sat cross-legged on her bed while Violet lounged on her own across the room. Violet's side had strings of beads and dried flowers decorating the walls to match her purple quilt, while Vivian only had an undecorated bookshelf, a brown quilt, and bare walls.

"Do you want to see the new dress I made for Roman's birthday ball tonight?" Violet asked her twin, twisting around to look at her.

The grating sound of Vivian sharpening her knife halted, and she looked up. "Is it frilly like the last one?"

"A lace border is not frilly," Violet protested. "Mom bought me real beads for my birthday." Usually Violet made her own out of stones and pebbles, but that took forever and they were never smooth or symmetrical.

Vivian scoffed. "Beads? Maybe if you wore normal clothes you'd have a boyfriend to take you to the ball instead of tagging along with Mom and Dad."

Violet counted to ten in her head before speaking again. "A lot of girls dress like I do." She'd had enough of Vivian's insults.

"You act as if I'm an outcast because I've never had a boyfriend. What do you care if boys like my dresses or not? I don't make you feel stupid for fighting or wearing nothing but neutral colors all the time."

"I'm trying to help you," Vivian snapped back. The older they got, the worse she treated Violet, and Violet didn't understand where her sister's growing hostility came from. "If the truth hurts your feelings, that's on you." Vivian sniffed and went back to sharpening her dagger, the sound making Violet want to scream.

Violet refused to admit it, but the fact that no boys showed interest in her hurt. No one knew Viv and Roman were mates, and boys flirted with her incessantly, but not Violet. "If you're going to be rude, keep your opinions to yourself. I'll wear what I want, *frilly* lace and all."

Vivian turned murderous eyes on Violet, taking her aback. "You're just trying to get Roman's attention," she sneered. "It's obvious you're jealous that I'm his mate. Wearing flashy clothes and throwing yourself at him isn't going to work."

Violet's mouth fell open. *Roman?* Where did that come from? She and Roman were only friends. How was that throwing herself at him?

"Are you insane? When have I given you the impression I was jealous?" Yes, Violet had been jealous when they were younger. She'd have an occasional fleeting thought here and there, but she'd always respected their bond. "If I wanted to ruin your relationship, I would have told him about your secret boyfriend," she seethed. "You are the only one of us who is disloyal."

The blood drained from Vivian's face, and Violet smiled with smug satisfaction as her sister scrambled for something to say. "You don't know what you're talking about."

Violet snorted. "You're not as stealthy as you think. Roman

is my friend, but you're my sister, and I wouldn't betray you that way no matter how horribly you treat me. Don't ever accuse me of something like that again."

Vivian ran a hand through her hair, her skin still a deathly pallor. "It's Roman." Violet's brows lowered. "My boyfriend," Vivian clarified.

Violet knew her sister had lied. It hadn't been Roman's voice Violet heard through the door a year and a half ago, nor had it been Roman her sister slept with last year, according to him.

Judging by her sister's reaction, she and her mystery boy were still together. "Why would you need to hide your relationship with your mate?" Violet challenged.

Vivian laughed bitterly. "It was his choice. 'For my safety,' he'd said. Until we graduate and he's stronger, we can't reveal our bond."

Lies. There'd be no reason for them to hide the relationship from their families.

It insulted Violet that Vivian thought her dumb enough to believe the blatant lie, but Violet let it go.

"Your clothes *are* pretty," Vivian said with a sigh. *More lies.* Vivian hated Violet's clothes. "Even if I don't understand why you'd want to spend hours sewing that weird stuff on. I'm sorry for what I said."

"You're terrible at apologizing," Violet muttered under her breath, wondering what happened to her sister along the years to turn her into the nasty, dishonest person she'd become.

Roman tugged at the collar of his green formal jacket, hating how it itched. He wore a shirt underneath, but it didn't help. The ballroom looked like a golden goddess threw up on it with ridiculous silks lining the walls and over-the-top gold statues he hadn't known his family possessed. Roman's birthday balls were the perfect excuse for his mother to go wild, and the large ballroom suffered the price.

After greeting every nobleman in attendance, Roman started toward the balcony doors, in need of fresh air, but stopped short when a burst of anger and hurt punched him in the gut.

He clutched at his jacket and sucked in air to combat the swirling emotions within him. They didn't affect his mood, only his physical body, meaning they weren't his emotions at all. *Vivian.*

He might not have felt romantic affection for her, but he was still supposed to marry her one day. His father had noticed the distance between Vivian and Roman and started drilling the importance of prioritizing his mate's safety and happiness into him. The feelings coming down their bond did not include fear or pain, so physically, she was fine. Ordinarily, her stronger emotions consisted of giddiness and triumph, and this swift change worried him.

Straightening slowly, he scanned the room for her familiar dark auburn hair. The large room brimmed with guests dressed in their finest, milling around to rub shoulders with those they deemed important. Moving along the outside of the crowd, his worry grew.

There. He caught sight of Vivian slipping into the ballroom through a side door. The dark green gown she wore fit her muscular frame well, and Roman could see why the other guys wouldn't shut up about her, even if she didn't appeal to him. Her hair hung loose instead of tied back in its usual braid, but the thick locks did nothing to hide the fury on her face.

Roman watched her search the room, and when their gazes collided, determination slithered down their bond. Whatever worry he'd had for her evaporated, replaced with the need to disappear.

Vivian wove her way through the crowd toward him, and he forced himself to stay put. They didn't speak much outside of school, training, and their weekly dinners, and he didn't know why she sought him out now.

"I've been looking for you," she said breathlessly. "Can I speak with you outside?" Vivian glanced over her shoulder. Roman followed her line of sight, but there were too many people to see what, or *who*, she was looking at. Smug satisfaction, strong and potent, traveled down the bond, and he had to fight to tamp down his own contempt.

He opened the door to the small balcony and ushered her outside. Before he could close the balcony door, Vivian tenderly cupped his cheek. The gesture took him by surprise, and he wrapped his fingers around her wrist.

"I've been wanting to do this all night," she murmured and kissed him before he could yank her hand away from his face.

Revulsion filled him as she stole his first kiss. It felt *wrong*, not only to him, but to Vivian as well if the unease flowing down the bond was any indication.

He jerked back, and Vivian sighed. As he started to ask her what the hell she was doing, someone cleared their throat and stepped out of the far shadows of the balcony.

Violet.

Roman's world tilted. Pain flashed in her big blue eyes, and he wanted nothing more than to shove Vivian over the railing. He and Violet were nothing but friends, but the need to beg for her forgiveness rode him hard.

Violet laughed nervously. "I'll give you two privacy."

Vivian giggled shamelessly and malicious glee zipped down the bond. "Sorry, Vi. I didn't realize you were still out here."

Roman's gaze snapped to Violet, and his body stiffened at the wooden smile plastered on her face. "Hiding?" he tried to tease.

They always met on this small balcony during his birthday balls, and had he known what Vivian intended to pull, he would have kept the viper far away. Roman thought that in her vulnerable state, she might have needed his help.

What a fool he'd been.

Violet laughed lightly again. "Always. I'll see you two later."

Miserable, he watched Violet leave, and when the door snicked shut behind her, he took a step away from Vivian. "What was that about?"

Vivian had the nerve to glare at him. "I wanted to see if there was a spark yet. We're only a few years away from graduation."

"Bullshit," he accused. "We're supposed to keep a low profile, and you just fucking kissed me in front of everyone."

She patted his cheek and winked. "I'll tell everyone my sister dared me to kiss the prince. They won't know we're mates." Vivian threw open the door, waltzed inside, and looked around. Roman watched as she theatrically swiped a thumb across her lips. "I'll see you later, Rome."

Then it hit him like a bolt of lightning. Vivian had used him to make someone jealous. The little serpent.

His fingers clasped around her upper arm to stop her retreat, and he leaned down. "I can feel your stronger emotions," he reminded her. "Something upset you earlier, and when you kissed me, you wanted to recoil as much as I did." She stiffened and turned a dark shade of red. "We have a lifetime together. Let's not start lying to each other now."

Vivian turned to face him so that the room was at her back and lowered her voice. "Fuck you, Rome."

He smirked. "I can feel when you do that too." The air between them grew heavy with tension. "We're not together, and as long as you're discreet, I don't care who you sleep with, but do not ever use me again."

Without waiting for a reply, he stepped around her and left.

Violet hurried from the ballroom and realized with absolute horror that she was in love with Roman Covington. The proof lay in the way her heart beat erratically, pumping the painful venom of heartbreak through her body. Her insides hollowed out, and a prickling sensation crawled across her skin.

How did this happen?

Roman belonged to Vivian, always had, and Violet had only ever wanted happiness for them, but seeing Roman kiss Vivian tore Violet to pieces. Her feelings were the worst kind of betrayal to her sister, whether her sister liked Roman or not.

Violet's throat tightened. Ridiculous, all of it. Another thought, worse than the last, struck her. Vivian *hadn't* lied about dating Roman. Perhaps at one time she'd dated someone else, but not now. That means she *did* cheat on Roman.

Oh gods. The sob Violet fought hard to contain escaped and echoed off the stone walls of the hallway. She felt sick and guilty and confused all at once, and the need to be far away from the palace overwhelmed her. If anyone happened upon her in this state, she'd die of embarrassment if the pain didn't kill her first.

Twin trails of warmth slid down her cheeks, and she swiped her sleeve across the evidence of her foolishness. *I'm crying over my sister's boyfriend. Gods, please forgive me.*

The quiet pat of her slippers against the marble floor were

soon joined by quicker, louder footsteps behind her, and she swore inwardly.

"Violet, wait."

Of course it had to be him. She swiped at her cheeks again and slowed her steps, turning to Roman with a forced bright smile. "Skipping out on your own party?" Her voice sounded stuffy from crying. *Damn it.*

He fell in step beside her and studied her face, taking in every detail. She knew what he saw: bloodshot, puffy eyes and a pink nose that hopefully wasn't dripping.

Dear gods, if you would kindly pull me to the heavens now, I will never ask for anything again.

Roman touched her elbow to stop her, his expression tortured. Violet's breath hitched. *Can he see how I feel?* His pity would be her undoing. If he tried to let her down with a valiant speech, Violet would disappear into the wild and never return.

"You should go back to your party before your mother sends the entire battalion looking for you," she suggested lightly.

Roman grimaced. "I don't know why Vivian kissed me."

Violet's brows lowered, wondering why he felt the need to pacify her with a lie. A pity *"we're just friends"* talk would be better than the insult of an untruth. "That's what mates do, is it not?"

His eyes searched hers, but she didn't know for what. Heartbreak, shame, and humiliation were the only things he'd find. "We're not supposed to in public," he reminded her.

Violet smiled softly, hating the way his confirmation of their relationship cracked her chest wide open. "I'm not the public. You can kiss her all you want." Tears threatened to make an appearance, and she wanted to scream. *I swear to the gods, eyes, if you leak in front of him, I will pluck you out myself.*

Much to her dismay, they didn't heed her warning, and a bead of moisture escaped.

Roman reached up and swiped away her tear with a gentle stroke of his thumb. "Why are you crying?"

"I've had a bad day," she admitted, not even having to lie. Watching him kiss Vivian ruined any joy the day had granted her. "And I'm tired."

Did he step closer or had she imagined it?

Roman had yet to remove his hand from her cheek; his thumb still moving softly across her skin. "What happened to make it bad?"

There was no concern in his question, but a challenge. She stared at him, trying to figure out his meaning. Did he want her to admit what she felt to further her humiliation? *No.* Many things could be used to describe Roman, but cruel and arrogant did not make the list. What, then?

"I had trouble with our arithmetic homework," she fibbed. "You know how terrible I am at it."

The corner of his mouth twitched. "We didn't have any arithmetic homework this week." This time, he *did* step closer, forcing her to step back. "In fact, we haven't had any homework this week in preparation for the ball." His head tipped slightly. "Tell me," he murmured.

But she wouldn't—couldn't—because in every scenario she came out the loser. When all's said and done, Rome and Viv would marry, have a beautiful warrior baby, and live out their happily ever after while Violet watched from the shadows.

With stark clarity, she realized they could no longer be friends. It hurt, possibly worse than seeing Roman and Vivian kiss, but it had to be done. If she didn't put an end to it now and give herself time to get over Roman before they forced her to watch him live out her dream with Vivian, there would be nothing left of her heart to give someone else.

So, she would end their friendship until her idiocy passed.

But not tonight. Selfishly, she wanted one more night with him before she confessed her sins and distanced herself; one more happy memory to tuck away for later. Besides, a lot of thought went into her birthday gift to him, and it'd be a shame to waste it.

Pushing down her swelling emotions, she wrapped her hand around his. "I have a gift for you, but you have to give up the rest of your party for it." She'd planned on pulling him away after midnight when the party died down, but now seemed as good a time as any.

Roman opened his mouth to say something but closed it with a snap and squeezed her hand. "I'd give up anything for you, princess."

Roman knew he'd look back on this night as one of the happiest of his life. He'd wondered if Violet felt the same way he did, but he'd seen her hurt expression before she'd fled the ballroom.

The tears streaming down her face only cemented his suspicions, and while he wanted to kill Vivian for being the catalyst to Violet's tears, they were proof his feelings weren't one-sided.

Only one thing stood in their way, but he vowed to find a way to transfer the mate bond from one twin to the other. Lore suggested identical twins were one soul torn in two. If their souls were once one, why couldn't the bond transfer from one half of the soul to the other? There had to be a way.

The palace library contained an unfathomable amount of

history books, some of them centuries old. They were kept in exclusive rooms not available to anyone except scholars and royals to avoid over-handling and to preserve them as long as possible. When age wore them down, scholars copied them into new books to avoid losing the information to time.

There might be something useful in them about bonds. He'd check old fables and faerietales too. As a child, when his mother would read to him, she'd said they were real tales passed down from person to person. Roman knew she'd only been fueling the imagination of a small child, but what if the old stories were rooted in truth?

Deep down he knew if something existed allowing a royal to bond to someone other than their gods-blessed mate, the knowledge would have leaked by now, but he had to try.

Roman adjusted his hand and threaded his fingers through Violet's. "Where are we going?"

She smiled beautifully over her shoulder and led him through the wide, ornately decorated hallways. Paintings framed in gold hung from the smoothed and polished stone walls, lit by oil lanterns encased in golden sconces. Roman hated it, but his mother thought the gaudier, the better.

"It's a secret," Violet said cryptically. "We're almost there."

They turned toward the stairs leading to their classroom, and a grin stretched across his face. "What scheme have you cooked up tonight, princess?"

Roman's favorite girl released his hand, pulled a few tools from her dress pocket, and crouched in front of the door. "We're going to flip everything inside." The mischievous smile she flashed him before starting on the lock made him laugh.

"What exactly does flipping everything entail?" he mused and leaned against the wall beside the door.

When the lock clicked open, Violet pushed open the door and tugged him inside.

After closing the door behind him, he turned to her and folded his arms across his chest. "How long have you been planning this without telling me?"

"Almost a month," Violet replied slyly, flitting from lantern to lantern to brighten the room. She waved her hand around, gesturing to the entire room. "We're going to flip all the furniture, paintings, and whatever else we can, upside down. It will look like the world flipped on its head."

It took a moment for her meaning to register, and when it did, he burst out laughing and Violet brightened with delight. "How do you come up with these things?"

She shrugged and tapped one of the desks. "I'm not strong enough to do the desks, but I can start on the paintings."

Roman raised an arm and flexed his muscles. "I won't let you down."

Together, they turned the room upside down, laughing and talking in hushed whispers as they worked. Roman paused to observe Violet as she flipped every book on the bookshelf. The flush of her cheeks from laughing, the excitement in her eyes, the way she bounced on her toes when she moved—*beautiful*.

He was hers completely and irrevocably, and he would do whatever it took to make her his, too.

8

A few days later, Roman lay on his bed and stared miserably at the black satin canopy above. He'd told his mother he didn't feel well and locked himself in his rooms all day like a petulant child. Truthfully, he *didn't* feel well, just not in the way he'd led her to believe.

He slid his gaze guiltily to the untouched soup his mother had delivered earlier. Perched neatly on a meal cart with his favorite sweet bread, the "feel-better" meal taunted him. He hated lying to his parents, but he couldn't bring himself to deal with anyone today.

The day before yesterday, Violet hadn't shown up to his weekly dinner with the Maekins. Meri said *Slayton* had invited her for dinner at his house. Yesterday, Roman looked into the guy. Slayton was their age, lived in town, and worked at the grocery store his father owned. Her mother hadn't mentioned Violet having dinner with Slayton *and* Griff or any of Violet's other friends. Only Slayton.

It could be nothing, but what if Roman misread things and Violet had feelings for this other guy and not him?

Roman had warned everyone in the palace school against touching Violet, but he hadn't thought she'd meet a guy from town.

To make matters worse, Violet barely looked at Roman in class, not even when Ms. Bonner squawked in outrage at the sight of the upturned classroom the morning after the birthday ball.

Alarm bells rang through the air, snapping him from his miserable thoughts. The deep chimes echoed off the stone walls, and Roman strained to decipher the code. His heart sped up with recognition. *Rebels.*

Rebel factions attacking the kingdoms were an ongoing problem throughout Eden—always had been, always would be. The rebels wanted to end the royal bloodlines. They believed the throne should be earned, not inherited, but their selfishness only proved how ill-suited they were to rule. The throne passed down the royal bloodlines because non-royal fae were too weak to properly defend an entire kingdom under attack. There had never been an assault large enough to require the use of their most powerful magic, but if there ever was, they'd be ready.

If someone sounded the rebel alarms within the palace, then rebels had already breached the palace walls.

I have to find Violet. Roman rushed to his dressing room, threw on his leathers, strapped on his weapons, and skidded to a halt halfway to the door. *Shit.*

Vivian's safety should be his top priority. His father might disown him if he failed to protect her. Mate bonds were the sole reason the royal bloodlines stayed strong, and if Roman couldn't find a way to transfer the bond from Vivian to Violet, he'd have to marry Vivian to keep his kingdom safe.

Still, Roman would check on Vivian after he ensured Violet's safety. Vivian should be in the arena training with the other junior warriors, and he didn't feel pain or fear through their bond. Only nervous excitement.

Not surprising Viv would think a rebel attack is exciting, he thought incredulously.

Roman ran down the hallway and skirted around the corner nearest the stairs, smacking into a maid with a meal cart. She shrieked and the contents of her cart went crashing to the ground.

Roman grabbed the maid's arms to keep her from falling and familiar eyes stared back in shock. Not a maid. *Violet.* "What are you doing here?" he asked with a shaky, relieved breath.

"Mom said you weren't feeling well. I made you soup." She pointed with a shaky hand to the mess on the floor, "and I wanted to see if you'd have dinner with me when you're feeling better so we could talk."

Violet's daunting words hung over him like a sharp blade waiting to strike, but he didn't have time to demand an explanation. With great difficulty, he slammed his warring emotions down and locked them up tight. Now that he knew Violet was safe, he could move his focus to finding Vivian and his parents.

"The alarms mean the rebels are inside the palace walls, don't they?" she asked him. "I-I need to find my mother. She knows I'm here and will be beside herself looking for me." Trembling fingers fiddled with one of the beaded bracelets adorning her wrist.

The chance of rebels getting inside the actual palace was low, but Roman couldn't leave Violet to wander the halls alone. *Think.*

"It's not safe for you to walk around by yourself. The guards will have already ushered your mother and the other staff into safe rooms." Taking her hand, he dragged her down the hall and into his rooms, not stopping until they reached his bedroom. Roman bent next to the bed, lifted part of the black damask bed skirt to tuck under the mattress, and gestured underneath. "Hide under here and don't come out until I tell you to."

Violet dropped to the floor and scooted her lithe body underneath the dark cherry wood frame. She rarely did what he said on the first try, and her submission stirred something inside him.

Roman lowered to his knees to peer under the bed, and the terror on her face took him aback. He tried to sound reassuring when he said, "I'll be back."

He started to stand but she latched onto his arm with a clammy hand. "Please, don't leave me."

His fists tightened on the bed skirt at her desperate plea, and every instinct screamed at him to hold her until the warriors neutralized the threat. "I have to find Vivian," he explained instead, "and they might need my help to fight." As a royal fae, even at sixteen, his physical strength and skill outmatched most of their strongest warriors. "You'll be safe here."

Scared eyes begged him to stay, and he averted his gaze. "I'm scared, Rome." *Godsdammit.*

The increasing terror in her words cut through him like a knife. "I know, princess, but I have to check on your sister and find my parents." The words sounded harsh as he battled his growing trepidation at leaving her there, and she flinched.

She freed his wrist and dropped her arm to the floor with resignation. "I understand." It felt like something broke between them, but Roman didn't know what or how to fix it. Violet had to know he didn't want to leave her, right?

If Roman shirked his duties, his mother and father would

never forgive him, and if something did happen to Vivian, he'd never forgive himself. *But if Vivian dies, the bond breaks.*

Appalled at his unsavory thoughts, he rose abruptly. "I'll be back for you. I promise."

"Rome," Violet called out softly.

He hesitated, knowing if she asked him to stay again, not even the gods could make him leave. Kneeling again, he peered under the bed. "What is it?"

"Keep Vivian safe."

The whispered words cracked something within him, and it took all he had to nod.

Roman plucked the section of bed skirt out from under the mattress, stood, glamoured himself and Violet to be invisible, and bolted from the room, locking the door on his way out. He knew his glamour wouldn't hold all the way to the training arena where Vivian should be, but it should stretch at least to the palace walls. The last he'd tested his glamour's strength, he could glamour the entire palace and courtyard, but not beyond. At some point he would be too far away from Violet for his magic to keep her hidden, and he cursed himself as he raced down the wide staircase.

Glamour training had always interested him the least, and he put most of his focus into the political and battle aspects of his training. He wanted to slam his fist into a wall at his own stupidity.

As Roman ran through the halls, he noticed guards methodically moving from room to room, calling out as they cleared each one. "Did any rebels make it inside the palace?" Roman asked a guard nearest the palace entrance.

The middle-aged woman bowed. "No, Your Grace. Only a handful of rebels made it over the walls, and we dealt with them." As if hearing the woman's words, the alarms stopped.

Roman offered his thanks and jogged outside, pulling up

short to stare, perplexed, at the small number of dead bodies being dragged into a pile. In the distance, guards knocked on every cottage in the warrior compound, clearing every home and ensuring the people's safety.

The bodies littering the pristine pink grass were easy to identify as rebels by their black-market weapons and armor. They weren't poor quality, per se, but they were made from scraps of various metals melted together. The crown monitored steel, iron, and other precious metals, and rebels had to smuggle scraps or use things like old iron stoves to make what little weapons they had.

As he surveyed the bodies, his confusion grew. It made little sense to send so few fighters into a palace crawling with guards and warriors. The plan reeked of decoy, but for what? Rebels caused chaos in attempts to cause unrest in the citizens by proving that the royals couldn't protect them. It never worked because Roman's parents *did* protect their people, and they protected them well.

The only other aim would be to kill the royals, and seeing as there were only three, Roman and his two parents, all of whom could handle a rebel with one hand tied behind their backs, the simplicity of the attack confused him further.

He scanned the courtyard and warrior compound for his parents. They were likely already discussing the attack with their council.

Frustrated, he stalked off toward the palace gates. Palace security was unmatched, and the top of the palace walls had spikes embedded in them four years ago after the queen of the Mountain Kingdom was murdered. Rebels had snuck over their walls and killed her in the palace garden.

Roman had never seen the Mountain Palace's walls, but his father said they should have been impossible to climb. The next day, modifications on the Tropical Palace walls began.

Rebels should not have been able to infiltrate their court-yard today.

"*Where are you?*" War's voice demanded, breaking into Roman's spiraling thoughts.

"*I'm on my way to the arena to find Vivian.*"

"*Vivian and the other trainees are well protected,*" War assured him.

Roman knew that, but if one of his parents happened to be at the arena and knew he didn't check on Viv, he'd never hear the end of it, otherwise, he'd still be in his bedroom. "*Violet is hiding under my bed. Will you stay with her until I can return?*"

"*I'll take care of Violet,*" War promised. "*Stay on guard. The attack could have been a distraction.*"

Roman cut the connection and jogged toward the palace gates. He feared the same thing.

He left me, was all Violet could think as she laid shaking under the bed. Roman had responsibilities as the prince, especially to his mate, she knew that, but she couldn't help feeling abandoned.

A loud bang sounded on the door to Roman's rooms, and Violet's lungs seized. *Please be a guard doing room checks.* Seconds later, the sound of wood splintering made her jump, and two sets of heavy footsteps clomped through the sitting room. Guards wouldn't break down the door, would they? She didn't know the protocol for the royal quarters. It would make sense to not give anyone a master key, but breaking down the door? No. *Something's wrong.*

Violet covered her mouth and squeezed her eyes shut. *This can't be happening.*

Heavy footfalls made their way into the bedroom, and

Violet concentrated on keeping her breathing as quiet as possible.

"Kincaid said the prince took ill this morning," a scratchy voice said.

"He's not in his bed, but the bedding is still rumpled. Check every room," said the other as a door banged open. These men weren't very bright. Breaking down a door and stomping around in the loudest way possible would have alerted Roman to their presence immediately. If he *were* here, he would have killed them.

After a few minutes of banging around the other rooms, the men returned to the bedroom. When two worn black leather boots appeared next to Violet's head, she sucked down a gasp and tried to creep backward toward the headboard.

"He's not here." The bed dipped, followed by an exasperated sigh and the sound of Roman's bedside drawer opening. "We outta see if there's anything expensive that's small enough to carry."

"We don't have time," the other replied angrily. "The diversion won't last long. I knew this wouldn't work on such late notice."

"We'll regroup and try again. If we kill the brat before he has a kid, the royal line ends."

Violet had heard her father talk enough about the rebels to know their primary goal had always been to extinguish the royal bloodline and take over. They'd tried for generations but never succeeded. To hear them speak so callously about killing a teenager they'd never met sent sickening chills down Violet's spine.

"We need to leave before they clear this floor," the man across the room told the other.

"A ring," the man on the bed said, sounding pleased. "We could sell it for a pretty price." A small box clattered to the ground and a large, gold ring rolled under the bed toward Violet.

Dread unlike any other crashed through her, and she tried to curl herself into a tight ball at the head of the bed.

The man rose from the bed, grumbling, while the other urged him to leave the ring. "Leave it, Clay. We have to go, *now*."

Please, leave, Violet silently begged.

"That ring could buy us a few new weapons," Clay argued. He lowered to the ground beside the bed and lifted the bed skirt. His shaved head and cruel eyes peered under the bed in search of the ring, and when his gaze landed on Violet, his mouth spread into a malicious grin. "Well, well, well."

She shook violently, her ears and head pounding as her limbs began to tingle. They were going to kill her. Or worse.

"There's a girl, Abe," Clay called over his shoulder.

Abe walked toward them and bent down to look at Violet. Where Clay's eyes were bloodthirsty, Abe's were calculating. He was a handsome man in his twenties with shoulder-length dark brown hair, light olive skin, and the palest grey eyes Violet had ever seen. For a moment, she thought he'd spare her.

That hope died a quick death when he said, "Seems the gods are on our side. That's the prince's mate, Vivian Maekin."

How does he know about Viv? No one knew Vivian and Roman were mates outside of family and the council. *No one.*

Clay laughed, and the sound was the ugliest thing Violet had ever heard. Abe stood, and she heard metal slide against leather. "We need to kill her and leave before anyone finds us. Drag her out."

Clay reached a meaty arm under the bed to make a grab for Violet's arm. Screaming, she pushed herself against the wall. His attempts to reach her were futile, and Violet thanked the gods for Roman's oversized bed.

"Come out, girl, and we'll make it quick," Clay sneered. He reached for her again, but his shoulders were too broad to fit under the frame. "I can't reach her."

Abe ripped up the bed skirt on the other side of the bed and jammed his arm under the frame. Abe was leaner than Clay with longer limbs, and his fingertips brushed against Violet's skin.

She screamed again but had nowhere left to go. "I'm not Vivian," she sobbed. "I swear."

Shoving his shoulder completely under the frame, Abe reached for her again as she screamed and begged him to leave her alone, to not kill her, to let her go. He ignored her pleas, and with another grunt, he shoved his entire upper body under the bed. When they both realized he had her, her screams and sobs became pure terror.

A beastly roar thundered through the room just as Abe's hand closed around Violet's wrist. Clay yelled something, but Violet couldn't make it out over her own screams.

Abe released her, eyes wide with fear, and tried to push himself under the bed, but something *ripped him* back with blinding speed. The bed skirt fell, obscuring her vision, but screams and violence echoed through the air. Violet slapped her hands over her ears to muffle the horrifying sounds of death. Her body curled back into a ball, her muscles tightening to the point of pain, and breathing felt impossible.

She didn't know how long the decimation lasted, but after a while, the room filled with an eerie silence. Soft thuds neared her and a bloodied white paw reached under the bed, followed by a few huffs and whines.

War.

Violet crawled toward the tigon and laid her quaking hand on his large paw. He tried to stick his head under the frame but couldn't go any farther than his nose. "Is it safe?" she whimpered, hating how her voice broke.

War purred and his tongue darted out to lick her hand.

"I'm coming out," she told the big cat, and he moved so she could inch her body out into the open.

A nightmare surrounded her, and she had to swallow another scream.

Violet slammed her eyes shut, not wanting any details of the bloody massacre to sear into her brain. She dropped to the floor beside War and blindly reached for him, needing something to anchor her. "You saved me." Her body trembled harder as the adrenaline wore off, and she squeezed her arms around the beast's neck as she cried.

Roman released a breath of relief when he saw the junior warriors sequestered in a weapons room with a wall of guards blocking them in. "The juniors are all accounted for and safe?" he asked Latton, the new sparring instructor.

"Yes, Your Grace. All but you," the man deadpanned.

Roman classified as a junior warrior, but his royal title and extra training put him high enough to not only fight alongside his men, but to call the shots if his mother and father weren't around. It irked some of the other warriors and guards, Latton included.

Roman ignored the instructor and scanned the juniors, finally spotting the top of Vivian's auburn hair. She chatted with the guy next to her, and Roman felt ridiculous for worrying. He closed his eyes and connected with War to check on Violet.

The moment they connected, he stumbled, watching helplessly through his *familiar* as a man tried to force his way under Roman's bed while another stood on the other side.

War ripped the man out from under the bed and attacked in a whirl of teeth and claws, but it was Violet's screams as she begged the men to not kill her that embedded themselves into Roman's soul. He would never forget that sound as long as he lived.

What have I done?

"Rome!" Vivian yelled. "What's wrong?"

Roman cut the connection with War and took off in a full sprint, ignoring Vivian's calls. He could feel her anxiety and fear mingling with his own, but he didn't have time to explain. Vivian had always been safe. He'd *known* that—had been able to feel it—but he let his sense of duty override his instinct, and Violet paid the price.

If anything happened to her, he wouldn't survive it.

Nothing prepared Roman for what awaited him when he stepped inside his bedroom.

There wasn't much in way of furniture because he liked space and despised clutter, but what little he had, namely his bed and nightstands, glistened with darkening blood spatter.

The two rebels lay mauled and dismembered on the red-stained rug, as if War had thrown their severed limbs around like discarded chew toys. Bloody quills dotted the floor, some embedded in bits of flesh.

Roman found Violet on the other side of the bed, kneeling beside a blood-soaked War with her arms wrapped around the tigon's neck.

"Princess," Roman rasped and crossed the room in a daze. He reached out for her, but she flinched away from his touch, breaking him even more.

"I thought you'd be safe here," he whispered helplessly, yet she still wouldn't look at him.

He glanced back at the remains on the floor, absorbing the reality of what almost happened. A tether inside of him snapped, freeing a darkness full of hate.

I almost lost her. He blamed himself; blamed the rebels; blamed the gods.

Footsteps ran into the room. "Oh my gods," Vivian choked out and pushed him aside to grab her sister.

Violet turned and threw herself into Vivian's arms, and Roman stared numbly as Vivian rocked her sister back and forth, whispering soothing words into her ear.

Vivian's chaotic emotions—fear, relief, and confusion—tangled together in Roman's chest. His own emotions threatened to crush him, and he wondered if they were crushing her too.

Did she feel the utter devastation and fury so potent he could taste it on his tongue?

He stared at the Maekin sisters, knowing Violet would never be the same.

And neither would he.

9

Roman sat across from Vivian in one of his mother's ostentatious drawing rooms. Paintings of his ancestors lined the walls, separated by large golden sconces. Rugs with busy patterns of rich reds and golds covered every inch of the floor and contrasted with the bright colors of the chairs and settees littered around the room.

Roman knew he looked haggard. His hair was a mess, accompanied by dark circles from lack of sleep, and his anger still simmered under his skin like a living entity.

He hadn't spoken to Violet since the attack a week ago, and he wanted to rip the Maekins' cottage to shreds until he stood in her room. Meri and Edgar kept her out of school and wouldn't let him in to see her. He'd tried to pull rank, but Edgar wouldn't budge, saying she needed her rest.

Roman couldn't take it, and he'd resorted to glamouring himself invisible to slip inside their cottage. His girl looked as haunted as he felt. Violet's ashen skin resembled death, and her vacant eyes stared at her bedroom wall. Seeing her like that broke something inside him, destroyed it so thoroughly that he'd never be the same.

"Why was Violet in your rooms the day of the attack?" Vivian demanded, bringing him back to the present with her curt tone.

Roman glared at the ground. An interrogation about the worst day of his life had him precariously close to throttling the contrite look off Vivian's face. "She'd heard I was sick and brought me soup." If he could go back, he would never have feigned ill, and this nightmare would have never happened.

Vivian lifted a skeptical brow. "You didn't seem sick." He decided not to answer, and she pinned him in place with her inscrutable gaze. "Your *friendship* with my sister needs to stop."

The darkness Roman tried to keep at bay swelled, forcing him to restrain himself from telling her to go fuck herself. "Excuse me?"

Vivian's face darkened to match Roman's mood. "You heard exactly what I said. I've seen you two together at home, and it needs to stop."

Roman threw his head back with an incredulous laugh, and Vivian jerked back. "You have no right to demand anything of me. Do you think I don't know that you're still seeing someone else?" He leaned forward and infused his words with venom. "Watch your fucking tone."

She recoiled and backed away. "How dare you?"

"How dare *me*?" His voice rose with every word. "I can feel your emotions, or did you forget? You have no right to ask me to give up a friendship when you are in a romantic relationship with someone else."

"See whoever you want," Vivian sneered. "I don't care, but not her." He stared at her. She was out of her fucking mind if she thought any amount of threatening would keep him from

Violet. "The gods chose me," she reminded him. "I won. I am who they blessed as your queen, not her."

I won. Roman almost laughed in her face again at the audacity of it all. "A mate bond isn't a prize to be won," he snarled. "You don't care about me, you only care about besting your sister. It's pathetic." Not wanting to be in her presence any longer than necessary, he stood to leave.

Had he not been able to feel Vivian's love for another, guilt would insist he grant her request. He wouldn't, but he'd feel bad about it. Violet meant everything to him. Vivian meant nothing.

Would Violet have loved another man if she'd been fated to Roman? The thought made him murderous. If she were his, he would kill anyone who stood between them, no matter the consequences.

Vivian stood silently, watching him leave, and he could feel her bitterness melding with his own. "We're not married yet, and I'll not take your happiness from you," he said from the doorway. "Love whomever you want, but until we are married, *n*ever deign to dictate who I keep in my life. I am the future king, no matter what, but your only tie to the crown is through me."

A week later, Roman cornered Griff during training. Violet's best friend towered over most, but not him, and the boy had to tilt his head, his shoulders tense as if ready to flee. Griff's rich russet skin sported a layer of sweat, and he squinted his black eyes against the afternoon sun.

"Is something wrong?" Griff's voice cracked, as most boys' did at their age.

Griff was an excellent fighter and rarely intimidated, but Roman didn't miss the rigidness of his stance.

"Do you know when Violet is returning to school?" Roman inquired as cavalier as possible. He'd skipped class the day before and went to Violet's house to check on her, only to find her gone.

Griff lifted a single brow. "She didn't tell you? I thought you two were friends."

Roman rolled his neck and reminded himself that beating the answer out of Griff would win him no favor with Violet. "I haven't been able to speak to her since the rebel attack." He pushed away the image of Violet clinging to War's bloody neck.

"You haven't been to see her?" Griff's tone took on a hard edge.

"Where is she?" Roman ground out, losing all patience. He'd rather not speak to her with her entire family present, but if he couldn't get her alone during the school day, he would have to.

Griff crossed his arms with a smug smirk. "She switched schools to the one in town. The one near the post building."

Roman reared back. "What? Why?"

Glancing side to side, Griff lowered his voice. "If you tell anyone this, I'll try to beat your ass," he warned. "I know I'll lose, but I'll inflict as much damage as possible." Despite wanting to pummel the guy, Roman admired and appreciated his protectiveness of Violet. "If someone finds out, they might tease her around the compound, and then I'll have to fight them too."

Roman's jaw tightened. "I would never betray her."

Griff's sigh was sad and full of pity. "Since the attack, she refuses to set foot inside the palace." He waited for Roman's response, but all Roman did was stare back dumbly. Griff shrugged. "It reminds her of the attack."

Roman would burn the palace to the ground when he took the throne if it would ease Violet's fears. He hated that a horrific memory ruined a place containing some of his most coveted ones. "I won't tell anyone," he vowed. "What time does her new school let out?"

"They only go until one o'clock," Griff replied. "They let out soon."

Roman nodded and spun on his heel to leave, throwing a thanks over his shoulder.

Roman waited outside of the small school building on the western-most part of Saltu. Violet moving schools meant less time with her, but if the palace frightened her, he'd not try to convince her to come back.

He would ask his father if he could switch schools. Roman already knew the answer, but trying never hurt. Since the attack on the palace, his need to be around Violet had become an obsession born from a need to keep her safe. What little spare time he had, he spent glamoured invisible at Violet's side. Having let her down once, he'd not do it again.

When the school bell rang, Roman stepped aside as the stream of students filed out of the building. He searched every face for his favorite freckles and blue eyes.

The sun glinted off a familiar head of silky auburn hair, and he couldn't stop the relief and elation coursing through him. Releasing his glamour, he called out, "Violet!" ignoring the startled cries of those around him.

Violet turned at the sound of her name, and the content look on her face faded. Roman stalked forward, dread trickling through his veins. Seeing her face fill with regret made him want to knock everyone over to get to her faster.

"What's wrong?" he asked roughly. Roman had never possessed patience.

Her delicate throat bobbed. "We need to talk."

Dread settled low in Violet's gut at what she had to do. Like a coward, she'd put off the conversation, but here Roman stood, staring at her, looking worse for wear.

Without a word, he tipped his head to the right and guided her through the other students. Slayton, one of her friends who attended her new school, caught her eye, silently asking if he needed to intervene. Violet subtly shook her head. The boy tipped his chin and left in the opposite direction.

Roman stared after Slayton with a murderous expression, and his hand on her lower back tightened around the fabric of her dress. "Are you dating him?" he asked through gritted teeth.

Violet peered up at him, hating how his jealousy made her feel. The way her heart preened only further solidified her decision. "We're friends. He's the only person I know at my new school."

Roman's hand and shoulders relaxed as he led her into the trees lining the road. The jungle and shore were her favorite places to be, and she didn't want to taint her happy place with this memory, but no other place offered privacy from prying ears.

Roman guided her toward a large tree with a brilliant bright yellow trunk, large, flat pink and green leaves, and bright purple vines hanging loosely from the top. They sat down on two roots, facing each other, and he rested his elbows on his thighs.

"Why do I feel like you're about to break my heart?" No anger tinged his words, only sad resignation, and Violet resisted throwing her arms around him.

She swallowed past the knot in her throat, praying she wouldn't cry. "We can't be friends anymore."

He straightened, displaying every emotion Violet knew in rapid succession. "I don't understand."

This might be the most humiliating thing to ever happen to me, she thought, but if she didn't tell the truth, he wouldn't let her go. Taking a deep breath, she straightened her shoulders and met his questioning stare head on. How did one tell a friend they were inappropriately in love with them?

When Violet had first learned to climb trees, she'd been afraid of falling. Seeing the hard, unforgiving ground below had made anxiety ripple through her system and kept her from climbing high.

One day, she fell from a lower branch and cried the entire way home. Her father intercepted her, kissed her bruises, took her back to the forest, and encouraged her to try again. It took quite a bit of coaxing, but once she'd shakily scaled the tree to the lowest branch, he'd told her to jump.

"If you pay attention," he explained. "You can jump before you fall to protect yourself on the way down."

She'd always respected her father's wisdom, and as always, he'd been right. Violet learned to predict when she needed to jump, even from one branch to another, to avoid falling.

Yet, somehow, she'd missed all the signs with Roman.

Violet had thought they were only friends, she really had, but apparently her heart missed the message; a dangerous thing when you're up so high.

No one had explained the dangers of falling in love—

infinitely more dangerous than falling from a tree. When you fall in love and the other person doesn't catch you, you break more than a bone when hitting the ground. You break everything. Your heart. Your soul. Your confidence in yourself. It all just *shatters*.

They must call it falling because when it's over, you can feel your heart fall to your feet right before it breaks against the hard truth.

Violet hadn't a clue how to tell Roman how she felt, something her mind couldn't differentiate from a life-or-death situation. Blood roared in her ears, and her heart tried to crack her ribcage as if personally offended by their existence. Better to just blurt it out before she passed out. "I'm in love with you."

Roman's nostrils flared and his chest heaved. He looked furious at her admission. Violet's heart hit the ground. *Hard.* She'd known he didn't return her feelings, yet a small part of her thought he might. *No.* It was better this way.

It wouldn't matter, anyway. They'd still have to end their friendship. "Having to watch your relationship with Vivian develop will be too hard if I feel this way. I need to get past it if I'm going to be able to be around you two in the future."

Roman jerked back. "Get past it? What does that mean?"

For being one of the smartest people Violet knew, the prince sure did have trouble grasping simple concepts. "It means I need to get over these feelings, and I can't do that if you keep," she searched for the right words, sputtering, "being you."

She gasped when Roman shot to his feet. "No."

Stunned, Violet leaned her head back to stare at him. "No?"

One step and he'd crossed the distance between them. One second and he'd dropped beside her. "No."

"You can't say no," she argued with bewilderment. "It's inappropriate for me to feel this way. It's *wrong*." Her lower lip tried to tremble, but she willed it to hold steady. "I'm a terrible person," she whispered. "Who falls in love with their sister's future husband?"

Roman stabbed a hand through his hair and tugged on the short strands. "You don't get to decide for me if we stay friends or not," he informed her with finality. "What about me? You can dispose of me that easily?"

Violet scoffed, her anger rising. "I am making this decision for *me*. Being in love with someone promised to my sister is wrong and *devastating*."

She jumped to her feet, throwing up her hands and letting them fall. "You're not listening. I love you, Roman. Giving you up will hurt more than anything I've experienced, but watching you fall in love with Vivian will destroy me. I need time to get over you before I'm subjected to that. Why can't you understand? How can you ask this of me?" She swiped at her stupid tears, hating that she cried so easily.

He glared at her and maneuvered her around a large root until her back hit the tree. "Did it ever occur to you that I love you, too?"

His words sank in. *No.*

"Did you ever think of what losing you and watching you fall in love with someone else will do to me?" His strong arms caged her in on either side of her head. "You might get over me, but I won't get over you. How can *you* ask that of *me*?"

A pain like she'd never known enveloped her, weighing her down, like being buried under a pile of stone. Despair beat at her until there was nothing left. Roman was everything she'd ever wanted. Having him tell her he loved her too, knowing she could never have him, altered something inside her. If she thought unrequited love hurt, it had nothing on this.

He loved her, yet she would watch him fall out of love with

her and in love with his mate. Nothing hurt more than knowing she had his heart but couldn't keep it. *Nothing.*

Imagine starving, having foregone food for a week, then being presented with a juicy steak, only to have it yanked away after one bite. "You're going to marry my sister," she whispered. "Loving me doesn't change that. She's your *mate.* The gods made you for each other, and one day, you will love her and she'll love you." The muscle in his jaw flexed. "When that day comes, I want to be happy for you. I want you two to be happy, but in order to not taint that happiness with hurt and resentment, I need to move on." She closed her eyes. "And so do you."

Roman pressed his forehead to hers. If he kissed her, she wouldn't have the strength to push him away. If he asked her to be his, she'd give in. Part of her wanted him to, and the other part screamed for him to let her go.

He pushed off the tree and stepped back. "I'll give you anything you want, princess." His voice held no emotion, but his eyes gave away his every thought. The hurt they held made her want to take everything back. "If space is what you want, space is what you'll get." He spun on his heel, and she swore she heard him whisper, "for now," as he walked away.

Violet watched him leave and gave in to the sinking feeling pulling her down. There, on the forest floor, she released her anguish, crying until her throat grew raw. Everything in her dimmed, and she knew there was no bouncing back from this within a day or two.

Despite never wanting to speak of this again, Violet went home and told her mother part of the story, just not the who. She'd considered faking sick instead, but then they'd call a healer. Going with half-truths seemed to be the best option, and she could only pray her mother would understand.

Looking back on her conversation with Roman, she realized her foolishness in thinking she could ever get over him.

Roman pressed his forehead against the cool glass of Violet's window as he strained to see against the afternoon glare. For a week he'd watched through her window as her beautiful complexion paled from staying inside and the light in her eyes dulled from grief. The same grief that held him prisoner.

Their souls were anchored to the ocean floor, weighed down by their confessions.

Roman had fought his every instinct to pull her into his arms when she'd sobbed on the ground after breaking his heart. The next day, when she stayed home from school, claiming illness, he'd skipped his own classes and sat outside her window.

Meri opened the curtains during the day to let in the light, allowing Roman to observe Violet. During the night, his access to her closed, and all he could do was listen to the sounds of her soft cries.

Accusing her of being able to give him up easily was cruel. The girl he watched day in and day out mirrored what he felt inside. His soul had fallen into a dark and lonely abyss, taking the joy out of everything he'd once cared about.

He didn't need a bond to tell him Violet was his true mate. Every royal found their soulmate at thirteen years old, but Roman had found his at twelve, only to have her ripped away.

For two weeks he and Violet wallowed in their grief, as star-crossed lovers do. Meri finally coaxed Violet into attending school, and Roman vowed to break thousands of years of tradition to marry her at any cost.

Nothing would stop him from having her, not even the gods themselves.

10

Roman raced toward the palace, his heart pounding in his ears. Violet needed him. Faceless figures tried to slow him down, but nothing mattered more than getting to her.

Violet's terror-filled scream pierced the air, urging him to run faster. He shoved past the broken door of his rooms and sprinted across the sitting room. "Violet!"

Roman burst into his bedroom and her tortured screams grew louder. The vacant room stood eerily still, save for Violet's screams ricocheting off the walls. "Violet?" Roman dove to the ground and peered under the bed.

She lay on her stomach, screaming and sobbing until she noticed him. Her hand reached for him, and her voice trembled. "Are you going to leave me?"

Roman shook his head and wrapped his hand around hers. "Never."

"Then why did you?" Her words pierced his heart like a well-aimed sword.

Why did you?

Why did you?

Why did you?

A decayed hand grabbed her from the other side and ripped her away. "No!" he screamed and shot to his feet.

He watched helplessly as a hideous man dragged a dagger across her neck. Roman dove across the bed, but the man vanished. Gathering Violet into his arms, Roman rested his head against hers, and for the first time in years, he wept.

Violet's death violently tore Roman from the nightmare. His sweat-slicked body stuck to the sheets, and he kicked to untangle himself from the covers.

Every night Roman dreamed of that day, and every night, the nightmares worsened. In the past, he'd woken up before Violet died, but tonight he'd watched his greatest fear unfold. The image of her smooth neck blooming with red and the light draining from her terrified eyes burned itself into his memory.

What if the gods are trying to warn me?

With that grisly thought, he dressed quickly, donned his boots, and glamoured himself invisible. Roman made his way to the compound, taking care not to make noise when he passed the guards.

He stood in front of the Maekins' cottage and told himself to go home.

In the Tropical Kingdom, homes had large, open vents to cool the interior with fresh air, but iron bars protected the homes from unwanted visitors and animals. Right now, he hated the ingenious design and tried every unbarred window he could reach.

Each locked window chipped away at his hope, until the window to their laundering room slid open without resistance.

Roman hoisted himself onto the sill and quietly climbed

inside. He only needed to confirm she was alive and well, then he would leave. He'd not expected her peaceful, sleeping form to calm the raging storm inside him.

Standing beside her bed, watching as she slept, brought him more peace than he'd felt in a year. His fingers twitched, itching to reach out and touch her to make sure this wasn't another dream.

He spun around at the sound of movement behind him, having forgotten Vivian slept across the room. The other Maekin sister rolled over, mumbled something in her sleep, and fell back into a deep slumber.

I need to leave.

But he couldn't. Roman eased the dressing table chair to Violet's bedside. After lowering himself onto the worn-out cushion, he leaned forward and rested his elbows on his knees.

He didn't know how long he sat there, watching her sleep, but eventually his lids grew heavy. If he fell asleep, he didn't think his glamour would hold to conceal him.

Then he left, vowing to never return.

Except he did return.

Every night.

SIX MONTHS LATER

Roman wandered out of the trees and stalked across the shore toward Violet. She looked beautiful with her long hair billowing in the breeze. One day he'd be able to join her without glamour, but for now, he'd resigned to watching her in secret.

After pouring over every book in the palace library, he'd found nothing of use about mate bonds, but he'd not give up until his father forced him to marry Vivian. As it was, he'd already asked his parents to extend their engagement another year. Instead of marrying at twenty-two, they'd marry at twenty-three. His father had said no, but to both his and Roman's surprise, his mother said yes. The king knew better than to go against his wife, and that was that.

If the time came and Roman hadn't found a way, he'd ask to push it back again. If they said no, he'd find another way. A royal refusing to marry their mate defied the gods and put their kingdom's future safety at risk, but selfishly, he didn't care.

Violet tied up the end of her dress and waded into the water, her movements slow as she pushed against the small waves lapping at her shins. Roman removed his boots and socks and rolled up his pants to join her.

He drank in her beauty, always greedy for more. Assessing all of her while she slept proved difficult, but following her around allowed him to study her more closely.

She bent at the waist and reached into the water with utter determination. Tipping forward to see her hands through the clear water, Roman watched Violet's fingers dig through the sand for buried treasures to add to her bucket sitting on the shore. He'd watched her do this countless times and wished he could be the one holding her bucket every single one of them.

Violet straightened and held up a clear horn-shaped shell that reflected the sunlight in an array of colors. Everything in the fae lands burst with color, and the trinkets in the ocean were no different.

The smile she blessed him with lit up her entire face, and Roman wished he could capture it in a painting to carry with him everywhere. Happiness didn't exist in his life outside of these coveted moments, and he'd not give up a single second unless necessary. Even then, he sometimes shirked his duties to soak her in.

There was nothing normal about following her around, obsessing over her every move, but it didn't matter. Not having her in his life wasn't an option. It hadn't been since the day he'd crashed into her and broken her shells.

Violet faced the shore, pushed her legs through the water with big steps, and carefully placed the shell into her bucket before heading back out.

Her cheeks and nose were red, and Roman tilted his head toward the sun with a frown. *How long has she been out here? Did she forget to put on sun protectant?*

"Violet!"

Roman whipped around at the male voice and glowered at the medium-height boy with pale, peachy skin and white-blond hair jogging across the white sand. A lock of tow-colored hair fell in his face, and Roman cursed the handsome fucker.

Slayton Robbins.

Violet grinned widely. "What are you doing out here?"

Slayton set down his bag, took off his footwear, rolled up his trousers, and picked up Violet's bucket. "My father let me leave the store early today. I was hoping I'd catch you out here."

How many times had this half-wit accompanied Violet without Roman knowing? Roman glared at the bucket in Slayton's hand. If it hadn't held Violet's precious finds, he would have knocked it out of his grasp.

Violet trekked back into the ocean with both he and Slayton on her heels. "Was it slow today?"

Slayton shrugged. "It comes in waves. The rebel attacks in the Mountain Kingdom have a lot of people scared. They come in and buy enough food to last them for a while so they don't have to leave their homes unless necessary."

Violet's posture stiffened, and Roman considered drowning Slayton for mentioning rebels in her presence. It wasn't like anyone would know his death was Roman's doing. Violet would only see Slayton fall and struggle beneath the surface.

Roman shook off the notion, unwilling to traumatize her further by making her watch her friend die.

As much as Roman loathed to admit it, Slayton's information intrigued him. Rebel attacks were increasing across Eden, but an increase in attacks every few decades was nothing new. Roman's mother claimed it was because they either switched leadership or needed to rebuild their factions from their previous failed attacks. The Mountain Kingdom dealt with the most increased activity as of late.

If the Tropical Kingdom's people were frightened, the king and queen needed to know. Roman glared harder at Slayton, annoyed he'd been useful.

Violet leaned over and dug around the ocean floor. "That makes sense. Is Griff still in training?" Her quick subject change did not go unnoticed by Slayton, and he had the good grace to look guilty.

Slayton held out the bucket. "Your mother stopped by earlier to drop off the new chest binders you made me. I like the new buttons. I've never seen the long flat ones before."

Violet dropped a few pebbles into the bucket. "Did you see the different button slots on the underside of the cloth to make it tighter? That way, if you lose all of those big muscles, you can size it down."

Roman smirked at her teasing and sized up Slayton's stout, muscular frame. He had a farmer's strength from lifting heavy sacks of grain as opposed to the fighting strength of a warrior.

Slayton held up his free arm and flexed. "Don't think I didn't notice the other slots you put in to accommodate my muscles *expanding*."

Roman took a step toward the scoundrel, forgetting his stealth, and both Violet and Slayton whipped around when the water splashed with his movement.

"I think it's just a fish," Violet dismissed and redirected her attention to Slayton's chest. "Are you wearing the new one now? You really have bulked up since the last time I made you one, and I wanted to make sure there was enough fabric, but not too much to ruin the compression."

"Not yet," Slayton replied. "I'll try it on when I get home. I need my mother to help me the first few times until I get used to the new style."

Violet motioned to Slayton's things in the sand. "Do you have them with you? I can show you how to use them."

Roman saw red. In no world would he watch Violet touch another man's bare chest, no matter how innocent the reason.

Slayton opened his mouth to reply, but Roman, now close enough from his misstep earlier, kicked him square in the ass. The force sent the man toppling forward, face first into the water. Violet shrieked and reached for her friend. Slayton struggled to stand, even with Violet's help, and Roman muffled a laugh.

"Something shoved me," Slayton insisted and glanced around looking uneasy.

Good.

Violet nervously studied the surrounding water. "Are you alright?"

Slayton rubbed his backside, and Roman could have sworn the man looked right at him before flicking his gaze to the water. "I must have tripped," he decided.

"Gods," Violet breathed and placed a hand over her heart. "You scared me."

Slayton gained his bearings and glanced down. "Shit, Vi, your bucket."

Roman's smug smile faded. Violet's shoulders drooped as she watched her bucket float farther away from the shore. He hadn't thought about her treasures when he'd kicked Slayton; he'd only thought about Violet helping the man remove his clothes.

The image still infuriated him. Roman knew there might come a day she would touch other men intimately and they'd touch her, but that day wasn't today.

It wouldn't be tomorrow either.

Roman crept into Violet's room and watched her chest rise and fall. He released a long breath. *She's alive.*

Across the room, Vivian lay buried beneath her blankets. The substantial happiness radiating down the bond suggested pleasant dreams. *Very* pleasant dreams.

Must be nice.

Roman set down Violet's bucket filled with new shells and pebbles. Swimming into the vast ocean to retrieve her bucket took no time at all, but collecting new treasures took all afternoon because he wanted them to be perfect.

Next to the bucket, he left a glass jar of sun protectant on Violet's pale yellow dressing table and crossed to her bed. Looking down, Roman bit his tongue to keep from laughing. The princess lay on her side, mouth open, with half of her face smooshed against the pillow. She looked adorable. The pink tint to her tan cheeks killed his mirth. Just as he suspected. *Sunburn.*

A half-finished string of beads on her side table snagged his attention, and he picked them up as quietly as possible.

The left sleeve of his shirt pulled up with the movement to reveal the green stone bracelet she'd given him for his thirteenth birthday. Replacing the strand of beads on her night-stand, Roman lifted his wrist to examine the scratched-up beads and worn string. If his bracelet ever broke, he would be devastated. It was the most precious item he owned.

Tugging his sleeve down, he picked up her bright pink dressing table chair and moved it beside her bed. He pulled a shifting puzzle from his pocket and sat down to settle in for the night. Footsteps in the hall halted the swift movements of his fingers. Roman glamoured the room to look exactly as it had when he walked in, but his heart rate kicked up regardless.

The door to the bedroom pushed open quietly and Vivian tiptoed inside. He watched with curious interest as she lifted the blanket on her bed and pulled out pillows he'd mistaken for her body. She removed her boots, and when she reached for her shirt, Roman averted his gaze.

Breaking into someone's house to watch them sleep was one thing, but watching someone undress without their consent was a line he wouldn't cross. Not that he desired to see Vivian naked.

He had to give it to her. She'd learned to move around quiet as a mouse. Vivian's blanket rustled as she climbed into bed, and Roman faced her again.

As his betrothed, he should care where she'd been and who she'd been with, but he felt nothing. The fact that he could not care less about Vivian or her comings and goings further proved he needed to correct the gods' mistake.

11

EIGHTEEN YEARS OLD

"Hold still," Violet chided War as she tried to braid the quill sheaths on the back of his head. She'd seen a new style of braid on a woman in town that she wanted to learn.

War visited Violet most afternoons, and today she'd taken one look at his long, soft sheaths and begged him to let her practice. He'd huffed loudly, turned his back to her, and sat in front of the settee in her parents' living room while she practiced repeatedly.

"I'm almost done," she promised, earning a rumbling purr in return.

A forceful knock on the front door ruined her concentration and sent a spike of fear through her. Violet scrambled to the floor and tried to slide under the settee, but the decorative scrollwork on the frame made it too tight a squeeze. If she could just lift it and slide under, she'd be fine.

Rolling onto her back, she grabbed the wooden frame and lifted it high. War, realizing her plan, put his nose under the frame to take some of the weight off. Ever so quietly, she slid under and lowered the settee, hoping the intruder left.

War never hid with her. She'd attempted to coax him into her bedroom closet a few times, but he always resisted. The cat was terrifying, but she couldn't help but worry.

After another knock went unanswered, Violet heard the front door open, cranking up the pounding of her heart. Her family wouldn't have knocked before entering, and the knowledge a stranger had entered her home uninvited sent Violet into a bigger panic. Heavy steps thumped across the wooden floor, akin to the way Clay and Abe had stomped through Roman's rooms.

What if the rebels discovered she'd outed the rebel spy to her father? It'd been years, but *what if?*

She clamped her lips together to keep from screaming. *Stay quiet and they won't find you.*

"What are you doing here?" Roman's deep voice took her by surprise. It took her a second to realize he spoke to War. She almost cried with relief, just as she did every time something like this happened.

Rolling her head to the side to stare at War's paws, she focused on slowing her breathing until her hands stopped tingling and lost that heavy feeling. If the gods had any mercy, Roman would take War and leave.

"What do you mean?" Roman demanded. Violet had witnessed Roman and War's conversations before, and she'd always wondered why the prince never responded in his mind. Assuming he could. She didn't know.

"Violet?" Roman called out.

She stayed quiet, not wanting to face the embarrassment of being found hiding under a piece of furniture like a child.

And by Roman of all people.

Roman's voice dipped lower. "Under the settee?"

War, you traitor.

Roman's boots appeared, followed by his knees, then his

hands and face. "Hey, princess. What are you doing under there?"

She sniffled, mad at herself for almost crying, and turned her head the other way. "Taking a nap."

Silence followed the lie, and she thought maybe he'd leave. No such luck. "Will you come out?"

"I'm trying to sleep," she clipped. "Please lock the door on your way out."

"Either you come out or I'm coming under there," he warned.

Dammit.

"You wouldn't fit," she muttered half-heartedly. Roman stood at *least* six foot four with broad shoulders and defined muscles everywhere. She'd be surprised if his arm fit past his elbow.

Defeated, she pushed at the settee's underbelly to lift it. Roman stood and the entire piece of furniture levitated. Violet crawled out from under it, and Roman set it back in its place. She motioned to the settee. "Thank you. What are you doing here?"

He considered her for a beat, and she nervously smoothed down her hair. They'd said little more than short greetings since their conversation in the woods two years ago, and every encounter they had exuded awkwardness.

"Looking for War. I saw he was in your house." Violet hated that Roman could spy through his *familiar.* She slitted her gaze at her feline friend for allowing the prince to spy, and Roman leaned over to run a finger down War's quill sheaths. "Did you braid his sheaths?"

She lifted a shoulder. "I needed to practice."

Roman rubbed a hand over his mouth to hide a smile, and she instinctively reached out to flick his forehead. His hand shot out and caught her wrist like many times before. The familiarity pricked at something deep inside her.

"You're still too slow," he teased. She rolled her eyes, and Roman dropped her wrist with a tip of his head toward the settee. "Why were you hiding?"

Violet busied herself by fussing with War's sheaths to stall. She'd never been a good liar and decided to try her hand at deflection. "I'll unbraid these and you can leave. It won't take long."

Roman touched her elbow gently, and she resisted the urge to shake him off. Pity was the last thing she wanted. "Talk to me, princess."

And pity was what she got.

It made her want to punch something. His perfect nose seemed like a good place to start. "I'm fine." She needed him to leave. Over the last two years she'd moved past her infatuation with the prince, but not completely. She suspected a piece of her would always belong to him, so she avoided him at all costs, even at their weekly dinners. "I want you to leave."

He folded his arms across his chest. "No."

She froze. "No? You can't say no." *Is that his favorite word?* she thought sourly. "Go. Away."

War looked between them, and Violet considered asking him to drag Roman out by the scruff of his neck. Roman stared at her long enough to make her fidget, and she glanced at the door. If she opened it and pushed him hard enough, maybe he would stumble and she could close the door before he regained his footing.

"Is there something fun under there?" Roman mused.

She bristled at his teasing tone. "I will drag you out myself."

Roman's slow grin promised a fight if she tried, and she turned to War. "Are you strong enough to drag him out?" The beast nodded, and Violet pointed at the infuriating prince. "I will give you all the juicy steaks you could ever want and pet you for an hour every day if you'll get him out of here."

Roman shot forward and hauled Violet over his shoulder. She shrieked and struggled to escape his hold, but it was futile. He tutted. "That wasn't very nice."

"Put me down," she ordered, trying to see around the prince's body. "War, a little help would be nice."

"He won't hurt me while I'm holding you," Roman informed her. She could practically feel his shit-eating grin. To his credit, War looked disgruntled at the fact. "We can do this one of two ways. Either you tell me willingly, or I tote you around for the rest of the day until you do."

"Grow up and put me down," Violet commanded, pointing at the ground.

He squeezed her thigh. "No."

"Is that the only word in your vocabulary?" she asked tartly.

"Only when you make demands of me that I cannot deliver," he affirmed. "I won't let this go."

Resigning to her fate, she dropped her arms and hung like a dead body. "I feel safe under things, especially my bed."

Roman lowered her to the ground, wrapped one of his hands around the back of her neck, and tilted her chin to look at him with the other. "What's frightened you?" She tried to extract herself from his hold, but he wouldn't budge. "I'm not letting you go until you tell me who has you scared enough to hide." The way he spoke promised of death, and it sent a chill down her spine.

"When you knocked, I thought it might have been rebels," she admitted.

Roman's murderous look turned stricken. "Princess," he whispered and pulled her against his chest. "Nothing I say or do can make up for leaving you under that bed." He buried his face in her hair and held her tight. "I'll never forgive myself for doing this to you."

He thinks it's his fault? She pushed back and he reluctantly let her. "What happened wasn't your fault. You know that, don't you?" She watched him carefully, astonished to realize he *did* blame himself. "Your duty is to the people of this kingdom. You couldn't protect any of them had you stayed with me. The *rebels* tried to hurt me that day, not you."

"What's going on here?" Vivian's sharp voice cut through the air from the kitchen doorway. Violet tried to jump back, but Roman tightened his hold. *How did I not hear her open the back door?* Her sister must have seen Roman's horse outside and deliberately snuck inside.

Violet tried to free herself again, but Roman simply stared down at her as though Vivian didn't exist. "Let me go," she whispered hotly.

Broken from his trance, he unwrapped his arms and faced his mate. "I scared your sister."

Vivian's astute gaze slid between Roman and Violet. Fighting with her sister was the last thing Violet wanted. They didn't have much of a relationship to begin with, and Vivian's barbed tongue always hit its mark when they squabbled. "He banged on the door, and I hid under the settee," Violet explained.

Vivian pinched the bridge of her nose as if Violet exasperated her. "You can't hide every time you hear a loud noise, Vi." Violet ground her teeth together and reminded herself Vivian could beat the shit out of her, but gods did she want to grab Vivian's braid and yank her to the ground. "She hid under her desk once at school and the teacher had to send for our father," Vivian told Roman. "It's ridiculous."

Two years ago, Violet hadn't known they were renovating

the school building's roof. The workers scaled the building undetected, but something slipped and a loud crash sounded against the roof, followed by yelling and footsteps above. Violet's vision had tunneled and she'd fallen to her knees to hide. Slayton had crouched on the floor beside her and held her hand until her father arrived.

It had been humiliating, but Slayton had threatened everyone in class within an inch of their lives when they'd laughed. Violet couldn't prove it, but she suspected someone told her classmates about the rebel attack after she left because other than the day it happened, no one made fun of her again.

Violet didn't want to be gossip fodder, and until now, she hadn't thought about that day in a long time.

War snarled and his blade-like quills shot out of his mane. Vivian stumbled backward and tried to hide behind Roman, but the prince slid out of the way.

"What is wrong with you?" he fumed. "She is *your sister*."

Vivian regained her wits and whirled on Roman with vehemence. "Rebels are a part of our lives, and she needs to be ready to defend herself instead of running to hide at every little sound." She motioned between herself and Violet. "How long until a rebel confuses her for me again?

"Everyone in the kingdom knows what I look like. Your parents made sure of that on our eighteenth birthdays when they sent a royal announcement to every news post in the kingdom with our pictures," she said bitterly. "As long as I'm a target, so is she."

Violet sucked in a sharp breath at the truth in her sister's words. Not only had the rebels thought she was Vivian, but being mistaken for each other had happened their entire lives. A lot of people in the capital knew Vivian and Violet were twins, but there were still people who approached her thinking she was Vivian, especially now that everyone knew Viv would one day be queen.

Every time it happened, Violet debated coloring her hair. It wouldn't change her face, but at least it would help distinguish her from the prince's esteemed mate. She never followed through because she liked her hair—a perfect mixture of her mother's bright red and her father's black.

"What is your problem?" Violet tried to demand hotly, but to her chagrin, her voice wobbled with embarrassment. How dare her sister try to embarrass her this way? Vivian hadn't almost died. Violet had.

Roman gently grabbed Violet's shoulders and stooped to her eye level. "Hey. No one is going to hurt you. I promise."

Violet slid her gaze from Viv to Roman. He shouldn't make promises he couldn't keep.

"Dad wants to train her to defend herself, but Mom won't let him because of how skittish she is."

Dad wants to train me? He'd never mentioned anything.

Vivian's lip curled with disgust. "Everyone walks on eggshells around her, and I'm sick of it." War growled again and positioned himself in front of Violet, *encouraging* Vivian to move back, and judging by the look on Roman's face, he wanted to rip Vivian's head from her body.

I hate you, Violet wanted to scream, even if her words held no real truth. Their parents told her healing didn't have a time limit, that she'd been through a great ordeal and they understood. Were they secretly as frustrated with her as Vivian? She wrapped her arms around her stomach, wanting to disappear.

"Enough." Roman's lethal command stilled the air. He gave his full attention to Vivian, and uncertainty flashed in her eyes. "You saw the dismembered body parts of the men scattered around my room, but Violet heard them get *ripped* apart. Do you have any idea what it sounds like to hear bones torn from their sockets as a man begs for his life?

"You might know how to defend yourself, but you've never been near a rebel. Your sister had one wrap his filthy fingers around her. You might be able to fight for your life, but you've never had to, and you have *no right* to tell *anyone* to get over almost being murdered."

Vivian's face paled with Roman's conviction, and so did Violet's. She tried her best to block out the images that accompanied the memory.

Abe forcing his way under the bed.

War's roar followed by agonizing screams.

War soaked in blood.

Body parts everywhere.

"You cannot begin to understand what she has been through," Roman went on. "A queen must have compassion for their people. Not disdain because they perceive them as weak."

Roman defending Violet threatened to rekindle the fire she'd worked so hard to put out. With one last glance in her direction, he motioned for War to follow him out. War licked Violet's hand, growled at Vivian, and trailed the prince out of the cottage.

The air thickened with awkward tension, and Violet searched for words. But what *could* she say to her sister? *Fuck you?* Those were the only words that came to mind.

"I'm sorry," her sister sighed. "I might not like you, but I do love you."

Violet stared unblinking at her sister, unsure whether to focus on the fact that Viv apologized or the admission that followed.

While Violet had always known Vivian didn't like her, the confirmation from the horse's mouth stung.

"I don't want someone to hurt you because of me," Vivian

explained, "and I get so *frustrated* when you run and hide. If you continue on this way and you're attacked, you won't survive it." With one last parting glance, Vivian grabbed a dagger out of her nightstand and left without a word.

Later that night, as Violet lay in bed, she couldn't shake the feeling that Vivian's words weren't an apology; they were a warning.

Roman slammed his fist into the man's ribs, relishing in the satisfying crunch of the bones giving way. The captive's desperate pleas and gasping breaths echoed off the damp stone walls of the palace dungeon. The man's screams melted like a calming balm over the shredded parts of Roman's sanity.

Hit. Hit. Hit. Roman dropped his hands and stared at Kincaid, the rebel spy responsible for the attack that almost took Violet from him. Violet had told her father what she'd heard while hiding under Roman's bed, and Edgar had relayed the information to the council. They'd apprehended the spy, a cook in the palace kitchens, and Roman had convinced his parents to keep the man alive under the guise of extracting information.

The council assumed by now the prisoner had died, but Roman had moved the man to an unused area of the dungeon and instructed the guards to keep the rebel alive and to mention his presence to no one. They didn't dare question their future king.

Roman had been visiting Kincaid for years, determined to make him regret every decision leading up to the day he'd betrayed his kingdom.

The tremble in Violet's voice as she asked Roman to stay rang in his ears, and he hit Kincaid again. The image of her peeking at him from under the bed as she told him she was scared *wouldn't go away*. He reared back and knocked the man unconscious.

Violet showed no signs of distress when he watched her, and her sleep seemed peaceful. How had he missed her lingering fear, and why hadn't War told him?

Vivian's mockery made him hit Kincaid's limp form again. He had no doubt she'd hurt Violet because she'd found her in Roman's arms, innocent as it may have been. He and Viv weren't together. They had an understanding to put on a show for the public, but romantically, they couldn't care less about the other. Vivian still had a lover, and Roman still followed Violet, but Vivian didn't know that, and her treatment of Violet was unacceptable.

"You're useless if you break your hands," Ares remarked as he sauntered into the cell.

Roman wanted to ignore his friend, but the man spoke true. Fae had magic, but that magic did not include rapid healing or immortality. Broken hands wouldn't stop him, but they would make fighting more difficult.

Roman stalked out of the cell and addressed the guard outside of it. "Have him cleaned up and treated. We can't let our friend die from an infection." Death would be too easy.

Ares caught up to Roman quickly in the dark hallway of the dungeon. "Do you want to talk about it?"

He asked the same question every time they visited Kincaid, and as Roman did every time, he changed the subject. "I think Vivian is seeing someone," he replied, using her as a scapegoat. "Have you heard anything about it?"

"No." Ares eyed Roman with an annoyingly perceptive look on his face. "I'm surprised you care. Have you asked her about it?"

Roman swiped at the speckles of blood on his face. "She

denied it." Lying to his best friend felt wrong, but confessing his obsession with Violet was out of the question. Roman thumped his chest. "I can feel it. I'm going to confront her again tonight."

"If she is, she's convinced him to keep quiet because fucking the future queen would be something anyone would brag about." Ares tilted his head side to side. "Or they don't want to be charged with treason."

Roman cracked his neck. Tonight, he'd demand Vivian put a stop to her affair. He didn't give a shit who she fucked, but he'd not allow her to hurt Violet without consequence. Taking away her ability to be with the person she wanted seemed like a good start. "Let me know if you hear anything."

Ares handed Roman a towel to clean himself. "How's Violet?"

"How would I know?" Roman challenged. He scarcely spoke to Violet in public, and he ensured no one saw him follow her around. Ares couldn't possibly know anything.

His friend grinned from ear to ear. "Because I saw your eyes glaze over to connect with War earlier, and he's always with her in the afternoons."

Roman made a mental note to glamour himself before connecting with War. "I wanted to see what *he* was doing," Roman lied again. He lied a lot these days.

Ares slapped him on the back. "Can you tell the big guy to put in a good word for me?"

Roman went rigid, unable to feign nonchalance. "Why?"

Ares laughed loudly, the sound grating on Roman's nerves. "I'm just fucking with you." He flashed perfect teeth that Roman wanted to knock out of his head. "I can ask her out myself." Roman stopped walking, and Ares followed suit. "Is there a reason you don't want me asking out your future sister-in-law?"

Roman eyed Ares up and down. The man had light sand skin with dark brown hair and almost matched Roman in height. Most people attracted to men found him appealing. *Does Violet?*

Roman blanked his expression. "Why do you want to ask out Violet?"

"Why wouldn't I?" Ares lifted a hand and counted on his fingers. "She's one of the prettiest girls I've ever seen. She's funny." He grinned widely. "Have you heard the little jokes she tells? They're ridiculous, but she looks damn cute telling them." Roman's muscles readied to attack. How did Ares know about her jokes? "I like her style. She's smart."

"I get it," Roman bit out. Not many men asked Violet out; he'd made sure of it over the years because he needed more time to find a way to make her his. He'd considered more than once begging her to secretly marry him to break his bond with Vivian, but he knew Violet would never do that to Viv, no matter how badly she treated her.

Roman had stopped threatening them over the last year, and stopped altogether when his parents announced Vivian as the future queen. It wouldn't take long for gossip of an affair to spread, and he'd not put that on Violet.

He had no intention of marrying Vivian, but it'd do him no favors for the citizens in his kingdom to know their future king pined for another woman. Some people were royalists and zealously worshipped anything to do with the royal fae, including mate bonds. Some royalists thought if they could touch a royal or their mate that some of the gods' blessing would transfer to them. If they suspected Roman intended on breaking that sacred bond, they would do anything necessary to keep it from happening.

"You should do it," Roman suggested through gritted teeth.

If Violet said yes, he'd reassign Ares to another kingdom. The Mountain Kingdom sounded nice. And far.

Ares burst out laughing as they ascended the stairs out of the cool dungeon. "I'm kidding, Rome."

Roman considered snapping his best friend's neck. He didn't think he'd miss him that much. "You think Violet is a joke?" he asked without an ounce of humor. "Do you not think she's good enough?"

Ares held up his hands, all jesting gone. "I meant what I said about her, but I'd never touch her. I don't know what your deal is with your mate's twin, but I respect you too much to go there."

Roman needed to mask his emotions better. Her safety depended on it, and that meant until he either found a way to transfer the bond or convince Violet to marry him anyway, he needed to pretend better with Vivian.

That night, Roman placed his hand on Vivian's back and ushered her into her favorite tavern. "I'm glad you agreed to join me," he said, forcing a smile for the benefit of their audience.

Vivian fluttered her lashes, putting on an excellent show of the doting fiancée. "Me too."

The woman was a wildcard, and he had no idea how she'd react to what he had to say.

Once they had their food, Roman leaned back and drummed his fingers on the table. "Are you still seeing someone?" *So much for easing into it.*

Vivian stopped chewing and Roman saw the wheels turning in her mind. She swallowed her bite and licked her lips. "Why would you ask me that?"

He relished in her unease, and even though this conversation would end in them having to step up their farce in the eye of the public, he couldn't wait to crush her happiness in his palm. "Answer the question."

Her chin lifted. "No, of course not."

He huffed and pinched the bridge of his nose. "I know you're lying, and it's time to call it off."

She set down her fork and sat back. "I told you I'm not seeing anyone."

Leaning forward, Roman's voice took on a hard edge. "I don't believe you, and I suggest you break up with them immediately. I will not hesitate to hunt them down and charge them with treason. We made an agreement that you'd stop seeing them once my parents announced our bond."

Roman picked up his silverware and tucked a bit of food into his mouth to keep from laughing at the proverbial steam coming out of Vivian's ears. "Surely you weren't stupid enough to fall in love," he couldn't help but add with a sardonic smile.

Vivian's cheeks flushed maroon, and there looked to be tears gathering in the corners of her calculating eyes. He should feel lucky to have garnered such a response; after all, she deserved to suffer for how she spoke to Violet, but bitterness consumed him at the injustice of it all. Neither of them wanted this. The gods had made a mistake and Roman and Vivian had to pay penance.

After composing herself, she beamed at him from across the table. "You're right. I'm sorry." She sighed woefully. "I'm excited for us to start our lives together, but I wanted to experience a relationship first. I never loved him."

It didn't escape Roman's attention that she only mentioned one man, and he wondered if it'd been the same one all these years. Against his better judgement, he pitied her.

Viv smiled demurely. "We'll be in a *real* relationship, then?"

He nearly snorted at the false hope she displayed. "As far as anyone is concerned, yes, but not in private. There's no need for it until we are married." *Which will never happen.*

Vivian leaned forward and lowered her voice suggestively. "I can't wait to *feel* each other at the same time." Roman would have recoiled if he'd thought she meant it. Did she honestly think he believed her act? He'd add delusional to her long list of faults.

He worked hard to shut down his disgust, lest she sense it through the bond. "Not until we're married," he said with too much force.

Vivian tilted her head with a look of surprise, her sharp mind hard at work. "You've never fucked anyone, have you?" She chuckled. "When I felt you, I assumed you had, but that's not correct, is it?"

"What I've done is none of your business, just as what you've done until now is none of mine."

She was correct in her assessment, though. The only pleasure his cock experienced had been by his own hand, but his lack of experience didn't bother him. He only hoped it wouldn't bother Violet, either.

12

NINETEEN YEARS OLD

Violet secured the last pin to the lace top, stepped back to examine Griff, and clapped. "It's perfect."

Griff glanced down at the sheer shirt with nothing but embroidered flowers to cover his nipples. "Can I take it off now before someone sees? I'll never hear the end of it."

Violet gestured for him to lift his arms.

"VIOLET IT'S JUST ME. I'M COMING IN," Lydia, Griff's cousin by marriage, yelled through the front door before walking into Violet's home. Violet lived in a small two-bedroom cottage on the edge of town. She'd rented it just after graduation and loved the independence it afforded her.

"Dammit," Lydia griped when she entered the room. "I wanted to see him in something pretty."

Violet snickered at the cousins' banter. She and Lydia weren't close—they'd been a year apart in school—but the girl popped up occasionally to spend time with Griff.

Today, Lydia had her golden-blonde hair in a bun to show-case her ample cleavage that spilled out of her tight, low-cut shirt. The pale blue fabric complimented her alabaster skin.

The revealing top paired with fitted leather pants made her look like a walking, curvaceous sex goddess.

Violet had tried to wear the same style once, but it did nothing for her lanky frame. She felt more like a twelve-year-old boy than a woman. It was for the best. She hated the restriction of pants. The dresses she favored had slits that allowed full range of motion, whereas the prospect of ripping the crotch of trousers while climbing a tree to retrieve certain flowers terrified her.

Griff glared at his cousin and donned his own shirt. "I'd hate to make you jealous because it looks better on me than you."

Lydia threw him a crude gesture and pulled up a stool to sit.

"IT'S JUST ME," Slayton announced seconds before opening the front door. He entered the room, panting, and swore. "I ran all the way here to see him in a dress." He threw his hands up.

"I missed it too," Lydia lamented. They both knew Griff had agreed to help Violet out today, and Slayton had poked fun at him all week.

Griff shoved Slayton's shoulder. "Fuck off. At least I'm nice enough to help her. That's why I'm her best friend."

"I'm her best friend," Slayton argued. "And you have more free time in the afternoons than I do."

Being a warrior, Griff trained from before dawn until right after midday. Occasionally they trained from dawn to dusk if rebel attacks escalated. Attacks in the other kingdoms had ticked up, but thankfully, the Tropical Kingdom remained in a lull.

Violet didn't know if each kingdom had different rebel factions with no association to the others or if they were one big group working together, but the varying degrees of attacks would suggest the former.

"Did you talk to Dominic today?" Lydia asked Violet, waggling her eyebrows. "Rumor has it you two are together a lot."

Violet suppressed a giddy smile. "He walked me to work this morning."

Lydia bobbed her head and plucked at the lace top folded on the table. "Are you wearing this for him on your next date?" She shimmied her shoulders. "Can I wear it next?"

"This is for one of my customers at the pleasure house, but I can make you one too," Violet offered.

Violet's cheeks heated when she mentioned the salacious establishment in town. The first time she'd dropped off an order to one of the performers, she'd discovered she enjoyed watching the shows. A lot. The sensuality of passion captivated her. The performers moved like dancers, and she often wondered what it felt like to experience that level of pleasure.

"Stop stalling and tell us about lover boy," Griff griped.

Violet perked up. "Things with Dom are good. He's taking me on a picnic under the stars."

Dominic was a guard in the battalion, as were most people she knew, having grown up in the battalion compound. He'd pursued her relentlessly and finally wore her down about a month ago. Standing just over six foot, he had handsome features with warm tawny skin, dark brown hair, and hazel eyes that looked at her like she was the most tantalizing thing in the world.

"You really like him," Lydia observed with a sly smile.

"I do." Violet couldn't help smiling like a giddy schoolgirl. "He's funny, and he likes me."

"And he's hot," Lydia added helpfully.

"That too," Violet agreed.

Griff looked affronted. "I'm hot and funny, and you never wanted to date me."

"She's too good for you," Slayton chimed in. He grabbed a ball of yarn off the closest table and threw it at their friend. "I wouldn't allow it."

"You made fun of me for falling." Violet took a hanger from her closet. "That is not the way to get a girl."

"You should have seen yourself, Vi," Griff protested and waved his arms around. "Your arms windmilled all the way down."

Lydia stood and smacked the back of his head on Violet's behalf. "Every day, I thank the gods I'm not attracted to men, because I would kill a man if I had to date one."

Slayton threw his hands up. "What did I do?"

"I need you guys to pull it together and help me decide what to wear tonight," Violet said seriously while placing the hanger through the lace shirt. "Should I wear something like this since we'll have to ride horses to get there?" She gestured to Lydia's outfit. "Or do I wear one of my normal dresses?"

Lydia stood and crossed the room to Violet's closet. "Definitely a dress with high slits." She grinned wickedly. "Easy access."

Slayton snorted. "You're going to get bitten by a bug if you try to fuck him on the ground."

"Gods," Griff mumbled at the same time Violet gasped.

Lydia raised a perfectly shaped brow at Violet. "You're not going to sleep with him?"

Violet hung the lace shirt in her closet and fell back on her bed with a groan. "I don't know. Maybe?" She raised her head to look at her friends. "I kind of want to get it out of the way, and we've been dating for a little over a month now." More like she wanted to feel the same ecstasy as the performers at the pleasure house.

"I bet he's experienced," Lydia offered.

"I'm experienced," Griff added, raising his hand.

"No, you're not," Slayton shot back as Lydia and Violet said in unison, "Shut up."

The gruesome training Roman took on after graduation boasted longer, more intense drills that took up most of his time. Their training started before sunrise, and while most warriors finished by midday, those of higher rank trained all day.

Next week they'd meet with another battalion in the kingdom for a sparring tournament, and as a royal and the future king, everyone expected Roman to win. If he didn't, the generals would work him harder.

Ares had sparred with him all morning in preparation, and they were both covered in dirt and sweat. Miserable.

Ares shrugged out of his leather top. "Damn, it's hot today." Fighting in leathers felt like dying a slow death, even in the shade.

Roman spit on the ground to expel the dirt from his mouth. "At least it's not raining." It rained often in the Tropical Kingdom, and while the rain cooled them down, it made the air thicker and the ground a mud pit.

They approached their training group and saw Dominic, another warrior their age, talking to a few guys who listened intently, enraptured by whatever he said.

"Her virgin pussy was the tightest I've ever felt," Dom told the others, and Ares' lip curled with disgust. "And the sounds she made…" He groaned. "One of the best fucks I've had."

Everything around Roman faded away, and nothing existed but the prick in front of him. Dominic spent a lot of time with Violet, and if he meant her, Roman didn't know what he'd do.

"I knew it," another warrior said. "Maybe she'll give me a ride next."

Dominic shoved the guy. "Violet's my girl."

White hot anger seared across Roman's vision. Dominic continued to speak, but it faded into background noise. Roman had a vague awareness of Ares grabbing his arm and saying something, but his friend's attempts to calm him were useless.

Roman crossed the distance between him and Dominic in seconds, wrenched the man's head back by his hair, and slammed him to the ground.

His fists rained down on the man's face repeatedly, hot liquid splattering in every direction. He didn't know how many men it took to pull him off, but by the time they had, the piece of shit lay unconscious on the ground.

Ares grabbed the sides of Roman's blood-speckled face and shook him. "Calm down before you kill someone."

His words brought Roman back from the brink of insanity, and he heard Vivian yelling his name. She sprinted across the arena with a worried expression and gaped at Dominic's unmoving form on the ground.

Roman hoped the fucker died.

"What in the hell happened?" she demanded. "I thought my chest caught on fire."

"Dominic was bragging about having sex with your sister," Ares explained, and Vivian's face reddened as her anger rose. "Then Dominic said he wished he'd fucked you too, when he had the chance, and Roman lost it."

Vivian looked almost gleeful before morphing her demeanor into one of fictitious concern. Roman felt her pleasure snaking around his own fury, and it disgusted him.

"They're just words, Rome. I wouldn't let him touch me. You know that."

Ironic, seeing as she'd fucked another guy for years, not that he gave a shit. Roman cursed himself, knowing a future king must keep his emotions in check, but it seemed an impossibility with anything concerning Violet. He would've killed the man had the others not pulled him off.

He'd let them believe the man's words about Vivian set him off, but in truth, he hadn't heard Dominic mention her at all.

Griff jogged toward Violet and Slayton from the direction of the palace grounds, still in his leathers. Slayton and Violet were supposed to meet him later for dinner. He shouldn't have been out yet.

Their friend picked up speed when he saw them, and the look on his face spoke of nothing good.

He slowed to a stop in front of them, barely winded, and shot her a wary glance.

"What's wrong?" Violet probed, scared to know the answer.

"Your boyfriend almost died today." He attempted to keep his words light and teasing but failed spectacularly.

The air whooshed out of Violet's lungs.

"What do you mean?" Slayton demanded as Violet's brain caught up.

Griff swiped at the sweat on his forehead. "Roman beat Dominic within an inch of his life." That jerked Violet back to reality. He scratched his jaw and avoided her gaze.

"Why would he hurt Dominic?" Violet wondered aloud. It didn't make sense. "Roman never fights." She spoke more to herself than her friends, trying to work out what had happened.

"It wasn't a fight." Griff grimaced. "Dominic never stood a chance. I thought Roman would kill him."

"Stop with the fanfare and tell us exactly what happened," Slayton said, losing patience. The two men were best friends, but they annoyed each other like brothers.

Griff looked apologetically at Violet, and she knew whatever he had to say was going to make her sick. He tried to gentle his words, but loathing seeped into them with each syllable. "I'm sorry, Vi. He had a large group of warriors around him, and he—" he hesitated. "He told them how good your pu —how good you were in bed."

A large group of warriors. How good you were in bed. "He told everyone?" Did her voice sound weak to them or just her? Had she spoken aloud at all? Why would Dom do that to her? Her ears rang, and she stared at nothing as she tried hard to rationalize the funny and sweet Dominic she knew from the Dominic Griff presented now.

"That fucking prick." Slayton pounded his fist into the palm of his hand. "I don't like the prince," Violet glared at him, and he held his hands up, "but I'm glad he stood up for you." He reached over and ruffled her hair, and she swatted his hand away. She knew he wanted to make her laugh, but her body wouldn't allow her, even if she wanted to.

Griff rubbed a hand down his face. "That's not what set him off." Slayton and Violet stopped their bickering and waited expectantly. "Dominic made a comment afterward about wishing he'd slept with Vivian when he had the chance, and Rome lost it."

Violet took the words like a physical blow. *He wished he'd slept with Vivian? Am I not good enough?* For Dominic to brag about their intimacy was one thing, but for him to wish it'd been Vivian instead of her was unforgivable. She and Dom had sex last week for the first time and one other time since. When he'd taken her home after their first time, he'd asked her to be his girlfriend.

If Violet had known she was runner up, she'd have told him to go kick rocks barefoot. A knot formed in her throat, and she fought to swallow.

Griff reached out and tugged on a piece of Violet's hair. "If it's any consolation, he said you were the best he's had."

Slayton punched Griff in the shoulder. "What the fuck is wrong with you?"

"She's about to cry!" Griff protested. "Knowing I was the best someone ever had would make me feel better."

"You are a jackass," Slayton muttered.

"If you two will excuse me, I'm going to shut my head in a door so I don't have to face anyone tomorrow," she joked weakly and stepped back. *Maybe War will bite my head off for me.*

Slayton wrapped his arm around her shoulders and pulled her in. "Don't let that asshole get to you."

As if summoned, War came barreling toward them. Knowing the drill, Slayton and Griff moved out of the way, and Violet squatted down. War poked and prodded her with his nose, purring loudly to soothe her.

"How does he always know when you're upset?" Griff asked, staring thoughtfully at War. "Can he read minds?"

Violet kissed the top of War's giant head. "I don't know. Maybe he can smell it. I'm alright," she cooed against the cat's fur, "but you need to go to Roman and try to calm him down." War shook his head. *Stubborn beast.* Trying to convince him to leave her alone was pointless and she didn't bother further.

Griff looked torn. "I have to return to training. The distraction from the fight gave me time to slip away to give you a heads up, but if they realize I'm gone, I'll have to run sprints." He turned to War and Slayton. "You two stay with her until I'm done."

"I planned on it," Slayton assured him.

"I don't need a babysitter." Violet planted her hands on her hips. "Dom and I only dated a handful of weeks." *Five to be exact.* War sat next to her feet looking as stubborn as Slayton. "Slay, I really need to be alone right now."

His nostrils flared. "I don't want you wandering through the forest when you're upset. Anything could happen."

"No," Violet replied sharply and adjusted her satchel. "Dominic isn't important enough to upset me that much, and War will be there."

"Fine." Slayton pointed at War. "If you see that dick, rip his arm off."

Griff clucked his tongue. "I don't think Roman left enough of him to rip."

The thought made Violet's stomach clench. Roman hadn't torn Dom to pieces for *her*, he'd done it for Vivian, and that hurt more than Dominic's betrayal. They'd been friends once. Didn't that warrant sticking up for her? She'd never let anyone seriously speak ill of him.

Violet didn't know what made her hate herself more: still wanting Roman to a degree, or wishing someone would fight to the death for her honor.

She and the men said their goodbyes, and War and Violet made their way to the forest. The duo meandered along a winding path through the lush foliage toward the shore. "If I tell you something, do you promise not to tell Roman?" she asked the beast at her side.

War stopped and peered up at her with a nod. His bright orange eyes unsettled most people, but not her. "He's not in there with you, is he?" War shook his head and her shoulders drooped, unable to hold up the heaviness of the day. "Did you hear what happened?" War nodded and nuzzled Violet's side. She plopped down on a large, blue tree root, and her voice dropped to a whisper. "It hurts, War. I can handle him telling everyone about us." She stopped to collect herself. "But he's just another person who wanted my sister instead."

She dropped her head and the first tear fell. "I get Dominic couldn't have Vivian, or missed his chance with her before they announced her as Roman's mate, but why did he have to say that?" She sniffled. "What good did it do him to let everyone know he'd settled for a look-alike?"

Tears fell faster down her cheeks. "He's not the only one, you know." She sniffled. "At school, no boys paid me attention until they announced Vivian as Roman's mate." She met War's tangerine gaze. "They never wanted me before even though Vivian and I are identical." Her voice broke and she pressed a hand to her chest. "That means it's *me* they don't like. Even the gods." Roman might have wanted her once upon a time, but the gods chose Vivian for him. What was so wrong with Violet that even the gods chose selfish Vivian over her?

Violet put her head in her hands and salted War's fur with her misery. She wasn't one for self-pity, but she'd allow herself this.

She picked up her head and looked to the gods. "I won't change." The words came out nasally from crying. "One day I'll be enough as I am, whether you think so or not."

Roman laid on his bed and closed his eyes, reaching down the bond for War. The moment they connected, Violet's tear-stained cheeks ripped him wide open. The anger he'd worked hard to snuff out returned tenfold.

Dominic would die.

"*Get out,*" War growled.

The *familiar's* tone took Roman by surprise. "*Where are you? I'm coming.*"

"*Roman, I know you still hold a candle for Violet, but if you aren't going to defy the gods to keep her, then you need to stay gone.*"

"*You told me going against the gods was impossible,*" Roman reminded him. "*Do you know something? Is there a way to mate her other than marriage? She'd never betray Vivian.*" War stayed silent for too long. "*What do you expect me to do?*"

"*I don't know,*" his *familiar* admitted, "*but she is heartbroken over something deeper than what that boy did to her today, and the last thing she needs is you as a reminder of her pain.*"

Roman cut the connection and stared at nothing.

If you aren't going to defy the gods to keep her, then you need to stay gone.

The last thing she needs is you as a reminder of her pain.

If he could reach into the heavens and drag the gods to Eden, he would. He would kill the gods with his bare hands to have her as his own, if he could. If he couldn't find a way to transfer the bond, he'd find a way to break it, consequences be damned.

She might not need him, but he needed her.

And wanted her.

And loved her.

He always had.

Violet woke the following morning with swollen eyes, a headache, and a weight in her chest. Feeling sorry for herself did her no good, but her mother always said a good cry now and then was therapeutic.

She rolled to her side, and a burst of color on her nightstand caught her attention. She rubbed her eyes to clear the sleep away; the small bouquet of violets and scattering of shells didn't disappear, and she sat up to lean forward and feel the light purple petals. They were real.

Throwing her legs over the side of the bed, she picked up the entire bouquet and examined the sloppily tied string around the stems. She set it aside and carefully picked up each shell in awe. They were exactly what she would have searched for. Things had mysteriously appeared in her room before, and she'd chalked it up to forgetting she had them, but this solidified her suspicions. Someone snuck into her home at night.

Only her mother had a key. They could be from her, but that didn't make sense. She would've just given them to Violet during the day. Violet gathered her new things, deposited the shells safely in the box where she kept her others, and found a vase to hold the flowers.

After placing the vase on her nightstand, she sat on her bed and stared at the violets. The gifts should frighten her, she knew that, but they didn't. Odd, seeing how everything scared her. Though since her father started teaching her self-defense techniques, she felt more confident in her ability to protect herself.

Sometimes, she'd swear the prince's scent lingered in her room. At first, she'd chalked it up to her imagination or a trick of the senses, but it was just a lie she told herself. A part of her *knew* it was Roman.

Violet sat at her dressing table and stared at herself in the mirror, her emotions at war with one another. How often did the prince sneak into her home in the middle of the night, and why?

Picking up a hairbrush, Violet set to work on fixing her hair, wishing she could catch the prince in the act to prove she wasn't going crazy, but he likely used his glamour. A sane woman would be scared.

So why wasn't she?

13

TWENTY YEARS OLD

Lydia squeezed Violet hard enough to cut her in half, her excitement palpable. "Are you sure you don't want to come with us to get away from these two?" she teased. "Victoria and I would love to have you live with us."

"Stop trying to convince my only friend to leave me," Slayton grumbled.

"Hey," Griff protested. "I'm your friend too."

Lydia waved Slayton off. "Whatever girl you're dating this week will keep you company."

Slayton pulled Lydia into a quick hug before passing her off to Griff.

Griff squeezed his cousin for a long while. He played tough, but Lydia leaving affected him. He viewed her as a little sister. Releasing her, he cleared his throat. "I'll miss your smartass mouth."

Tears pricked the corners of Violet's eyes. She was a crier and hated seeing her friend upset.

Last year, Lydia met her new wife, Victoria, and they were moving to the Garden Kingdom to be closer to Victoria's family. Her sister's husband had died suddenly, and Victoria needed to move home to help with her three nephews.

Victoria had left for the Garden Kingdom a week prior, wanting to get there as soon as possible. Lydia, having all her family and friends here in the Tropical Kingdom, needed longer to tie up loose ends and say goodbye.

With a last round of quick hugs, Lydia hopped into the carriage and left them all behind for a new adventure. *What would it be like to travel out of the Tropical Kingdom?*

"Are you alright?" a familiar deep voice asked from behind them.

Violet shrieked and flipped around. Roman stood impossibly close, his words laced with concern. *Where in the hell did he come from?* Her question died on her tongue as she took him in. As handsome as ever, he wore a fitted, long-sleeved, beige shirt that clung to his chest like a second skin. It only had a few buttons at the top, all of which were undone, and he ran a hand through his short blond hair, making his biceps bulge.

Her mouth dried; her farewell to Lydia momentarily forgotten. She'd moved on from Roman, no longer harboring a painful love for the boy who'd stolen her heart at twelve years old, but she wasn't blind. Good gods, he got sexier every time she saw him. Royal fae were tall, and she guessed he stood at least six foot four or six foot five by now. Perfect for climbing.

Slayton elbowed her in the side to break her trance, and she cleared her throat, feeling like an idiot. *What the hell is wrong with me?*

"Yes," she replied. "Just telling Lydia goodbye. She and her wife moved to the Garden Kingdom."

But Roman wasn't listening to her. At least she didn't think he was, because his gaze narrowed at Slayton's arm that had elbowed her in the side.

Griff snorted, and Roman looked over at him before

turning his attention back to Violet. "I'm sorry, princess. I saw you crying and wanted to make sure you were okay."

It touched her he'd taken the time to check on her, but it also made her feel guilty for ogling him like a piece of meat. "Thank you. These two promised to take me out for strawberry cake."

Roman rubbed his jaw, his gaze never wavering from hers. "If you need anything, let me know." He turned to Slayton. "If you hit her again, I'll break your arm."

Slayton, who clearly had a death wish, smirked with a mock salute. "Yes, Your Grace."

Without another word, Roman nodded and walked off, leaving her to stare after him.

"Is it just me, or does he get moodier the older we get?" Griff asked when the prince was out of ear shot.

Slayton shrugged as they started back toward the bakery. "He's always been like that. At least as long as I've known him."

"No, he hasn't," Violet argued, feeling defensive. "Serious? Yes, but never moody. He's actually really fun once you get to know him."

"Violet and Roman used to be best buddies when we were younger," Griff told Slayton. "They'd get in trouble for laughing in the back of class."

Violet smiled to herself, remembering the silly notes they'd send back and forth, and she couldn't help but miss their friendship, even before her pesky heart leapt from her chest into his hands.

Maybe now that they were older they could.

Maybe.

A few weeks later, Violet fastened Ares' leather training shirt and moved back to examine her work. "What do you think?"

He inspected the absorbent panel she'd added to the outside forearm area of his sleeves and smiled. "It's perfect. Sorry I wore out the last one." He dug into his pocket and handed her a few coins.

Over the last year, Violet had created a profitable business altering and customizing the guards' fighting leathers, amongst other things. With the queen's permission, Violet's father helped her set up a tent near the training arena, and from there, things took off.

Her most requested item was a thick, absorbent cloth sewn to the forearm panel to wipe the sweat from their faces. Apparently, swiping leather across dirty, sticky skin was uncomfortable, and after hearing Griff complain a million times, she'd fixed the issue for him. Before long, warriors were approaching her, asking her to do the same for them.

It allowed her to cut back her hours at the dress shop in town. She made enough to quit the dress shop altogether, but Maggie, the owner, had been all over Eden and knew everything there was to know about the fashion and techniques of the other kingdoms. Each kingdom had vastly different tastes due to the varying climates.

Lydia's move to the Garden Kingdom had sparked a fresh desire in Violet to follow in her boss' footsteps, but Maggie said it had taken her almost two years. Traveling Eden itself didn't take years, but staying in each kingdom long enough to learn their ways took time. Violet didn't think she could handle being away from her family and friends that long, so the next best thing was Maggie.

Violet deposited the money into her bag and waved in the next person. A tall, handsome man with curly brown hair, sunkissed skin, and bright green eyes stepped inside. He stood a little over six feet tall and had a lean, well-built frame, and her breath caught when their gazes collided.

The handsome man stared at her with parted lips as his eyes roamed over her face. The two stared at each other for an eternity before Violet snapped out of it.

"Hello." She scanned his clothes, noting the lack of leathers. "Are you a warrior?" She couldn't tell. This man had a warrior's build, but warriors wore fighting leathers during training, and this man wore a simple linen shirt tucked into dark brown trousers.

He walked farther inside her little tent and extended his hand. "Titus. I'm the new weapons master." He ate up her appearance as if she was an anomaly he'd never seen before.

Violet tentatively took his hand. "It's nice to meet you."

"Forgive me," he apologized. "No one warned me the battalion seamstress was beautiful. You took me off guard."

She scrunched her nose at his terrible attempt at flirting. "Does that work on many women?"

He laughed and shook his head. "Not yet. Did it work on you?"

"No." She beamed. "But I'm flattered all the same. What can I help you with today?"

He held out a black jacket and pointed at the pocket. "My jacket is torn."

"Ahh." She accepted the garment and inspected the hole. "Do you carry sharp tools in here?"

Titus smiled sheepishly. "Yes."

She tsked and folded the jacket. "You could cut yourself, you know."

"It's a terrible habit," he agreed. "One I'm suddenly glad I haven't been able to break."

She bit the inside of her cheek to suppress a grin. "I can line the pockets with leather to protect the cloth from tearing in the future."

His lips pulled into a slow smile. "Pretty *and* smart."

"Your lines are getting better," she praised with a light laugh, making his smile grow. "I can have this finished by tomorrow morning. Will that work?"

"Take your time. I have other coats I need to rip the pockets on too." He winked when she burst out laughing.

Violet jotted his name and what he needed on a piece of paper and attached it to his jacket with a pin.

He started to leave but stopped, and said, "I didn't catch your name."

She looked up, surprised. Her eyes met his, and the way he looked at her made her stomach flutter. "Violet."

"Violet." He murmured her name as though testing it out. "It was nice to meet you, Violet."

"You, too, Titus."

He lifted the flap of the tent, paused, and dropped it, spinning toward her again. "I'd like to take you out."

Violet tossed his jacket into a basket and lifted an amused brow. "Was that supposed to be a question?"

He blew out a shaky breath. *Is he nervous?* "I'm messing this up. Violet, oh beautiful seamstress who will save me from stabbing myself, would you do me the pleasure of allowing me to take you to dinner?"

Trying not to seem like a giddy schoolgirl, she shrugged one shoulder as nonchalantly as possible. "Sure. I'm free tomorrow night."

The way his face lit up sparked a new kind of excitement within her. "Tomorrow sounds perfect. Do you live in the compound?"

She picked up another piece of paper and wrote down her

address. "I grew up in the compound, but I live on the outskirts of town now."

Titus glanced at the paper and slid it into his pocket. "I'll pick you up at six o'clock." He opened the flap and looked back one last time. "Goodbye, Violet."

He disappeared outside, and she stared after him with a goofy grin on her face. How long had it been since she'd gone out with a man?

Too long.

Titus seemed different, and what was better, he wasn't a warrior or guard. She'd written off her sister's colleagues long ago, not wanting to relive the Dominic incident. At least she'd never had to face him afterward. He had supposedly tucked tail and ran after Roman beat him half to death.

The next person walked in, and Violet composed herself, already thinking about what she'd wear on her date.

Roman brooded as he and Vivian walked through downtown toward the theater. His parents insisted they meet them for the opening night of a new play, adamant the future monarchs needed to be seen together. Roman did everything in his power to avoid Vivian outside of his weekly dinners that they now had at the palace with his parents.

Not for lack of trying on Vivian's part. Roman held no interest to her, but being future queen did, and he hated how she acted when they made public appearances, like the world should bow at her feet. She no more deserved to be queen than a contrite toddler.

"Ares and I are sparring with the generals from Henton tomorrow," he told Vivian, needing something to talk about other than Vivian herself before he bashed his head against the closest wall. Henton, a neighboring village of Saltu, boasted a reputation for their ruthless battle training techniques. "It should be a good show."

"You and Ares are attached at the hip," Vivian griped. "There are plenty of other men in the battalion to befriend."

Vivian hated Ares, not that he liked her any better. They often squabbled at training, and Ares told Roman that on the occasion they argued during Roman's absence, she threw around her position as future queen to get her way.

Roman's patience wore thin, and he came to a sudden stop. "Whatever your issue with Ares is, put it to rest."

Vivian's face screwed up. "Then tell him to show me respect," she rebutted hotly. "I am his future queen, and he's always challenging my decisions in training."

The entitlement this woman had astounded Roman. Any time Ares challenged her, it was to show her a better way of doing something, and it pissed her off. Her skill level did not compare to his.

She started to say more, but Roman's attention snagged on Violet walking their way on the arm of a man. *Where do I know him from, and why is he looking at Violet that way?* Roman had never seen them together or heard her talk about him to her friends.

Violet laughed at something the man said, and jealousy tried to consume Roman, but he tamped it down to keep Vivian from feeling the full force of it.

Vivian frowned at him and followed his line of sight, her breath hitching right before indignant fury blasted down the bond. He looked down at her, but her attention belonged to the couple before them. Roman's lip curled. Vivian's disdain for Violet pissed him off more than any of her other shortcomings.

Anytime someone brought up her sister, Vivian either made a snide comment or changed the subject. The last time she'd made a disparaging comment about her sister in his presence, he'd almost threatened to cut her tongue out. But he knew if he showed Violet favorable attention, Vivian might try to hurt her. Roman didn't think Vivian would hurt Violet physically, but there were many other ways to harm a person.

Vivian only remained in possession of her life because Roman didn't think Violet would take her death well, despite their strained relationship.

Violet and the man glanced up, both looking like they'd seen a ghost. The man looked from Vivian to Violet and back again, no doubt shocked at their likeness. He didn't know Violet well, then, if he didn't know she had an identical twin.

Roman pasted a smile on his face and sauntered forward, prepared to find out everything he could about the man foolish enough to touch the future queen.

No. Of all nights to run into her sister, why did it have to be tonight? Violet didn't miss the way Vivian glared at her as they approached. No relationship existed between Vivian and Violet other than random encounters when their parents had them both over for dinner, and every word out of Vivian's mouth contained a tinge of negativity aimed at Violet.

Titus looked between Violet and her sister several times and whispered, "Is that your sister?"

"Can't you see the resemblance?" she joked back. Hopefully they could say hi and leave as quickly as possible.

"You don't look happy to see her," Titus observed.

"It's not that." She pushed a strand of wayward hair out of her face and tried to take an inconspicuous deep breath.

Titus ran his thumb soothingly over the back of her hand. "Want me to make an excuse to leave immediately?"

Her eyes snapped to his, finding them full of mischief. Violet felt the weight of her sister's presence lift. She hadn't realized it, but part of her worried Titus would see Vivian and wish he'd been with her instead. "We'll say hi, and if they try to lock us into a conversation, can you fake a medical emergency?"

He barked out a laugh. "I'll do what I can."

"Hey!" Everyone turned toward the shout across the street. Slayton waved and jogged over, and Violet breathed a sigh of relief. If anyone could make a situation more comfortable, it was him.

He threw his arm around Violet. "There's my girl." He smacked a theatrical kiss on her cheek.

She side-eyed her friend, and Titus playfully tugged her closer. "Is there something I should know?"

"Yeah, there is," Slayton played along and puffed out his chest. He made to kiss her again, but she covered his face with her hand and pushed him back. "I'm going to loosen all the crotch seams of your pants the next time you ask me for alterations."

"I'm Vivian," her sister interjected and held out her hand to Titus.

Titus shook it with a polite smile. "Titus." He held his hand out to Roman. The prince watched him closely and took his proffered hand.

"Roman." He withdrew and turned to Violet. "Where have you two been?"

Titus gestured toward the building behind them. "Gus' Tavern. They have the best steak."

"I could go for steak," Slayton butted in before Roman could reply. He gestured toward Gus' and asked Roman, "Do you two want to grab dinner?" Violet held back a laugh. Those two weren't friends in the least, and Slayton *hated* Vivian.

Vivian's contemptuous glare would have scared a lesser man. "No." The woman tossed her glossy hair and batted her lashes at Roman. "We have a date at the theater tonight." Roman pursed his lips, and Vivian snuggled into his side, or tried to until he smoothly adjusted his stance, blocking her attempt to burrow against him.

Slayton snapped his fingers with feigned disappointment. "Damn."

Everything about this impromptu meeting made Violet want to jump in front of a carriage. Awkward did not begin to describe it.

Titus sighed noisily. "I hate to cut our conversation short, but Violet and I have plans. It was nice meeting you two." Titus nodded to Slayton. "Good to meet you."

Slayton shook Titus' hand and smirked. "I'm sure I'll see you soon."

Roman tipped his head to Titus. "I'll be by the armory to more properly introduce myself." It sounded like a threat.

The prince stepped forward and pulled Violet into a quick hug that stunned her into paralysis. "It was good to see you, princess." He glared at Slayton. "Bye."

Slayton laughed like Roman had told a joke only they understood. "Bye, Your Grace."

Roman ignored him and guided a silent Vivian toward the theater.

"That was interesting," Slayton remarked.

Violet glanced at the future king and queen, and mumbled, "That's one way to put it."

Roman milled around Violet's cottage, searching for evidence indicating Titus had been there after their date.

The only men's items were the clothes with names pinned to them piled high in a basket by the door. Roman's lips twitched into a ghost of a smile. Her success made him proud. She did excellent work and everyone loved her. He frowned and thought back to Titus. Perhaps they loved her a little too much.

Satisfied Titus had not been there, he wandered back to Violet's room. As was his ritual, Roman stood at the side of her bed, checked her breathing, and planted himself in a cushioned wing-backed chair in the corner, a new addition to her room as of late.

Roman had his night routine down to an art. He'd go to bed early in his rooms, have the same nightmare, wake up around three in the morning, and slip into Violet's cottage to check on her.

And watch her sleep.

There had been times when Violet stayed up all night, sitting in her bed as if waiting for something or someone. Those nights he stayed poised to attack. He didn't know what he'd do if another man showed up, but he knew they'd never make it to the bed alive.

Roman flushed hot with anger. It was selfish to keep Violet from finding happiness with another man, and he'd told himself on the way over here that until he could be the one to make her happy, he'd force himself to be okay with her *dating*, but there would be no fucking.

Roman would kill someone before he'd allow them to touch what was his. Because she *was* his, and he was hers. He'd never touched another woman, and he never would.

14

TWENTY-ONE YEARS OLD

Roman sat on the row behind Violet in the gallery at the pleasure house, watching her observe the couple on stage. She used to sit toward the back, but over the years had moved close enough to hear the wet sounds of the man's tongue as he ravaged the writhing woman whose thighs wrapped around his head.

Normally, Roman drew the line at invading Violet's intimate moments, but here, he didn't have to deprive himself. There were people everywhere, watching, playing, performing, and Violet sat out in the open, enjoying every minute.

The first time she'd seen him there, her eyes had widened, and to his surprise and pleasure, she hadn't left. Instead, she'd shot him a cheeky grin and continued to watch the show.

Roman hadn't sat right behind her at first. He'd stayed in the back and observed her closely. He knew Violet's tells when she saw something she liked. Her breath would hitch, and she'd squirm in her seat, crossing and uncrossing her legs. It became too much, being that far away from her in that state, and the next time they were there, he'd sat directly behind her, neither saying a word to the other.

The woman on stage had her hands bound to the bedpost, and she yanked against the restraints as the man's movements against her cunt sped up. He lapped at the woman's center with fervor, the wet sounds of his tongue reaching into the audience. Violet's hand fluttered to her neck and drifted down her breasts.

Some patrons rented out private viewing boxes with their partners to fuck while they watched, and Roman had fantasized about taking Violet against the glass more times than he could count.

Her breathing picked up when the woman on stage ground herself against the man's face with a long, tortured moan. Violet's hand slid to the top of her thigh and clutched at the material of her dress for dear life. He wanted her to push her skirt aside and let him watch as she finger fucked herself.

A lot of people pleasured themselves as they watched, but not Violet. His girl waited until she got home. Roman wondered if she *liked* to edge herself; if she refused to allow herself the release she desperately craved until she got home. He didn't watch her make herself come. Seeing her come for the first time would be a gift she gave to him freely.

But he listened.

Gods, did he listen.

Hidden just outside of her bedroom door, he'd relish in her moans and wonder if she licked her fingers and rubbed her clit, or if she pushed her delicate fingers into her soaking pussy and fucked herself into a frenzy? Did she gush, or did she drip, waiting for him to lick her clean?

He wanted to feel her wet cunt choke his cock as she cried out for him. The tightness in his pants grew, and he worried he would spill just from the thought.

The woman performer's screams rose, and Violet shifted restlessly in her seat. It snapped the last of Roman's restraint. Leaning forward, he hovered his lips over her ear and broke their unspoken rule, murmuring, "Does Titus not eat your pussy well enough, princess? Is that why it's your favorite part of the show?"

He knew Titus had touched nothing but her mouth. It worked out well for Roman, because as long as Violet stayed with Titus, he didn't have to worry about killing anyone else for touching her body. For some reason, her *boyfriend* wouldn't lay a finger on her. Roman knew because there wasn't a single second Titus and Violet were in private without him there.

He'd assigned one of his most trusted warriors, Marissa, to tail Violet whenever Roman couldn't. Marissa didn't know the truth about his mating or his obsession with Violet; she thought Roman wanted protection on his mate's defenseless sister.

Not that Violet couldn't defend herself; Edgar had been teaching Violet self-defense for the last couple of years. Watching her disarm her father had Roman beaming with pride.

Once her shock wore off, Violet turned to him, their faces inches apart, and whispered, "Does Vivian not scream loud enough when you eat hers? Is that why it's *your* favorite part?" A perfect brow ticked up in defiant challenge and he had to physically restrain himself from throwing her over his shoulder and spanking her ass raw. He loved it.

"I've missed that sharp tongue of yours, princess." Leaning back a little, he rested his elbows on his knees. "I miss the days when we were friends, and you were crawling around in chicken shit."

"I miss those days too," Violet murmured. She paused before pivoting toward him fully. "You're with Vivian now, and

I'm with Titus." Her hand waved between them. "All of that childhood infatuation and puppy love is in the past. I don't see any reason why we can't be friends."

Hearing her say she didn't love him anymore hit hard, but it didn't matter. The way she looked at him, giving him the opportunity to be around her again without hiding, made him want to bellow out a victory cry.

He had two years left to devise a way out of his marriage to Vivian that didn't involve killing her. Since he knew Violet wouldn't agree to marry him and break the bond that way, the only other option he'd found was Vivian's death. If killing her meant he could marry Violet, he would do it, but he'd rather find a way that wouldn't upset his future wife. In the meantime, he'd take Violet in whatever way he could.

Violet sat across from Roman at the bakery with a giant piece of strawberry cake in front of her, laughing at the look of sheer horror on his face.

"I'm not eating that," he protested.

She pointed to the bowl of lumpy cottage cheese and strawberries. "You agreed to try whatever I wanted you to if I came here with you."

Roman ignored her and pointed to the flower crown on her head. "I haven't seen you wear one of those in years." His expression held a hint of fondness, and she chuckled lightly.

"I never take time to make them anymore. My closest neighbors have an eight-year-old son. Yesterday, when I stepped outside to leave, he came tromping up the stairs of my porch, holding this out like a grand prize." She touched the crown, remembering how cute he'd looked. Roman studied her crown thoughtfully, drumming his fingers against the table.

"It's one of the sweetest things anyone has done for me," she stated. *Other than the mysterious gifts that occasionally appear in my room.*

One day Violet would gather the nerve to ask Roman about them, but their rekindled friendship was new, and she didn't want to ruin it.

It'd been two weeks since they'd decided to try being friends again. *Friends.* If someone told teenage Violet being platonic friends with Roman Covington made her happy, she'd laugh in their face... and probably cry a little too.

But it's true. Violet did enjoy being friends with Roman again. She loved Titus and wanted to marry him someday, and she thought he wanted to marry her too. When they'd first started dating, Titus had been honest. He didn't want to have sex until after they married.

The sentiment was unusual for fae, practically non-existent, but she respected his choices. Every time they kissed, he stopped before it went too far and told her he couldn't wait until he could have her. That meant he planned on marrying her, right? They hadn't talked about it, but they'd been officially dating for almost a year.

Which reminded her... "How is the wedding planning going? Only five more months and you'll be a married man." Roman looked away and tried not to laugh but lost the battle. "What's so funny?" Violet demanded.

His face brightened with amusement. "Our twenty-second birthdays are in three months, not five."

Violet held up her fingers and silently counted. *Damn.* "Just answer the question." She grabbed Roman's spoon, dipped it into his bowl, and held it out for him to grab.

He reared back and pushed her hand away. "We aren't getting married next year," he said, shocking the hell out of her.

"Did you move the wedding up?" She held out the spoon again, and he glared at it.

"I'm not eating that, and we agreed to push the wedding back a year."

Violet's brows shot skyward. "And they let you? Why would you want to?" Traditionally, royals married their mates on their twenty-second birthday, whether by the gods' decree or a kingdom tradition, Violet didn't know.

"What's the rush?" He plucked the spoon out of Violet's hand and stuck it in the bowl. "Most non-royal fae don't get married until they're in their mid to late twenties. As long as I'm married at some point, it shouldn't matter."

Violet took a long drink of her juice and licked the remnants from her lips. "Will they smite you for your defiance?"

Something flashed in Roman's eyes, and he casually leaned back in his chair, looking for all the world like a king lounging on his throne. "I guess we'll see."

15

TWENTY-TWO YEARS OLD

Roman watched Titus leave Violet's apartment, thankful he'd headed out early. The man's life held no excitement outside of Violet, yet he left her every night. It spared his life, but he didn't know that.

Roman instructed Marissa to follow Titus a few nights a week under the guise of needing to know who would possibly be marrying into the royal family. Titus worked, spent time with Violet, and went home. That's it.

That is exactly what you do, a small voice in Roman's head reminded him, but he shoved it away. He had friends outside of Violet; Titus did not, according to Marissa.

Roman vanquished all thoughts of the man and observed Violet as she washed the dishes from their dinner. His lip curled. Her boyfriend should have stayed to help. Violet wouldn't lift a finger without Roman by her side once they were together.

A darkness clouded his soul at the reminder that time was running out. Four months. That's all he had left to find a way out of mating Vivian without killing her.

He wished, more than ever, that he'd let Vivian continue her dalliance with the mystery man because the woman hunted him down and harped on him constantly about their wedding. She'd been furious about delaying it for a year, but nothing she said changed Roman's mind.

If he hadn't been hellbent on putting her in her place, she'd probably be too preoccupied to care about their wedding, or lack thereof. She might have even run off and married the poor man.

Roman stilled. *That's it.* Why the fuck hadn't he thought of it sooner?

What if he could convince Vivian to marry the man she loved? If the guy already wed another, maybe she'd take another lover and fall in love. It might be a long shot, but Roman had to try.

With one last look at Violet and a silent promise to see her later, he slipped into the night to find Vivian.

"I need to speak with Vivian," Roman told Meri when she answered their cottage door. "It's important."

"Of course, come in." His future mother-in-law stepped aside for him to enter, closed the door behind him, and disappeared up the stairs.

Minutes later, Vivian floated gracefully down the stairs with a curious look in his direction and Meri on her heels. "What are you doing here?" Blunt and to the point; her usual mask gone.

"I need to speak with you privately." He looked apologetically at Meri.

"Edgar will be home soon," she said and crossed the room toward the door. "I'll intercept him on the porch, and you two can talk in Vivian's room."

"Thank you." Roman held out his arm, indicating for Vivian to go in front of him.

They climbed the stairs in silence, and once in Vivian's room, Roman closed the door with a soft click. He hated being in here. Violet's bed no longer stood on the opposite side, replaced by a custom-made weapons rack. The vibrant colors that once adorned the walls were noticeably absent with nothing in their place. It depressed him.

"What is this about," Vivian queried, getting straight to the point.

Roman had spent the entire way from Violet's cottage rehearsing what he would say. Vivian was no fool, and he had to plant the seed without her realizing his manipulation.

"Has my mother spoken with you about training?"

Vivian's eyes slitted. "Why would your mother need to speak with me about warrior training?"

"Not warrior training. You'll be stopping that after we marry." *Lie.*

"What?" she screeched, and he stared blankly while she sputtered. "I'm not quitting training."

"Yes, you are," he deadpanned. "You'll begin training with my mother on how to be queen." If his mother knew he'd insinuated women couldn't fight as a warrior and be queen, she'd rip his head off.

"That's bullshit," she seethed. "Your mother fights alongside your father."

"My mother trained as queen from the time she was a child," he reminded her, "and she doesn't train with warriors anymore. She fights if we're attacked."

Vivian's face reddened with rage. "I'm not stopping what I love."

Roman chuckled humorlessly. "Yes, you are. No general will allow you to set foot inside the arena if I tell them not to."

"Fuck you!" she yelled and shoved him.

He stuck his hands in his pockets and blew out an exaggerated breath. "We can't go on like this, Viv. Neither of us is happy, and I don't want to live the rest of our lives resenting each other."

Vivian stiffened. "Are you fucking kidding me?" Her arms dropped, hands fisting at her sides. "I don't know where this is going, Rome, but you can't toss me aside. I'm your mate."

Roman stepped back, putting on the best performance of his life. "If anyone knows that, it's me. The gods bonded us, whether we like it or not, but we don't have to be miserable." He raked a hand through his hair and paced the length of the room. "Do you think I like having a mate who hates me?"

Vivian tracked Roman like a hunter watching its prey. "Do you think I want a mate who is in love with someone else?" she countered.

Roman stopped abruptly and looked at her in surprise, forcing his real emotions down. He'd mastered suppressing them over the years to keep her from knowing his every thought. *Easy to do when you feel dead inside without the love of your life.*

"Vivian, I barely have time to take a shit, let alone fall in love with someone. If I'm not training with the warriors, my parents have me in council meetings and going over fake political scenarios with them or the scholars." *Lie.* He'd completed that training years ago, but she didn't know that. "What little spare time I possess, I spend with the few friends I have. When would I fall in love with someone?"

"I've felt it," Vivian stated matter-of-factly and tapped her chest. "Or did you forget?"

Time to see if his emotion suppressing skills were as good

as he thought. "And when was the last time you felt it? *Really* felt it? A couple of years, right?" He scrubbed his hands down his face and dropped them, feigning defeat. "I can feel your sadness, Viv. I know you miss your old boyfriend." *Truth.* It gave him pleasure to know she was suffering, and now he thanked the gods for her still holding a candle for this mystery man.

She shifted, a look of uncertainty flitting across her features for the first time. "I still feel spurts of affection and happiness from you."

Shit. He rubbed his forehead and feigned disbelief. "You do know that I love my family and friends, right? Gods, Vivian, look at us."

They stared at each other, Roman waiting for the perfect opportunity to strike. "It doesn't matter," she conceded. "We're mated, and that's that."

"But you can still be happy," he murmured. "It was wrong of me to put an end to your relationship when I had no intention of starting one with you."

Her eyes flared. "What are you saying?" He thought of Violet to garner affection and push it down the bond, schooling his face into one of sympathy, hoping Vivian would mistake it as him caring about her happiness.

"I'm saying I won't stop you anymore." The crackling of a candle was the only break in the silence of the room. "If you want to be with him, or anyone else, I give you my blessing."

"Violet won't have you," she informed him, her words cracking like a whip.

He snorted. "Violet is in a committed relationship. It's only a matter of time before Titus proposes to her. I can assure you, this has nothing to do with your sister."

Vivian's face paled, and she wandered over to her bed and sat down. *That isn't the reaction I expected.* Her sister being happy while Vivian lived *not miserably* at best got to her. She'd unknowingly given him the perfect weapon to wield against her.

"It's funny." He smiled wryly. "You once said you'd won because the gods chose you as queen." He forced her to look at him, pushing as much sympathy and pity as he could down the bond. Truthfully, he did pity Vivian. She might be a spiteful, arrogant nightmare of a person toward Roman and Violet, but she'd had her choice taken away too. "In the end, Violet is the only winner," he whispered. "She gets to marry someone she loves and be happy for the rest of her life; and look at us." He gestured between them.

Vivian's jealousy shot hot and fast down the bond, but Roman pretended not to feel it. *Predictable.* "And when we're married?" she demanded.

Roman crouched down in front of her and turned her face to his. "Our arrangement still stands." He hesitated. "Viv..."

She rubbed her chest, brows pushing together. "I can feel your uncertainty. Just say what you need to say."

"If you decide to marry him, I understand," Roman murmured. "I won't stop you."

He grunted when her shock, anger, hope, and confusion assaulted him. "That's treason," she hissed and stood, nearly tipping him over. "And what of the future of the kingdom, *Your Grace*? They would hunt me down for jeopardizing their future safety."

"No," he said sharply. "I wouldn't let that happen. I'm not saying I want you to do that—no royal has ever married anyone other than their mate in the history of Eden—but I'm not a fucking monster. I won't force you to marry me and sign yourself up for a life of misery. We've tried to be friends, and it doesn't work. We're too different." Tried was being generous. More like he'd pretended to try for three seconds when they were teens. "You can have your affairs. I won't disparage your happiness anymore, and I don't want to put my kingdom at risk, but if breaking our bond is the only way you feel you can live without hating your life, I won't begrudge you that, either."

Roman walked to the door and opened it. "I'm not the soulless asshole you think I am," he intoned quietly. "I'm giving you back the choice the gods stole from us."

He closed the door behind him and prayed Vivian's feelings for her ex-lover were stronger than her desire to be queen.

16

THREE MONTHS LATER

Violet stood on her toes and planted a kiss on Titus' lips. "Are you sure you don't want to stay?" The corners of his mouth tightened, and she added, "Not for sex. Just to stay."

He pulled her close and smoothed back her hair. "I wish I could. More than anything."

The strain in his voice caught her by surprise, and she leaned back to look at him. "Is everything okay?"

His lips, warm and soft, pressed tenderly against her forehead. "Stress from work. That's all."

"I'll make you your favorite sweet rolls tomorrow," she promised and stepped back. "Have you decided what you're wearing to Vivian and Roman's wedding? If your clothes need to be altered, I'll have to start on them now."

If it weren't for Roman, Violet doubted she'd attend the wedding at all. Supporting her friend was the only reason she planned on attending the grand affair. Vivian ignored her more than before, but she and Roman saw each other at least once a week. Sometimes he had lunch with her, Griff, and Slayton, and every now and then, he even came to dinner with her and Titus.

Violet didn't know much about Roman and Vivian's relationship. Asking Roman about Viv resulted in him changing the subject. Every. Single. Time. Violet hoped they were as content as she and Titus.

Who knew, she might have a wedding of her own soon, if Marissa spoke true at lunch yesterday. According to her, Titus walked out of the jewelry shop last week carrying a small, square box. When Marissa and Roman left the sandwich shop, Violet had squealed like a schoolgirl.

Not even the fact Marissa delivered the news could put a damper on her excitement. A tall, statuesque woman with cool ivory skin, bright red hair, and the prettiest face Violet had ever seen; Marissa checked all the boxes on the *ideal woman* list. Griff's words, not Violet's.

The woman tagged along with Roman sometimes, and while Marissa had never given her a reason, Violet didn't like her. It made Violet feel rotten because she couldn't put her finger on why. She said nothing to Griff about it because they were friends, but she'd confided in Slayton.

He hadn't said much other than he'd keep an eye on her, and that if Violet ever felt uncomfortable or threatened to tell him or Roman straight away. It hadn't escaped her notice that he didn't mention Titus. Violet had a sneaking suspicion Slayton wasn't her boyfriend's biggest fan. He hadn't seemed happy, either, about what Marissa saw, but Violet knew he'd support her no matter what.

Titus didn't answer her question about the wedding, his eyes filling with something akin to regret. *What's going on with him?*

"I understand if you can't go," she assured him, trying to mask her disappointment.

"I'll be at Vivian's wedding." He kissed her again, his lips lingering on hers. "You know I love you, right?"

She chuckled and patted his chest. "I do, and I love you too." She gestured toward the front door. "Now go before I tie you to my bed."

He smiled and opened the door before looking back at her again. "I do love you, Violet."

She shooed him outside with a teasing smile. "You said that already." As she shut the door, she couldn't help but sense doom looming over her.

The next day, Roman waited for his mother and father in his sitting room, pondering how they would take his refusal to marry Vivian in three weeks. He'd hoped by now she would have gotten cold feet and run off with her lover, whom Roman knew she'd started seeing again if her love and orgasms traveling down the bond were any indication.

Elated did not begin to describe what he felt when she'd fucked the mystery man again for the first time. It meant Roman's plan had worked, but she'd not disappeared and broken their bond yet. He couldn't hold off on canceling the wedding any longer and sent a request that morning for a meeting with his parents about his upcoming nuptials.

He mentally went over the reasons him marrying someone else wouldn't harm the kingdom. It mattered not to him, but his parents cared.

1. The bloodline wouldn't end if he married someone else, it would only weaken, but even a weak royal fae was stronger than the strongest non-royal fae, and when his child married their mate, it would strengthen again.

2. There were no other royal heirs to take his place if

Roman denied his mate because royals only had one child. The gods couldn't kill him or the Tropical line would die out. *Maybe.*

No one knew what the gods might do. They were ethereal beings who'd created Eden, left instructions to the first humans and fae, and left. They'd only come back once, thousands of years ago, to erect the magical barrier separating the humans from fae and hadn't returned since.

3. He would kill Vivian if he had to.

Surely those three reasons were enough to placate them.

"Knock, knock," his mother sang as she walked into his sitting room with a bright smile.

Roman stood and met her halfway, kissing her on the cheek. "Thank you for coming."

She pulled back. "Why are you being formal?"

"Sarah, leave the boy be," his father interjected and guided his wife to one of the plush chairs against the wall. When his father took his own seat, he indicated for Roman to sit down. "Tell us what this is about, Son."

Right to the point then.

"I'm not marrying Vivian."

His mother huffed, her mouth turning down at the corners. "I know marriage can be scary, honey, but we cannot postpone the wedding again."

"None of the other three heirs have married yet, and they're older than he is," Roman's father countered.

Roman's brows rose. Royal fae heirs not marrying on their twenty-second birthday was unheard of. But all four? Unfathomable.

"I'm not postponing the wedding," Roman cut in. His parents' bickering came to a halt. The queen looked confused, but his father's eyes narrowed. *Here goes nothing.* "I'm not marrying Vivian at all."

The words silenced the room in their wake. His father's face reddened with fury, and his mother's paled with shock.

"What do you mean?" his mother asked, rising from her seat. "She is your mate. You must marry her."

"Why? Because gods whom we haven't seen nor heard from in thousands of years said so?" he challenged.

"Because it will put our kingdom in danger," his father bellowed and stood. "Of all the selfish, immature things you've done, this is too far. You *will* marry Vivian."

Roman stepped closer and snarled, "No, I will not."

His mother's voice quieted. "Why, Roman? What could be important enough to forsake your kingdom and defy the gods?"

Roman shifted to look at the woman who'd taught him the importance of love. He'd planned to wait until Violet agreed to marry him to reveal his true reasoning, but he knew the only way to win his mother over was to tell her the truth.

"I'm in love with Violet." He stared at her, imploring her to understand. "I always have been. The gods made a mistake. I know they did."

"Love?" the king scoffed. "You would put your entire kingdom at risk because of an infatuation? Son, think about what you're saying."

Roman's head twisted eerily slow to look at his father. "There is nothing in this world more important to me than Violet Maekin. Nothing. Not even you two."

"And how does Violet feel?" his father asked snidely. "She has a serious boyfriend. Confident of you to think she'll give him up."

Roman threw his head back and laughed maniacally. "You think I'm worried about Titus?"

At the same time, his mother surprised the hell out of both men by saying, "People disappear all the time."

Roman gaped, and his father blanched. "Sarah, do you hear yourself?" the king asked his wife.

"What?" She placed her hand over her heart. "I knew he loved her when they were kids. Even *I* thought the gods were mistaken, but eventually they outgrew their young love." Her warm fingers wrapped around Roman's, and the king mumbled to himself as he paced the length of the room.

"I thought you outgrew it," his mother continued, "but had I known, we could have announced her as your mate instead. No one in the kingdom would have been the wiser."

The guilt in his mother's voice made his heart swell with gratitude. But none of this was her fault. The gods dealt Roman a shitty hand that he must rectify himself.

He smiled wryly. "I'll have her. Even if I must kill any man who stands in my way."

His father's head whipped around so fast, Roman thought it might snap off. "Dear gods, there are two of you."

Sarah smiled sweetly up at her son, ignoring her husband. "Okay, honey, but we can just as easily send him to another kingdom. It wouldn't be the first time."

The king looked between his wife and son. "You two cannot go around killing and exiling people for dating the ones you love."

The queen's face darkened. "Tippy Glenn did not *date* you, and if she had, more than her grabby hands would be fertilizing my garden."

Roman's father rubbed his forehead. "Maybe diluting the bloodline wouldn't be the worst thing in the world," he mumbled under his breath.

Roman stared at his mother, wondering how she'd kept animals from digging up the remains in her garden. It was the main reason he didn't leave bodies there, like Kincaid. The man's body had finally given out, and Roman had been forced to get creative with his disposal.

Roman's mother sniffed and lifted her nose in the air. "Hush. We need to meet with the scholars and come up with a plan to lessen the blow when we announce Roman's decision."

Roman stared longingly at his bed the next morning. His nightly routine, while worth it, left him tired most days until he had his morning coffee. Each night after Titus left Violet's house, Roman came back home for a few hours of sleep and would wake in the early hours of the morning from a nightmare. He'd then slip back into Violet's house to check on her and watch her sleep until just before dawn.

If he thought he could survive on no sleep, he'd stay with Violet all night, but he couldn't. He'd tried a few times.

Roman rubbed at his sternum, annoyed with Vivian's giddy excitement laced with a strange sort of anxiety. *Odd.* If there was one thing about Vivian, she rarely experienced anxiety or fear.

A knock on his door interrupted his thoughts. He passed through his sitting room and opened the door to find his parents on the other side. He stepped aside and waved them in. "To what do I owe the pleasure?"

His mother bustled into the room in a flurry of pale pink skirts. "We need to discuss the situation with your mate."

Roman led them to the small dining table in the corner of his sitting room and pulled out a chair for his mother before he and his father joined her. "I assume you have a plan."

His father leaned back and crossed one leg over the other, looking deceptively relaxed. "We have, and the council agrees."

Roman wanted to slam his fist on the table. The fewer

people who knew about this until they had the logistics figured out, the better. "You didn't think to check with me before involving the council?"

"The council helped concoct the plan," his mother explained, pushing an stray piece of hair out of her face. "And we agreed."

Roman looked between the two. "Why do you both look as if you're delivering a death blow?"

His parents exchanged a wary glance, and his father answered, "Because we know you won't like it."

"I'll not marry Vivian." Roman asserted and stood. "End of discussion."

"Sit." His mother tapped his chair. "I would never force you to marry when you're in love with another."

The tension in Roman's shoulders loosened a fraction as he eased into his seat. "Then what is it?"

"You'll marry Violet," his father began, "but to everyone else, she will be Vivian."

Roman shot to his feet again. "No," he snarled. "I'll not have my mate pretend to be someone she's not. Especially not her unworthy sister."

"Vivian is your mate," his father snapped. "This is a compromise that allows you to *risk your kingdom* without them knowing."

Over Roman's dead body would he hide Violet behind Vivian's mask. "No one in the capital would buy it. Everyone knows the twins are night and day."

His mother adjusted the sleeve of her dress. If she was avoiding his gaze, he really wouldn't like the next part of their *plan*. "Vivian will leave the kingdom, and Violet will train with your father, Edgar, and me to pass as a warrior; learn to act and dress the part of Vivian publicly. We will announce Vivian's retirement as a warrior in lieu of her taking over as queen."

Roman scoffed and moved to the center of the room before he threw something. "I never took you two for fools."

His father straightened and leaned forward. "Watch it."

"No, *you* watch it," Roman returned with a lethal note in his deceptively calm voice. "I will marry Violet. If our people refuse to kneel before her, I will cut them off at the knees. They will have no choice but to kiss her feet."

A searing pain tore through Roman, and he cried out, clawing at his chest as he lurched toward the table to steady himself. His mother screamed and jumped out of her seat to kneel at his side.

The sound of her voice was a distant murmur, muffled by the blood roaring in Roman's ears. He couldn't speak or breathe, and he gritted his teeth against the sharp pain. Were the gods punishing him for his disobedience?

A sheen of sweat broke out on his forehead. How long would their useless punishment last? Not even the greatest pain imaginable could force him to give up Violet.

It didn't make sense that they'd punish him early, and fear gripped him. What if something happened to War? He closed his eyes and reached for his *familiar,* greeted by nothing but darkness and silence.

"*War?*" he bellowed down the bond.

The beast's vision blinked open until Roman stared out at an array of colorful trees. He watched through War as the cat jumped from a tall branch and ran toward the palace. Roman breathed a sigh of relief.

"*What's wrong?*" War demanded.

"*I don't know. My chest feels like it's being destroyed from the inside out, and I was worried something happened to you.*"

"*I'm on my way.*"

A vague awareness of his parents yelling his name and his mother's hands fumbling over his torso teased at the corners of his mind. The pain dissolved as quickly as it came, and he sat back on his heels, panting. *What just happened?*

"Roman, speak to me," his father's strong voice ordered.

Roman pushed to his feet. "It was like being ripped apart from the inside out. I thought something happened to War, but he's fine."

Deep lines formed between his father's brows until his face paled. "Where is Vivian now?"

"Vivian?" Roman's face matched his father's. "How would I know?" A pause, followed by hope. "Do you think she broke the bond?"

A triumphant smile tried to tease Roman's lips, but he pushed it down, too scared to truly hope. He connected with War and told him to find Vivian.

He reached inward for Vivian's emotions, but they were gone. Not even a whisper of her remained.

Opening his eyes, he stopped fighting his grin, and his mother gasped, covering her mouth. "She either married another or she's dead," he confirmed, answering the question on both his parents' faces.

And he cared not which one.

17

Roman pounded on the door to the Maekins' cottage with his parents at his side, but no one answered. Racing around the house, he climbed through the laundering room window and searched every room.

He stopped short when he entered Vivian's bedroom. Tidy, as always, but nothing adorned her desk or weapons rack. Moving quickly, he opened her drawers to find them completely empty. His plan worked; she'd married her lover.

Roman left the empty house and met his parents on the porch. "No one's here and Vivian's room is bare. Did she have her trunks delivered to the palace already?"

"I'm unsure," his father replied, "but we need to find her. I'll have someone check with her sister."

"*I'll* check with Violet." Roman switched course toward the stables. He rubbed at his chest. It felt strange to not have Vivian's unwelcomed emotions as background noise after years of trying to tune them out.

"Roman." Something in his father's tone made him stop. "Try not to look so happy."

Roman looked past his father to his mother, who was grinning like a child in a sweets shop. He winked at her and nodded to his father without a word. He could no more hide his happiness than he could deny his love for Violet.

Whether Vivian was dead or married, he didn't care if it meant the bond no longer existed. His cheeks hurt from smiling. When was the last time he'd openly smiled over something that didn't involve watching Violet? Years. He knew he deserved hell for his apathetic thoughts, but they couldn't be helped.

I will suffer the deepest ring of hell if it means one lifetime with her.

At the stables, his mother took her horse from the stable hand and shooed him away when he tried to help her mount.

His father rubbed his forehead with a heavy sigh. "I'll inform the council."

War appeared from the direction of the training arena with Tilly, his mother's lorix *familiar,* running beside him. Lorix were small monkeys with big round eyes and light blue fur. They looked harmless, but their venomous incisors and claws grew when aggravated. Vicious little things.

Violet stared at her ceiling, still groggy from sleep. The sun shining bright through her window indicated she'd slept later than usual. The perks of having the day off. A soft knock on the front door startled her, and she sat up in bed, her heart beating wildly.

She took a moment to gather herself, breathing deep. With her father's help, Violet had successfully begun combating her need to hide at the slightest sound. During their self-defense trainings her father insisted on strengthening her mind. He claimed knowing how to defend yourself from ailments of the mind was just as important as knowing how to protect yourself.

Violet still hid under her bed from time to time, but the impulse lessened with each passing day.

The knock sounded again, and she crept into the front room to peek through the curtains. A man in the post carrier uniform stood on her porch with his hands behind his back. *What in the world is a postman doing here this early?*

"Good morning, Miss Violet," he greeted when she opened the door. "I was asked to deliver this to you." He held out an envelope with her name on it.

"Thank you," she said with a polite smile and glanced at her post box, wondering why he hadn't left it there. She'd never had a post carrier knock before.

Understanding her silent inquiry, the man motioned to the letter. "A man came into the post yesterday and paid extra to have his missive delivered to you directly this morning."

She recognized Titus' sloppy handwriting and frowned. Why would he mail her a letter yesterday when he could have given it to her himself?

Violet thanked him and shut the door. The letter burned her palm as she walked into the kitchen to put a pot of water on to boil before tearing open the envelope with a pounding heart.

Violet,

This is the hardest thing I have ever had to do, and if I were a stronger man, I would have told you in person.

Before I say this, know that I do love you, and part of my heart will always be yours, but the rest has always been elsewhere. That day I walked into your tent and saw your face, I was stunned into silence. You look just like her, but different in your own, beautiful way.

I am ashamed to admit that when I asked you to dinner, it was with revenge in mind. Vivian and I have been in love since late childhood, and when the prince announced her as his mate, I'd never felt such betrayal and heartbreak in my life. She never told me why she wanted to keep us a secret, but I loved her too much to deny her anything.

When I took you out for the first time, you surprised me. You are so full of life, and you made me laugh more than I thought possible. The more time we spent together, the more I realized I didn't care about hurting Vivian anymore. I cared about making you happy, and bit by bit, I fell in love with you too.

But Vivian still haunted me, and when she came to me weeks ago and begged me to run away with her, it felt right. You must understand that fate forced us apart, not our own choices, and it wouldn't have been fair to you if I'd stayed.

I will never forgive myself for breaking your heart, but you deserve a man who can give you their all, and that man isn't me. ~~I wish it had been you.~~

With Love,

Titus

The paper slipped through Violet's fingers and joined her on the old wooden floor. She didn't know when she'd slid to her knees, but she knew the exact moment the shards of her heart pierced her lungs on their way to the ground.

The betrayal didn't cut deep, it sliced her all over in a thousand tiny knicks, drawing blood and pain from every piece of her.

Her dinner from last night evacuated her stomach, and she

alternated between shaking, crying, and cursing the two people responsible.

A strangled sob ripped from her throat as a gaping hole formed in her chest.

She'd never hated someone before, but in that moment, she hated her sister more than anything in the world.

"*Violet,*" a deep voice rumbled on the other side of her front door. "*It's Roman, let me in.*"

Violet hung her head and cried harder. If she ignored him, he'd go away eventually. Falling back on her butt, she leaned her head against the cabinet behind her. A muffled curse followed by footsteps pounded down her porch steps.

Did Vivian leave him a note? Is he devastated like me?

Violet's kitchen window crashed open, and she screamed, her broken heart beating erratically. She scrambled across the floor on her hands and knees, narrowly missing the vomit, and tried to hide under the table.

Large hands wrapped around her waist and stopped her escape. She thrashed around, but they pulled her against a warm body. "It's me, princess," Roman murmured and settled on the ground with her still in his arms. Tugging her into his lap, he moved one of the chairs and tried to scoot them both under the table, but his large frame wouldn't fit. Instead, he held her tight and whispered apologies.

Fur brushed against her leg, and she lifted her head to see a fuzzy blue lorix blinking back at her. She pressed closer into Roman. Lorix were cute, but they were deadly.

"Tilly," Roman said sharply. "You're scaring her." He ran a soothing hand down Violet's back. "She's my mother's *familiar.*" The lorix ignored Roman and scooted closer to Violet.

The adrenaline wore off, and Violet tried to move out of Roman's lap, but he refused to let her go. "What happened?"

Violet sniffled. "You don't know?" Her watery eyes raised to his.

"Is Vivian dead?" he asked cautiously.

She jerked back. "What?"

"The bond is gone," he explained. "I thought maybe something happened to her."

He thought Vivian died and looked not the least bit upset. *The bond is broken.* Violet's breath hitched and a fresh wave of tears swarmed her. If their bond broke, then Vivian *married* Titus.

I fucking hate *her.*

"Sh-she ran away with T-Titus," Violet hiccupped. The lorix climbed into her lap and wormed its way under Roman's arm to snuggle against her stomach.

"She *what*?" Roman boomed, making her wince. Funny, he seemed more upset to know she'd married another man than he had thinking she'd died.

"If you'll let me up, I'll show you." Violet was proud of herself for managing not to blubber her words. Roman reluctantly released her, and she retrieved Titus' letter from the floor. "Last night Titus paid the post extra to hand deliver this to me this morning."

Roman snatched the paper from her and froze. Without reading the letter, he dropped it to the floor and grabbed her hand to inspect it. "The paper didn't cut you, did it? I didn't mean to grab it like that."

A surprised laugh bubbled out of her. "I'm fine, but *you* won't be when you read that note." She forced back a new onslaught of tears.

Roman picked up the discarded letter and scanned the contents, his face contorting with fury. "How could he do this to you?" He wrinkled the paper in his fist, violence rippling off him in waves. "I will fucking kill him for what he's done to you."

Violet leaned forward and took the crinkled paper. Smoothing it out, she held it in front of him. "What *they* did to *us*. He left with Vivian."

Roman pushed the letter away. "You think I care your sister left?"

Violet tried to make sense of his response but came up short. "Um, yes? If your bond no longer exists, then they *married*. Your *mate* married *someone else*." Right before their wedding. What a fucking bitch.

"And she will lose her head for her crimes," he said stoically.

She blanched. "You can't kill her."

The prince took back the paper and folded it neatly to place in his pocket. "Yes, I can. She committed treason, and so did Titus. They *will* die for what they've done." Violet shook her head, and he cupped both sides of her face. "What they've done to you is *unforgivable*."

She ripped her face from his hands. "They're assholes," she agreed, "and right now I hate them, but I don't want them to die."

The tender look Roman afforded her took her aback. "For you, I'll let them live, but they cannot go unpunished."

It was the best she could ask for. As far as Violet knew, a royal mate bond had never been severed, and she didn't know what it meant for the future. "Thank you."

A knock on the door mpade her jump back into Roman's arms. "It's just my mother and War," he soothed and picked her up.

Violet wiggled as he stalked to the front room. "Let me down," she ordered. He obediently lowered her feet to the ground. Straightening her dress and wiping her nose, she hastened to the front door to open it.

Queen Sarah took one look at her face and gasped. "Is Vivian dead?"

Roman's chest pressed to Violet's back. "No. She married Violet's boyfriend."

The queen gasped again and looked between Violet and Roman. "How do you know?"

Roman reached into his pocket and held out Titus' note. The queen skimmed the contents and raised her shocked gaze to theirs. "Oh, honey." She wrapped Violet in a motherly embrace, squeezing the life out of her. "I am so sorry. We'll kil—"

"No," Roman interrupted her, and they shared a silent exchange.

War nudged the side of Violet's leg, and she released Roman's mother to squat beside him. He nuzzled her face with his giant head, purring loudly.

She encircled his massive neck with her arms, reminiscent of the day in the woods when she'd broken down over Dominic. Did War remember that day too? A dam within Violet broke, and loud sobs wracked her body.

Roman pried her away from War, lifted her effortlessly into his arms, and carried her into her room.

After Violet cried herself to sleep, Roman reluctantly released her and crept out of the room.

"Honey, are you alright?" his mother asked when he entered the living room. She reached for him and pulled him into a hug. "I know seeing her hurt hurts you."

He freed himself from her arms and held both of her shoulders. "She refuses to let me kill them."

His mother's mouth turned down. "Why?"

Roman shrugged. "I don't know, but I'll not upset her more."

Violet might not want him to kill them, but that didn't mean they would get off without punishment. He would send Ares on a scouting mission to find them.

His mother nodded curtly. "If that's what my sweet girl wants."

Keeping the queen from killing Vivian and Titus would be a feat. Her innocent face didn't fool Roman for a second. How many people had his mother made *disappear*, he wondered.

"If they're found, I want them brought to *me*," Roman added. "They're mine to deal with."

The queen smiled brightly. "As long as I can watch."

Low murmurs and a closing door roused Violet from a fitful sleep. The morning's events crashed into her, and she stared blankly into the abyss. Vivian might not like her, but this was unforgivable. All she'd had to do was tell Violet Titus had once been hers and Violet would have backed off from the start. Instead, she'd waited until Violet fell in love before she ripped him away.

Titus wasn't innocent either. He'd lied their entire relationship and had the gall to spend time with her and tell her he loved her while secretly meeting Vivian. The hurt in her chest burned to ash, engulfed by her rage.

She sat up and grabbed the closest thing she could reach, her alarm clock, and threw it against the wall with a scream.

The metal bells clanged loudly along with the shattering of the glass face.

The door to her room slammed open and Roman's wild eyes landed on her, assessed her for injuries, then traced the room. He glanced from the broken clock on the floor to her and lifted a brow. "I didn't take you as a thrower."

She raised her chin. "There's a lot about me you don't know." The smirk on his face taunted her as if to say, *No there's not.*

He backed out of the room and Violet fell back on her bed, jumping when War's tongue coated her hand in slobber. "*Ew.*" She shot up and glared at him. "You know I hate when you do that." She didn't have proof, but she was certain he could produce extra slobber on demand.

Things clattered in the other room, piquing her curiosity until she climbed out of bed to investigate. The queen and her lorix were nowhere to be seen, and the afternoon sun sat low in the sky. *How long was I asleep?*

She stalled in the kitchen's doorway and stared slack-jawed at the battlefield of Roman's making. "What the hell are you doing?"

The four-person rectangular table lay on its side, the flat tabletop surface facing the far wall. Her wall décor was missing, and the shelves on the side wall, once filled with extra dishes, were now empty. Said missing dishes sat in neat little stacks on the underside of the turned-over table.

Roman twirled around with an armful of plates and lifted them. "Getting ammunition." He strolled to the table and set the plates next to the other dishes, then tapped the floor next to him. "Get down here."

Too shocked to argue, she grabbed one of the table legs and lowered herself to her knees. "Have you lost your mind?"

In lieu of an answer, he passed her a ceramic teacup. "As

soon as you throw it, duck behind the table so the shards don't bounce back and hit you."

She stared at the teacup in her hand. "Throw it?" Her brain worked hard to catch up to the absurdity.

"Like this." He rose to his knees, took the teacup from her, cocked his arm back, and let the very breakable object fly. The cup collided with the far wall just as he ducked back down behind the table.

Violet gaped at him, disarmed by his boyish smile. She peered over the table to where the ceramic shards littered the ground. "You broke my teacup."

Roman jerked his thumb over his shoulder, in the direction of her room. "You broke your clock."

Her heart swelled, which surprised her, because she thought it'd been smashed to bits like her innocent little teacup. Holding out her hand, she said, "My turn."

Chuckling, Roman grabbed two saucers and handed her one. "On three?"

She grinned. "One. Two. Three!" The plates soared through the air, and Roman pulled Violet down behind the safety of the table. The satisfying crash of the dishes shattering against the wall released another sliver of the anger threatening to implode her world.

They locked eyes, and a plate appeared between them, slotted in Roman's giant hand. Violet held out her own and wiggled her eyebrows. "Again, prince."

Roman barked out a laugh, and she realized she'd not seen him laugh so freely in years. Sure, he'd laugh, but not like this. It never reached his eyes as it had when they were kids. She'd thought it was who he was now but watching him hide behind an old table with a stack full of dishes, she wondered if he'd been happy with Vivian after all.

Armed with more plates, Roman counted them down, and

for the next hour, they broke down the rest of the barrier Violet had erected between them years ago.

Roman picked up Violet's massive kitchen table as if it weighed nothing and flipped it upright.

A knock pattern rattled the front door. Announcing their presence for the entire world to hear to keep from spooking Violet wasn't sustainable, so her friends and family created their own secret knocks. Roman didn't have one yet, a fact she was reminded of when he frowned at the door seconds before Slayton burst through.

He opened his arms wide to pull her into a hug, but a massive hand shot out above Violet's head and landed on Slayton's forehead to push him back. "Touch her and I'll kill you," Roman warned.

Violet tilted her head back and frowned. "What is wrong with you?" She pushed his arm away and hugged Slayton, ignoring Roman's grumbles.

"If I see Titus, I'll beat the shit out of him," Slayton vowed. "I knew there was something off about him."

Marissa waltzed through Violet's door behind Slayton, her flared hips swaying. She gave Violet the world's most awkward hug before moving to Roman's side, running a soothing hand down his arm. "I came as soon as I heard."

Oh, gods. Had word gotten around to everyone? Violet tried her best not to order Marissa to leave. Of all the people she wanted to see right now, Marissa held firm at the bottom of the list.

"Who told you two?" Roman barked like a guard dog.

Marissa flinched and stepped back. "Everyone in town knows."

Slayton reached for Violet to pull her away from a fuming Roman, but the prince snatched his wrist midair. "Stop touching her," he ground out.

Violet held her hands up between the two. "Will everyone calm down?"

"Oh, sweetheart," Violet's mother wailed from the doorway, hurrying in a whirlwind of skirts. Marissa and Slayton stepped back to allow Meri to pull Violet into a hug. Violet liked hugs, but if she had to hug one more person, she might throw herself into the ocean and let the sea creatures have her.

Violet's father, Edgar, walked in next, bringing her into his arms. More pity hugs. "It's going to be okay, monkey," he murmured against her hair. The childhood endearment almost made her cry again, but she'd sworn earlier not to shed another tear. He kissed the top of her head and addressed Roman. "We'll do everything we can to find Vivian and bring her back to you."

If Violet's father had slapped her, it would have hurt less. "Bring her back to him?"

"I don't want her back." Roman stepped slightly in front of Violet as if shielding her would soften the blow of her father's words. "I was never going to marry Vivian, and since she married another and broke our bond, she did me a favor."

Everyone in the room gasped, and all eyes turned to the prince. "The bond is broken?" Violet's mother asked, her voice barely a whisper. "That can't be. Her note said nothing about getting married."

Violet tried to step around Roman, but he held fast, so she pinched his side until he moved with a deep scowl. "What note?" she questioned her parents.

Her father grimaced. "Your sister left a note that she and Titus were leaving together, but we didn't think she'd be foolish enough to marry the man. If the mate bond is broken—"

"I'm marrying someone else," Roman finished for him and flicked his gaze to Violet before returning to Edgar.

"I thought the gods made the bonds," Violet mused.

"If they want to keep the bloodline strong, they'll bond me to whomever I marry." His words were absolute, as if saying it made it so.

"You can't know that," Violet's father argued. "Vivian might have broken the bond, but she is still who the gods chose. If you two marry, I'm sure—"

"No," Roman cut him off harshly. "Vivian and Titus have committed treason. I wouldn't marry her if she came crawling to me on her knees, royal bloodline be damned."

Violet's mother whimpered. "You mean to kill them?"

"The only reason I won't separate their heads from their bodies for what they've done to Violet is because she's asked me not to."

A deep line formed between Edgar's brows, and he and Meri exchanged a loaded look.

The prince's declaration made Violet's head spin. The conviction with which he spoke peppered goosebumps down her arms. Why did he care so much? They did the same to him, yet he focused solely on her.

The room filled with tense silence. No one knew what to make of Roman's declaration, and to his credit, he looked completely comfortable as if he'd told them about a new horse.

Violet's mother nodded. "We understand, and thank you for your mercy."

He laughed humorlessly. "Do not mistake me for a kind man. It is not me you should be thanking."

Marissa and Slayton remained silent, watching the

exchange, Slayton with a speculative look, Marissa with one of... anger? What did *she* have to be angry about?

Roman turned to Violet and bowed slightly. "We'll give you three privacy, but I'll be back to check on you later."

"Okay," Violet acquiesced. "Thank you."

Roman said his goodbyes and signaled for Slayton and Marissa to follow him out. Slayton hugged Violet one last time, but Marissa left without looking back.

Violet's father pulled her into another hug. "Please do not think our concern for Vivian means we are excusing what she's done to you, monkey. I am ashamed to call her my daughter, but she *is* our daughter, and the last thing we want is to see her dead for a selfish mistake."

Violet leaned into his chest to convey her understanding. She had no plans to ever speak to Vivian or Titus again, but she couldn't bring herself to watch them die, either.

18

TWENTY-THREE YEARS OLD

Violet hurried down the sidewalk toward the pleasure house, eager to watch tonight's show. Two of her favorite performers would be on stage, and she didn't want to miss it.

Roman said he'd meet her there after meeting with the council. Word about Vivian breaking the mate bond had spread like wildfire, and the fear and unrest amongst the kingdom's citizens hit an all-time high. Personally, Violet thought the reasoning strange.

So what if a royal at their full power could glamour an entire kingdom? There had never been a large enough scale attack to warrant that level of protection. I guess *familiars* were useful because they could spy undetected, assuming they weren't a giant like War. Imagine a great tigon tromping through the Desert Kingdom for intel.

The gods likely had a good reason thousands of years ago —perhaps a lot of unrest in the early settlements—but now it felt stupid. Unfortunately, royalists believed the royals had the blood of gods running through their veins and that the gods would rain hellfire on the world if they dared taint their godly blood.

All hogwash, if you asked Violet, but it didn't matter what she thought. There were enough of them that they'd spread fear throughout the Tropical Kingdom.

A man she'd never seen before stepped in front of her. "Violet?"

She pulled up short, almost crashing into him. He looked to be around ten years older than her twenty-three years, with pale skin, and light brown hair peeking out from under his brown, wide-brim hat. "Yes?"

He took his hat off and raked a hand through his hair. "I don't mean to bother you." He waved his hand across the street. "I saw you walking and just wanted to introduce myself. Paul." Paul stuck his hand out.

Violet shook it, feeling awkward. "It's nice to meet you, Paul."

"Look, I've been through what you have," he started, his words coming out in a rush. She tensed. *I can't deal with this again.* "My wife had an affair with my best friend and left me and my two kids," Paul went on, replacing his hat. "If you ever need someone to talk to or have a drink with, I'm a good listener."

Violet would like to say this was the most awkward thing she'd encountered since her sister ran off with Titus, but that would be a lie. People stopped her often, offering her words of pity, encouragement, or vitriol, depending on if they mistook her for Vivian or not. The latter were the worst. She'd considered wearing a sign around her neck that said, "VIOLET. NOT VIVIAN."

"Thank you, Paul, that's very kind of you." She nodded in the direction she was headed. "I apologize but I have to go. I'm meeting someone."

Without waiting for his reply, she hurried off. Something else she'd learned: if she tried to carry on a conversation to be polite, it either never ended or it got *weird*. She'd rather not stay to find out.

She heard Paul cry out behind her, followed by a loud crunch. Momentarily distracted, she tripped on a loose cobblestone and went tumbling to the ground. Something snatched her out of thin air seconds before her face collided with the hard ground.

"Gods, princess, are you trying to give me a heart attack?" Roman mumbled as he put her back on her feet and started to fuss with her twisted skirts.

"Quit, you mother hen," she chided and pulled her skirt from his grasp. "And thank you for saving me. One of the stones is loose and I caught my toe."

He dropped to his knees, already reaching for her feet. "Let me see."

She brushed him off, tucking her foot under her dress. "My toe is fine."

He glanced at her from his spot on the ground, face level with her chest due to his massive form, and a small spark flared in her heart; something she'd thought Titus had smashed to bits. A movement over Roman's shoulder caught her interest, and she gaped at Paul moaning on the ground, his face bloodied.

"Oh my gods," she started toward him, but Roman stopped her. "He's still alive."

She balked at her friend. "I'd hope so. What did you do to him?"

"What I had to," Roman responded, refusing to look away from her. "He won't bother you again."

"You cannot go around smashing people's faces for

speaking to me," she insisted, secretly thrilled at his obvious jealousy. *What is wrong with me?*

His brows rose. "Yes, I can."

"Roman," Marissa's grating voice called from across the street, making Violet want to scream. The woman popped up everywhere, and it drove her crazy.

To Violet's delight, Roman seemed annoyed. "Please don't invite her to come with us," she whispered to herself, but not low enough because Roman's large hand found her chin and pinned her with a heated stare.

"I would never let anyone encroach on our time at the pleasure house," he avowed. "*Never.*"

For years, the pleasure house had been their thing, even when they never spoke about it aloud. After seeing him there two or three times, Violet went on the same day, at the same time, every week, hoping he'd be there too. At the time, there was nothing romantic to it, but it had been nice to know someone she knew and respected had the same *special interests* as her.

Lately, it felt like *more*. She wasn't ready to date again, and even if she was, Violet didn't know what came next for Roman. Would the gods give him a new mate? Would he get to choose? *Would he choose me?*

Other than his extreme protectiveness, he gave no indication that he wanted her. That could just be him wanting to protect a friend. *He* did *get jealous just now*, a little voice reminded her. But he refused to discuss Vivian, said he didn't care where she was or what she was doing, but Violet wondered if he masked his hurt.

"I've been looking everywhere for you," Marissa said once she'd joined them on their side of the street.

Roman tensed. "Why?"

Marissa looked hurt at Roman's curt tone. "I bought tickets

to your favorite play at the theater tonight. It's opening night, and I thought we could go."

Roman softened, and Violet hid her surprise. *Roman has a favorite play?* Why didn't she know about it? As much as Violet disliked Marissa, she didn't want to keep Roman from seeing something he enjoyed since he enjoyed so little.

"We can go there instead," Violet offered. "I can buy a ticket when we arrive."

"They're sold out," Marissa said apologetically. "If I'd known he'd be with you, I would have bought three."

Roman dug into one of his pockets and pulled out a few coins. "To cover the tickets. I appreciate the offer, but Violet and I have plans."

Violet feigned interest at the shop window behind them to hide her smile. It was nice to be chosen for once.

"Are you jealous of Marissa, princess?" Roman murmured in Violet's ear after they took their seats side by side at the pleasure house.

Roman took note of the chills cascading across her neck. What he wouldn't give to suck the delicate skin into his mouth, see how long he could keep the small bumps on her skin.

"I'm not jealous."

Roman grinned, his mouth still next to her ear. "Liar. Did you think I didn't notice your cute little smile when I turned her down."

She lifted a delicate shoulder. "I won't speak ill of your friend."

Interesting. "Being jealous of someone does not equate to insult. Do you not like Marissa?" He'd never speak to the woman again if she'd upset his future wife.

Violet paused before waving him off. "She's fine. I just didn't want to cancel our plans."

Roman cursed the dim lighting preventing him from seeing whether she spoke the truth or not. There were few secrets between them. Why would she lie now? "I would let nothing keep me from watching you rub your pretty little thighs together." He should pull back, lest he send her running, but her jealousy had him on a high. "Tell me, princess, are they slippery?"

Violet's breathing picked up, and she adjusted herself in her seat. "We aren't supposed to discuss the pleasure house." Her throaty voice went straight to his cock.

All he wanted was to run his hand up her thigh and see for himself. Would she let him? Was it too soon? Did she still love Titus after what he'd done?

He leaned down and softly kissed her neck. "One day I'll change your mind and hear every dirty thought you have."

The hand she held nearest him twitched, and she fidgeted again, murmuring, "One day."

Two days later, Violet hurried down her porch steps to head to work. "Of all the days to be late," she muttered to herself. She'd overslept and was late meeting with a new client who wanted a custom wedding dress.

Hanging on her post box was a sloppy flower crown full of bright purple flowers. She grinned, the gift from her tiny neighbor lifting her mood. He'd been leaving her random flower crowns for the past two years. When she'd see him coming or going with his mother, she'd wave and thank him for the pretty crown. The boy always nodded and left in a hurry with red-stained cheeks.

After plucking it off the box, she situated it on her head and bounded down the stairs but came to an abrupt halt, groaning. An obscene number of workers lined the streets, ripping up the cobblestone. There was a narrow walkway on each side, and when she got closer to town, more people were trying to squeeze into the small space to get where they were going.

Drat. She'd have to wake earlier on the days she worked at the dress shop to account for the foot traffic. Hopefully the construction wouldn't last long.

Only it *did* last long because the crown had ordered every single sidewalk and street to be rebuilt.

19

Roman's hand rested on Violet's back as they walked down the cobblestone sidewalk of Gruene, a small village outside of Saltu. Both wore light cloaks with the hoods pulled up. The weather in the Tropical Kingdom stayed the same year-round; warm during the day and a little cooler at night beneath the thick jungle canopy.

Saltu had festivals sometimes for this reason or that, but they didn't compare to Gruene. Fae traveled from all around to attend the tiny village's summer solstice festival. Occasionally, humans would too.

Violet didn't venture outside of Saltu much, but Gruene held a famous craft fair every summer solstice. Merchant carts lined the main street that ran through downtown, a lively band played music as people danced, and the street lanterns burned bright enough to light the night.

Violet loved it. She'd only been one other time with Slayton, and when Violet announced she was going again this year, Roman had insisted on accompanying her.

Violet bounced with each step as they passed the dancers

twirling around in front of the stage. "Dance with me," she begged the prince who looked like he would vomit at the prospect. "Please?"

He surveyed the dancers and turned back to her. "I only know ballroom dancing."

The villagers and visitors from all over the world swung each other around, twirled under another's arm, held each other close, and every other imaginable dance move one could think of.

"No one knows the steps," she insisted. "Slayton and I danced with multiple people, and each time it was something different. We just did what felt right. *Please*. It'll be fun."

"You danced with other men?" he asked in a low voice, glaring at every man within eyesight.

Got him. "I did, and it was *so* much fun. It's okay if you don't want to dance, I'm sure I can find another partner."

His head turned so fast, she wondered if it hurt his neck. "You're playing a dangerous game, princess."

Violet grinned mischievously and pretended to survey the crowd. "I just need to find a man without a woman. Let's see…"

The world turned upside down, and she squealed as Roman carried her over his shoulder toward the other dancers. "That man doesn't have a partner," she taunted, referring to a gentleman standing to the side. "If you could be a dear and put me down so I can ask him to da—ow!"

Roman slapped her on the ass, hard. "Be a good girl and stop trying to get other men killed."

He set her in the middle of the dancing area and stood awkwardly. Violet grinned so wide her cheeks hurt. Roman held out his hand, and when she grabbed it, he winked and yanked, then curled his arm around her so that she spun into him. "Do you enjoy training me like a monkey?"

Violet spun out and threw her head back, laughing. "I

always wanted a pet," she joked and stepped toward him to rest her hand on his shoulder.

"You have War." He moved them around the dancers, spinning and laughing.

"I'm going to tell him you called him a pet." She tsked. "I'll bet he bites you for it."

The world blurred around her with each spin. Upon colliding with Roman's chest again, he leaned down close to her ear and whispered, "The only person I want biting me, is you."

Fire burned under her skin, and the silky sound of his chuckle did more than the pleasure house ever could. She looked at him coyly. "One day, prince."

The future king of the Tropical Kingdom looked happier than Violet had ever seen him as they danced around and laughed without a care in the world. She made a mental note to ensure they came back every year for the rest of their lives.

"I'm thirsty," she panted and tapped her mouth.

Roman re-situated both of their hoods that'd fallen and ushered her through the crowd toward a refreshment stand. Something in the distance caught his attention, and he leaned down. "You wait here, I'll be right back."

"What do you want?" she asked. "In case I'm up to order before you get back."

"A dark ale." He kissed the top of her head and disappeared through the crowd with her staring dumbly after him.

Shaking herself, Violet surveyed the different carts around her to keep busy in line. Her eyes brightened when she spied a jewelry cart next to the refreshments. Even from here she could tell the pieces were beautiful.

Violet eyed the jewelry cart. The *lineless* jewelry cart. Popping over to take a look wouldn't take too long, and she could be back in this line before Roman returned.

Coming to a decision, she slipped out of line and approached the jewelry merchant. "Hi," she greeted the woman behind the cart with a smile. The woman looked up, but her own smile fell and her eyes widened. *Strange.* "Do you have any bracelets with shells?"

The woman's mouth pulled into a sneer and her voice rose. "You're her."

Violet stared back, bewildered at the hostility. "I'm sorry, have we met?"

A man standing behind the cart with two other men glanced in their direction. "Everything alright, Maye?"

Those around them started chattering and the three men focused on Violet. Then it hit her. *Oh, shit.* "No," she tried to explain to the woman, shaking her head. "I'm not Vivian, I'm her twin sister."

Maye turned to the men behind her. "It's the prince's mate."

The men studied her until one nodded. "It's her." He advanced toward Violet. She backed away and checked over her shoulder for Roman. That's when she noticed a tattoo of a seraphim on the approaching man's forearm.

Religious fanatics believed the gods were a type of angel called seraphim, who possessed three sets of wings covering their face, back, and legs. She'd heard a few royalists in the streets of Saltu, yelling for all to hear about her sister's transgressions. They believed Vivian to be equivalent to the devil for shitting on the sacred mate bond.

This wouldn't end well.

Violet turned to run, but someone grabbed her by the hair and yanked her back. She screamed from pain and fear. Her feet came out from under her, and her body slammed into the ground, stealing her breath. "I'll find the general," the woman told the men.

Her father's words came to the forefront of her memory. *Never give them your back.* She sat up and rotated to face the man.

He came at her again, and she pretended to cower. When he got close enough, she grabbed his thigh and hit his kneecap with the heel of her palm as hard as she could.

Pain radiated up her arm, and the man screamed and stumbled back. "Demon!"

"Stop!" a woman from the crowd cried. Violet saw her try to run forward. "She's telling the truth!"

Another man grabbed the woman around the waist and hauled her back. "Quiet, Bea." The woman fought against him, insisting what Violet said was true, but the men didn't listen.

One of the men grabbed Violet's hair during the distraction, and she clawed at his arm. He started to drag her, and she cried out as her body scraped against the gravelly stone.

The hold on her hair released, and her head slammed against the ground. People around them screamed and backed away, and a loud thump, followed by a grunt, sounded from the man behind her. She pushed herself up in time to see Roman running to her side. "Are you okay, baby?" He tugged her into his arms, running his hands over her hair.

One of the other men, fool that he was, attacked Roman from the back. The crazed look on the prince's face should have sent the fiercest of men skittering to hide, royal fae or not.

He spun, pushing Violet behind him, and grabbed the man by the head, then twisted it forcefully enough to rip it half off. Violet heard more screams from the crowd, children crying, and someone puking.

The last man tried to run, and Roman ripped his own hood down. "ENOUGH," he boomed, silencing the crowd. "Seize him by order of the crown."

People close enough to see his face gasped, and murmurs

flew through the crowd. Two men caught the fleeing attacker and dragged him back to Roman.

Roman yanked him from the men's hold and threw him to the ground. Onlookers tried to run, but the prince would have none of it.

"I am Roman Covington, your prince and future king," he announced to the crowd. "Stop your retreat or you will meet your end." Everyone froze. Some made it impressively far, but not far enough to escape his wrath. "This is what happens to anyone who dares touch what is mine."

Roman lifted his foot high above the third man's head.

No. Violet screamed Roman's name and ran to his side.

He reached for her and grabbed both sides of her face. "I'm sorry, princess." His voice trembled with rage. "I'll make every single one of them pay." Blood spatter coated his face and body, ruining his pristine white shirt. He looked like an avenging angel.

"There are children here," she tried to reason with him. "You have to stop."

His jaw ticked. Two men dragged Maye forward, and Roman stood to face the crowd. "I want all children under the age of nineteen removed. One parent or guardian may take them home."

Parents yanked small children into their arms and ushered the older children away. Roman watched the crowd, and when they'd gone, he turned to the man on the ground and crouched. "The only reason I am not grinding your skull into the gravel is because of the *kind* and *generous* woman you attacked." He stood and snapped his fingers at someone close by. "Bring me a sword or a butcher's knife."

The man on the ground started screaming and tried to crawl away, but Roman slammed his boot down on his chest. "You will not die today, but you *will* pay."

A man hurried to Roman and handed him a large meat cleaver.

"Roman," Violet whispered, at least she thought she had. Did she say it aloud at all?

Roman moved next to her and kissed her forehead. "Turn around and cover your ears until I tell you to stop."

Without protest, she whirled around and slammed her hands over her ears, but nothing in all of Eden could muffle the man's screams as Roman doled out his form of justice.

Muffled protests filtered through Violet's fingers, and she spread them to hear better. "You touched her?" Roman demanded of someone.

"N-no, Your Grace," Maye, the jewelry vendor swore. "I only told them she was your mate who'd forsaken you and the gods."

A beat of silence. "She is not the one who broke the bond; She is Vivian's *twin sister*," he roared.

"I-I didn't know, Your Grace, I swear it!"

"She's lying," the woman, *Bea*, who'd tried to stop them said, stepping forward. The man who'd held her back tried to clamp a hand over her mouth.

Roman crossed to the woman and ripped the man's hand away from her. "Speak," he ordered Bea in a softer, but terrifying, tone.

"Violet told them, Your Grace," Bea stated. "I grew up in Saltu. Violet was a few school years behind me." She glared at the man still whimpering on the ground behind Violet. Violet envied her for not shying away from what was certainly a grisly scene. "I tried to tell them she was telling the truth, but they didn't listen."

Violet dug through her memories but still couldn't place the woman.

Roman pivoted to the sobbing jewelry merchant. His steps

were slow and measured as he walked toward her. Violet followed him with her eyes, mesmerized by the power rolling off him. "She tried to tell you, yet you spewed lies anyway."

Maye apologized repeatedly through her sobs. Violet twisted around to face Roman and Maye. Whatever he was about to do, she knew she couldn't stop him, and as sick and twisted as it was, she didn't want to.

Bending down, Roman discarded the bloodied cleaver in his hand. Violet glanced at the man on the ground and tried not to scream at the sight of his hands lying a few feet away.

Roman grabbed a dagger from his boot. "Apologies don't take back what you've done." He pointed his dagger at Violet. "Do you see what they did to that beautiful woman?" He wrenched Maye's mouth open, grabbed her tongue, and cut it off.

The woman cried out in agony and fainted, her slack body sagging. The two men dropped her and moved away with equal looks of horror. Screams rose from the crowd and Roman tossed her tongue next to the other man's severed hands.

He turned in a circle, looking at the entirety of the people surrounding him. "Take this as a warning. Whoever touches what is mine will suffer dearly for it. You stood by and watched as an *innocent woman* suffered." The words tore from his throat with the fury of a thousand men. "Imagine if she was your sister or daughter or wife. If you see who you think is Vivian Maekin, you handle her with care because if anyone lays a finger on Violet again, I will kill not only them, but any bystander who let it happen."

Whoever touches what is mine will suffer dearly for it. Violet shivered.

Roman returned to Violet and lifted her into his arms.

"I can walk," she protested, but stopped when his dangerous eyes met hers.

"Let me do this. Please." Violet nodded and wrapped her arms around his neck. He buried his face in her hair and breathed deep. "Fuck." He found the woman who'd spoken in Violet's defense. "You, come with us."

Bea scurried after them without a word. Luckily, the town's inn was close by. The people inside must have seen or heard everything because no one said a word. A man hurried out from behind the check-in desk. "I'll have extra towels sent up. Penny, call the doctor," he urged a woman who looked on with horror.

Roman nodded. "Thank you."

Bea and Roman filed into Violet's room and shut the door. "Have a seat," Roman told the other woman and nodded toward the bed. "We're filthy, and you're not. I don't want to sully the sheets."

Bea nodded and sat delicately on the edge of the bed, staring at the prince with a mixture of fear and awe.

What he'd done would mark him as a gruesome king, one to be feared, not loved. Violet shut her eyes against the guilt of what he'd sacrificed to avenge her. She could only hope he hadn't inadvertently recruited more people to join the rebels against him.

"What's your name?" Roman asked the woman.

"Bea." She gazed at Violet. "I tried to stop them, but they held me back. I'm sorry, Your Grace."

Roman tried to rub the tension from his forehead, but all he could see was Violet screaming on the ground, her beautiful hair in that man's filthy hand. "You did what you could, and for that I owe you my gratitude." He gestured to the armoire that sat opposite the modest bed.

The room didn't have much. A bed against the wall beneath the window; two nightstands; an armoire; a large, overstuffed chair; and a dressing table. "Please grab the small wooden box at the top of the armoire."

"I can grab it," Violet tried, but he shushed her with a scathing look. His sanity dangled by a thread and holding her was all that kept him hanging on.

Bea retrieved the box and tried to hand it to him, but he refused to take it. "What is your last name?"

"Trenton."

"Bea Trenton, if you ever need anything, contact me, and you will have it." He pointed to the box. "For now, take this as my gratitude."

Bea peeked into the box and gasped. "I cannot accept this for doing what is right."

Roman arched a regal brow. "You will."

He could tell she wanted to argue but thought better of it. "Thank you, Your Grace."

"Forgive me for my rudeness, Bea, but I need to be alone with Violet." It was a wonder he'd remembered his manners at a moment like this.

"I understand. Thank you, again." She stepped forward to say goodbye to Violet and hurried from the inn like her shoes were on fire.

Violet's body quaked, and Roman pulled her closer. "I shouldn't have left you." Every time he did, she suffered for it. *Never again.*

The weight of her head settled against his shoulder. "It's not your fault. We were at a festival. Everyone was having fun." She reared back and swiped at the side of her face. Blood from his shirt had smeared across her cheek. He'd forgotten it coated him. "Gods," she whispered.

He stood and carried her into the bathroom. Setting her on

the side of the clawfoot tub, he filled it with warm water and scented oils. "Do you need me to help you?"

"No. I'll be okay," she promised with a weak smile.

"I'll be right outside if you change your mind."

Against his better judgement, he stepped out and closed the door, resting his forehead against the cool wood. How could he let this happen? He swore he'd never let anything happen to her, but it had.

Killing two of the men and mutilating two others in front of the villagers was irresponsible, but he would do it again a thousand times over.

20

Roman's panic clawed at his insides as he stood in front of Violet's cottage, willing her not to go. "Please don't leave yet. In a little over a year, I'll be able to leave the kingdom. I'll go with you."

"I've always wanted to do this," she said softly, "and with what happened at the festival two weeks ago, it's not safe for me here right now."

Maggie, the seamstress Violet worked for, once traveled Eden to learn about the other kingdoms' clothes, or something like that. Violet had decided to take the trip herself, leaving Roman for a year, if not longer. "I swear on my life, no one in this kingdom will harm a hair on your head again." He wanted her to be happy, but not without him at her side.

"Don't make this harder than it already is," she begged. "I'll write. I won't spend as long in each kingdom as Maggie. She's already taught me a lot, so I won't need to stay as long as she did." She threw her arms around his middle and buried her face in his chest. "I'll miss you. I promise I'll be back for your coronation."

Roman wrapped his arms around her, knowing he couldn't change her mind, and if he chained her to his bed, she might hate him. "Griff and Ares are going with you."

She stepped out of his hold, leaving him empty. "You're already sending War with me." The tigon at her feet nudged her leg. "I don't want to take them away from their families and friends for a year."

He'd already spoken with Griff and Ares in the event he couldn't convince her to stay. He'd been trying since she'd announced her plans shortly after her attack. "This is non-negotiable. I won't let you leave unprotected."

"I can go, too," Slayton offered from behind them. He, Griff, Ares, and Violet's parents stood around them to see Violet off.

"I will gut you if you set foot in that carriage," Roman warned.

Slayton's cat-like grin made Roman want to knock his teeth out. "No, you won't," the man retorted.

Violet huffed and pointed at Slayton. "Stop antagonizing him." She turned back to Roman. "And you, stop threatening my friend."

"*Best* friend," Slayton added.

Roman bristled. "I'm her best friend."

"Sorry, prince, *I'm* her best friend," Griff goaded with a smile to match Slayton's.

Violet hiked her thumb toward the tigon. "War is my best friend. Stop acting like children."

Roman raked a hand through his hair, resigning himself to his fate. "I prepared another carriage to accompany you."

"What do I need an extra carriage for?"

"You'll need more than you can carry in one carriage," he explained.

Violet tilted her head. "Like what? I'm only taking two trunks."

That morning, Slayton had helped Roman load a carriage with money, buckets of seashells, beads, food for their first leg of travel, and anything else Roman could think of that Violet might need. He'd also written to each king and the human queen to ask that they provide her with extra protection and a place to stay.

The Garden Kingdom was her first stop, and its king, Dean, ensured Violet's safety. Roman expected the same from Rennick, the Mountain King, Amos, the Desert King, and Charlotte, the Human Queen, but he'd instructed Griff and Ares to keep her in the Garden Kingdom until Roman sent word that he'd received their replies.

Ignoring her question, he glanced over her head at the others. "Violet and I need a minute alone."

They made themselves scarce without protest, and Roman took Violet's face in his hands. Leaning down, he brushed his lips against hers. "I'll miss you, princess. Promise to come back to me."

Her stillness worried him. He shouldn't have kissed her, but he refused to regret it. Finally, she nodded. "I promise."

They made their way to the others waiting by her carriage in time to greet Ares, who'd arrived with the second carriage.

Violet said her goodbyes, and Roman stood with the Maekins and Slayton, watching everything good in his life fade into the distance.

"Protect her, War. If anything happens to her, Eden won't survive my wrath."

"With my life," the tigon vowed.

"Thank you," Roman responded. *"I'll check in tonight."*

War's amusement trickled down the bond. *"I expect nothing less."*

Slayton's hand squeezed Roman's shoulder. "Come on,

prince. There's a bottle of liquor at my place with your name on it."

Sighing, Roman followed Slayton into town, toward the small loft he inhabited above his father's grocery store. "She's going to love seeing the other kingdoms," Slayton assured him. "You did the right thing by not keeping her here."

Roman stopped and closed his eyes to call on his *familiar*.

"War."

"Yes?"

"When she sees something that makes her happy, call for me. I want to see her happy, too."

He could feel the tigon bob his head. *"You won't miss anything, Roman. I swear it."*

THE LETTERS

21

Happy Birthday, Princess.

I made you something (with Meri's help), and you can't laugh. I tried my hardest to do it on my own, but my hands were too big to thread the string myself. It's a necklace with purple stones. (I have it on good authority from thirteen-year-old Violet that it's your favorite color).

The bracelet you gifted me for my thirteenth birthday is in desperate need of repairs. I've had to stop wearing it to prevent it from breaking. When you're home, I have every intention of begging you to fix it for me. I'm afraid if I try, I'll destroy it.

The Garden Kingdom looks beautiful. What is your favorite thing you've seen so far? I'll make a list, and when you return, we'll plan a trip together so I can see them with you.

Three hundred and sixty-five days.

Yours,

Roman

P.S. Thank you for letting War sleep with you. I feel better with him at your side.

22

Roman,

King Dean and his mate, Fawn, arrived at the palace yesterday morning. The king left two weeks ago to attend the Mountain King's coronation with no mate. Griff, the gossiping hen, told me Dean's mate died. His information was either incorrect, or Dean met his second mate during his travels.

Lydia and Victoria arrived yesterday as well. The contrast between the two is entertaining. Victoria is the calm to Lydia's crazy.

I woke in the middle of the night a few days ago and found War staring at me. It scared the shit out of me. I told him it wasn't polite to stare at people when they were sleeping, but maybe you should tell him too. I don't know if you've ever opened your eyes in a dark room and saw glowing orange eyes staring back, but it's terrifying.

After Lydia and Victoria leave next week, Ares said we're going to the Human Kingdom. I'm excited to see their foliage in real life. Do you remember the paintings Ms. Bonner had of their kingdom? The colors were dull, but maybe they aren't as dreary in person.

Want to hear something strange? This morning, at breakfast,

Fawn wore a cuff attached to a strap around her wrist, and the king held it like a leash. She didn't seem happy about it, either. When she tried to take it off, the king's familiar, a giant serpent named Lilith, wrapped around her and pinned her arms to her sides. Fawn was <u>*pissed*</u>*.*

Other than that, King Dean dotes on her, and she seems to like him too. I'm sad we'll miss their upcoming wedding, but I'm excited to see the other kingdoms.

I have to go. Griff just threw an apple at me (he missed) for making us late to Ares' fight. He's competing in a sparring competition with the Garden warriors. He seems excited about it.

I miss you.

Always,

Violet

P.S. If the gods grant you another mate while I'm gone, tell me, please. I'd rather know ahead of time instead of arriving home as the last to know.

Griff,

If you ever throw an apple at Violet again, I will cut your fucking arm off.

Roman

P.S. Stop taking her to watch sweaty men fight.

Princess,

I hope your travels to the Human Kingdom are going smoothly. I'm unsure how long it will take for you to receive this, but I needed to tell you as soon as possible. The last thing I want is you worrying that I'll take a mate while you're away. I planned on telling you this face-to-face when you returned, but your last letter made me realize there's a possibility you'll meet a man who interests you during your travels, and I can't let that happen.

There will be no news of another mate while you're away.

Since Vivian left, you are the only woman with whom I will plan a wedding. The only woman I will call my wife and mate. I am yours, and you are mine.

Three hundred and thirty-seven days.

Yours,

Roman

P.S. Don't fall in love with someone else. Come back to me.

Violet sat at the small desk in her room at the inn, just inside the Human Kingdom border, and read the letter again. *Roman wants to marry me 'since Vivian left?'*

She'd heard people say they got butterflies in their stomachs, but reading his words again turned her organs to ash. Her anger was a tangible thing, igniting everything within her.

Did he think a few flowery words would convince her to be a stand-in for Vivian?

Red clouded her vision. *"Since Vivian left."*

"That fucking *asshole.*"

Jumping up, she stomped to the door connected to Ares' room and threw it open without knocking. He and Griff each had a room on either side of Violet's and had insisted on keeping the connecting doors unlocked in case of an emergency. This was an emergency.

Violet pulled up short at the sight of Ares' muscular body slamming into a woman from behind.

He looked up, met her eye, and paled, his stunned expression matching hers. Neither moved nor spoke at first until Ares composed himself. "I know you and Rome like the pleasure house, but he'll kill me if he finds out you saw me naked."

The woman whipped her head to the side and shrieked, attempting to cover herself with her hands.

"*Violet*," Ares pleaded, his voice shrill enough to make her cringe. "I am begging you to leave."

Shaking her head, she crossed the room, Ares' fearful eyes bulging with every step. "Don't worry, your delusional friend won't hear about this from me." She shoved Roman's letter into Ares' chest. "I don't intend on writing him again. Tell the prince he can find someone else to replace Vivian. Just because we're identical twins doesn't mean I'm her fucking backup."

Spinning on her heel, she almost fell over War. "You can tell him what I said too." Weaving around the giant tigon, she marched into her room and slammed the door behind her.

Had Ares known about Roman's plan? Had War? Not that War could tell her, but it still embarrassed her.

Roman hadn't seemed to care about Viv leaving, but he'd always hidden his feelings well. He'd given Violet no indication he wanted her as more than a friend, but now that he was afraid she might meet someone else, he'd decided to tell her he wants to marry her?

"*Since Vivian left.*"

Fuck. Him.

"Are we still on for dinner tonight?" Marissa asked Roman as they trekked out of the training arena.

"*What did you say to Violet?*" War's voice came through the bond, stopping Roman in his tracks. "*Whatever you're doing, stop and watch this.*"

Marissa moved in front of Roman, the picture of concern. "Rome? What's wrong."

He ignored her, glamoured himself invisible, and closed his eyes to connect with War. Violet stomped away, a piece of paper in one hand, and threw open a door.

War followed close on her heels and immediately closed his eyes. *"What are you doing? Open your eyes,"* Roman commanded, shooting his frustration down the bond.

"You don't want to see this," the tigon replied, amused.

"I know you and Rome like the pleasure house, but he'll kill me if he finds out you saw me naked."

Ares? Hot, jealous rage pumped through Roman's veins. *"War, open your fucking eyes."*

A woman, not Violet, screamed, and War gave in, showing Roman the sordid scene. Ares, the handsome bastard, stood naked, his cock lodged into a frantic woman trying to cover herself.

Violet stood stock still, staring at him. *Did she like watching him?* Roman would kill him.

"Violet," Ares half-yelled, sealing his fate. How dare he fucking yell at her? *"I am begging you to leave."*

Violet shook her head, her beautiful hair swishing with the movement, and walked toward Ares. *"Fucking rip his head off,"* Roman commanded War down the bond. The disloyal beast merely huffed in return.

She slammed the paper into Ares' chest. *"Don't worry, your delusional friend won't hear about this from me."* Violet might as well have spewed venom. Delusional? She planned to hide this from him?

"War, if you don't kill Ares now, I will torture him into a slow death when he gets back."

"You are focusing on the wrong thing. Listen to her."

"I don't intend on writing him again," Violet assured Ares.

Roman's heart stopped. *"Tell the prince he can find someone else to replace Vivian. Just because we're identical twins doesn't mean I'm her fucking backup."*

She thought he wanted to replace Vivian?

"War, bring her home right now," Roman ordered.

"I cannot speak to her," War reminded him wryly.

"Fuck." Roman's palms grew damp, and his breathing shallow.

Violet turned and almost ran headfirst into War. *"You can tell him what I said too."*

Roman opened his eyes and dropped his glamour. "Roman, is everything okay?" Marissa asked carefully.

He made to leave, but she caught his arm. "Tell me what's wrong. Let me help you."

Grabbing the back of his neck, he tipped his head skyward. What had he put in the letter to make his girl think she was a replacement for Vivian? The idea was laughable.

"Nothing. I have something to do, and then I have an appointment, but I'll meet you at the palace for dinner with my parents."

Roman, Slayton, and Marissa hung out a lot now that Violet, Griff, and Ares were gone. The king and queen had invited the three for dinner tonight, but Slayton told Marissa he had to help his father stock the store.

Without waiting for her reply, Roman trotted toward the small cottage on the outskirts of town.

23

Princess,

It seems you misunderstood my last letter. Let me make myself perfectly clear. You are not a replacement for Vivian because Vivian was never going to be my queen. I decided years ago, when you stood in the forest and tried to do right by your kingdom and sister, that no matter the cost, you would be my wife.

I spent years researching ways to transfer the bond from her soul to yours, and when I realized the impossibility of it, I lost my mind. Knowing you would never agree to marry me while still bonded to someone else had ignited a new type of desperation. I would have done anything to keep you.

I waited for inspiration to strike to avoid my last resort plan. I won't tell you what it was because you wouldn't approve.

I realized the only thing Vivian loved more than the idea of being queen was herself. I played on her jealousy. She once told me she'd won by being mated to me. I told her you'd won, not her, because you were happy and in love with Titus while she was stuck in a loveless relationship neither of us wanted.

I gave her my blessing to continue with her lover and told her that if she broke the bond, I wouldn't charge her with treason.

I didn't know her secret lover was Titus. He would ultimately have had to go, but I never wanted it to be at your expense. If he'd died or disappeared, you would have been heartbroken, yes, but not betrayed. I would have killed them both before I let them hurt you. They will pay for what they've done.

You are not a replacement. You are my true mate, and I'm done caring if telling you what's on my mind scares you. You're my obsession, Violet Maekin. You always have been, and you always will be. You have owned me completely since we were children running through the palace halls.

Three hundred and twenty-nine days.

Obsessively Yours,

Roman

P.S. You signed Ares' death warrant when you stepped through that door. I suggest you knock when visiting Griff.

Violet gaped at the letter in her hands, unsure which part to process first: Roman trying to transfer the bond, him threatening to kill everyone, or him calling her his true mate.

She'd thought the same thing when they were kids, that maybe the gods made a mistake, but as an adult she knew it was a childish notion.

Rereading the letter, she wondered if her heart would explode. She didn't dare question whether he meant it; she could see his conviction in every stroke of ink.

Roman said Violet was his obsession but stated nothing of love; but he didn't have to. He'd told her he loved her years ago, and she'd pushed him away.

With shaking hands, she set down the letter and called out for War. The tigon stood and stretched before loping across the gigantic room. Slipping from the chair, Violet lowered herself to her knees. "Call Roman, please."

War closed his eyes.

Roman examined the shell in Slayton's hand and grumbled, "Are you purposefully picking out the ugliest ones you can find?"

Slayton scowled at him. "Who made you king of the shells?"

Something slimy brushed against Roman's calf, and he jabbed his hand in the water, yanking out a flailing rainbow trout. Slayton screamed like a howler monkey and tried to back away.

Roman looked from the fish to Slayton with a mischievous glint in his eye.

"Don't you fucking dare," Slayton warned.

Roman started after Slayton, who yelled creative threats over his shoulder, but War's call made Roman drop the flailing fish in the water. *"Violet's asking for you."*

He jogged to the shore and plopped down in the gritty sand. *"Show me."*

Violet sat on the floor in front of War expectantly. *Waiting for me.* It'd been almost seven weeks since she'd walked along the shore, and the freckles on her nose were fading.

His gut churned with apprehension, knowing she'd read his letter. If she rejected him, he'd lock her in his rooms until she fell in love with him again, and he didn't know how long that would take.

"Is he here?" her sweet voice asked War. The tigon nodded, and she rubbed her palms on her thighs.

"Hey Rome." She huffed out a laugh. *"This is strange."*

Roman grinned when she shook out her hands. *Nervous, princess?* If only he could speak back to her. Too bad War wasn't a parrot.

War growled down the bond.

Violet pulled her shoulders back and looked War dead in the eye. *"I got your letter."* She waved the paper in her hand, and Roman's heart stuttered. *"You sound like a psychopath."*

You have no idea.

"You should speak with your mother about your proclivity for threatening people's lives. Someone level-headed needs to calm you down."

Roman full on laughed, and he heard Slayton, who'd sat beside him at some point, mutter something about Roman being unstable.

Violet leaned forward and cradled both sides of War's face, holding Roman captive with her delicate hands. *"I want you to know that I love you too."*

Every nerve ending in Roman's body sparked with elation. *She fucking loves me.*

"She was talking to me," War uncharacteristically teased.

"I'll turn you into a rug."

"Hey man, are you okay?" Slayton asked, sounding far away. "You're shaking."

Roman dismissed him with a wave of his hand and concentrated on Violet. Someone knocked in the background, and Ares' muffled voice called out, *"Vi, are you ready to go, yet? We're starving."*

That fucker. War growled at Roman's frustration, and Violet narrowed her eyes at the beast. *"Did Roman make you do that?"* War nodded.

"Where is your loyalty?" Roman grumbled, and War chuffed in response.

"Roman, if you hurt Ares, I won't marry you." Violet folded her arms across her chest. *"Are we clear?"*

"Did she just threaten to not marry me if I kill Ares?" Roman asked War with disbelief.

"I believe she said if you hurt *him."*

The little minx. She'd pay for that later.

Violet reached out and tapped War's nose. *"Answer me, Roman Covington. Are we clear?"*

She could have asked Roman to bring Dominic back from the dead and he'd have found a way. He'd do anything if it meant she'd marry him.

"Nod your head," he instructed War, who dutifully obeyed.

The smile that spread across her face would make the gods weep. *"She is beautiful."*

"She is," War agreed.

Violet leaned forward and placed a kiss on War's forehead. *"I love you, prince."*

"I love you, too, princess."

24

Roman whipped off his shirt and laid back on a bed in the palace infirmary.

"Are you sure you want *another* tattoo?" Marissa asked, eyeing Roman's chest, where his newest addition would go.

Roman glanced at her sideways. "I wouldn't be here if I didn't."

His friend reached out to trace the swirling lines on his left arm, and he absentmindedly shook her off. "Don't you think both arms are enough?" Her eyes raised to his. "There's no need to cover up all of this beautiful skin."

"You don't like them?" he tried to joke, but something in the way she looked at him rubbed him the wrong way.

She dropped her hand and sighed. "I like tattoos, but yours are all the same thing." Leaning closer, she examined the design going down his arm. "Why don't you mix it up?"

Roman surveyed both arms, twisting them. "Because I don't want anything else."

Marissa dropped down on the stool beside him like a bored child and frowned at his arms.

What is with her lately? Wherever he went, Marissa either wanted to accompany him or happened to be there, too. She sought him out during training, always asking him to be her sparring partner, and lately, she'd been touching him more than he thought she should. Which was never. Perhaps she was just lonely. She didn't have many other friends, if any.

Roman made a mental note to ask Slayton what he thought.

Alexander, the tattoo artist, waltzed in, took a seat, and cleaned Roman's chest with soap and a damp cloth. "Okay, boss, show me which direction you want them to go."

Roman tapped his *familiar* mark that covered the left side of his chest. "Toward my heart."

Alexander bobbed his head and dipped the needle-point tool in an inkpot. "You didn't strike me as the sappy type."

Marissa stood abruptly. "I forgot that I promised my father I'd meet him this afternoon."

"You needn't explain yourself, Riss," Roman said dismissively. "I'll see you tomorrow at training."

Her face fell. "We're not meeting at the cafe tonight?"

Roman shook his head. He didn't remember making dinner plans with her tonight. "No. I'll see you tomorrow."

The woman fled the infirmary in a whirl of red hair and resentment. "I take it the tattoos aren't for her."

Roman would have recoiled if Alex weren't holding a needle over his chest. "They're for my mate."

Alexander's hand froze. "I thought your mate married another man. Broke the bond. Put our entire kingdom in danger, if you believe the old religious texts."

"The gods bonding me to Vivian was a mistake," Roman replied matter-of-factly. "Her identical twin sister, Violet, is my true mate."

Alexander chuckled. "Makes sense." He began puncturing

Roman's skin, leaving tiny trails of fire in his wake. "The townsfolk will be glad to know the gods gave you another mate." He leaned back and dipped his needle in the black ink again. "Why haven't you announced her yet?"

If the people wanted to think the gods bonded them, Roman would let them. "She's traveling right now. We were going to announce her when she's back home."

Alexander hummed. "Does she know about all this?" He waved a hand over Roman's upper body.

Roman looked down at the intricate artwork that would soon cover his entire upper body. "They're a surprise."

In hindsight, he should have asked Violet if she liked tattoos before having his entire torso covered in them.

Princess,

How was your first week in the Mountain Kingdom? Two weeks ago, I sent a carriage with more money, shells, and warmer clothes for you. By the time you get this, it should already be there. I hate that the Mountain Kingdom is so far away. Waiting weeks for a letter back is excruciating.

To answer your question in your last letter, yes, I still go to the pleasure house, but not to see the shows. I go because I remember how you looked, flushed and squirming, fighting off the need to slip your hand under your dress and stroke your slick little cunt.

Sometimes I rent out one of the elite boxes and imagine pressing your front against the glass while I eat you from behind. It always was your favorite part of the show.

Would you like that, princess? Or would you rather I fucked you against the glass instead?

Fuck, I miss you.

One hundred and eighty-one days.

Obsessively Yours,

Roman

P.S. There's a sweets shop in town that makes a new chocolate I want you to try. It's become my favorite indulgence, though I think your pussy will replace it once I've had a taste.

25

Violet tapped her coal pencil against her sketch pad, trying to figure out what reason the Mountain Queen had for sewing her dress hems above her ankles as opposed to the full-length dresses everyone else in the Mountain Kingdom wore. Was it rude to ask?

Amelia had taken Violet under her wing, and her female companionship was a nice reprieve from Griff and Ares. Violet loved them, but they got on her damn nerves sometimes.

Amelia's unique fashion drew Violet to her. One seamstress Violet had visited in the Mountain Kingdom claimed the dresses to be human fashion, but that couldn't be further from the truth. Violet had just been in the Human Kingdom, and no one wore the *interesting* fabrics the queen donned at least twice a week.

Amelia's dresses were always in the traditional Mountain Kingdom style—tight long sleeves and bodices with full skirts —but the shorter hems hovered well above her ankles in the front and were never straight. Sometimes her dresses were in the common cool-toned colors of winter, but three of them were made of the ugliest fabric Violet had ever seen, and she always wore tall leather boots in a green the color of vomit.

She also wore a gold necklace with a trout fish pendant. None of it matched her personality, and once, Violet had heard Rennick grumble something about Amelia's necklace, but the queen had silenced him with a scathing look.

Despite Amelia's odd taste in fashion, she was fun to be around, always on the go and talking about whatever book she'd read.

King Rennick, on the other hand, could not be more different. Or terrifying.

A loud knock startled Violet from her thoughts, and when she opened the door, a disgruntled giant glared down at her.

Rennick was about an inch taller than Roman with lightly tanned skin, dark hair, and light eyes. His shoulders were so broad Violet wondered how they fit through doors. Her slight fear dissipated at the sight of a small fennec fox in a sweater held tightly in the king's arms. It was a sight to behold, and she tried her hardest not to laugh.

"Why does Roman want me to behead Finn?" the king demanded without greeting.

Finn? Finn was King Rennick's right-hand man, who had a great sense of humor. He took Violet to meet all of their warriors so she could see the differences between their uniforms and the Tropical Kingdom's. She'd told him about the absorbent strips she'd added to the sleeves back home, and he'd loved the idea. Excited that it impressed him, she'd told Roman.

Oh no. She'd told a *very jealous* Roman.

Violet steadied her breathing to keep calm. She should want to kill Roman for asking Rennick to kill a man out of petty jealousy, but it only made her want him that much more.

It was strange, starting a relationship in the midst of a

separation, but it also made the anticipation grow to a point that Violet considered going home early. Some of the things they wrote each other in their letters...

Amelia appeared in the doorway beside Rennick, breathing hard and stealing the king's attention. "I told you to wait on me. You're probably scaring the crap out of poor Violet."

He lifted the small fox. "That's why I brought Eddy. You were with Birdie, and I didn't want to disturb you."

"Birdie had to leave," Amelia replied, still a little out of breath. "Finn and I grabbed lunch instead, and you could have waited ten minutes."

Rennick's eyes narrowed dangerously. "Lunch with Finn?" He thrust Eddy into Amelia's arms and stalked off, throwing over his shoulder to Violet, "Never mind. I'll take care of it."

Amelia sighed. "I'm sorry. Was he terribly rude?"

Violet stared after the king, suddenly concerned for Finn. Were all the kings insane? Amos, the Desert King, was the only one she'd yet to meet, but so far, the unstable king count was three for three. "Uh. Actually, you might want to go after him. I think he's going to kill Finn."

Amelia swore colorfully and muttered, "Not again," before taking off after her mate.

Roman,

Instead of getting angry at whatever poor man made the mistake of speaking to me, perhaps you could turn that jealous heat elsewhere... As my trip comes closer to an end, I can't stop thinking about seeing you again, kissing you, and finally being with you intimately.

You always speak of things you want to do to me, which makes me wonder: what is the first thing you'll do to me, prince?

Only a few months left.
Always Yours,
Violet
P.S. Rennick tried to kill Finn today, and were it not for Amelia, he would have. No more kidding around about murdering people.

For the first time, apprehension about seeing Violet again hit him hard. *What is the first thing you'll do to me, prince?*

Roman banged on Slayton's door relentlessly until the man threw it open. "Knocking once would suffice, Your Grace."

Roman shoved past him and paced the length of Slayton's living room, nearly knocking over the overstuffed leather chair in his haste.

Slayton steadied the piece of furniture and pointed at it. "Sit. You're too big to be stomping around."

With an exaggerated sigh, Roman fell into the chair and laid his head back. "How am I going to last longer than three seconds?" he blurted out without giving a care if it made him sound lacking.

Slayton made a choking sound. "Please tell me you're not talking about fucking Violet. I don't want to think about that."

Roman scowled at him. "Don't say fuck and Violet's name in the same sentence, and yes, I am." He sat forward and rested his elbows on his knees. "I want it to be good for her, and I've heard that the first time is usually quick. How do I fix that?"

Roman expected ridicule, but Slayton just nodded thoughtfully. "I can't help you, but I bet my brothers can."

"No," Roman said quickly. "I don't need rumors of the virgin prince needing sex advice floating around the kingdom."

"But you are a virgin prince who needs sex advice," Slayton

pointed out unhelpfully. "My brothers won't tell anyone. They're two of the most trustworthy men I know."

Reluctantly, Roman agreed. He'd do anything to ensure Violet's first time with him was enjoyable for her.

And that was how Roman ended up with what Rodge, Slayton's oldest brother, deemed the "fist cunt." It consisted of a tube made of soft leather, filled with rice, that you heated up. Once it became warm, you slathered the inside with oil.

"Tighten your fist so it's hard to push in. The tighter the pussy, the shorter you'll last. It's not like fucking your hand. I can't explain it, but you'll see," Rodge had explained matter-of-factly.

And fucking hell, was he right.

OBSESSIVE LOVE

26

(ALMOST) TWENTY-FIVE YEARS OLD

Roman,

You should get this letter a week or so before we're home. I wanted to tell you our plan (if Griff or Ares haven't already). King Amos and Queen Clover will be escorting Griff, Ares, and me back to Saltu. Amos insisted since he would travel to Saltu for your coronation anyway.

As I'm sure you know, because I know you like to spy, I sent the extra carriage and War ahead of us. I wanted War to be there with you while you prepare for the big event. He doesn't know it yet, but I made him a tigon-friendly royal coat to match yours. I might (most likely will) need your help to coax him into wearing it.

He's basically becoming king of the animals in the Tropical Kingdom, and he needs to dress the part. Really, I just want to see him in clothes after seeing a fennec fox in cute sweaters.

I can't wait to see you. I've missed you more than I thought I would, and I promise to find you the moment I set foot in the capital.

See you soon.

Always Yours,

Violet

P.S. I love you.

Roman grinned down at Violet's letter and traced his fingers over her signature. *Always Yours.* His smile widened.

"You look like an idiot," Slayton remarked as he approached. "Did Violet send you a naked drawing of herself?"

Roman's smile fell, and he scowled. "I will kill you where you stand."

Slayton laughed loudly, and Roman's scowl deepened. "The carriage and horses are ready to leave."

Roman, Slayton, and six other guards would leave shortly for the Desert Kingdom border. If his mate thought he'd let her go one day on Tropical soil without seeing him, she didn't know him very well.

"Don't you think six guards is overkill?" Slayton eyed the other men readying their horses. "She's traveling with the Brutal King. I doubt anyone is stupid enough to try to attack him."

The Desert King had earned his nickname when he'd brutally slaughtered his father and most of his father's closest confidants. Amos' father was an evil man who treated women like second-class citizens. What surprised Roman was that Amos hadn't killed his father sooner.

"It's not uncommon for rebels to attack close to a royal's coronation," he explained. "I'll not risk Violet's safety."

Roman's parents approached his small convoy. "I wish you'd wait," his father insisted. "She'll be here soon. There's no need for you to risk missing your own coronation."

Violet making it to the coronation was the only thing that guaranteed Roman himself would attend. If something happened and she didn't return in time, he'd be at the border, waiting to step across at midnight on his twenty-fifth birthday. "I'm not waiting an extra week."

His mother swatted his father's arm. "Stop. If the roles were reversed, would you allow me to be within reach and not see you right away?"

The king contemplated the question, and his wife's eyes flashed with outrage. Before she could tear into him, he chuckled. "You know I wouldn't, dear, but we're mates."

If he'd thought that would placate her, he'd been wrong. Before Roman could crack his father's jaw, his mother reached up and grabbed her husband's neck. He hissed as she dug her nails into his skin. "If you insinuate Violet isn't Roman's mate again, I will choke you until you pass out."

Roman's father smirked and leaned forward. "Don't tempt me, Sarah. You know I like it—"

"*Hey*," Roman snapped, wanting to scrub his brain of the past few minutes.

The queen released her husband's neck with one last warning glare and turned to Roman. "Be safe and come home quickly. Having to reschedule your coronation would be a pain."

Violet peered out the window of the carriage, watching the small border town pass by. Their group had been traveling for a few hours.

She popped her head through the window. "How much longer?" Violet called to Griff. He either didn't hear her, or he ignored her. If they hit one more bump, her bladder would ensure there'd be an embarrassing mess to clean up.

"What's wrong?" Clover, the Desert Queen, asked Violet

quietly. She didn't speak much, and when she did, you sometimes had to strain to hear her.

She and Clover had become quick friends, despite the other woman not caring a lick about fashion and Violet not liking to read. Clover possessed a pleasant, albeit shy, temperament with everyone except her husband.

Violet didn't know the full story, but for some reason, Amos sent Clover to the Human Kingdom after he'd found her at thirteen. He'd begged her to come back when they were sixteen, but unbeknownst to him, she'd heard from her brother that he'd claimed another girl to be his mate. Even though romance hadn't factored into Amos' engagement, it had destroyed Clover, and she'd tried to kill him when she saw him again.

"A lover's quarrel," he'd told Violet.

Regardless, the two complimented each other perfectly. They were a golden god and goddess come to life, rebuilding their kingdom King Amos' father destroyed. Amos stood as tall as Roman with a leaner build, sun-tanned, whey-colored skin, and golden-blond hair that curled at his ears. Clover had wild, curly blonde hair and skin a shade lighter than the king's. They were beautiful together.

"I need to relieve myself," Violet grumbled. "I don't think I can wait."

Clover poked her head out the carriage window for a moment. "We're close to the border. I can see the wall in the distance."

If Violet knew Roman, he'd be at the border waiting for her, unable to wait until she made it to the capital. "If Roman is at the border, he'll yank me into his arms before I can say anything." At least, she hoped he would. "I'd rather not wet myself in front of everyone."

Clover afforded Violet a rare smile and stuck her head back out the window. "Amos, tell everyone to stop."

The Desert King, never far from his mate's side, called for a halt, and the moment the carriage stopped, Violet hurried outside.

"Why are we stopping?" Griff griped. He was a terrible traveling companion. "The wall isn't much farther."

"I need to relieve myself," Violet answered. Her bladder hurt too much to care if Amos and Ares heard her.

Thank the gods they were close enough to the Tropical border that tree groupings appeared on the Desert Kingdom's side. The vegetation wasn't as dense as in her kingdom, but enough to give her privacy.

Ares jumped from his mount. "I'll go with you."

"Roman will kill you if he finds out you were within ten feet of her exposed ass," Griff deadpanned.

Ares sized up Violet. "He'll mutilate me if he finds out I let her wander into the woods alone."

"I can go with her," Clover offered, reaching into the carriage for her sword. The queen's skill outmatched both Ares and Griff, and they both knew it.

Ares nodded, but Amos jumped from his horse. "The hell you will."

"Is that so?" Clover asked, her deceptively soft voice promising a painful death.

He halted and narrowed his eyes. They had a silent battle of wills before he sighed. "I'm scouting the area first."

Clover's lips quirked to the side. "Fine."

In the distance, Violet saw the vague outline of the border wall separating the Tropical and Desert Kingdoms through the thickening trees. The thing was enormous, and she didn't know if they were fifteen minutes or an hour away.

A few minutes later, Amos appeared through the trees and

signaled for the women to go. They hiked far enough in so as not to be seen, then Clover stood guard with her hand resting on the pommel of her sword.

After Violet finished and Clover denied needing to go, they picked their way back toward the road.

"Took you long enough," Griff complained. "Golden God over there was three seconds from barging through the trees like an angry bull."

The king did not look amused.

An all too familiar voice screamed from behind them, "RUN!" They whipped around and Violet's eyes widened at the woman sprinting toward them from the trees. For a second, she thought it was Vivian. *Surely not.* Why would Viv be in the Desert Kingdom?

Her doubts were decimated when her sister grew closer and screamed, "REBELS!"

Without hesitation, their group moved. Clover grabbed Violet's hand, dragging her to the far side of the carriage horses and out of sight of the rebels. Ares mounted his horse and steered toward Violet, but he whipped around when battle cries rose in the air. She couldn't tell how many there were, but the rebels outnumbered their small party of five.

A tidal wave of fear crashed through Violet, and her hands fumbled with the horse's harness. "Shouldn't we be in the carriage?" she asked Clover, proud of herself for speaking coherently.

"We'll be faster on horses," Clover explained, transforming into a war general.

Violet thanked the gods her father had taught her and Vivian how to ride. *Vivian.* She scanned the mayhem around them, spotting her sister fighting alongside Ares, Griff, and Amos.

A man in tattered armor charged toward the carriage and raised his sword. Violet screamed. "Clover, watch out!"

Clover flipped around in time to block the man's attack. Amos appeared at her side and shoved her out of the way, but the queen drove her sword into the rebel's side. "Go help the others," she shouted at her husband above the grunts, cries, and clangs of the battle raging around them.

The two sides collided, and to Violet's horror, arrows flew toward them. She knew she'd only hinder the fight and looked around for a place to hide. In the carriage she'd be a sitting duck, but if one of the rebels saw her sneak into the woods, she'd have no chance of outrunning them.

As it was, the horse hid her from sight, but she could never forgive herself for using a living creature as a shield if something happened to it.

"Move to the border!" Griff instructed the others, and Clover grabbed Violet's hand, dragging her toward the men's horses, leaving the carriage horses behind. They'd not been able to unhook their harnesses, and Violet's heart wrenched.

She could see the border guards sprinting toward them, tipping the scale in their favor, and she almost cried out in relief. Griff appeared at her side, swung her onto his horse, and galloped toward the wall.

They weren't as far from the border as she'd thought, and they gained ground quickly. *We might make it.* She glanced over her shoulder, thankful the others followed suit while dodging the arrows flying their way.

But they weren't fast enough; an arrow struck the side of Griff's horse, and it stumbled to the ground, sending Violet and Griff rolling across the rough road. Sharp stones cut into Violet's face and hands, but her adrenaline numbed the sensation. The horse took off running with an arrow protruding from its back flank.

"Stay down," Griff grunted as he climbed to his feet, fighting off a rebel who'd caught up to them. Amos, Griff, Ares, Vivian, Clover, and the border guards surrounded them, fighting off the rebels on all sides. *I'm worthless here*, she thought with despair.

A beast's resounding roar filled the air, followed by a savage voice. "VIOLET!"

Violet looked through those around her toward the wall. War ran full speed in her direction as Roman pounded against an invisible barrier, yelling her name.

Violet screamed and ducked just in time as an arrow flew past her. War pounced on one of the men nearing Violet, and Ares swung his sword to behead another rebel attacking him from the side.

Violet watched the man's head fly through the air and collide with the ground. His unseeing eyes stared at her as it rolled across the grass.

I'm going to pass out.

The magic kept Roman firmly on the other side, and Violet thought, *If I can make it to the border, he'll keep me safe.* Griff and Ares stood protectively in front of Violet, charging and killing any rebel who got too close. Here, amid the fight, she hindered the others. *A helpless person they felt obligated to protect.*

Griff broke from the line and looked at two of the border guards, hoisting Violet to her feet. "Get Violet to the border."

One grabbed her arm and told her to run, but War barreled into Violet's side. She collided with the rough ground again, and her vision blacked as more gravel sliced her skin. She fought for breath and tried to shake the haze from her vision.

She watched in horror as War slammed to the ground beside her with an arrow speared between his ribs. Her scream rose above the raging battle. "War!"

Violet crawled toward the tigon, and pain shot up her arms

with every slap of her shredded palms against the gravel. His quills retracted, and his chest moved in quick, shallow breaths.

Violet's hands moved over his bloody fur to assess the wound, but she didn't know what to do. *Don't you push arrows through instead of pulling them out? Or is it the other way around?* The arrow pointed toward his heart. She couldn't risk piercing it. *If the arrow hasn't done so already.*

The guards who were taking her to Roman searched the ground, their gazes passing right over her. One cursed. "Where is she?" They both surveyed their surroundings. *Who are they looking for?*

Vivian tripped over Violet and tumbled to the ground beside War's body.

One guard hauled Vivian up, confusion on his face. "Weren't you in a dress?"

Violet looked to Roman, close enough to see his face. *I can make it.*

Vivian yanked out of the guard's hold and looked around frantically, calling Violet's name. Roman spotted his ex-mate, sending him from frantic to rabid as he raged harder against the barrier.

"EVERYONE TO THE QUEEN! PROTECT YOUR QUEEN!" he roared, his words cracking through the air. Dread crawled across Violet's skin as all but Ares and Griff sprinted toward Vivian.

"*No,*" Violet whispered and turned terror-filled eyes to Roman. He'd said he loved her, yet he'd left her unprotected in favor of Vivian.

Her gaze collided with his, his eyes alight with fear and rage. "*PROTECT YOUR QUEEN!*" he screamed again, his desperation palpable.

A sob ripped from Violet's throat, and she hung her head over War's body in resignation. She couldn't drag the beast to safety, and she had no combat skills to protect them. Leaving War while he still breathed wasn't an option. He'd never left her; he showed up and saved her time and again. She'd not leave him here.

Roman continued to scream as Griff barked out orders, but Violet no longer heard them. Her despair was a living thing pressing down on her.

Shadows fell over her, blocking out the midday sun, and she looked up, astonished to see a tight ring of guards surrounding her and War.

She glanced around, searching for her sister. *The guards think I'm Vivian.*

Ares broke from the circle and felt around blindly. "Where are you?"

Violet cried harder. "Vivian is out there," she said ruefully and leaned over War again. Ares' hands bumped against her back.

"Thank the gods," he breathed, pulling her up. "I need you to wrap your arms around my neck."

Bewildered, she looked at him. "I'm Violet." *Why did I say that? Let him take you to safety.*

"I know who you are, Vi. Roman glamoured you, and I can't see you. Wrap your arms around my neck and tuck your head against my shoulder so I can take you to him before he bloodies his hands trying to claw through the barrier."

Her stomach bottomed out. She should have known Roman wouldn't betray her, that the words he'd told her repeatedly were true. Guilt like she'd never known weighed her down.

Ares lifted her into his arms. "I've got her!" he yelled at those around them. "Move!" The warriors and guards surrounding them created an opening, and he took off.

Violet looked back to War and panicked. "We can't leave War."

"He'll be fine," Ares panted as he ran.

"No," she pleaded and struggled against his hold. "We can't leave him!"

Her breathing grew erratic, and her hands began to tingle as her panic climbed. Ares vanished, yet he still held her. *Roman's glamour.* She shut her eyes tight, the sensation of floating on air turning her insides. Ares shot across the border into Tropical territory. Seconds later, Roman yanked her out of his arms and sprinted in the opposite direction.

Grief and shock set in as she watched the fighting continue over Roman's shoulder.

War didn't move.

Roman ran until he reached the closest house on the outskirts of the border village. An older man stood outside brushing a horse, and he startled when he saw Roman approach.

"I'm Roman Covington, crown prince, and I need a bed immediately," Roman insisted roughly.

The man's eyes widened, and he tossed his brush onto a nearby haystack. "Yes, Your Grace. Is she hurt?"

Roman took stock of Violet's injuries. "I don't know." Every emotion clawed at his insides as he prayed to the very gods he hated.

"I'll send for a healer."

Roman hurried through the man's front door, and a young woman on the couch jumped with a squeak. The knitting supplies in her lap scattered on the ground with a loud clank.

The man motioned to Violet. "Fayline, get something to clean her up, please."

"Yes, Papa." She hurried into the kitchen while the man led Roman into a bedroom and motioned to a small bed barely big enough for two people. The modest room had wooden floors with no rugs, two side tables, and a small fireplace opposite the bed.

Violet shook uncontrollably in Roman's arms, and he knew if he didn't calm her down, she'd go into shock. "Is there anything under the bed?"

The man hesitated and bent down to look under the wooden frame. "There are a few boxes, Your Grace. Old clothes, mostly."

"Pull them out."

Roman kissed the top of Violet's head. "You're safe, princess. I've got you." Her soft cries gutted him. He'd never felt more helpless than he had watching her from the other side of the barrier. Especially when Vivian had appeared. Had she hurt Violet, there wasn't a place in Eden she could hide from him.

Roman thanked the gods for Griff, who'd instructed his team to surround War. The guards couldn't see Violet through Roman's glamour, and when they'd started toward Vivian, Roman saw Violet's devastation, thinking he'd called her vile sister his queen. The image would haunt him forever.

Once the man had pulled everything out from under the bed, Roman kneeled on the floor and gently laid Violet down. "Can you crawl under on your own?"

She looked from him to the bed, nodded, and tucked her body underneath.

"Here, Your Grace," Fayline said, handing him a wet cloth.

He murmured his thanks and tried to crawl under the bed, but the frame was too low for his broad chest. "*Fuck.*" Stretching out his arm, he covered Violet's hand with his. Her cries stopped, replaced by sniffles and quiet whimpers. "Can you come closer so I can clean your face?" Dirt and gravel clung to the blood and scrapes marring her skin.

She scooted closer, and he tried to release her, but she shook her head and squeezed his hand tighter. "Please, don't leave me."

Every piece of him broke. He'd done this to her. He'd made her think he would leave her like this. "I'm not leaving. I need to clean your face."

Her eyes bounced between his and she released him. Roman gingerly wiped away the few pieces of gravel still clinging to her face, flinching with every wince and hiss she made. Once he'd cleaned the cuts to the best of his abilities, he dropped the towel behind him and reached for her hand again.

"Go bring more towels," the old man instructed his daughter. Roman startled, having forgotten they were there.

Violet's shaking hand held his like a lifeline. "They shot War," she said on a broken whisper.

Roman wedged his head under the bed, his large body sticking out at an awkward angle, and brought her hand to his lips. "War is fine. He's on his way."

Violet's teary voice broke his heart. "How?"

Roman smiled tenderly. "*Familiars* have fast healing to prevent them from dying before their bonded. Decapitating them or cutting out their vital organs is the only way to kill them."

She graced him with a feeble smile, and Roman sensed her overwhelming relief.

No, he *felt* it.

His breath stalled, and he concentrated on the emotions coursing through him. The relief evaporated like a lingering dream, and disappointment hit him hard when he only sensed his own.

He didn't know how long they laid there, nor did he care.

He only cared about her safety, both mind and body. Everything else could wait.

Roman pulled his head out from under the bed and looked at the man and his daughter. "My tigon will be here any moment. Please open the front door or he'll break it down."

The man left quickly, but Fayline stayed rooted to the spot. Her cool, medium brown cheeks paled, and her brown eyes almost popped out of her head.

"He's friendly," Roman assured her, but when War prowled through the bedroom door, she yelped and backed into the wall. War ignored her, rounded the bed, and laid on the other side, sticking his paw underneath the frame.

More footsteps entered the room, and Roman glanced over his shoulder at Ares. "Is she alright?" his friend asked.

"She will be. Has the threat been neutralized?"

"Yes. I've never seen that many in a random ambush before." His calculating gaze looked out the window. "Vivian escaped."

Roman glanced under the bed at Violet. She'd turned her head to face War, and Roman lowered his voice. "Why the fuck was Vivian with them?"

Ares grabbed one of the spare cloths and wiped his hands. "I don't know, but she fought against them with us."

27

After a long night's rest in an inn located in the border village, Violet gradually returned to herself. Roman hadn't left her side since carrying her away from the battle, nor had War. Their steady presence soothed her soul in a way she'd not experienced before.

By the time they'd resumed their travels, Violet was a new woman. A traumatized new woman, but new all the same. She sat tucked into Roman's side in their carriage, the same horses alive and well. Saltu was a week's ride from the border village they'd stayed the night in, and she wanted nothing more than to be in her own bed to heal in peace.

The top of War's head bounced in and out of view as he trotted alongside the carriage, his irritation from not fitting inside with them evident.

Roman ran his fingers idly through Violet's hair. He'd not stopped touching her since last night, as if afraid she would disappear. If she so much tried to shift positions, he tightened his hold.

Eventually, Violet managed to free herself enough to

stretch and angle herself toward Roman. "Where is Vivian?"

Bits and pieces of Ares and Roman's conversation from the night before swam in and out of her memory. She remembered talk of her sister, but not the full context. Shock had rendered her ignorant of her surroundings, something she needed to work on since she had an unlucky streak with rebels.

A dangerous tension filled the carriage, the promise of violence heavy in the air. Roman didn't scare Violet, but judging by the look on his face, whomever held his ire should say their last goodbyes.

Staring out of the carriage window, Roman ground out, "Your sister disappeared." When he returned his focus to Violet, the intensity took her aback. "I will find her, and when I do, I will drag her back to Saltu if I must."

He studied her closely, and when her lips turned down, he continued. "I would have killed Vivian long ago to sever our bond, but I knew losing her would hurt you, no matter how much you two despise each other."

Violet moved to the bench across from him to face him fully. She had a lot of groveling to do. "I thought when you told the guards to protect their queen that you meant Vivian," she confessed, feeling lower than dirt. "When they started moving toward her my heart sank. I know you would never do that, but I lost faith in you, and I shouldn't have." She shrugged helplessly and whispered, "I'm so sorry. You've shown me time and again what I mean to you, and you didn't deserve my doubt."

Roman closed the distance between them and crouched down on the carriage floor. "Your adrenaline was high, princess, nor are you trained in battle. It's difficult to keep your wits about you in situations like that."

"Don't," she said forcefully. "Do not make excuses for me. I never should have doubted you, not even for a second, but I did, and I'll never forgive myself for that."

They sat with her confession heavy in the air until Roman lifted and brushed his lips against hers. "Apology accepted." Pulling back, his mouthed tipped up into a crooked grin. "But if you're hellbent on atoning, I know a few ways you can make it up to me." He waggled his eyebrows, and she burst out laughing.

He made to pull away, but she seized the back of his head and brought him close once more. His mouth moved tentatively against hers, like he'd never been kissed before, but soon he took charge, swiping his tongue against the seam of her lips for entry.

His hand trailed down her neck, sending a sensual shiver across her skin. It continued down her chest, grazing her breast, then teased its way down her side until it reached her hip.

"Violet," he whispered against her lips, breaking away. "Vivian has never been my queen. She never was going to be. It's always been you." He leaned back on his haunches and rolled up the sleeves to his long sleeve linen shirt.

Tattoos of intricate vines filled with flowers wound around his forearms and disappeared under his shirt sleeves. She picked up his arm to inspect them closely. "They're beautiful. Whoever did these is an incredible art—" The words caught in her throat, and she lifted her gaze to his. "Violets?"

The lines she'd believed were his *familiar* mark peeked out of the top of his shirt. She undid his buttons to reveal more vines. He'd covered himself in violets. "Why?"

"There's a violet for every day you were gone," he confessed, "and more for the days I missed you enough to need the pain as a distraction."

Heat licked at her skin. She needed him like she'd never needed anything, and before she could chicken out, she reached over and closed both curtains. Grabbing Roman's shoulders, she indicated for him to stand and pushed him backward onto the opposite cushioned seat. Smiling coyly, she straddled his lap the best she could, never dropping his gaze.

Roman gripped her waist, and the hard length of his cock pressed against her center. He trailed a hand up her side and brushed the underside of her breast with his thumb. The thin fabric of her dress did nothing to hinder the sensation, and she shivered. "I don't want the first time I have you to be in a carriage," he said.

Violet leaned forward and kissed him again, pouring everything she felt into it. "I can't wait. I need you."

Something in Roman snapped at the pleading in Violet's voice. He'd wanted their first time to last hours as he savored every inch of her with his tongue, but he'd deny her nothing. If she wanted to fuck him in a bumpy carriage, he'd happily oblige. Thankfully, all royal carriages, including the one he'd given Violet for her trip, were custom built to accommodate his and his father's large sizes.

"Lift up," he commanded in a husky tone he didn't recognize. Blood pumped straight to his cock, which throbbed against the buttons of his pants. Her chest aligned with his face as she rose to her knees, still straddling him on the bench. "Fuck."

Roman leaned forward and licked her nipple through the thin fabric of her dress, groaning when he realized she wore no breast band. With one hand, he worked her dress down her shoulder, then switched sides until the fabric fell away and her dusky brown nipples blessed him with their appearance.

Could a man die from need? Unable to hold back, he ran his tongue over her left peak and bit the tender skin of her breast.

She gasped and thrust her chest forward until he took her into his mouth, working his tongue against her pebbled skin.

Tasting her was second nature, and the desperate sounds she made encouraged him. He skimmed his fingers down her spine as he switched to her other side, moaning against her sweet skin. He didn't think he could remove his mouth from her tits, and the need to fuck her with his fingers as he'd seen done at the pleasure house overwhelmed him. His hand continued its descent over her backside, and underneath, until he reached her center.

Slowly, he ran his fingers over her entrance, circling the sensitive skin. Violet cried out and pushed her hips down. "Please, Roman."

Gods. If he came in his pants, he'd never forgive himself, but his name on her lips tested his control.

He bit her soft flesh, and she jerked and pressed closer. Roman smiled against her skin and moved between her breasts. Skimming his other hand down her front, relishing in the way her stomach twitched beneath his touch, he found her clit and rubbed gentle circles with his thumb.

Her body quivered, her breathing picked up, and when he pushed a long, thick finger inside her cunt from behind, she cried out. "Sit down and ride my hand."

Without preamble, she dropped, impaling herself further on his finger, and he covered her mouth with his to swallow another cry. "Quiet, princess. I don't want anyone else hearing sounds meant only for me."

She clapped a hand over her mouth and tried to get up. Roman removed his thumb from her clit, grabbed her chin, and forced her to look at him. "Stay with me. Don't worry about them. Keep those pretty lips on mine and no one will know that your needy pussy is riding my hand."

Her entire body flushed, and he grinned, pulling her face to his. He added another finger, and she gripped his shoulders tighter as she rocked her hips.

"More," Violet begged breathlessly.

He released her chin and returned to her clit, running his fingers lightly around it as he pumped in and out of her. "Gods, please." The corner of his mouth tipped in a smirk at the strain in her voice. Pride swelled within him.

"What's wrong?" he asked innocently as he continued to circle her clit, ghosting over it occasionally.

"I swear to the gods, Roman," she groaned and rocked her hips harder to force his thumb where she wanted it.

He took mercy on her and touched her where she wanted. She pitched forward and panted into his neck. Turning his head, he hovered his lips above her ear. "I'm going to add another finger."

She shuddered and nodded. With one finger inside her from behind, he used his other hand to insert another finger from the front. Her dripping cunt allowed it to slide in easily, and once fully seated, he pressed his front palm against her clit.

"Look at me," he commanded. Violet eased back with hooded, glassy eyes. "Ride."

Violet moved her hands around the back of his head and yanked his mouth to hers. She rocked herself on his fingers, his palm rubbing against her clit. The kissing stopped, and she panted against his lips. It was the most beautiful thing he'd ever seen.

Her movements became jerky, and her pussy pulsed around his fingers as he moved them in tandem with her body.

"That's it," he crooned. "Take what you need."

She buried her face in his neck and bit down hard enough to make him hiss as her orgasm rolled through her. The pain mixed with her cum coating his fingers was too much, and he groaned as his cock jerked, his own cum coating the inside of his pants.

Violet's chest heaved as she gulped down much needed air. Slight aftershocks from her orgasm still moved through her limbs, leaving tingles in their wake. Roman said he'd never been with another woman, but the way his hands had worked her into a sopping mess suggested otherwise.

But she had no reason to doubt him and decided he possessed a gods-blessed talent for sexual favors. Sitting up, she groped at the buttons on his trousers. If she didn't have him inside her, she'd die.

His hand covered hers. "We can't." She snapped her head up, and he cleared his throat. "*I* can't."

Were his cheeks turning pink? "You don't want to?" Did he not like his first experience? It'd been years since Violet had done more than kiss a man. Perhaps her skills were rusty.

"I want to more than anything," he said roughly, "but I can't for a little while."

Violet sat back and lowered her arms. "Okay..."

Roman adjusted the crotch of his pants, and the redness in his cheeks darkened. Violet followed his gaze and noticed a large wet spot on his pants. Realization hit her, and she looked up with a wicked grin. "That's flattering."

Roman huffed out a laugh and redressed her before moving her to the bench beside him. "It's embarrassing."

Violet caressed his arm and planted a quick peck on his cheek. "It's your first time fooling around. I'd be suspicious if you lasted long."

Roman leaned his elbows on his knees and glanced over at

her. "I've been practicing to ensure I last longer than sixty seconds." He snorted. "A lot of good that did."

Violet's blood boiled, and she grabbed a fist full of his hair, forcing him to look at her. His eyes widened.

"Practicing? Who is she?" If he said Marissa, she would kill them both.

The violence coursing through her took her by surprise, and she released him, scooting back, terrified of her own reaction. That wasn't like her. She didn't want to kill people. Usually.

He grinned wickedly and reached for her. She pushed his hand away, but it did no good. Roman evaded her attempts to ward him off and wrapped a hand around her knee, yanking her to him. "Jealousy looks good on you, princess." He tried to kiss her, but she snapped her teeth at him. "I didn't use a woman."

"Then who are *they*," she corrected herself through gritted teeth.

His smile widened, and she wanted to scream. "It is what Slayton's brother calls a fist cunt." Violet blinked at him. "It's a toy of sorts that men use to mimic the feel of a pussy."

Violet's jaw dropped. "A *fist cunt*?" Roman nodded. "What kind of stupid name is that?"

The prince shrugged. "It's a pretty accurate description." Blond strands stuck up in every direction as he ran a hand through his hair. "Feels great, but not great enough, apparently, if feeling you fall apart on my fingers made me soak my pants."

Violet couldn't get the mental image of Roman fucking a fake pussy out of her mind. "I want to watch you," she whispered.

"Fuck." He said the curse so quietly she almost hadn't

heard it. "Keep talking like that and I'll be ready to go in no time."

The carriage came to a halt, interrupting their conversation, and someone knocked on the door. "We're stopping for the night." The sound made Violet's heart pound, and she clung to Roman in desperation. The abrupt noise thrust her back into her teenage self, hiding under Roman's bed.

Roman pulled Violet into his side, running a soothing hand over her hair. "It's just Griff or Ares," he murmured. "You're safe."

The beat of Violet's heart slowed, and the embarrassment at her reaction filled her cheeks. "Sorry. I've gotten better, but the attack at the border stirred up old habits."

"Never apologize," Roman ordered. "Never."

"We're stopping for the night," Ares called through the door.

Roman looked at his pants with dismay, and Violet covered her mouth to keep from laughing.

"It's not funny," he grumbled, but it only made her laugh harder. "You know this means they'll know we did something when they see it, don't you?" He grinned.

The color drained from Violet's face. Mortified, she looked around the empty carriage for a solution. "Climb backwards out of the carriage and I'll jump into your arms. My dress will cover your pants, then you can change in our room."

The mischievous glint reappeared in Roman's eyes. "No. I think I'll let them see."

"*Roman Covington, I swear to the gods,*" she whisper-yelled.

He winked and opened the carriage door. It would sadden her to lose him now that she had him as her own, but it couldn't be avoided because she was going to kill him.

28

Violet sat at a lavish table in a private room of the inn where she, Roman, Ares, and Griff were staying for the night. She thanked the server as he placed a plate in front of her. Amos and Clover had dined in their room, and War had disappeared into the jungle to hunt for his own dinner.

"I'm starving," she said to herself and picked up the roast sandwich to dip in the gravy.

Roman stiffened. "You never said you were hungry."

Violet lifted a teasing brow. "I was preoccupied."

"I'm trying to eat here," Griff complained across the table. "I don't want to hear about you two fucking in the carriage. It's bad enough we had to hear it in real time."

Violet gasped, and Roman's hand shot across the table, wrapping around Griff's neck. "You will forget every sound she made."

Roman released Griff, and the man rubbed his throat with a few coughs. "I'm trying. Maybe next time wait until you have a room to yourselves, yeah?"

Violet wanted to crawl under the table. "Can we talk about something else?"

Ares nodded and swallowed a bite of chicken. "If we pick up the pace, we can reach Saltu in three more days."

"Three days?" Violet asked. "It's a week's ride from the border to Saltu, and we've only been traveling a day."

"That's with a normal pace and frequent stops to rest," Ares pointed out. "We can travel dawn to dusk with fewer stops and make it in half the time." Chicken fanned out from the bone when he tore it off with his teeth. "We can knock another day off the ride if you ride a horse instead of the carriage. Griff can stay with the carriage and lead it home."

The thought of being stuck in a carriage for fourteen hours a day with few stops sounded miserable, but so did traveling for another six days. Riding a horse all day sounded worse, and she wouldn't want to leave Griff alone with the carriage. The horses were trained to pull without a driver, so it wouldn't be too much work, but it'd be lonely. Griff was too social.

Violet bit into her sandwich as she weighed the pros and cons of each, but immediately gagged with the wretched taste of the devil's spit hit her tongue. She spit out the sandwich, shoved back from the table, and leaned over to dry heave.

"Violet?" Roman's alarmed voice broke into her internal panic, reminding her he did not know her hatred for the putrid condiment that had assaulted her senses.

She waved him off. "I'm fine." She gagged again.

Someone—Griff—shoved a drink in her hand and patted her back. "There must have been mayonnaise on the sandwich," he explained to Roman.

"What does that mean?" Roman asked as he crouched next to her.

"She hates it." Griff's voice wavered with barely suppressed laughter. "Our queen can't even handle smelling it."

Violet gulped down the water and glared at Griff. "It's fucking disgusting. It should be outlawed."

"You don't like mayonnaise?" Roman asked. "I didn't know." The last words were spoken with a tinge of sadness.

A horrid thought struck Violet. *Is my boyfriend a mayonnaise lover?* They'd have to break up. She reached over and grabbed Roman's ale, taking a long swig to burn the terrible taste from her tongue. "It's not something that comes up in conversation."

"One time she bit into a chicken sandwich and puked all over the table," Griff continued. "My mother was mortified."

Roman picked up her plate and quietly entered the kitchen.

Griff snorted. "He's going to kill the cook."

"What?" Violet snapped her head toward the kitchen door. "Why?"

Griff lifted a brow. "For making you act like you swallowed a slug."

"I didn't ask for no mayonnaise. They couldn't have known."

Roman returned with a new sandwich and set it on the table. "I asked the cook to make you another one."

The cook stuck his head out of the door. "My apologizes. We should have reviewed the ingredients when you ordered."

She waved him off. "No harm done." The man disappeared back into the kitchen, and Violet squeezed Roman's hand in thanks. The prince might be terrifying in his own right, but he also possessed a thoughtful sweetness he never showed to anyone else. "Thank you for the new sandwich." A whiff of mayonnaise hit her, and she fought another gag. "I can still smell it."

Roman motioned to his mouth. "That's because you have some on the corner of your mouth."

Violet's stomach turned.

"You've done it now," Griff mumbled right before Violet puked all over Roman's boots.

Later that night, after Roman burned his clothes and shoes and scrubbed his body raw, Violet crawled into bed and patted the mattress beside her.

Roman folded his massive body under the blankets and rolled to his side to face Violet.

She ran her nails through his still wet hair. "I'm sorry about your boots."

"I've never seen anyone have such a visceral reaction to food before," Roman teased, his hand gliding down her back, leaving the slightest tingle in its wake.

Violet shrugged. "I've hated mayonnaise since I was a child. I can't help that it makes me sick to my stomach." She sighed and changed the subject. "Do we have to get up early?"

He tucked her head against his chest and kissed the top of her hair. "We do. You should get some sleep."

Running her hand down his side, she tried to slip it under the band of his briefs. "I don't want to go to sleep."

Roman moved quickly, jumping out of bed like his ass was on fire. "You have no idea how hard the ride home to Saltu will be. As much as it pains me to say this," he adjusted the bulge in his sleep pants, "you need as much rest as possible while we're on the road."

She sat up. "Why did you get up? And I can sleep in the carriage."

Roman grunted and adjusted himself again. "Because if you keep touching me, I'll give in. I won't risk your well-being."

Violet ran a hand down her chest, a pretend pout playing on her lips. "My well-being is declining as we speak." Her hand continued its descent to grab the hem of her nightgown.

He crossed the room in record speed and caught her wrist. "Don't you fucking dare, princess."

Got him. "Or what, prince?"

Pulling her to her feet, he directed her to the small fainting couch in the corner. "Sit here, you little minx."

Within seconds, he'd removed one of his shirts from his trunk and began ripping it into long strips.

"I know you like to sleep on your side with your hands tucked under your pillow," he said conversationally as he continued to tear the shirt, "but tonight you'll have your arms around me. Understood?"

The fainting couch might come in handy if he kept speaking to her that way. "How do you know how I like to sleep? I barely slept last night." Instead, she'd dozed off a few times in the carriage.

"That's not important," he replied, shrugging her off.

She stood from the couch and closed the distance between them. "It is important." The gifts. She'd forgotten how he'd snuck into her house from time to time to leave gifts over the years. "You remember from the times you snuck in at night to leave me gifts," she guessed softly and smiled.

Something flashed across his face—guilt maybe—and he hesitated too long before saying, "Yes."

Alarm bells rang in her head. He was hiding something. "Roman, how many times did you break into my house at night?"

"Break in?" He chuckled. "Two seconds ago you said I snuck in. Now it's breaking and entering?"

"How many," she repeated slowly.

The intensity in his gaze pinned her in place. "Seven times."

Seven? More than seven gifts were left over the years. She stepped back. "Stop lying."

He narrowed his eyes at her retreat. "A week."

It took her a moment to put together his meaning, and when she did, she gasped. "You watched me sleep every night?" she shrieked. "For how long?" Her heart pounded. What had he seen? Racing through her memories, she tried to remember if she'd done anything embarrassing on nights she couldn't sleep.

Roman prowled toward her. "For years."

Her mouth opened and closed, and her back hit the door behind her. "What is wrong with you? Normal people don't break into other's homes and watch them sleep!"

He cocked his head to the side and considered her reaction. "It's not breaking in if you left your window unlocked. Which is dangerous, by the way. You're lucky I was there."

"It is most definitely breaking in," she argued. He'd lost his mind from one too many hits to the head during training. That had to be it.

"It's not a big deal."

Violet balked at his nonplussed tone. "Yes, it is!" She waved her hands around wildly. "It's illegal!"

The bastard smirked. "I am the law, princess. If I want to follow you around every day for the rest of your life and watch you collect shells or sew Slayton new chest binders, I will, and not a person in this world could stop me."

"You're not the law yet," she said, poking him. "Definitely not when you were breaking into my house for... for years!"

Violet paused, his words replaying in her head. "...*watch you sew Slayton new chest binders...*"

"How do you know I sew Slayton's binders?" Violet doubted it had come up in casual conversation between the two men. "Have you been stalking me? That's an invasion of privacy, Roman. Have you no morals?"

Roman's grin turned feral, and he leaned down to graze his lips across her cheek. "You're not only my queen, Violet. You're my obsession. You have always been mine, and I have always been yours. Not even the gods succeeded at keeping you from me. What makes you think something as trivial as morals would?"

"You're insane," she whispered, ashamed at the thrill and arousal that pounded through her blood at his confession. Maybe she was insane too.

He straightened with a loving, serene look on his face and caressed her cheek. "Get in bed."

She obediently crossed the room and climbed into bed, wondering what was wrong with her. Who got off on knowing someone had creepily stalked them for years? He'd watched her sleep every night, for fuck's sake.

Lost in thought, she hadn't registered Roman wrapping the strips of shirt he'd torn around her wrists until it was too late. She grunted in protest and tried to tug them from his hold, but he shook his head and tsked. "Be a good girl and hold still."

"What do you think you're doing?" she demanded, still trying to free her wrists. Glaring at the offending fabric, she cursed the intricate knots her loving prince had secured.

Seemingly satisfied with his work, Roman brought her bound hands to his mouth and kissed them gently. "You're the one who decided to play with fire, princess." She tried to whack him in the mouth, but he laughed and dodged her weak attempt.

Laying down beside her, he looped her arms over his neck and situated them into a comfortable position. His earlier words made sense. He didn't mean they'd cuddle all night, he meant he'd hold her hostage.

"We both need sleep, and we won't get it if you keep trying to entice me by playing with your pussy."

"You can't tie me up," she huffed and yanked on the ties again.

Roman settled against the pillow and winked. "Yes, I can."

29

Roman grinned down at the dried drool staining Violet's cheek. Last night, after putting up a good fight, she'd given up and melted against him, falling into a deep sleep.

Nothing this woman did bored him. From the way she slept to the way her eyes blazed with fury. The woman seduced him without trying, but when she *did* try, gods. He bit back a groan. Watching her trail her hand under her nightdress... *fuck.* His cock hardened again at the thought.

He lifted her arms over his head to untie the strips of cloth. Violet stirred and blinked slowly into consciousness. She sat up so fast, Roman had to swerve to avoid a busted lip. "Easy," he chuckled.

She glared. *Still mad, then.* "You tied me up."

Flashes of lovers tying each other up at the pleasure house assaulted him, and his lips curled into a slow smile. "The last time I checked, you couldn't rub your legs together hard enough during the bondage shows."

Every exposed inch of Violet's skin turned cherry red. "You tied me up to *not* have sex. It's not the same." She rubbed her wrists and slid out of bed. "Besides." She gazed at him over her shoulder. "You'd be tied up, not me. We'll see how much you like not being able to touch."

Over his dead body. Roman launched across the room and threw Violet over his shoulder. Shrieks of laughter and protest filled the air until his hand came down on her ass with a resounding slap.

"Shit," she hissed. "That stung."

"Good." He slapped her ass again, causing her to yelp. "The next time you threaten to keep me from touching you as I please, remember this." Another slap, followed by a tender caress over her red, heated skin.

"You refused to fuck me because you didn't want me to be tired and uncomfortable during our ride today, yet you're spanking my ass raw." She unsuccessfully swatted at his backside from her upside-down position. "How do you think sitting on a sore butt all day is going to feel?"

"I'll get you a pillow."

Huffing, she let her arms hang limp, turning into dead weight on his shoulder. The skin of her bottom was warm under his lips when he placed a gentle kiss there. He hadn't hit her hard enough for the pain to linger longer than an hour. Still long enough to learn her lesson.

Half an hour later, he heard Violet cursing as she dug through her trunk.

"What's wrong?"

She stood and turned with a groan. "I can't find my underarm crystal."

Roman reached into his own trunk and pulled out his. "Use mine."

You'd think he'd offered her a mayonnaise covered serpent by the way she recoiled. "I'm not using yours. That's disgusting."

"Why?" Slight offense laced his tone. "I don't stink."

"I didn't say you did, but sharing an underarm crystal is not sanitary."

He raised his brows. "I'll have you sitting on my face at some point, and you're worried about sharing an underarm crystal?" Her mouth fell open, and he stepped forward, placing the stone in her hands. "Use it."

Violet climbed into the carriage, wiggling on the cushion to find a comfortable position. Her skin was still tender from Roman's *love taps*, but she'd be lying if she said she didn't like it. Damn him.

Violet froze when she heard Roman say, "Marissa?"

"Roman, thank the gods," Marissa's breathy voice returned. "I've been worried about you."

Violet popped her head out of the window just in time to see Marissa throw her arms around Roman's neck. The woman beamed at him, her gaze dipping to his lips. Roman had Violet's full trust, but Marissa did not.

Violet remained in the carriage only because Roman didn't return the woman's embrace; he pried himself away and took a step back.

"What are you talking about?" he asked the redheaded woman who stared at him with big doe eyes.

"I heard about the rebel attack at the border," she explained. "I came as fast as I could."

Violet's lips flattened. That didn't make sense. Ares said if they rode sunup to sundown with minimal stops, it'd take them three days to get home, and a day less than that if they left the carriage behind. The attack was two days ago.

Two days ago. Is that all? Violet had effectively blocked out the trauma from that day. If she allowed herself to dwell on it, it would break her like all those years ago. She'd made so much progress, and she refused to back pedal. Only time would tell if her bravado would hold.

How could news of the attack have made it to Saltu fast enough for Marissa to hear and meet them? It couldn't have. Three days to Saltu to deliver the news and another three back, give or take a day to adjust for speed, it'd take at least eleven days.

No, that wasn't right. Three days there, three days back. Violet counted on her fingers but stopped when Ares voiced her own concerns. "It's impossible for news to have traveled that fast."

Marissa fidgeted with the end of her braid, looking decidedly embarrassed. "I was already on my way to the border."

"Why?" Griff mused.

Marissa blushed furiously and flitted her gaze to Roman. "Can I speak with you privately?"

That's enough. Violet couldn't kick Marissa's ass because the warrior would beat the crap out of her, but the old, complacent Violet no longer existed. She swung open the carriage door and stepped down. "Hello, Marissa," she sang and made her way to Roman's side. His lips twitched when he saw her sauntering toward him. "Had I known you missed me enough to meet me at the border, I would have written you while away."

The tips of Marissa's pointed ears turned red, but her face remained impassive. "Roman kept me updated on you," she replied smoothly and smiled at the prince. "We kept each other company."

"No, we didn't," Roman protested and glanced warily at Violet.

Marissa tilted her head with a faint smile. "We hung out

every day. What would you call that?" She turned to Violet with a saccharine smile. "We really did miss you. You would have loved to watch Roman get all those tattoos." She waved her arm over his torso. "The first time the needle touched him, he almost came out of the seat." She laughed good-naturedly, and Violet wanted to rip her hair out.

Roman's stance loosened at Marissa's friendly tone, but he clamped his hand around Violet's, a movement that did not go unnoticed by the other woman.

That's right. He's mine.

Griff threw his arm around Marissa's shoulders and squeezed. "I missed you, Red."

Marissa's lip curled. "I hate it when you call me that."

Griff, the traitor, picked up Marissa's braid and dropped it. "It's fitting."

"Who told you about the attack," Roman's voice cut through their friendly banter.

Marissa jerked her thumb over her shoulder toward Saltu. "I passed the messenger sent by the border guards yesterday. He was riding like hell, so I stopped him to see what was going on."

All plausible. Dammit. Violet tended to take people at face value and see the best until they proved the worst, but Marissa rubbed her the wrong way. The warrior wanted Roman, that much Violet knew, but as far as her excuse for getting here so fast, it made sense. Yet, Violet couldn't shake the feeling that she'd lied.

"You never said why you were already on your way to the border," Violet said, going for casual.

Marissa's eyes slid briefly to Roman. "It didn't feel right being in the capital without Rome. I don't really have any other friends." She shrugged. "I left a few days after him."

"It's not safe for you to be traveling alone right now,"

Roman interjected. "The rebels are growing bolder. They openly attacked the Desert King and Queen with me on the other side of the border."

"It's not like them to be that stupid," Ares added. "There were five of us and a dozen border guards within running distance. They only had eleven fighters. It doesn't make sense." He looked disapprovingly at Marissa. "It was foolish of you to come alone."

Marissa threw her hands up. "There hasn't been a rebel attack in the Tropical Kingdom in years. The attack at the border happened after I left. How was I supposed to know?"

"It doesn't matter now," Griff butted in before addressing Roman. "Are Amos and Clover travelling with us?"

Roman shook his head. "I've asked them to go back home."

Everyone froze. "They're not coming to the coronation?" Ares asked.

"I'm not having a public coronation." Roman looked calm, which was absurd because he might as well have said he was setting the entire kingdom on fire. "It's too dangerous to have that big of a gathering after what just happened. I've already sent word to the other kingdoms and to every general in our kingdom."

Griff whistled. "People are going to be pissed. That's all anyone in the capital has talked about for the last few months."

"We'll have a public celebration," he explained, still calm, "but not until later, once we have the issue with the rebels under control."

"I get it," Griff assured him. "All the royals in one place is like a barrel of fish."

"It's never been a problem in the past," Ares pointed out. "All the royals together are unstoppable. They could easily glamour themselves invisible and then slaughter every rebel one by one."

"*If* they see the rebels coming," Marissa said thoughtfully. "I agree with Roman. Having a private ceremony is safer." She smiled warmly at Roman, but he ignored her, his mind already on his next task.

To Violet's delight, the woman looked thoroughly annoyed.

By the time their party stopped for good, Violet wanted to lie in front of the carriage horses and tell them to trample her. Her hips and back hurt from sitting for hours on end with little reprieve. They'd only paused twice, just long enough for Violet to relieve herself. Roman had stocked the carriage with food that morning and the others had food in their pack saddles, so they'd not have to stop for meals.

The trip might not have been so unbearable if she had someone to talk to, but Roman explained that the lighter the carriage, the faster the carriage horses could go. He could have at least ridden close enough to the carriage for her to speak to him out the window. Instead, he hung back to bring up the rear. All in all, she was sore, cranky, and bored out of her mind.

It didn't help that she could hear the others chattering amongst themselves. She'd tried to talk to them through the window opening, but she'd had to yell for them to hear her over the road noise.

The only one who'd stayed close to the carriage was War, and he could do nothing more than offer her pitying looks.

The rumble of Roman's voice followed by Marissa's laughter had Violet's mood darkening. Fumbling with the door handle, she almost fell face first to the ground when Ares opened it from the other side.

The man's quick reflexes saved her from embarrassing herself more, and he chuckled. "Easy."

Roman appeared at their side in seconds, tugged her out of Ares' hold, and tucked her into his side. Fire would have burned Ares alive slower than Roman's glare did. Ares held his hands up. "Someone had to help her out of the carriage."

Violet didn't miss the challenge in his words, and neither did Roman, if the stiffening of his body was any indication. "I was about to."

Marissa stood in the background with a smug smile on her face. In times like these, Violet wished she had trained with Viv so she could attack the woman properly. Her father had only taught her defense.

Reaching up, Violet grazed Roman's jaw to grab his attention and tapped her lips teasingly. "I haven't spoken to you in hours, and this is how you greet me?"

His face softened, and he leaned down and kissed her deeply. "Next time, wait for me to help you out of the carriage."

She arched a brow. "Next time, don't take so long."

Satisfaction graced her lips when Marissa stormed off. Roman realized her game and huffed out a laugh. "No need to stake your claim, princess. She knows I'm yours."

Violet patted his arm. "You poor, dense man. That won't stop her from trying to take you away."

Roman's brows pinched together. "Marissa doesn't want me. She's just clingy because she doesn't have any friends other than Griff and me." He paused. "It's annoying, but she's harmless."

"You don't believe me?" Violet tried to step back, but he pressed her tighter into his side.

"I don't think she's a threat to you," he replied. "If she were, she wouldn't be breathing."

"I didn't say she was a threat, but when she oversteps, and she will, I hope you're ready to face the consequences."

Roman's head popped back. "What is that supposed to mean?"

Violet succeeded in extracting herself from his hold and shook out the skirt of her dress. "It means that I'm telling you she has feelings for you, and if she kiss-attacks you, I'll never let you live it down."

He frowned at her. "I want you to trust me."

"I trust your faithfulness," she informed him, "but I don't trust your judgement, and I don't trust her."

Roman reached forward and ran a thumb across her lower lip. "If she has upset you, I'll take care of her."

Violet balked. "You make it sound like you'll kill her." The prince merely stared back at her. "Okay, calm down. It's not that big of a deal, just don't be alone with her. Actually, don't stand close to her either."

Roman looked away to hide a smile. *Glad he thinks this is funny.* "I'll stay away from her, but if she upsets you, let me know."

Violet beamed and brushed her lips across his. "Thank you."

"And I want you to stay away from every man in Eden."

A laugh burst out of Violet, and he scowled. "Come on, prince. I'm hungry and in dire need of a bath."

30

After grueling days on the road, Violet nearly wept when the outskirts of Saltu came into view. Chances of her never traveling outside of the capital again were very high, and she desperately wanted to walk around for longer than a few minutes at a time.

The swaying of the carriage stopped, and unable to wait for Roman to help her out, as he insisted on doing, treating her like a helpless child, Violet threw open the door and jumped down just in time to see Marissa's foot get stuck in her stirrup.

Her arms windmilled comically, and she shrieked, "Roman, help!"

Roman stood beside her horse, and when Marissa inevitably fell backwards, he stepped to the side and watched her smack into the ground.

Violet slapped a hand over her mouth to stop her laughter, as did Ares. Griff had the good grace to only allow his mouth to twitch. He held out a hand. "You're supposed to step down, not fall."

Marissa gasped for breath, grappling at Griff's hand.

"You should be more careful," Roman deadpanned.

"You think this is funny?" Marissa snapped. "You deliberately let me fall. What's gotten into you?"

Violet hurried to Roman's side. Did Marissa make a habit of trying to fall into Roman's arms?

Roman's face hardened. "Watch the way you speak to me, Marissa. The only reason you're still here is—"

"That's enough bickering, you two," Violet cut in. The last thing she needed was Roman publicly threatening catty women's lives on her behalf. "I want to walk around before my legs stay permanently numb."

Roman tore his death glare away from Marissa. The woman shot Violet a malicious sneer and stormed off.

"You let her fall," Violet said to Roman after the others left toward their respective homes.

Roman hiked a shoulder. "I told you I'd stay away from her."

Violet turned her face into his arm to muffle her laugh. Tilting her face back to look at him, she blew him a kiss. "Let's go surprise our parents and eat dinner. I'm starving."

Roman's mother hurried out of the palace gates toward them, her purple skirts flying around her legs. "You're home!"

He moved forward to meet her halfway, but she flew past him and threw her arms around Violet. Roman spun around, grinning when Violet's eyes flared. She patted Sarah's back awkwardly. "I missed everyone too."

His mother stepped back and waved her hand. "Come on, honey, your parents are right behind me. They can't wait to see you."

"Hello to you, too, Mom," Roman said dryly and approached the two women.

She held out her arms, pulling him against her with a hearty squeeze. "I'm glad you're home safe." She moved back to Violet's side. "Your father and the council are waiting to be debriefed on the attack."

He moved to Violet's other side, having somehow entered a silent battle with his mother over who got to stand closer to Violet. "They'll have to wait. I need to feed my mate and take her home to rest."

Violet waved her hand. "I'm right here, and I can feed myself. You won't believe this, Roman, but I can find my way to my own cottage."

His mother's face fell. "You're not staying in the palace?"

Violet looked from the queen to Roman, clearly confused. "We haven't discussed it yet," Roman replied for her.

"I hadn't thought about it," Violet admitted softly. "We haven't even had time to discuss the wedding."

Roman beamed with pride at how freely she spoke of marrying him.

"There won't be time for a wedding before Roman's coronation," Sarah said ruefully but soon perked up. "That just means we'll have two coronations!"

"Two coronations?" Violet parroted.

"Oh, gods," Roman groaned. "You're just looking for an excuse to throw two more events. We can marry tonight and be crowned together." Violet looked uneasy, and Roman's elation deflated. "You don't want to marry me tonight?"

"It's not that," she assured him, softening her words. "I just..." She blew out a breath. "I always wanted to plan my wedding. You know—flowers, cake, inviting my friends."

The queen beamed, and Roman sighed in defeat. "If a grand wedding is what you want," he pecked the top of her head, "then you will have one. Though I think we can still crown her at my coronation."

"I don't think that's a good idea," his mother remarked.

"Mom!" Violet cried suddenly, breaking away from Roman and Sarah to run toward Meri and Edgar. The Maekins hustled down the palace steps, and Roman glanced sideways at his mother. She must have run full speed to reach Roman and Violet once she'd received word they were in the capital.

Meri burst into tears, babbling about the rebel attack and how Violet could never leave again. Edgar wrapped his arms around his daughter, murmuring something for only them to hear.

"Don't I get a hug?" an annoying voice asked Violet. Slayton and Roman's father stood behind the Maekins, and when Violet saw her friend, she threw her arms wide.

Unfortunately for her, Roman was faster, and before she could wrap her arms around Slayton, he'd wrapped his arm around her waist and hauled her against his chest. She frowned up at him. "Let me go."

Roman grunted. "No."

"Aww, come on, Rome." Slayton held his arms wide. "I'll let you hug me first."

"The only way my arms are going around you is to rip you in half," Roman muttered.

Violet tried to pry Roman's arm from around her. "I won't marry you if you don't let me hug him," she threatened.

Roman lowered his lips to ear. "If you thought binding your wrists was bad, you're going to be thoroughly upset when I chain you to my bed until you change your mind."

"You wouldn't dare." He stared down at her until she sighed with resignation. "Yes, you would. I'm going to hug him at some point. It might as well be with you standing here."

Roman instantly released her, shooting daggers at Slayton.

The man yanked Violet into a tight embrace and smirked over her shoulder.

"I will kill you," Roman threatened.

Slayton released Violet and winked at Roman. "You love me too much to kill me."

Roman almost growled like a feral dog but stopped himself. The king chuckled and wrapped an arm around Violet's shoulders. "I'm coming to discover my son is intense like his mother. We're glad you've all arrived home safe."

The queen harrumphed and walked around them toward the palace entrance. "I had the kitchens prepare extra food in the event you arrived before dinner. Dinner should be ready."

They all filed inside the palace, and it didn't escape Roman's notice that Violet leaned closer into his side, gripping his hand like a vise. She'd entered in the palace more over the years, finally overcoming her reservations for the most part, but the events of the past week must have brought forth old fears.

"If you'd rather have dinner elsewhere, the others won't mind."

His mate straightened her shoulders. "I'm done running, and if we're to marry, I need to be able to walk through the palace with ease."

Roman admired her courage, but the fact she had to be courageous about walking through the fucking palace in the first place pissed him off.

The table and chairs in the private palace dining room were taller than Violet remembered. There were even rungs used as footrests at the bottom of the chairs, but what confounded

Violet more was that the table and chairs weren't the only things with added height.

Once she'd taken note of the dining furniture, she began cataloguing other things when they passed through the halls after dinner. Benches and settees stood at a taller height as well; not as tall as the table and chairs, but noticeably taller in their own right.

Roman tugged Violet through the palace until they reached the courtyard. "I want to show you something, and if afterward you still want to stay in your cottage, we will."

Violet shot him a quizzical look. "What does the surprise have to do with my cottage?"

"It's a surprise." A horse waited for them at the palace entrance, and after he'd set her atop his mount and climbed up after her, he led them around the side of the massive palace and past the warrior compound.

"Has that gate always been there?" she asked when they approached the palace wall. A small door-sized gate with two guards on either side stood in the middle of what Violet could have sworn was a flat, gate-less wall.

Roman dismounted, helped Violet down, and handed the reins to one of the guards. He pulled out a key and unlocked the gate, ushering her through. While Roman locked the gate back, Violet tried to grasp what she saw.

A stone house in the same style of the palace, only much smaller, stood tall in front of them in the middle of a miniature courtyard, surrounded by its own stone walls. These walls, however, had even more weaponry adorning the top, and trees had been cleared from the vicinity, creating an impenetrable fortress.

The building itself looked to be the size of one wing of the palace. Six stone pillars lined the porch, with large windows placed between each, and massive, cherrywood double doors with intricate designs carved into the wood. Surrounding the porch were flowers of every kind. Some Violet recognized, and others she didn't.

Roman placed a gentle hand on her back. "Do you like it?"

Speechless, Violet turned to him fully, noting how nervous he looked. "Roman, this is beautiful, but what is it? I've never heard of this place."

He rubbed the back of his neck and smiled sheepishly. "I had it built for us while you were gone."

She stood staring between him and the house. "You built us a house?" He chewed the inside of his cheek, looking unsure, and nodded. "Why?"

His shoulders drooped. "I know you get scared in the palace, and I thought if I built you a new one just for us and a select few staff, you'd feel safer." He'd stunned her speechless, and without preamble, she threw herself into his arms. "We can live in your cottage, princess. We don't have to live here."

"Are you kidding?" she mumbled against his chest. "I love it." Lifting her head, she tried to force every ounce of her gratitude and love into her words. "I'm making sure this goes in the history books. I want everyone to know how thoughtful you are." She twisted to look at the house again. "I can't believe you built us a house because I was scared."

Roman slid both hands to the sides of Violet's neck and framed her jaw with his thumbs. "There is no limit to what I would do for you."

Running her hands up his chest, she lifted on to her toes and slanted her mouth over his. He deepened the kiss, his lips caressing hers with slow, deliberate tenderness. His tongue slid against hers in a sensuous dance.

Once they came up for air, he rested his forehead against hers. "I want to show you the rest before this goes any farther."

Violet huffed out a laugh and pecked his cheek. "Lead the way, prince."

Violet trailed after Roman, having long let go of his hand to stop and look at the flowers around the porch. Porch was too small a word. Her entire cottage could fit on the "porch."

Once she'd thoroughly inspected the foliage, she bounded up the stairs to where Roman waited for her by the huge double doors. Detailed carvings swirled across the wood, stopping her up short with a gasp. "Violets," she breathed.

Roman tapped his forearm peeking out from his rolled-up sleeves. "Drawn by the same artist who did these."

A dark feeling of inadequacy almost overwhelmed her. All these years, he'd never lost hope in them like she had. While she'd traveled the world to chase her dreams and run from fear, he'd stayed behind, building a life for her, not them. Everything he'd done had been for her comfort, but what had he done for himself?

A calloused hand slid around the nape of her neck and into her hair, grabbing a handful to tilt her head back. "Are you hurt?"

Roman's gaze, so earnest and full of concern, almost turned her into a watering pot. Taking a deep, shuddering breath, she moved away from him and gestured around. "You did all of this," she motioned to his tattoos, "and this, and gods knows what else. You stalked me, you watched me sleep, which in retrospect is really fucking weird, but it's also sweet, and what have I done?" She held her hands up with a shrug and dropped them helplessly. "I've done nothing but stand here and cry on the beautiful porch of the beautiful house you had built for me."

Silence stretched between them like a gaping canyon, separating them. Pointing out their one-sided relationship wasn't her best idea. What if she lost him? "I'll do better," she swore. "I'll play strategy games with you every day."

"You cheat," he reminded her pointedly.

Sniffling, she flicked her hand dismissively. "I don't cheat. I'll read those boring books you like so we can talk about them, and I'll—"

"Stop."

Violet snapped her mouth shut, her lip trembling as Roman took measured steps toward her. "You really don't know, do you?"

She swiped her nose with her sleeve and steadied her voice. "Know what?"

Roman huffed out a quiet laugh, and once he stood toe to toe with her, he tucked a piece of hair behind her ear. "Do you remember the first time we met? You ran into me in the hallway."

"You ran into me," she replied with a sniffle.

His lips split into a beautiful smile. "That morning when I woke, I'd hated my life." Violet sucked in a sharp breath. "I love my parents, and they meant well, but they kept me on a tight leash. Too tight. I didn't have any friends or much contact with anyone my own age."

"Roman," Violet whispered, her heart breaking into a million pieces for the young prince forced to wear the heavy crown.

He idly traced the outline of her face as he continued to speak. "When I started training with the junior warriors, I didn't know how to speak to the other kids. That didn't stop them from wanting to be around me, but it stopped me from wanting to be around them." His fingers trailed down to her neck and tenderly stroked her pounding pulse. "And then I met you. You made me feel like I was normal." Roman dropped his head forward and laughed. "You threatened to kill me within the first day."

A laugh bubbled out of her upon remembering their back and forth. "That was thirteen years ago."

"You got me a birthday gift," he went on, ignoring her protests. "A beaded bracelet in human-grass green that sits in a box in my room because I wore it until it nearly fell to pieces. No one other than my family has ever gotten me a gift other than you.

"I don't know who I'd be had I not met you. I was a shell of a boy who didn't know how to laugh, then you came along and forced me to. Hell, you made me sneak out in the middle of the night to smuggle half-dead chickens into our classroom."

"The chickens were fine," she laughed through her tears, playfully swatting his arm.

He released her and stepped back. "I have loved you since the day I watched you crawl around in chicken shit, Violet Maekin, and now that I have you, I'm never letting you go."

"I'm sorry I gave up on us," she whispered. "I loved you so much and didn't think I could compete with a mate bond, but that's no excuse."

"Don't," he replied, his voice sharp. "Don't blame yourself for being the rational one out of the two of us. Someone has to balance me out."

Violet burst out laughing, thinking he was kidding, but the deadpan expression on his face told her he wasn't. She laughed harder and walked into his embrace. "I love you, Roman, and I swear I'll do a better job showing you."

31

Roman watched as Violet looked around the inside of their new home, relishing in the way her eyes lit up with excitement. He'd paid the crew to work around the clock to finish everything before his mate returned, and he'd been as involved in the process as he could.

Walking through the front entrance, the foyer had white marble floors to complement the light stone walls. He'd had as many sconces, chandeliers, and lamps installed throughout the house as he could, wanting everything to be open and light, just like her.

He'd commissioned paintings of faerietale scenes from old storybooks, adding a whimsical feel to the dwelling. Violet had always been a dreamer with a joyful outlook on the world around her, and he wanted their home to reflect as much.

"The furniture," Violet mused, running her hand along the back of a chaise lounge. "It's all taller than what you'd normally see. Longer, too." Moving on to the coffee table in the middle of the settees and chairs in their main sitting room, she bent over to look under it. "I first noticed it in the main palace. Is it a new trend?"

Roman walked to the other side of the coffee table, stretched himself out on the ground, and scooted underneath it. Violet stooped down to peer at him, and he patted the floor beside him. "I had them all commissioned to fit us." After being unable to fit under her kitchen table the day Titus left, Roman knew something needed to be done. He'd not let her hide on her own ever again. It was slightly difficult to sit on their settees and benches, and he'd had to add steps to their bed, but he didn't care.

Looking out from both sides of the coffee table, he realized the flaw in his plan. "I guess it isn't much for hiding. I can have tablecloths made to cover the sides and skirts added to the settees."

Violet laid down and rolled under the table, grabbing his hand. "I can't believe you did this." She choked on her words, as if speaking by sheer force. "I love you."

Before he could respond, she rolled toward him. One of her hands cupped his cheek, and her lips collided with his. The kiss brimmed with passion, conveying everything Violet felt. He knew because her feelings stirred inside him like the mate bond, but not quite.

There wasn't much room under the table to pull her on top of him, but gods, did he want to. "I need you," he murmured against her lips. Because he did, more than anything. He'd waited over a decade to have her, but he didn't think he could wait another minute.

Breaking their kiss, he moved out from under the table, reached under to hook his arm over her waist, and slid her out until he could hover over her. Violet giggled, and it was the most beautiful thing he'd ever heard.

He reached between them and ripped her dress open, the pretty beads she'd sewn to the neckline shooting in every direction. His deep groan at the sight of her perfect tits drowned out her gasp, and he dove to suck a beaded nipple into his mouth.

Breathy words slipped from her lips, and her fingers dove into his hair. The way she squirmed beneath him stoked a fire of need. He needed to bury his cock so far in her cunt she'd feel him forever, but with his inexperience, Roman knew he needed to make her come first.

After paying both breasts ample attention, he kissed and licked his way down her stomach, dipping his tongue in her belly button. Violet jolted and half-heartedly slapped at the top of his head. "That tickles."

He grinned against her. "Good." The journey to the apex of her thighs sweetened the farther south he went, briefly stopping at her slender hips to rip the lacey underwear denying him the sight of her.

His tongue ran across the tender flesh of her left hip, and she lifted her bottom, pressing herself into his face. "Please," she begged.

How could he deny her?

"Spread for me, princess. Let me look at the pretty cunt I'll be eating tonight."

She moaned and pushed her legs wide, showing the darkened skin of her slick pussy. Seeing her bared to him for the first time like this almost made him come in his pants again. He whispered a thanks to the gods for making this perfect creature for him to devour.

Lowering his head, he brushed his lips along the inside of her thigh. "Is this what you want?"

"Roman." She pleaded with him now.

"Here?" his deep voice rumbled as he stuck his nose against her dripping pussy and pulled in a deep breath. His cock jerked and throbbed. He tried to think of anything unsavory to stave off his climax. *Fuck. Fuck. Fuck.*

He flattened his tongue against her opening and swiped up in one, long lick. Her taste exploded across his tongue, and her cry rang in his ears. Everything around him narrowed to the arousal flooding his tongue as he stroked her over and over. He knew right then that there wouldn't be a day in his life he wouldn't have his head buried between her thighs.

Her hips ground against his face, and he wrapped his hands under her to hold her steady. Deeper he dove, ravenous for what he'd been denied for so long. His tongue alternated between fucking her entrance and licking her clean, only to start over again.

Her cries grew louder, and she tried to slip her hand to rub her clit, but he bit the tip. She yelped and yanked her hand back. "Your clit will get the attention it deserves when I say it does, princess. Let me play."

She tossed her head back and tried to push against his mouth again. "Roman, *please.*"

Ignoring her, he dipped his head, running his tongue everywhere but where she wanted it. Her protests grew louder and her movements more erratic, until he granted her mercy and sucked her clit into his mouth.

Her back bowed with a scream, intensifying when he slipped two fingers inside her. Roman flicked his tongue quickly as the performer at the pleasure house had instructed him to do, switching to sucking just as he curled his fingers.

Her walls quivered around his digits, and her body convulsed, ripping a loud scream from her throat. He continued to move them in and out, dragging them along her fluttering walls.

Once she came down, he removed his fingers and sucked them into his mouth. He wanted nothing more than to clean her cunt with his tongue, but she'd need the mess to help accommodate his size.

"I need to be inside you," he rasped and reached for the back collar of his shirt to pull it over his head. Violet sat forward and worked on the buttons of his pants, freeing his aching cock from its confines.

Violet's mouth fell open. "Oh."

Roman removed his pants and crawled over Violet's body, forcing her to the ground. "You can take it, princess," he said, his voice low and throaty. "Your pretty little pussy will stretch for me like it was made to do."

Violet shivered and her nipples puckered. Roman shifted his hips and rubbed his dick against her folds, grunting at the mess his words made. "Fucking hell, Vi. You like when I tell you what I'm going to do to you?" She nodded, uncharacteristically quiet, hanging on his every word.

"First, I'm going to slide into your tight cunt, inch by inch." He punctuated his words by notching the head of his cock against her entrance and pressing slowly. A hiss slipped through his gritted teeth.

Violet lifted her hips and whined. "More."

"Your greedy cunt is choking me, princess." Another two inches and his girl started to writhe beneath him. "I'm going to fill you, baby. Are you ready?" *Am I ready?*

"If you don't, I'm going to explode," Violet cried, still moving beneath him for friction.

In one long stroke, Roman bottomed out and entered paradise. They both moaned long and loud. "I need a minute," he ground out.

Violet reached for his neck, their gazes connecting. "Kiss me."

He didn't need to be told twice. Swooping down, he sucked her bottom lip between his and bit lightly until she opened. With each swipe of his tongue, her pussy loosened, accepting him. Her soft thighs wrapped around his waist to bring him closer.

"I have to move."

She nodded, and he dragged his cock through her hot channel. When he thrust back inside, she moved her hips in time with his. The sound of their slick bodies slapping together filled the room.

"I can't last much longer," he told her tightly. It surprised him he'd lasted this long. Guess the fist cunt worked better than he'd thought.

Bringing his hand to his mouth, he spit on his fingers and moved them to her clit, rubbing in time with their bodies. The feel of her walls sliding against the hardness of his cock was euphoric. He'd never get enough.

"Roman," she cried as her movements became erratic.

Thank the gods. He wouldn't last much longer. A tingling started at the base of his spine. *Fuck.* He tried to control his movements, to stave off his climax until his mate came one more time.

Violet chanted his name like a prayer, the walls of her pussy quivering around his cock. It sent him over the edge. Cum shot out of his dick harder than anything he'd ever experienced, and he was faintly aware of Violet's soft cries. "Keep going," she begged. "I'm almost there."

His cock had yet to completely deflate, and he thrust harder. Working her clit the best he could, he sighed with relief when she screamed and came all over him.

The shaft of his cock deflated completely, and his arms burned with the effort to keep his body from crushing her.

"Are you sure you've never done that before?" Violet asked between pants.

Roman dropped his head and laughed. Never had he been so light and free, and it had nothing to do with the warmth still encircling his dick. "I learned a thing or two from the shows we watched."

Her mouth pulled into a beautiful smile. "We should go soon. I believe you once said something about a private room?"

Roman cursed the late hour. On one hand, the staff had taken off for the night, allowing him to fuck his mate anywhere he pleased, but on the other hand, the last show at the pleasure house would be nearing its end by now.

"Soon," he promised and kissed the tip of her nose.

"I love you," she whispered. His cock twitched inside her, slowly rising. She laughed, disbelieving. "So soon?"

Roman tested the waters, moving his hips, and shuddered. "If I try to fuck you again, I won't last longer than three strokes."

Violet covered her mouth to stifle a giggle, and he quirked a brow. "Is that funny?"

She shook her head, trying to hold in her laugh. He leaned down and nipped at her nipple, and she shouted in protest. Glancing up at her, he laughed against her skin at the contrite look on her face.

His cock stood erect, and gods help him, he had to have her again. Looping an arm around her back, he pushed himself up to his knees and into a standing position. Violet grabbed at his shoulders and tightened her legs around his waist. "What are you doing?"

Roman prayed the coffee table was as sturdy as it looked and sat on the end. He scooted himself back until his knees hit the edge and released Violet's back. Leaning back, he rested his weight on both of his hands and met Violet's inquisitive stare.

"Ride me, princess."

Grinning devilishly, Violet rocked her hips, and Roman swore colorfully. He forced himself not to move. If he didn't control the rhythm, maybe he wouldn't come in three seconds.

His mate rotated her hips in different ways, and he dropped his head back with a tortured groan. "This might kill me." The look on Violet's face made his balls tighten, and he shot his hand out to grab her hip. "You're fucking beautiful."

Violet's moans as she worked her hips faster were his undoing, and he sat forward, running his hands up her sides to her tits. He plucked at both of her nipples and watched with astonishment as her mouth opened with short bursts of breath.

"Roman," she sobbed as her pussy spasmed around him, and by some miracle, she came before he did. Only seconds before, but it was progress.

Her legs drew up and her body twitched while her pussy clamped around his cock, triggering his own release. Wet, sticky residue trickled over his groin and thighs, and he looked down where they joined.

"What a mess," Violet mumbled.

A mess indeed. He reached down and scooped their mixed cum on his fingers and held it in front of her mouth. "You need to clean it up."

She snorted. "I'm not licking that."

He turned his ear toward her. "What was that?"

Violet opened her mouth to reply, but before any words came out, Roman slipped his fingers past her lips and smeared them against her tongue. "I said, you need to clean it up." The blue in her eyes disappeared as her pupils expanded, and she closed her lips around his fingers. "Good girl."

Again, he swiped their releases up and fed them to her until only a faint residue remained. "I can't wait to have you on your knees," he murmured, smirking at the fresh slick coating his cock. "For now, I want to bathe you and put you to bed. It's been a long day."

He stood, still inside his future wife, and carried her to their room.

32

Once she'd slipped on her night dress and slippers, Violet looked around the large bedroom. A four-poster canopy bed with gold drapes, blankets, and bed skirt was against the back wall. It stood tall off the ground, and on each side were two little steps to help her climb up.

The rest of the room sported white walls with gold detailing and different paintings in golden frames. Instead of a set of rooms like in the palace, this was one space with a large sitting area in one corner, built-in armoires lining one wall with a dressing table and floor to ceiling mirror, and a glass door leading to the bathroom.

"Everything is so open," she commented as she inspected her new home and trailed back into the bathroom for a better look. "Anyone could watch me bathe."

Roman followed her into the oversized bathroom. A shower encased in glass stood next to a large marble bathing tub. *Are those gold handles?* A wash basin with a mirror and shelf for toiletries sat on the opposite wall next to the solid door of the water closet.

"That's the idea," he drawled. "I never want to take my eyes off of you." He put a hand on the small of her back and led her through their bedroom to the door. "As far as everyone else, no one has a key to our room except for us. There is no around-the-clock staff, and during the work hours when the staff is here, only one maid is approved to clean our room at a specific time each day."

Roman pulled out two keys and handed one to Violet. "If you do not want her to clean that day, lock the door." Coming to a stop in front of another white painted door, he slid the key in the lock and turned the knob. "No one will bear witness to your naked body but me."

The prince ushered her inside the room and every thought abandoned her. Five dressmaking mannequins lined a wall directly across from the window. During the day, the lighting would be exquisite.

A white wooden desk with gold hardware adorned the connecting wall, complete with a plush, velvet desk chair. Violet sat on the tall settee beside the desk and melted into the plush cushion. It was the softest piece of furniture she'd ever encountered.

On the opposite wall, a brand new sewing machine was nestled next to a large cabinet filled with bolts of fabric and organizational boxes containing various items, like beads, shells, and sewing supplies.

"Are there any more wonderful things in this place that are going to make me cry, because if so, I'd like to get it all done at once." She sniffled and threw her arms around Roman's middle. "I don't think I will ever be able to say this enough, but thank you. You didn't have to do any of this, and the fact that you put so much thought into it would make me love it, even if I hated it."

He stiffened. "Do you hate it?"

Huffing, she stepped back and held her arms wide. "This room is everything I've ever dreamed of. I *love* it. I promise." In a few steps she was at the door, and she looked at him over her shoulder. "Show me your special room."

He followed her into the hall and shut the door behind them. "What do you mean?"

Pausing, she turned to him fully and searched his handsome face, tanned from the sun and brushed with dark blond stubble. "What in this house is for just you?"

"Ah." He nodded at the door across the hall from her sewing room. "This is my study."

"Study?" Trailing after Roman, she stepped into the darkened room and surveyed the space. Where the rest of the house boasted all bright whites, golds, and pops of color, this room was all rich, dark colors with dark mahogany wood furniture.

A large two-sided fireplace stood in the middle of the room, dividing the study in half. One side contained his desk, cabinets, a table holding a detailed replica of Eden, and a few chairs facing his desk.

The other side of the room housed shelves filled with books and strategy games, a table with four chairs, soft reading chairs split by a table, and an overstuffed chaise lounge the size of a small bed.

One entire bookcase held slider puzzles in various shapes and sizes. Violet had never seen so many before, and she peeked at Roman from the corner of her eye. She knew he enjoyed them, but she hadn't realized how much. She filed the information away for later.

Violet quirked her lips to the side at how very *Roman* the space was. "This suits you," she remarked and studied the game set on the table. "Who were you playing with?"

"Slayton."

Violet's head snapped up in surprise. "My Slayton?"

Roman scowled. "He is not *your* Slayton."

Oh, this is too good. "You and Slayton are friends," she accused gleefully.

Roman stood firm and folded his arms across his chest. "No, we're not."

"You like him," Violet taunted with a laugh. Stepping forward, she pried Roman's arms apart and slid her own around his middle. "That makes me happy."

Tenderness filled his gaze. "You're delusional."

She chuckled and spun around. "Let's play a game." Grabbing a familiar game from the shelf, she went to her knees on the soft rug before the fireplace and started to set up.

Roman crouched down and stayed her hand with his. "It's late. We can play tomorrow."

"Oh." She sighed dramatically. "I was hoping we could play for articles of clothing, but I guess it can wait."

Roman's fingers curled around her wrist. Whatever he'd intended to say drowned out when a tinkering bell and clucking sound came from somewhere beyond the door.

Violet dropped the game pieces and pivoted to stare at the door. "What is that?"

The prince shot to his feet, mumbling under his breath before saying, "Babs. She must have escaped again and slipped in through War's door."

He made to leave, and Violet scrambled after him. "Who is Babs, and why does she sound like a bird?"

Roman peered over his shoulder, opened the door, and stared at a plump auburn hen with a pink string attached to the tiniest bell tied around her neck.

Violet jumped back, and the hen stared at Roman. She clucked with all the indignation a hen could possess and ran forward. Violet screamed and ran backward. The bird pecked Roman on the shin once and flapped her wings.

"You're being a brat again," Roman told the hen before picking her up and stroking her head gently. "Violet, this is Babs. Babs, this is my mate, Violet."

Babs clucked in greeting.

Violet stared warily at Babs. "Roman, why are you holding a chicken with a name?"

"I was speaking with the head cook about moving a cook to our house, and Babs ran into the main kitchen, sending the staff into a fuss. A few tried to chase her down." He chuckled. "She's a slippery little thing. Cook said to use her for dinner, and I don't know… It didn't feel right."

Violet's eyes ticked from Roman to Babs. "You eat chicken all the time."

He hiked a shoulder. "I didn't want anyone to eat her."

Violet rolled her lips together and took a tentative step forward. "You tied a bell to her."

"She likes to hide," he explained. "She's not supposed to come into the house, but she keeps breaking out of her coop somehow."

"If she poops in our house, I'm closing War's door permanently," Violet warned. The thought of stepping in chicken droppings made her want to puke. "I'm serious."

Roman frowned. "She doesn't come into the house often, and there have been no accidents yet." He petted her again, and to Violet's utter delight, raised his tone as if speaking to a small child. "You just wanted to meet Violet, didn't you girl?"

Roman looked up to say something, noticed Violet's barely leashed laughter, and frowned. "What's so funny?"

Shaking her head, Violet waved her hand at him. "This. All of it. I'm bringing in an artist to commission a painting of you and Babs."

"No, you're not," Roman grumbled. "Don't be ridiculous."

"I need to remember this forever," she informed him. "I'm hanging it up."

"I'm not sitting for a painting." Roman stalked down the hall with a bobbing Babs in tow.

"We'll see," Violet taunted and scurried after him.

How is this my life? she wondered to herself. *An attractive prince who loves me and saved an ornery chicken to keep as a pet?*

Giggling quietly, she floated down the hall alongside her mate, loving every minute of how her life had turned out. Every ounce of heartbreak was worth it if it meant getting to this moment with the love of her life.

Roman sat in the chair beside his and Violet's bed, watching his mate sleep. The sheer happiness he'd felt today overwhelmed him. Nightmares didn't keep him awake tonight. Elation did. Like if he slept, he'd miss something great with her.

"*Roman,*" War said, breaking into Roman's thoughts.

Roman sat up straight. War let him know when he was on his way to Roman and Violet's home, but he'd never connected in the middle of the night. "*What's wrong?*"

"*Vivian is near the capital,*" he replied gravely, sending Roman's anger into overdrive. "*I spotted her earlier and followed her.*"

Roman was already moving to get dressed. "*Is she with anyone?*" He didn't want to leave Violet alone, but no safer place existed than their small fortress. Even if someone killed the guards, the guards didn't have a key. Roman or Violet were the only two with keys, and only they could let people, including War, inside, so long as they remembered to lock the gate when they came and went.

"No."

Kissing the top of Violet's head, Roman gathered his daggers and set off to find War. *"Where are you?"*

"Deep in the jungle. You won't reach us before sunrise. I can try to corral her toward Saltu, but I fear that would include bloodshed."

"Fuck." Think, Roman. *"Does she know you're following her?"*

"Hard to tell." War paused. *"You should be proud of your generals and her father. They trained her well."*

"Not the time," Roman replied wryly. *"Leave her and stay with Violet at all times when I'm not around. She's following her sister, but if she thinks someone is on to her, she will retreat and regroup later."* Roman continued outside, locking the door behind him. *"Meet me in the council chambers."*

War's imposing presence lifted from the air. Vivian knew he wouldn't hurt her, even if Roman told him to, unless she actively attacked someone.

The cut on her hand smarted, and she shook it out. One of the rebels' swords had caught her across the knuckles at the border fight. He'd received a sword through the gut for his efforts.

If they got to Violet before Vivian, they'd kill her. Vivian hated Violet, and she hated herself for it. Resentment devoured affection, and watching people fawn over delicate little Violet while simultaneously expecting Vivian to be strong and controlled at all times had nurtured resentment like milk to a babe.

All Vivian had to do was get Violet alone, give her the sleeping tonic, and take her to the rebels herself. Then she'd be safe, and Vivian could reclaim her place on the throne before that bitch she'd once considered a friend could dig her claws into Roman.

A new enmity fueled by something more powerful than hate wound around Vivian's veins like an ivy over a stone wall. Everything was Titus' fault. How foolish she'd been falling for his act. For years. Every word out of his mouth since they were kids had been a lie.

The day he'd ran to her sister's side when Vivian accidentally hit her with her wooden sword should have alerted her to his schemes, but she'd been a foolish kid. She'd believed he'd liked her. They'd grown from children to teenagers to adults together.

She'd watched his light hair turn dark, his eyes melt from hazel to brown, his gangly, boyish build grow strong. She thought they'd fallen in love together, but she was nothing but a pawn.

A foolish, pissed off pawn.

33

A tinkling noise tickled the back of Violet's mind. She lingered in the floating space between sleep and consciousness until her brain registered the sound was real, coming from somewhere in their home.

Opening her heavy eyes, she reached over to find nothing but air and sat up. "Roman?"

Silence.

Looking around, she spotted a folded piece of paper with her name scrawled on the outside in familiar penmanship. The tinkling persisted in the background, but she ignored it and reached for the note.

Princess,

A pressing matter has come up. I'll be with the council most of the morning, but War will stay with you until I return. When he arrives, the guards will ring the bells to let you know he needs inside. Your keys to the gate and front door are on the bedside table. If you decide to leave, have War tell me where you're going.

The staff arrives just after sunrise and will need to be let in. Do

*not let them in without War at your side. I'll find you as soon as I'm
done.*

I love you.

Obsessively Yours,

Roman

*P.S. If you're sore, there are bath salts on the edge of the bathtub
to soak in. They should ease your muscles.*

A pressing matter? A cold sweat beaded Violet's forehead.
What if rebels were in the capital?

The tinkling still invaded the otherwise silent walls. Climbing
out of bed, she adorned slippers and a robe and grabbed the keys
from the nightstand, just in case. She ventured into the hall and
spotted clusters of tiny bells she'd not noticed last night hanging
along the walls, jingling incessantly. They reminded her of the
staff call bells and alarm bells in the main palace.

If she must let the staff in, that meant the bells were being
triggered from somewhere outside. Curious, she wandered
through the house and onto the porch. War, along with four
women and a man, waited patiently on the other side of the
gate.

Violet hurried down the long path, grateful Roman had
used smooth cobblestones and not gravel because the bottom
of her house slippers were not sturdy enough to keep sharp
rocks from stabbing her feet.

"War!"

The tigon dipped his head slightly, and Violet tried one of
the keys. With a soft clink, the gate opened, and she stepped
back to allow the beast in. War positioned himself in front of
Violet.

A guard with shoulder-length, curly, dark brown hair, pale

beige skin, and dark brown eyes moved into view and stepped inside. She tipped her head respectfully. "Do we have your permission to allow the staff in, Your Grace?"

Violet blanched. "I'm not the queen," she sputtered. The royal title didn't belong to her yet.

The young guard smirked, showcasing a dimple. "To us, you are. I'm Dani." The woman held out her hand for Violet to take. Releasing her, she gestured toward the gate. "Kaylan is right outside. We're the day guards."

A woman with a light rosy skin, mahogany hair with blunt bangs, and a wide smile poked her head around the corner. "You can call me Kaylie."

Violet waved awkwardly. "It's nice to meet you both. I apologize for taking so long. I was asleep and didn't understand what the ringing meant."

Dani hiked a thumb over her shoulder. "There's a pulley we use to ring the bells. A light ringing means there's a guest or someone who wants entry. There's another for emergencies. It's exactly like the palace alarms."

Violet's mind drifted to the day she'd heard the dreaded alarms, but she shook herself. "Thank you for letting me know." Eyeing the other four women in maids' attire and the man in work clothes, Violet lowered her voice for only Dani to hear. "I've never met the staff. How do I know it's really them?"

"Any guard protecting the bunker knows who the staff is," the guard whispered back.

"The bunker?" Violet looked back at her beautiful home.

Dani snorted. "This is the most secure place in all of Eden. Accurately nicknamed the palace bunker, or just the bunker."

Affection consumed her. Roman did this for her.

"Until you're familiar with the staff, you can ask War to confirm since you don't know Kaylie or myself, either," Dani suggested. "He's met them all." Violet decided she liked Dani, and if she had it her way, they'd be friends.

War nudged Violet's leg and nodded, then turned to the staff and nodded again.

"Thank you, Dani. You can let them in."

Dani stood aside and the staff filed in one by one, each introducing themselves to Violet as they passed. One of the maids looked alarmed when they took in Violet's attire, and Violet flushed scarlet. She'd forgotten she wore only a robe and nightgown.

"I would love to chat with you all later, but I need to change and run errands."

Khrista, one of the maids, smiled. "We understand. Oh, and please don't forget to lock the gate. The prince will have someone's head if it remains unlocked too long."

Violet nodded and locked the gate. "Thank you for reminding me. This will all take some getting used to."

Khrista nodded and followed Violet inside. "Did Prince Roman give you our schedule?"

"He had to leave before I woke this morning," Violet responded, "but I can write it down, if you don't mind telling me."

"Of course, Your Grace."

"Violet. Please, call me Violet."

Khrista looked uncomfortable. "I'm not sure Prince Roman would approve."

Violet dismissed her concern. "You let me worry about the brooding prince. I'll get your schedule and then get out of your hair."

Khrista finished explaining everyone's daily schedule, and Violet frowned down at the paper. "You all can't leave unless one of us is here to let you out?"

"No, Your Gr—Miss Violet. Only you and Prince Roman

have keys." Violet chewed on her lip. It wasn't fair for them to wait around if she had yet to return, but she wanted to see her parents and friends today, and it would eat the day. "Don't worry," Khrista added. "They informed us of everything that comes with working at the palace bunker. I assure you, we are more than happy to wait."

"I'll speak to Roman about increasing your pay," Violet decided. "It isn't fair for you to not be able to run to town or see your loved ones with no extra compensation."

Khrista grinned. "That is not necessary. I assure you, Prince Roman has more than compensated us."

"Oh," Violet replied lamely. Roman's thoughtfulness and consideration for others filled Violet with pride. "Well, I'll leave you to it. I must go."

With a final wave, Violet petted War's soft sheaths and headed toward the gate.

"Violet and I are going to see her parents," War rumbled.

Roman tapped his finger against the paper in front of him restlessly, wanting nothing more than to join his mate. *"Let me see her."* Roman's eyes defocused, and he entered War's consciousness. The beast turned his large head to look at Violet and nudged her with his nose. Roman released the tension holding him hostage when Violet smiled down at the tigon.

"I missed you, too, big guy." She ruffled his sheaths, and War returned his gaze to the path ahead.

"Roman," his father said brusquely, and Roman cut the connection to War. "This is serious, son. If Vivian is working with the rebels, she needs to be captured immediately."

"I'm not sure she is," Roman replied. "She fought against

them, and they had no problem attacking her." He tapped his finger again. "But it's possible."

His mother took a drink of water before saying, "Vivian might want you back."

"Vivian never had me to begin with," Roman replied icily. He recalled the first time rebels attacked Violet in his bedroom. When Vivian had held Violet in her arms, Roman had sensed her emotions. She hated Violet, but she loved her too. "I don't think she'd hurt Violet, but I won't take any chances."

His father sat back and rubbed his forehead. "Sarah, what did your family do to warrant a curse? That's the only explanation to this mayhem." The king dropped his hand. "There's no other explanation to a broken mate bond, escalated rebel attacks, and now a family feud between a mate and the future queen."

"Vivian is not my mate," Roman snapped, losing his patience. "And who's to say the curse isn't from your side?"

His father looked between Roman and the queen and moved his finger from one to the other. "I love you both more than my own life, but—"

"I wouldn't finish that sentence if I were you, Felix," Roman's mother quipped.

The king sat forward and leaned toward his wife. "Or what, minx?"

Roman scooted back his chair and stood. "That's enough for today. Mom, let me know if Tilly has news. Dad, inform the generals they need to prepare our warriors. The rebels are acting out of character. They're either playing a game we don't know yet, or they're acting rashly. Neither is good."

"I don't think we should have a private coronation," his father said for the one thousandth time that morning. "After what happened with Vivian, upsetting tradition will only cause more unrest."

"A coronation is the perfect place for rebels to attack," Roman explained. Tradition in the Tropical Kingdom dictated the monarchs from each kingdom be in attendance, customarily accompanied by members of their council, as well as the palace staff, warriors, and others who worked directly under the crown. After the coronation, a parade through the capital took place, and over the next month, a tour through the kingdom to every village.

"He's right," Roman's mother remarked to her husband. "The rebels recklessly attacked the Desert King and Queen in broad daylight. Having every ruler, their council, and all the battalion in one place would be the perfect place to attack." He sighed. "We'll send word to the other royals to not come. It's too dangerous."

By the time Roman stopped by the florist and picked out a bundle of flowers he thought Violet would like, War said Violet was on her way to dinner with her parents in town and then they'd be home.

Deciding to give her alone time with them after not seeing them for a year, he headed home to get started on Violet's birthday gift.

Their birthdays, and his coronation, were the day after tomorrow, and he wanted it to be perfect.

Violet and War approached the bunker's gate and slipped inside with a nod to the night guards. A clucking sound drew their attention to the left side of the bunker's courtyard, and War froze.

Babs strutted toward them, her sights trained on the large tigon. The sheaths on War's head shot straight as his quills made an appearance. Violet looked between War and Babs.

War's low growl had Violet taking a step forward to put herself between the chicken and cat. "It's just Babs," she said to War slowly, "Roman's pet chicken. Have you not met her before?"

Everything happened at once.

Babs shot forward with a battle cry, Violet dove toward the bird before War could eat her, and War ran.

You'd have thought lightning struck his ass with how fast he took off. Babs gave chase, and Violet stared slack-jawed after the two. Babs was fast, she'd give her that, but the devil's little legs were nothing compared to the tigon.

War roared and disappeared behind the bunker. Babs had a long way to go before she reached the corner, and Violet couldn't decide if she wanted to laugh or follow them.

Roman charged out of the bunker fit to kill until Babs squawked and he saw her disappear around the backside of the building. He chuckled to himself and walked to Violet's side. "I see Babs broke out of the pen again."

Violet pointed in the direction the animals disappeared. "Why did War look terrified?"

Roman smirked. "Because he is, and he knows he can't kill her."

A beat of silence followed, followed by Violet's burst of laughter. Roman watched her, a look of wonder on his face. "I missed you today."

She kissed his lips lightly and looped her arm through his. "I missed you too."

They passed through the large sitting room, and Violet noticed one of Roman's handheld puzzles, along with a few stray leaves. "What in the world were you doing in here?"

A flush crept up his neck, and he scooped up the leaves, stuffing them in his pocket. "Nothing." Grabbing his puzzle, he turned to leave, but Violet reached out to stop him.

"Show me."

He gazed over his shoulder at her. "It's nothing. Just something I do to pass the time."

Violet shook her head. "You have a lot of them, and I've seen you with one before." He turned to her with a curious look. "When we were younger," she clarified. "I saw you at one of your birthday balls. You were on the small patio. I didn't tell you I was there, but I watched you. You started twisting it fast, but King Felix came out looking for you. It was small enough to put in your pocket."

The flush on his throat spread to his cheeks, and he cleared his throat. "They're called shape shifter puzzles. You match the symbols or colors on each moving piece together." He twisted the pieces with quick precision, too fast for Violet to track.

The smile on his face held her captive. It started small, but the closer he came to victory, the bigger it grew. They were *fun* for him. Since they were teenagers, she'd worried he'd never find something that brought him joy. Watching him was like watching a beautiful flower bloom under the summer sun.

He finished and held up the puzzle with triumph. It no longer resembled a jumbled mess, but a white rose with green leaves hugging the bud. Reaching out, she took the puzzle from him, stunned. "Rome, this is incredible."

He shrugged like it was nothing. "I like doing them."

"Can I keep this one?" She wanted to remember the smile on his face when he held out the rose puzzle for the rest of her life.

His brows lowered. "Of course."

Holding the rose like a timeless treasure, she grinned back at him. "Thank you. I know just the place."

The sound of Roman's footsteps followed her through their home until they wandered through the door to her sewing room. She proudly set the rose puzzle on her sketching desk and stepped back to admire it. "I love it."

"I love you, Violet."

She encircled him with her arms and rested her chin on his chest. "I love you, too, Roman Covington. Take me to bed?"

His soft smile turned wolfish. "Yes, Your Grace."

34

The next morning, Violet strolled into Roman's favorite candy shop to buy a box of his favorite chocolate bars. He'd written her a letter while she was away about a new bar at the shop he couldn't stop eating. It sounded delicious, and she couldn't wait to try one and see the look on his face when she presented him with more chocolate bars than he could eat in a week for his birthday tomorrow.

Much to Violet's dismay, Marissa sat in the corner of the shop, shoveling tiny chocolates into her mouth as she cried. She held a letter in her hand, staring at its contents with despair.

The paper, Violet noted, looked well-worn. The sight made her heart pinch. She knew the look of heartbreak when she saw it.

Guilt followed the sympathy. Had Violet misjudged Marissa? Clearly the woman loved someone else, and Violet had accused her of trying to steal Roman.

Sighing, she wove her way through the tables and sat across from Marissa. "Hey, are you okay?"

Marissa jumped and hid the paper in her lap, but when her watery eyes landed on Violet, they filled with resentment. "No thanks to you," she spat in an almost whisper. "You ruined everything." Stunned, Violet stared at Marissa, unable to form a reply. Marissa revealed the paper again and shook it. "He loved *me* until you came back." Her shoulders slumped and she looked miserably at the letter again. "Or maybe he used me to pass the time until you returned."

Dropping her shoulders pitifully, she dissolved into another fit of sobs. *What in the fuck is she talking about?* Violet plucked the letter from Marissa's hands with no resistance from the mess of a woman across from her.

She instantly regretted it, for on the paper Marissa had so lovingly read repeatedly, was an all too familiar penmanship and signature. With each word, Violet felt to the urge to empty the contents of her stomach, or cry, or burn Roman's favorite bakery to the godsdamn ground with Marissa inside.

Marissa,

Today I passed the pleasure house and thought of you. Specifically, of pushing you against the glass of my privacy box and winding your red hair around my fist while I fed you my cock from behind. Gods, it will look beautiful wrapped around my hand. And with my name on your lips? Fuck, I can't wait. I'm counting down the hours until then.

The first time we sat together at the pleasure house was the night I purchased a privacy box of my own. I knew I'd have you in it one day. Thank fuck that day is soon and thank you for agreeing to it. It's all I've thought about.

My cock could cut glass at the thought.

Soon.

Yours,

Roman

Marissa's face twisted into a cruel smile. "He wanted me." Her smile morphed into a sneer. "And now he barely speaks to me."

It couldn't be true. Violet knew Roman, and he wouldn't lie to her. "This letter is forged," Violet said matter-of-factly, "because Roman would never betray me like this."

Marissa threw her head back with humorless laughter. "You really believe that?" She leaned forward and lowered voice. "No matter how many tattoos he has, your name isn't on him, Violet. You *left* him, while I was here at his side. He wanted me." The sound of her love-sick sniffle made Violet want to commit a crime. "The talks we had... he loved me."

Violet snorted. "Roman spoke to you as a friend. Men are daft. He had no idea his friendship gave you misguided notions of romance."

Marissa's smug smile made her pretty face ugly. "Has Roman told you anything about me? Because I know all about you." *Bitch.* "I know no one wanted you in school. I know that even your boyfriend who took your virginity wished he'd had Vivian instead."

Violet fought to keep her expression impassive and scoffed. "Everyone knows those things, but nice try."

Marissa tsked, the condescending sound grating on Violet's last nerve. "I know Titus wouldn't fuck you either, but he had no problem fucking Vivian. It seems you're always second best. Isn't it weird that Roman speaks to me about your intimate personal life, but doesn't trust you enough to tell you anything about anyone else?"

She had Violet there, but that still didn't mean the letter was real. Even if it looked real. *Extremely* real.

Looking back at the letter, she pulled the paper close and

squinted. It was Roman's handwriting. His signature. His vernacular. One would be hard pressed to deny he'd written it, but Violet sensed otherwise. She knew Roman would never write the letter to Marissa, but she also didn't know how the woman knew about Titus.

Violet had told Roman that tidbit one night as she'd cried on his shoulder shortly after Titus left her. No one else knew. She was going to kick his ass, but first she needed to get to the bottom of this letter.

Without another word, she stood and stomped out of the candy shop with the letter clutched tightly in her hands.

War, who'd waited outside of the shop for Violet, trotted alongside her as she stalked toward the training arena. The beast, sensing her soured mood, cast worried glances her way.

She'd not been able to form enough words to tell him what his idiot bonded had done. He'd not only given Marissa the impression there was something between them, if even unintentionally, he'd also spilled her secrets, and now there was this blasted letter.

Roman loved her, and she knew that. She trusted him. But she'd also told him this would happen. Marissa wouldn't stop until she either had him or was forced to leave. Well, she'd just earned herself the latter because Violet wouldn't stand for the other woman's constant challenge.

The letter crinkled in her fist. *The nerve.*

A guard at the gate of the training arena smiled kindly and started to say something, but with one look at her face, he snapped his mouth shut.

"I need to see Roman," Violet said hotly.

"Yes, Your Grace," the guard said just as Roman burst through the arena door looking frantic.

"What's wrong?" he panted.

Violet glared at War. "You couldn't let me surprise him this once?"

Roman's hands clasped her face, but she batted them away. "Don't touch me when I'm pissed." She shook the letter. "What have you gotten yourself into?"

The prince looked at a complete loss. "I'm going to need a little more information, and fast."

Violet held out the letter to read the contents. She would ensure every guard and warrior within earshot heard the lengths Marissa would go to. "Today I passed the pleasure house and thought of you. Specifically, of pushing you against the glass of my privacy box and winding your red hair around my fist while I fed you my cock from behind."

Lowering the letter, she stared at Roman and noticed the muscle in his jaw flex. His expression no longer held confusion, but murderous intent. *Wait.* "Did you write this?"

"Violet, do not read another fucking word," Roman warned her through gritted teeth. The guard who'd greeted her stepped far away from the prince.

She raised her chin defiantly, and continued, "*Gods, it will look beautiful pulled tight in my hand. And with my name on—*"

"Enough!" Roman thundered, and her head snapped back.

"Did you just yell at me?" she demanded. "It's your fault Marissa thinks you're in love with her, not mine."

Roman ripped the letter from Violet's hand and she made a grab at it, but he held it above his head. "Every man within hearing distance will lose their head if you keep reading," he warned.

Why? she wondered silently, then said aloud, "I wanted everyone to hear the lengths that woman will go to to come between us," she stated calmly. "I want them to see how shameless she is."

The warriors and guards around them seemed to lean in with interest. *Perfect.*

Violet was usually a kind person, but if she was to be queen, people needed to learn she would not tolerate disrespect. Hopefully, they wouldn't hate her. *No.* She couldn't think that way. Her days of being a people pleaser were behind her. Just look where that'd gotten her in the past: walked all over.

Roman stared at her like she'd told him War could fly. "Why would Marissa think I love her? I've given her no indication." His eyes lowered to the letter and bulged. "What the fuck?" Emotions ran a gamut across his face. "I didn't write this letter to her. I wrote it to you."

Violet chewed on her lip, losing a bit of her bravado. How had Marissa gotten a letter meant for Violet? Addressed to Marissa?

"I wrote it right before I left for the border," Roman mused to himself, "but not to Marissa."

"Someone clearly intercepted the letter and, I don't know, traced it and changed the name, hair color, and sign off."

Roman's eyes ticked to Violet's hair. "Your hair is red, but I think you're right."

Violet picked up the end of her hair to inspect her auburn strands that were more brown than red. Men were clueless.

"When the candlelight in the pleasure house hits your hair, it looks more red than brown," he said defensively, reading her thoughts.

"It's not just the letter," Violet told him. "She knew things she shouldn't and claimed you divulged them to her. She then informed me that my name wasn't on you, and I had no claim." Roman wasn't a toy or a novelty, and it sickened Violet that so many people treated him as such. Violet, Marissa, random strangers who only wanted to be his friend because of who he was and what he could do for them.

Roman stalked to Ares who stood in the background, looking thoroughly amused, and murmured something low. The man nodded and took off running. "Let it be known," Roman bellowed for those around them to hear, "I have only ever loved Violet Maekin, your future queen. Any woman who says differently will be considered a traitor to the crown. I'll not have anyone disrespect my mate with falsehoods." He looked Violet dead in the eyes when he added, "If anyone mentions what I said about my mate in that letter, I will mount your head above my mantle."

Watching rebels almost hurt Violet was the scariest thing Roman had experienced. Seeing the fire in her eyes, not knowing why she looked fit to rip his head off for his naivety, was a close second.

An all-consuming fury raged within him, and it was all he could do to not shred his way through the capital until he found Marissa. He didn't know how she'd done it, but somehow, she'd changed his letter.

A letter with his private thoughts. How many other letters did they steal? If he found out someone had kept a letter Violet wrote from him, they'd not survive to live another day. Her words were his and no one else's.

The things he'd written had been for his mate and no one else. Knowing his warriors heard them, that they were likely picturing their queen being thoroughly fucked, caused Roman's blood to boil. Had Violet kept reading, he would have ripped them all limb from limb to banish the vision from their minds.

His anger did not belong to Violet, it belonged to Marissa, but his emotions were impossible to tame. What if Violet had believed Marissa? He could have lost her.

As his inner turmoil settled, he could admit that seeing Violet pissed off and out for blood made him want to fuck her into oblivion. He'd seen her many ways, but angry beyond reason was not one of them. Witnessing her fire stoked his own.

"You're not in the clear," Violet informed him and dropped her voice to a whisper. "You told her about Titus and me. She was quick to remind me I've always been second best. Dominic. Titus. Every other man who showed interest then promptly ignored me." He saw it then, the flicker of insecurity and hurt in her eyes as she tapped her chest. "There's something about me that sends men running, and the fact that she knew about all of them because you told her. I am *not* happy."

Shit. Roman had not realized how her *dating history* might have affected her. Unable to allow her to think something was wrong with her, he knew he had to confess what he'd done, but first he needed to correct her assumption that he'd ever betray her confidence. "I didn't tell Marissa anything, princess, I swear it. And you didn't send the other men running. I did."

Her brow furrowed. "What are you talking about?"

Licking his lips and praying she didn't kill him in front of everyone, he confessed. "Boys started to notice you when we were fourteen." Roman drank in her beautiful face. "How could they not? I couldn't stand it. If they showed interest in you, I *encouraged* them not to."

Violet gasped but recovered quickly. "And Dominic? Did you force him to want to fuck Vivian after taking my virginity?"

Roman's mood darkened further. "Never remind me what

he stole from me again, and no, I didn't force him to say that. I didn't even hear him say it, but if I had, I would have killed him in front of everyone instead of waiting for suggesting your sister held a candle to you."

Violet assessed him like a puzzle that needed to be solved. "*Instead of waiting?* What does that mean?"

Double shit. "I don't think you want to know."

His curious little mate wouldn't be deterred, like a dog with a bone. "Yes, I do."

Roman looked at those who still watched their row. He could order them to leave, but if they heard what he'd done, they'd know not to fuck with what was his. "I killed him later."

It was the first time Roman had killed anyone. He'd laid in wait for Dominic to recover from his injuries, let the man think he'd escaped death, then he'd cornered him.

"You humiliated Violet," Roman said, deceptively calm.

"I didn't mean what I said about Vivian," Dominic insisted. To Roman's surprise, he sounded genuine. "I don't know why I said it." The man raked a hand through his hair. "I'll never forgive myself for embarrassing Violet, but I'm hoping she will. I really like her."

That did it. If Dominic thought Roman would let him anywhere near Violet again, he was sorely mistaken. Roman stepped forward and wrapped his hand around Dominic's neck. The man clawed at Roman's grip as it cut off his lifeline. "Ask for her forgiveness from hell. Tell Orcus hello for me."

Violet covered her mouth, and Roman wrapped his fingers around her wrist and pulled it away. "I couldn't let him live after disrespecting something so sacred."

She gaped at him. "You can't kill people for being assholes, Roman."

He snorted. "If I killed people for being assholes, Slayton would not be breathing, princess."

She dropped her hands and stared at him incredulously. "You *killed* a man, and you're making a joke?"

Roman frowned at her. "That wasn't a joke."

"And Titus?" she asked.

He heard her apprehension, knew what she feared. "No. I planned on killing him once I found a way to dissolve the bond with Vivian, but I never would have allowed him to hurt you the way he did."

The guard closest to him took a few more hesitant steps backward. *Good*, Roman thought. Every person in his kingdom should fear him where his mate was concerned.

"How many people have you hurt because of me?" Violet rasped. Her tone suggested condemnation of his behavior, but her eyes told a different story. The black of her pupils ate the blue of her irises, and her lids drooped slightly.

He tried not to smile, he really did. He invaded her space further, leaving nothing between them, and wrapped his hand around the side of her neck. "Hurt or killed, princess?"

"Oh my gods," she breathed.

"You are *everything* to me." Leaning down, he dropped his mouth to hers. "I will soak the earth beneath your feet with the blood of anyone who disrespects you." Roman straightened and spun to look at the small crowd. "I would lay my life down for this kingdom and any of you." He ushered a still-stunned Violet forward. "Except when it comes to your queen. I would not hesitate to make a necklace of your bones if she'd only ask."

He expected abject horror, but he saw none. His warriors and the few guards who stood around merely answered with variations of their understanding and respect.

Violet wondered how hot hell was because it would surely be her eternal resting place for the thrill that ran through her at Roman's declaration.

He'd scared off the boys in school. All these years she'd thought it was something about her they hadn't liked, but it'd been Roman's doing.

It should infuriate her.

He'd killed Dominic.

It should horrify her.

It should make her feel a lot of things.

More in love than ever shouldn't be one of them.

35

"I told you she wanted you," Violet said, smugness sneaking into her irritated tone.

"How was I supposed to know she thought I wanted her when I'd never said that?" he asked, perplexed. Never once had he given Marissa any indication he wanted anything more than friendship with her. Friendship was pushing it. She worked for him.

His stomach clenched uncomfortably. He'd had her follow Violet to protect her. Would she have intentionally allowed someone to hurt Violet? The thought stopped him cold.

Violet halted beside him and shook his hand clasped in hers. "Hey," she said softly, "I'm not mad at you. Irritated at your obliviousness, yes, but not mad. I know you'd never betray me that way."

Looking into Violet's eyes, his fear and anger subsided. "I can deal with your anger, but I can't deal with the thought of you being hurt because I trusted the wrong person." Her head tilted in question. *How many confessions will I make today?*

"Before you left to travel, I had Marissa follow you during the day when I couldn't to ensure your safety."

Violet paled. "You had *her* follow me?"

Maybe he should have lied; one time in their entire lives wasn't that bad in the grand scheme of things. "I wanted you safe."

"You could have assigned anyone else," she protested. "She is more likely to kill me than save me."

Roman's body tensed as if ready to strike. "I thought I could trust her. She'd proven herself trustworthy. I had no idea she would fall in love with me." Violet's mouth set in a hard line, and he smirked. "Can you blame her?"

His mate's nostrils flared, and she tried to pull her hand from his. When that didn't work, she whacked him in the gut with her left hand. "It is not the time to joke. I want her sent out of the capital."

Roman pressed his lips together. If he sent Marissa's body out of the capital, it wouldn't be a lie to promise Violet her request.

Slender fingers thumped him on the forehead. "What is that look?"

Sighing, he lifted her hand to his lips for a kiss. "Princess, I can't let her live."

"What is wrong with you?" Violet gasped. "Gods, Roman, as much as I love you, I cannot condone killing people for disrespecting me. I already have to live with Dominic's death on my conscience."

"Dominic's death is not your doing." He released her hand and grabbed her chin, forcing her to look at him when he said, "It is mine. They're all mine, as is every ounce of blood I will spill in your name. You would never kill someone, even if they deserved it." Leaning down, he pressed a kiss to the top of her head. "But you cannot ask me to change who I am."

Violet stared up at him, her mouth opening with the beginnings of a thought, only to close again. Another man might worry she would turn away from his dark nature, but Roman feared nothing of the sort. They were made for one another. She would no sooner turn from him than she would rip out her own heart.

At her resigned sigh and disgruntled expression, he grinned like a cat. "I don't want you to change," she admitted, "but will you at least try alternative measures going forward? Exile to another kingdom, maybe?"

"I'll try," he conceded.

Violet nodded and blew out another breath. "Thank you." She looked around them and frowned. "Where is War? I still need to finish shopping."

The subject change gave Roman whiplash, but he recovered quickly. "I can go with you."

"I need to pick up your birthday gift," she replied. "I ran into Marissa before I could buy it."

He suppressed a smile. Gifts didn't interest him, except from her. It was another memento to put in his closet to look at when he missed her. "I'll call War."

There was something he wanted to ask her, but it felt insignificant in light of the Marissa scandal. Surprising her had been the original plan, but he doubted she'd want another thing sprung on her out of the blue. "I have somewhere I want to take you tonight," he began, catching her attention. "I have a competition, a big one. The biggest one of the year, actually. Competitors from all over Eden show up."

She must have noted his nerves because she moved to stand in front of him. "What kind of competition?"

Roman licked his lips and dug a small shape shifter puzzle from his pocket. "A shape shifter competition. I've been competing in them for the last year." Heat prickled the apples of his cheeks.

Violet gingerly took the puzzle from his hand. "They have competitions? Why didn't you tell me? I'd love to go."

He'd been worried the idea of watching people race to solve puzzles would bore her. Hopefully she didn't laugh at the next part. He wouldn't blame her if she did. It was a bit ridiculous. "I compete in disguise. They call me the Masked Shifter."

He saw it, the moment Violet rolled her lips together to fight off the laugh, making his own lips twitch. "That's interesting," she said after a beat.

Roman hung his head and laughed. "It's horrendous, but I don't want people to know it's me."

Violet pursed her lips. "Do people tease puzzlers? I won't let that stand." She lifted her chin, looking every bit the queen she was. Gods, he loved her.

He coughed to cover a laugh. "Puzzlers?"

"I don't know what you're called," she mumbled, "but if you can kill people for disrespecting me, I can make a law that says people can't make fun of puzzlers."

Roman barked out a laugh. "An entire law?" Violet bristled and he picked her up. Her legs wrapped instinctively around him. "No one makes fun of us, princess. The competitions are quite popular, but I didn't want people treating me differently than the other competitors for being a royal."

Understanding dawned on her and she wrapped her arms around her neck. "Well, Mr. Masked Shifter, we better get home and get you ready."

Violet bounced on the balls of her feet as she stood in the royal viewing box with War sitting beside her. "Did you know he did this?"

The tigon nodded. Oh, how she wished the beast could communicate more with her because she had a million questions.

Roman and Violet entered the large complex separately so as not to give away his identity. The complex was a catch-all venue where large-scale events took place, such as concerts, popular plays, sparring competitions, and so forth. Never in a million years would she have thought puzzle competitions would be on that list.

Murmurs rippled through the crowd and heads turned in her direction. Most people gave her a wide berth with War at her side, but it didn't stop them from staring, though that didn't explain their abrupt attention now.

"He's nervous."

Violet jumped and flipped around to see Queen Sarah and King Felix standing behind her in the royal box. "You knew he did this?" she asked Roman's parents.

Felix chuckled and plopped his muscular body down in one of the throne-style chairs. "Who do you think helped him find the perfect mask?"

Violet glanced down at Roman's table. A skeleton mask covered his entire face except his eyes. "It's terrifying."

Sarah sat delicately beside her husband. "Intimidation is key." The queen exuded elegant grace. You'd never know she could rip your head off with her bare hands. Violet didn't know if it was true, but the queen was a fierce fighter and terrifying in her own right. It wouldn't surprise Violet to find out the queen could do it.

"It's hard to see from up here," Violet complained and

grabbed on the rail to lean closer. "I should have brought a mask."

"I can glamour you invisible," Sarah offered. "Roman will be able to see you, but no one else will."

Violet perked up. "You wouldn't mind? I've only seen him do a puzzle once, and I want to see his face."

Sarah smiled warmly. "Anything for you, honey. Take care not to bump into people if you can. It gives them quite a fright, and they start spouting nonsense about ghosts and spirits."

Violet giggled. "I'll be careful." She gave Sarah a quick hug and hurried to the box exit. "Thank you."

"I'm surprised you showed up after last month's ass-kicking," a cocky voice called out to Roman.

Grinning under his mask, he turned to Kelty, a short fae man with close-cropped dark brown hair, dark umber skin, and a stout build to match his square jaw. Despite being ten years Roman's senior, the man had a child-like quality about him.

He was obnoxious, brilliant, and Roman's biggest competition.

All year they'd gone back and forth, battling each other for first place. Used to being the best at everything he did, losing to Kelty had knocked Roman's ego down a peg or two. For the first time, Roman was truly nervous. Sure, he'd been nervous before his first match, but there was something different about today's competition. Not only did the winner earn the title of Eden's best shape shifter competitor, but Violet was in the crowd watching him for the first time. His head swam a little at the thought.

"Come to offer me your congratulations early?" he shot back and widened his stance.

Kelty grinned, his mouth stretching from ear to ear. "You've lost the last three competitions."

Roman's fingers itched to reach for one of the shifting puzzles to practice. Usually, he and Kelty went back and forth with their wins, but Violet's impending homecoming had distracted Roman the last few times. But not today. Today, she sat in the royal box, watching him, and he'd be damned if he lost. "I like to lull my enemies into a false sense of calm," he lied.

Kelty, the ass, saw right through him and clapped him on the shoulder. "There's always next year, Mask."

Roman pushed his hand away. "I won't lose today."

Kelty must have sensed something in Roman's demeanor, because he hung his hands on his hips and studied him carefully. "What makes you so sure?"

Roman swept his gaze over the crowd, snagging on Violet standing in front of the stands on the competition floor with War at her side. Spectators weren't allowed on the competition floor, but no one noticed Violet standing there.

When her eyes met his, she waved excitedly and gave him two thumbs up. His heart soared, and he tapped his heart, then pointed at her. Her smile widened, and he winked before turning back to Kelty. "Because my girl is here."

Kelty looked from Roman to the area behind him. The man's eyes skipped right over Violet, and Roman realized Kelty couldn't see her. No one could. He looked at the royal box and spotted his parents. *They glamoured her.*

Smiling wide, he brushed past Kelty to take his place at his assigned table, and called over his shoulder, "May the best man win."

The speed at which the contestants' hands twisted and pulled the puzzles made Violet's head spin. Every table housed five puzzles of various sizes, each one more complicated than the next, and Violet's voice scratched as she clapped and cheered each time Roman moved on to the next shifting puzzle.

Roman reached his final piece before anyone else, and Violet jumped up and down, clapping so hard her hands hurt. Another man she'd seen speaking with Roman before the match was mere seconds behind the prince. When he moved on to his last puzzle, people in the crowd stood, screaming. Some chanted Roman's alias while others yelled the name "Kelty."

Violet vibrated with anticipation. She wanted Roman to win more than anything. He'd been so nervous; he'd never admit it outright, but she could tell. This competition meant something to him, so it meant something to her too.

Minutes passed quickly as Kelty and Roman's puzzles took shape, and the crowd fell to a quiet buzz as everyone held their breaths. Never had Violet thought a puzzle competition would generate the same buzz as a sparring tournament, but it did.

Then it happened. Roman dropped his puzzle, an anatomically correct heart, and jumped back with his hands raised. The crowd went wild, but instead of basking in their screams, Roman turned, locked eyes with Violet, and took off running.

Her heart swelled, and when he closed the distance between them, she jumped into his arms, and he swung her around. With his head buried in her neck, he laughed, the sound so full of joy and excitement, Violet almost wept.

"You did it," she whispered in his ear. "I knew you'd win."

Roman pulled back and yanked off his mask to kiss her, his excitement spreading to every part of her. The crowd changed their tone, gasps of surprise and loud chatter rising around the arena.

Violet startled and shifted her head to look around. *Everyone is staring.* Sarah must have dropped the glamour on Violet. "They're going to know who you are," she hissed. He couldn't glamour them because having them disappear into thin air would be a dead giveaway.

Come to think of it, why hadn't he glamoured himself to look like someone else?

She must have asked out loud, because he replied, "I need to focus all of my attention on the puzzles, not glamour."

"Why did you take your mask off?"

He shrugged. "I needed to kiss you."

"Your Grace?" a voice said from behind Roman and Violet. They both turned to see the moderator of the competition holding a trophy. A golden cube-shaped shape shifting puzzle sat atop a black stand with a golden plaque that said SHAPE SHIFTING CHAMPION.

Roman beamed with pride and thought this might be the best day of his life, having his girl here while he won something he'd wanted since he'd first discovered the competitions existed.

Roman chuckled. "I guess the secret is out."

"Hiding your hideous face was smart, Your Grace," a boisterous voice boomed good-naturedly. "Wouldn't want to scare the others. It'd be an unfair advantage."

Kelty appeared from behind the moderator and stuck out his hand with a wide smile. Roman's large hand engulfed the other man's and he grinned back. "Don't be jealous because I'm prettier than you."

Kelty laughed, a loud, infectious sound. "It's been an honor going against you this year." He looked at Violet and winked. "I beat him more times than he beat me."

Roman tugged her into his side. The bastard was too charming for his own good. Violet held out her hand. "I'm Violet."

Kelty bobbed his head. "The queen."

Violet fidgeted with the necklace around her neck and laughed. "Not yet."

Kelty grinned from ear to ear. "Tomorrow is close enough. It's a pleasure to meet you, Your Grace."

Violet waved him off. "Please, call me Violet."

"Call her Your Grace," Roman interjected, "or I'll kill you."

Kelty threw his head back with a loud laugh and clapped his hands. "So I've heard. Don't worry, Mask, I won't touch your bride."

Violet jabbed Roman in the side with her elbow. "Stop threatening to kill people."

Roman looked down with a crooked smile. "No."

"Why'd you really hide your face?" Kelty mused, picking up Roman's mask from the ground.

Roman scrubbed a hand through his hair. "I didn't want people to treat me differently because of who I am."

Kelty snorted. "Confident in your importance, aren't you?" Violet giggled, and Roman cut his eyes to her. "Will you compete next year?"

"Probably not now that everyone knows." He looked pointedly at the crowd watching him with rapt attention.

Kelty twisted around the stare at the others on the competition floor. "They're looking at me." He pointed to his face. "This is a work of art."

Violet laughed again and Roman frowned, not liking another man's jokes summoning her laughter.

"Your Grace, we typically have the top three winners stand on the podium to have their pictured sketched," the moderator said and held out the trophy. "If that's okay?"

Roman accepted the trophy and clapped Kelty on the shoulder. "I don't mind at all."

"Congratulations, son," Roman's father said as he and the queen approached. "A perfect way to start your reign."

Roman's mother pulled him into a tight hug. "We're so proud of you."

A few palace guards surrounded the monarchs, forcing the crowd to keep a wide berth. The queen loved talking to the townspeople, but in large crowds such as this one, things could get dangerous fast.

Roman thanked them both and kissed the side of Violet's head. "Do you mind waiting with my parents while I pose for the picture?"

"Of course not," Violet said, shooing him toward the podium. "I plan on having one of the palace artists copy it to hang in my sewing room."

Roman shook his head lightly, kissed her once more for good measure, and jogged over the podium, wondering how his life could get any better than this.

36

Violet held open the door to the beauty shop for War to slip inside. After Roman's competition, she'd convinced him to let her escape for a while to get ready for their birthdays the following day. She needed her hair trimmed and wanted to pick out a new lip paint. Roman didn't know it yet, but Violet organized a surprise party for after his private coronation.

Only Roman's real friends and his and Violet's families would be there since Roman hated big celebrations. She couldn't wait to see the look of surprise on his face.

The moment she stepped into the shop with War, conversation ceased. They knew her here, she'd been coming for years, but today they looked at her differently. Word traveled fast, and everyone knew she was to be the next queen. Many still believed the crown should find Vivian and force her to marry Roman.

Despite Violet's newfound fame, people rarely approached her with War at her side. She'd never been more grateful for the terrifying beast.

Except when he'd saved her life. Twice.

Gunnar, Violet's usual stylist, offered her a bright smile. His light brown shoulder-length curls brushed the top of his shoulders, longer than the last time she'd seen him. His blue, flowy top floated around the top of his fitted pants. The click of his heeled boots against the stone floor quickened as he approached and opened his arms wide.

"Violet!" He beamed at her, his light olive skin glowing with excitement. She laughed and returned his quick embrace. "How long have you been back?"

"A couple of days," she replied. "How have you been? I missed you." She picked up the ends of her too-long hair. "My hair missed you too."

Gunnar picked up a lock of her hair to examine the ends. "Did you not get a trim this entire year?"

"No," she admitted sheepishly. He blanched. You'd think she'd told him she'd washed it with molasses. "I've only ever had my hair cut here, and it made me nervous. Do you have an opening for a trim today? I know it's late notice."

Gunnar's face fell. "I don't. Unless you don't mind coming back late tonight?"

Violet chewed on the inside of her cheek in thought. She'd planned on spending the evening with Roman, celebrating his win. "I have plans, but that's okay. Does anyone else have an opening?"

She'd let others at the shop cut her hair before and they'd done a great job, she just preferred Gunnar. He'd been cutting her hair for years.

"Cassie, do you have an opening for a trim?" Gunnar asked one of the other women in the shop.

A woman with strawberry blonde hair, fair skin, and a sassy smile looked up. Violet liked Cassie too, and she held her breath. Cassie's face fell. "No, but I can stay late."

"I have time right now."

No, Violet almost groaned aloud. Becks, another stylist with dirty blond hair, a square jaw, and deep-set blue eyes sauntered over. She and Violet had gone to school at the palace together, but they were never friendly because Becks and Vivian were friends. How, Violet didn't know. Becks didn't enjoy sparring any more than Violet did.

"I don't mind," the woman added with a faux smile.

Violet glanced at the bottom of her hair and back to Becks, weighing her options. She desperately needed a trim, the ends of her hair looked like a worn-out straw broom, but she didn't want to ask one of the others to stay late, nor did she want to cut into her time with Roman.

"That'd be great," she replied with a smile she hoped looked genuine.

What's the worst that could happen?

Roman sat back on the large lounger in his study, leaned his head back, and connected with War.

War, who'd been lying down, stretched, stood, and maneuvered himself to sit in front of Violet. He knew what Roman wanted before he'd even asked.

"Has anyone given her any trouble?"

"No," War replied. *"She is getting her hair cut."*

Roman's lip curled when he took in the scene. *"Why is Becks cutting her hair? Where is Gunnar?"*

Roman had watched Violet get her hair cut countless times over the years, and never had she let Becks touch her. He'd never seen Becks disrespect Violet, but neither was she nice.

"Oops," Becks gasped.

Violet stiffened, and Gunnar, who stood behind another

customer nearby, looked over with abject horror. "What happened?" Violet demanded.

"I snipped a bit more than I meant to," Becks replied, sounding apologetic, but the smirk she tried to hide said she was anything but. "It wasn't much." She held out a piece of hair about five inches long. "Just an inch or two longer than the trim you wanted. I'll just even it out."

Violet's chin wobbled and her eyes filled with tears. Roman watched as his mate fought hard not to cry. His girl swallowed hard, and whispered, "Okay."

Becks smiled and lifted Violet's hair, but Gunnar swooped in, moving her aside. "I'll finish it." The steely snap of his words took everyone in the shop by surprise. Never once had Gunnar sounded anything but peppy, until now.

Roman cut the connection to War. He had a certain stylist to see.

Violet smoothed a hand down her hair again, feeling another round of tears coming on. Her hair that once hung almost to her waist, now hovered around her chest. Still long by most standards, but much shorter than she'd adorned for most of her life.

What will Roman say?

Nodding to the evening guards at the bunker gate, Violet unlocked the gate and pushed inside. "Are you coming?" she asked War. The beast shook his head and trotted off once Violet shut and locked the gate.

"Roman?" Violet called into the quiet house.

"I'll be right there," his baritone voice answered back.

Unable to wait to see him, she followed the sound of his voice to the dining room. She gaped when she stepped inside and looked around. Flower garlands hung from the ceiling of the intimate dining room, petals were scattered on the floor and table, and Roman stood on a chair, attaching strings of beads to the wall.

"What is this?"

Roman jerked and dropped the beads. Violet had a feeling had it not been for his natural grace and impeccable coordination, he would have toppled over the arm of the chair.

"You're not supposed to be in here," he accused. "I told you I'd be out in a moment."

"I couldn't wait to see you." She rounded the small dining table and stood next to him, looking up at his six-foot-four frame balancing on the tall dining chair. "Come down and give me a kiss."

A boyish smile took over his face, and he jumped down to scoop her into his arms. "This was supposed to be a surprise for breakfast."

Violet wrapped her arms around his neck and kissed him. "It was a surprise, and I love it."

He looked at the decorations. "Yeah?"

She giggled and pecked his lips. "Yeah." Releasing him, she inspected the table, noting a flower crown, similar to the ones her neighbor's son used to make her.

Very similar.

Picking it up, she examined it closely. "Who made this?" Did he know about the little boy who grew up next to her cottage?

"I did," he said sheepishly. Her head snapped up, and red crept along Roman's neck. "You used to wear them when we were younger, and I always thought you looked like a faerietale princess."

Violet blinked as her mind put the pieces together. "You

left me flower crowns on my porch," she said dumbly. "Not Cooper."

The boyish grin returned. "And you always wore them."

Never had Violet experienced mortification and affection at the same time. Affection because Roman was, well, being Roman, and mortification because every time she'd received a crown over the years, she'd sought out Cooper and told him thank you.

"Oh my gods, he thinks I'm crazy," she whispered to herself.

Roman's smile faltered. "Who?"

Violet lifted the flower crown. "I thought Cooper made the flower crowns, and every time you left one, I found him and told him thank you." Roman pressed his lips together and his cheeks puffed out. "It's not funny," she wailed. "No wonder he gave me strange looks. He wasn't embarrassed, he thought I was randomly thanking him for that first crown years later."

"Why did you think a child made them?" Roman asked with a frown.

Violet set down the crown and covered her face. "I bet he told his parents how weird I am."

Roman removed her hands from her face and cupped the sides of her neck, tilting her head to look at him. "You'll be queen soon. Who cares if they think you're weird?"

Before she could protest, he claimed her lips. The soft kiss soon turned heated, and Roman lifted Violet into his arms. "Let me take your mind off of things."

Roman carried Violet to their room and laid her down on the plush bed. The look in his eyes set her body on fire. She'd never felt more alive.

Within seconds, he'd ripped her dress down the middle and shoved the fabric aside to take her in. "Beautiful."

Lowering his head to her left breast, he took one of her erect nipples into his mouth and tugged with his teeth.

Violet hissed and wiggled beneath him, unsure if she liked the pain or not. He ran his warm tongue over the stinging skin, soothing it. She liked it. Fisting his hair, she pulled him closer, his face pressing against her breast.

His deep laugh vibrated across her skin, and he sucked the peak into his mouth, gentle this time. The talented man alternated between sucking, licking, and biting. Using his right hand, he pinched her other nipple, then ghosted his palm over it to gently squeeze her soft flesh. Switching sides, he continued his assault, and Violet's pussy grew from damp to soaked in a matter of seconds.

"Roman," she pleaded and yanked on his hair.

"Tell me what you need, princess."

"I—I don't know," she breathed. "I need you everywhere."

Her glassy eyes found his, and a wolfish grin spread across his face. "If you want me in every hole, I'll need to fuck that pretty mouth of yours while I eat your perfect cunt. Is that what you want?"

It is now. "Yes, please."

Flipping her around, he maneuvered her until the world was upside down. The blood rushed to her head as it hung off the side of the bed, and she had an eye level view of Roman's cock springing free from his pants.

"If I push too hard, tell me." He waited for her okay before running his thumb across her bottom lip. "Open."

Violet darted her tongue across her lips, catching the tip of his thumb, and opened her mouth. "You mind so well," he murmured and grabbed his cock to guide it past her lips and over her tongue. His tortured groan made her grin. "Fucking hell, princess."

Leaning forward, he ran his tongue down her stomach, to

the juncture of her thighs. She heard him inhale through his nose and tried to close her legs. He tutted. "Spread your thighs or I'll make you."

Goosebumps peppered her skin, and more arousal leaked from her opening. "That's my girl," he praised and lowered his mouth to her pussy. Violet bucked her hips, which made her body scoot closer to Roman's hips. She gagged, and he pulled his hips back to let her breathe.

"Eager to choke on my cock, princess?"

She could barely fit him in her mouth, let alone answer him. A thick finger swirled around her opening and dipped inside. Moaning around him, she gripped his muscular thigh with one hand and encircled his cock with the other.

An intrusion pressed against Violet's back entrance, and she stiffened on reflex. "Relax," he commanded. "You wanted me in every hole. Let me do my job."

She released the tension in her muscles, and Roman worked his finger into her, pushing past her tight ring of muscles. Her body sucked him in, and his cock jumped in her mouth.

"I'm going to move now. If you need a break, tap my leg twice." He looked back at her under his arm. "Tap once if you understand." She tapped his thigh, and he winked. "Good girl."

He descended on her with the hunger of a man starved. She cried out just as he pushed the head of his cock against the back of her throat. Gagging, she squeezed his thighs, refusing to give in.

When his cock pushed to the back of her throat again, she swallowed to take him deep, concentrating on breathing through her nose. Though concentrating grew difficult with his tongue pumping into her pussy as his stubbled chin rubbed against her clit.

His finger still worked her backside, a sensation she'd not

yet experienced, and her body tingled with sensory overload. Her hips writhed beneath Roman's face, and her thighs quivered.

A tightness built in her core, and she unintentionally sucked his cock harder. Roman jerked and pressed his face into her pussy, momentarily stopping. "If you keep that up, I'm going to fill your mouth until it spills down your face." The barely leashed control in his voice urged her on, and she pulled his hips closer, sucking hard.

The thick head of his cock slid down her throat, and they both moaned. Their hips fucked the other's face, their paces increasing together. Another intrusion joined the first in her back hole, and the two fingers gently scissored.

She cried out and tightened around them, coming harder than ever. Roman sucked her clit into her mouth, intensifying her already explosive climax. Something spilled out of her, but she was too far gone to care because Roman quickly moved his tongue back down to lap up every drop he could.

He groaned against her, his cock jerking and shooting hot cum down her throat. His face rubbed against her pussy as his hips fucked her mouth in earnest. With his dick hitting her throat and the cum gathering there, she couldn't breathe. Violet tapped his leg twice, and he freed himself from her mouth, extracted his face and fingers from between her legs, and hoisted her up.

To her mortification, she coughed, spewing cum everywhere, including on his chest.

Roman rubbed soothing circles on her back, holding her hair out of her face. She didn't look up; she couldn't. *How fucking embarrassing.*

Roman kneeled beside the bed and moved into her line of sight. "Are you okay?" The concern in his voice made her want to die.

The first time she sucked his cock, she spit his own cum all over him. *Gods, just take me now.*

"Violet," he said with a sense of urgency. "Talk to me."

Finally, meeting his eyes, she nodded. "I'm sorry."

His head popped back. "Sorry? What the fuck for?" He motioned to his chest. "For this?"

She nodded again and chewed on her lip.

Roman's mouth gaped right before he laughed, and she wanted the ground to open up and swallow her whole. "Baby, that was the hottest fucking thing I have ever seen."

Violet's brows drew together. He had to be lying.

Reaching down, he ran the fingers that hadn't gone in her ass through the cum on his chest and brought it to her face. "I filled you with so much cum you fucking choked." He spread the cum on her lips. "I'm in you so completely that I'm spilling out. It will be hard not to do that every time."

He wiped more from his skin and stuck his fingers in his mouth. "Suck. Just because you spit it out doesn't mean you're not going to swallow it."

Violet's nipples tightened and her embarrassment subsided, replaced by a different kind of heat. Roman repeated his movements methodically until he'd wiped every drop of excess from both their bodies. "Now let me fill the rest of you. Turn around and get on your knees."

Roman stared at his mate's glistening cunt and thought he might blow before he even touched her. *Fuck.* He'd never get over the sight of her choking on his cock and cum. Godsdamn that was hot.

Unable to resist, he licked her from front to back, his eyes rolling back in his head. "Roman," she squealed, making him smile.

"You're my favorite taste, baby." He licked her again. "I'd rub you on my food before every meal if I could."

She looked over her shoulder and scrunched her nose. "I'm not sitting on your food."

Another lick. "I'll spread it with my fingers."

Every inch of Violet's skin flushed. "You're insane."

"We've already established that." Roman gathered up her silken hair, twisted it, wrapped it around his fist like a rope, and notched the head of his cock in the entrance of her cunt. "Brace yourself."

She tried to turn her head to look at him again, but he pulled on her hair and slammed into her heated body. A scream of pleasure tore from Violet's throat, and Roman wrapped his free hand around her hips.

Withdrawing, he slammed into her again, knowing he wouldn't last long. "Play with your clit," he commanded, pleased when she reached down to work herself.

He moved, and Violet called out his name as he thrust into her. Moving his hand from her hip to his mouth, he covered it in spit and pressed it into her tight ass. One day he'd fuck her there, but not yet. He'd researched the best way, and she needed to be prepped first.

Their moans and heavy breathing filled the room, and Roman worried he'd spend before her. "Come on, princess. Come on my cock like a good girl."

Violet pushed her hips back and moved her hand faster over her sensitive clit. The slick walls around Roman's cock quivered, and he almost sighed with relief. Seconds later, she screamed and squeezed her cunt around him, milking his own release.

Roman pulled out of her with a groan and climbed into

bed, dragging her into his arms. "That was incredible," Violet said around her panting breaths. "I've never experienced anything like it."

Roman tried to push aside the thought of her with another man and focused on her sentiment. "Same."

She burst out laughing and rolled on top of him. The still-long strands of her hair covered her perfect breasts, taunting him to push them away, but Violet interrupted his thoughts with a kiss. "I love you, Roman Covington."

Roman smiled and whispered against her lips, "And I love you. Obsessively so."

37

Roman watched Violet sleep, unable to fall under himself. He would turn twenty-five at midnight, a moment he'd been dreading since Vivian broke their bond. His parents speculated the gods could grant him another mate on his twenty-fifth birthday, since it was the next and final birthday blessed by the gods.

On an heir's twenty-fifth birthday, the magic trapping them in their kingdom released, and they took over their kingdom. Most heirs couldn't wait for the day, but not Roman. It could seal the fate of another woman. He couldn't lie to Violet, and if she'd not marry him anyway and break the bond, his new mate must die or marry someone else immediately.

Glancing at the clock, he blew out a shaky breath. A few seconds until midnight. Roman closed his eyes.

He stilled at the unease of ethereal voices whispering in his ear.

Violet.

His eyes flew open. The organ in his chest beat double-time, and his hands trembled. Could it be? Had they righted their wrong?

He tried to jump out of bed, but the sheets tangled in his feet, and he tumbled face first to the ground with a loud thud.

Roman heard Violet stir, the sheets rustle, and her melodic voice call out, "Roman?"

"Down here," he rasped, unable to move. If he'd imagined the voices, it would crush him. He'd marry Violet no matter what because regardless of what the gods said, she was his true mate, but Roman wanted, more than anything, to feel the bond with her.

Her hair swung over her shoulders as she peeked over the side of the bed, furrowing her brow. What happened next would have brought him to his knees had he been standing.

Violet rubbed her sternum. "I feel weird."

Roman cleared the knot from his throat and tried to control his breathing. He could *feel* her confusion, and a rush of relief cast out the nervous energy. "Did you feel like you were going to pass out from nerves?"

Seeing the realization take over her face, *feeling* her nervous excitement, followed by the prettiest smile he'd ever seen, brought the knot back to his throat. "Yes," she whispered. They stared at each other in awe until she laughed, the purest sound of joy he'd ever heard, and launched herself at him.

He caught her with an *oof* and rocked back on the floor. "We're mates?" she clarified.

He grinned and brought her in for a kiss. "We've always been mates, princess. The gods just took a while to catch up."

Their kiss slowed into something more than lust or love. Words couldn't describe how it felt to feel your partner's emotions, to know how much they loved you. The gods had deprived him of this, of what belonged to him, and he'd never forgive them.

Roman rolled them over until he hovered above Violet, his eyes boring into hers. "You're mine in every way," he told her softly. "Forever. In every lifetime. No god or man can take you from me without joining me in death, and if they send me to hell for my sins, I will claw my way back to you, princess. Always."

"What makes you think I won't follow you to hell?" she asked, and he *felt* her truth and conviction. "I gave you up once. I won't do it again."

Reaching between them, Roman guided his cock to her cunt and rubbed it along her seam, thankful they'd never gotten dressed. The head of his dick wept with precum, and he knew things would go fast. "I don't know how long I'll last," he warned.

In answer, Violet hooked one of her legs around his waist and lifted her hips. He sank into her until he bottomed out, both of them gasping at the sensation of not only the physical, but the bond. Their pleasure mixed together, feeding off the other.

"I don't think I'll last long either," Violet whispered. "I can feel you." Roman rotated his hips to grind against her clit, and he shuddered with the sensation from them both. "Oh my gods."

Roman pulled out and thrust inside over and over again, each pass stronger than the last. He couldn't stop the strangled sounds tumbling from his mouth any more than Violet could stop her screams. Everything throbbed and tingled and tightened.

"Fuck," he ground out.

Violet clawed at his back and wrapped both legs around his waist. "I'm close. I'm so fucking close."

Roman looked between them, where his cock disappeared into her swollen pussy. "Look how well you take my cock, baby." He pulled out slowly and paused until she lifted her head to see. The blue in her eyes thinned in favor of her dark pupils. "Your greedy little cunt needs me."

He thrust into her, hard, and she threw her head back with a scream. She thrashed and called out his name, begging for release. His thumb found her swollen clit and pressed tight circles until her legs drew up and her back bowed.

Her pleasure hit him like a ton of stone, and he almost blacked out from the intensity of it. Without warning, his release hit them both, and he didn't know if they'd survive it.

Roman didn't know how long it took to ride out their waves of pleasure; he didn't know how long he stayed inside her, catching his breath, and he didn't know when they'd crawled back into bed.

What he did know was that he'd never been happier.

"Happy birthday, princess."

Violet listened to Roman sleep, his deep breaths lulling her into her own slumber. The bond had soothed a part of her soul she hadn't known was raw.

She'd be lying if she said she hadn't been scared the gods would give Roman a second chance mate who wasn't her, and when she'd realized she could feel his emotions, she'd almost burst into happy tears.

Roman Covington belonged to her, and she belonged to him. She'd always wanted it, but he'd always known it.

And now Violet understood why Roman would kill, *has* killed, for her, and prayed she would never have to do the same.

Because she would.

Without hesitation.

38

Violet stood in a small room near the throne room, trying, and failing, to calm down. Today marked her, Roman, and Vivian's twenty-fifth birthdays, but instead of celebrating Roman becoming king, he'd asked her to marry him instead.

He'd promised they would have a grand celebration and redo the ceremony for the public so she could plan the wedding of her dreams. Violet didn't need a grandiose wedding, though she'd always wanted one. You couldn't torture that confession out of her, though, because she wouldn't risk Roman feeling bad for taking that from her. He didn't take anything; he gave her everything.

"Are you ready, monkey?" her father asked her.

Smoothing a non-existent flyaway, she turned and looked in one of the large, golden mirrors on the wall of the small sitting room. Turning from one side to the other, she checked that her gauzy white dress looked exactly as it had five minutes ago. The skirt billowed when she walked and dragged behind her. The loose, off the shoulder sleeves attached to the tight bodice, making it appear like she had curves when she absolutely did not. Her satin slippers whispered across the floor as she walked, and her hair fell in soft waves around her shoulders.

And on top of her head sat the flower crown Roman gave her last night, perfectly imperfect. And definitely not made by a child.

Satisfied, she nodded once and hooked her arm through her father's. "I'm ready."

Her father led her to the doors of the throne room, where her mother waited. The latter dabbed at her eyes for the thousandth time that day and kissed Violet's cheek. "You look beautiful."

"Thanks, Mom. You do too."

Her mother tittered out a stuffy laugh and handed her handkerchief to her husband. "I'm going to let them know you're ready."

She disappeared through the door, and Violet's dad held out her mother's used handkerchief, looking rightly disgruntled. "What am I supposed to do with this?"

Violet tried to not laugh and looked around. "Hide it under that bench and we'll get it later to throw away."

The older man tossed it under the bench, grumbling under his breath, and took Violet's arm again. Two guards opened the doors to the throne room from the inside and stepped aside.

No music played, no flowers or fabric hung from the ceiling, and no large crowd turned to stare at her when she stepped through the doors.

Only the council, Roman and Violet's families, and their closest friends stood in front of the dais, watching her walk toward them. It wasn't what she'd planned for her wedding as a girl. She'd been excited about the prospect of planning a beautiful ceremony with her mother and Sarah, but once the bond had snapped in place, she could tell waiting would eat Roman alive.

Violet's eyes met Roman's, and a blast of intense love burned through her. It took her breath away. He looked devastatingly handsome in his royal coat, the purple fabric contrasting beautifully with his skin tone.

Wait.

Violet halted and stared at Roman's coat, then at War, who looked pissed in a matching one. She'd made the beast a coat to match Roman's green one, but they both wore purple.

"What's wrong?" her father whispered, following her stare.

Realizing she'd stopped and feeling Roman's panic, she kissed her father on the cheek, dropped his arm, and walked as fast as she could toward her mate. Roman met her halfway, and she jumped into his arms, burying her face in his neck.

"I can't tell if you're upset or not," Roman murmured against her ear. "It feels like you're happy, but I'm going to be honest, seeing the woman you're supposed to marry stop in the middle of the aisle is worrisome."

He tried to joke but she could feel his nerves. "You're wearing my favorite color," she mumbled against his neck. "You're supposed to be wearing human grass green."

His chuckle and affection touched her both inside and out. "You said it was ugly," he reminded her, "and suggested I change our royal color to violet purple."

Popping her head back, she looked at him, trying to discern what he'd said. "You didn't."

"He did," his father, the former king, muttered from close by. "Had new banners made and everything. Cost a fortune."

"Shut up," Roman's mother hissed, hitting his arm playfully.

Or maybe not so playfully if his wince and smirk in her direction were anything to go by.

"That's absurd, Roman," Violet said, turning her attention back to her mate. "The Tropical Kingdom's royal color has been green since the beginning of time."

Roman shrugged. "The circumstances of our mating will be what the history books focus on, not the change in banner colors."

Violet kissed him and signaled for him to set her down. Walking to War, she kissed him on the head. "You look very handsome." He chuffed, looking fit to be tied, and begrudgingly licked her hand. *It appears someone didn't want to wear his new coat.*

Roman had done so much for her that she refused to deny him this. Standing in front of their loved ones, with no strangers other than the council, she appreciated the change.

It came time for the blood exchange, and Violet stared at the small dagger in her hand. "I don't think I can cut you."

To pass the royal fae powers from the royal heir to their mate, they sealed their marriage by wiping holy oil on a small part of each other's skin, nicking the oiled skin until it bled, and licking their partner's blood. *Gross.*

"I'll make the incisions," Roman replied and took the dagger. "You place the oil and do the licking." The way he said the last part made her squirm, and his satisfaction slid down the bond.

Glaring up at his smug smile, she closed her eyes and thought of everything they'd done the night before, working herself up. Popping her eyes open, she grinned deviously at her mate as he adjusted himself and promised retribution under his breath.

Roman leaned down, hovering his lips next to Violet's ear. "Where do you want to lick me, mate?"

"Our parents are here," she whispered with a warning

glare. Flicking her eyes to the dagger in his hand, she considered stabbing him with it.

He laughed loudly, much like he'd done their first day of class, and she couldn't help but laugh, too. "Your wrist," she decided and grabbed his non-dominant hand.

Amused disappointment trickled down the bond, and she couldn't help but tease him. "I'll lick you somewhere else later."

Apparently, she'd not whispered quietly enough, because Slayton groaned, "Come on, guys."

Violet's face heated, and Roman laughed even louder. *Jerk.* Dabbing a bit of holy oil on Roman's wrist, she watched him slice the delicate skin. The metallic taste of Roman's blood hit Violet's tongue, and she tried not to look repulsed. Why couldn't they just press their cuts together and trade blood that way?

Roman stepped into Violet's space, moved her hair to the side, and tilted her head sideways. The officiant dabbed a bit of oil on Roman's finger, and he ran a sensual trail down Violet's neck.

Everything happened in slow motion. Roman handing off the dagger and sinking his teeth into Violet's neck. She screamed and latched onto his shoulders, and the onlookers gasped in surprise. Roman's father was barking orders or scolding Roman, Violet couldn't be sure, all while Roman licked at the wound on her neck.

"What the hell is wrong with you?" she demanded, feeling his pride down the bond. Asking him questions did no good because his stare remained riveted on Violet's neck.

"I hope it scars," he said, finally looking at her.

She gaped at him. "You wanted to give me a scar?" *Where did that dagger go?*

He nodded and stared at the throbbing mark on her neck. "Everyone will know you're taken."

"Roman, everyone will know I'm the queen. Being taken is a given."

"Not if they're from another kingdom," he argued as if biting someone to permanently mark them was a sane thing to do. Another lick to her wound, more satisfaction down the bond, and a heated look thrown her way, made her pussy pulse.

What is wrong with me? She moved back and gestured to her neck. "What if it gets infected?"

The gleam in Roman's eye told Violet he'd already thought of that. Of course he had. "The holy oil heals the wounds quickly and keeps them from getting infected."

Griff stepped forward for a better look. "It looks like a rabid dog bit you."

"One did," Slayton added unhelpfully.

Roman scowled at him. "Who invited you? This is friends, family, and council only."

Violet huffed, grabbed his arm with the sleeve still rolled up, and sank her teeth into his flesh before she'd thought better of it. The taste of blood hit her tongue, and she jerked back. Holy hell, she was going insane.

Everyone stared at her in various stages of shock. Except Roman. The bastard stared at the bite mark on his arm like it held the secrets of the world.

A weird sensation coated Violet's skin and she held out her arms to examine them. As soon as it had started, it stopped, and she looked around. "Was that supposed to happen?"

"What?" Roman asked at the same time Felix said, "Yes."

"What?" Roman repeated, his voice rising.

"She now has royal magic," Sarah explained. "When a royal marries his mate, their magic increases to that of a royal."

Roman nodded in understanding. "I forgot." He grinned at Violet. "Congratulations, Your Grace."

Roman ignored the disapproving looks from his father and the council members. His father berated him for acting like an animal and biting Violet in front of everyone, and the council disapproved of his private coronation and wedding, insisting they'd involved the public.

They made good points. Some people would think they were lying about Violet being his bonded mate to appease the public, especially since word of Vivian's appearance during the rebel attack at the border had made its way through the Tropical Kingdom.

Vivian. The name alone made him want to destroy everything in his path. They'd yet to discover what brought her back. Roman wanted to kill her and be done, but his wife might not forgive him.

His mother's *familiar* still trailed her, and so far, she'd spoken to no one, but she watched Violet outside of the palace walls. Wherever Violet went, Vivian followed from a distance. In crowded places, Tilly couldn't follow, but if Roman wasn't at Violet's side, War was.

"We need to discuss Violet's coronation," Joffrey, one of Roman's councilmen said. "We've sent news to the post that a new queen will be crowned, but we didn't say who."

Roman swore he'd not let them ruin his wedding day with talks of politics, especially not at his wedding lunch, but if they were about to try to convince him to say Violet was Vivian, he would gladly spill blood. "Why didn't you put Violet's name?"

Joffrey cleared his throat. "Just a precaution for her safety," he answered. "And if there seems to be an uproar about it not being Vivian Maekin, then perhaps we could—"

"Enough," Roman bellowed. "I thought I made this clear, but it seems you need reminding." He pushed back his chair and stood to look down his nose at the men and women of the council. "I have already made it clear who the queen was to be. My warriors and guards know it, and by default, rumors have trickled through the kingdom." A council woman spoke, but Roman held up a hand. "I will not have my wife pretend to be someone she is not. Vivian has been selfish and undeserving of the crown since the day our bond snapped in place."

He glanced at his in-laws. "I would apologize for insulting your daughter, but it would be a lie. Violet is compassionate, kind, and great with people. Our kingdom is lucky to have her as their queen. Anyone who opposes her will be tried and convicted of treason."

He expected Violet to protest, to tell him to calm down and think rationally, but she did none of that. Instead, she looked up at him with hearts in her eyes, and her love and gratitude filtered down the bond. *"Thank you,"* she mouthed.

He stole a quick kiss and turned back to the table. "We will announce Violet Covington as my mate and wife, and every citizen will bow when my mother places the crown upon my mate's head. Understood?"

He met everyone's eye, demanding their agreement. When he met Slayton's, the man tipped his head, and Roman knew it was more than compliance. It was approval.

And dammit if that didn't mean something to him.

"Are you ready?" Roman asked, tugging on the blindfold.

After he'd scared the shit out of everyone in the dining

room, he'd blindfolded her, picked her up, and said he was giving her a wedding gift. The air grew heavy, and their voices echoed around them.

"Yes. I'm ready."

The blindfold fell away, and Violet stared slack-jawed at Marissa chained to the wall in the palace dungeon.

If you'd told Violet to guess what her gift would be, Marissa held prisoner would not have been in the top one million.

"You don't like it?" Roman asked, wrapping his arms around Violet from behind.

"I—what is this?"

"You get to decide her fate," the king replied, serving her a prisoner on a platter. "You can do whatever you'd like."

Violet turned quizzically to her husband. "What do you think I'll choose?" Because she truly didn't know what his threshold was. Imprisonment for another week? Working in the stables shoveling shit?

Roman shrugged. "Whatever you'd like, wife."

That got Marissa's attention. The chains rattled as she sat forward and tried to speak around the gag in her mouth.

Violet approached the cell bars and studied the other woman. "You didn't hear?" She pulled back her hair to expose the already healed bite on her neck. "Roman and I got married this morning."

Marissa spewed a litany of curses. Turning hate-filled eyes on Violet, she snarled something else.

"Remove her gag," Roman told a guard Violet hadn't seen.

"Don't," Violet countered. "Whatever she has to say isn't worth hearing." A bolt of lust shot down the mate bond, and she looked at Roman. "Really?"

He shrugged. "Turns me on."

Violet huffed out a laugh and rubbed at her breast bone.

"Feeling when you're horny might be a problem if you can't control yourself."

Marissa made a strangled sound, her face going from pissed to something else.

"Guess you haven't heard that we're also bonded mates."

Marissa sat back, stunned, and Violet smirked. Violet had never been cruel a day in her life, but seeing Marissa miserable and imprisoned gave her a sick satisfaction. Unfortunately, she still had a conscience. Sighing, she twisted to glance at Roman over her shoulder. "I think sitting in the dungeon taught her a lesson. Let her go."

Roman gave the guard a signal, and the man disappeared in the opposite direction. "I need to do something first," the king replied. The guard returned with some kind of iron rod in his hand and slipped into the open cell next to Marissa's.

The guard made all sorts of racket, and Violet couldn't resist poking her head into the enclosed area. The guard held the end of the iron in the beginnings of a fire. "What is that?" she asked Roman over her shoulder.

"Step back into the hall," her husband instructed. "I don't want you to get burned."

A sick feeling curdled in Violet's stomach. "Roman, you cannot burn Marissa. I won't allow it. She's a bitch, but I can't let you do this."

All the blood drained from Marissa's face. "I'm not burning Marissa," Roman grumbled. "Just wait."

The guard exited the cell holding the iron rod. The end had a flat scrolling piece of iron attached, and it glowed bright red. A branding iron.

Oh fuck. "Roman. Whatever you're about to do, don't."

Roman kissed her on top of the head and looked at Marissa. "Just so there's no confusion for you or any other women in the future."

Roman nodded to the guard and bared his neck. Violet watched in slow motion as the guard took the iron and rolled it across the side of Roman's neck. Roman made a sound like a wounded animal but stood still. The scent of burning skin filled Violet's nostrils, and even though it felt like a lifetime, the whole thing ended in seconds.

She covered her mouth to keep from screaming as she stared at her name branded into the side of Roman's neck. "What the hell is wrong with you?"

He took a calming breath, straightened his head, and met her bewildered gaze. "She said your name wasn't on me. Now it is."

"*You could have gotten a tattoo like a normal person,*" Violet shrieked.

"Tattoos can fade," he said simply, as if discussing the weather and not his melted skin.

To Marissa's credit, she didn't look traumatized. She looked annoyed. Violet motioned to the guard. "Can you take Marissa home?"

The guard nodded once. "Yes, Your Grace."

"Can we go home?" she asked Roman, eyeing his angry flesh. "I want to clean that before it gets infected."

"I've heard eating pussy is a great way to boost the healing process," he murmured and licked his bite mark.

She shivered and tried unsuccessfully to look vexed.

39

"HE MARRIED VIOLET?" Titus roared, praying Marissa had lied. "You had one fucking task, Riss. *ONE*. This is why father never trusted you."

Ice cold fury coated Titus. *Violet*. His sweet Violet, married to the fucking king.

"They're mates!" Marissa yelled back. "Not even the traced and forged letter worked. Violet didn't believe it for a second. I can't compete with the godsdamned mate bond."

Titus bent to his sister's level, seething. "I did. Do you think I wanted to court and fuck that incessant brat, Vivian?"

"He is obsessed with her," Marissa shot back. "If I thought you wouldn't kill me, I would have killed the bitch myself. I never stood a chance against her."

Titus heard the bitterness in his sister's voice. She'd fallen for the prince, but after what she'd said about Violet, he couldn't care less.

He grabbed her by the throat, cutting off her air. His sister slapped at his arm, to no avail. "Watch your fucking mouth," he snarled. "If you speak of her that way again, you will regret it."

He released her throat and retreated to the sounds of her falling to the ground, gasping for air.

From childhood, Titus and Marissa's father, head of the southern rebel faction, had trained Titus to take over for him one day, while their mother trained Marissa to be queen.

Rebels observed every female child born the same day as Roman Covington. The king and queen had kept his birth date a secret, but the southern faction had their ways of discovering information, unfortunately for the midwife sworn to secrecy. Once they discovered Roman's mate, another piece of intel their faction acquired before the public, Titus was to seduce and marry her, severing the mate bond.

The bond severance would create unrest among their people. Marissa was then to befriend and seduce the prince in his vulnerable state and marry him. She'd drug him to the point of compliance if necessary.

If at any time the opportunity arose to kill the prince, they'd take it, and Titus and the prince's mate would take the throne. The people would back them because mates were gods-blessed.

The shoddy plan had ample opportunities to fail, and the faction knew that, but no other strategy in their faction's, or any other faction's, history had succeeded.

Titus' father had observed the Maekin twins because of their close proximity to the royal family, and he'd taken Titus with him on many scouting missions.

From a young age, Titus knew he loved Violet. Watching her run through the forest in her pretty dresses, collecting things from the forest and sea, intrigued him. She possessed a freeing joy he'd never known.

Titus had often snuck out without his father to watch her,

and one day when the twins were ten and he was eleven, Vivian caught him. He'd feigned being lost, and she'd believed him. She'd also asked him questions about himself, and he'd fed her his cover story that his father had drilled into him for years.

She'd shown up at the smithy his father owned with obvious interest. His father instructed him to befriend her, giving him a natural in with the twins if needed. Titus kept his distance from Violet, observing her from afar, for he knew if the gods mated Roman to someone else, losing Violet would destroy him.

The day Vivian hit Violet with her sword, he'd broken his own rule, unable to see her hurt. Blue eyes, prettier than Vivian's somehow, met his, and he was lost.

The worst day of his life came after the prince's thirteenth birthday, sealing his fate with a girl he didn't want, and so began his relationship with Vivian Maekin. Vivian hated her sister, and in return, Titus grew to hate her.

After Vivian broke it off with him, his father suggested he date Violet to make Vivian jealous as a last-ditch effort. Titus both relished and dreaded the idea. He wanted Violet more than anything, but if their plan worked, he had to give her up.

He'd wanted to lay her down and make love to her every night, but if he'd allowed himself to have her completely, giving her up would've been impossible. The self-restraint he'd showed deserved an award. Never had he endured a more arduous task.

A year passed and he'd thought maybe, just maybe, Vivian wouldn't give in, and he'd get to keep Violet.

Their faction needed Vivian alive for their fallback plan of Titus taking over to work, but if Titus failed to break the bond, they'd kill her instead, giving Marissa a chance to ascend the throne alongside Roman.

Titus had asked his father once why they couldn't kill Roman and Vivian both.

His father sighed, patient as ever. "The zealots will cause less of a stir if we have one half of the mate bond on the throne. I'd rather you be king, but royals are next to impossible to kill. They're faster, stronger, and can glamour themselves invisible. The Mountain King's mother was the first royal killed by a rebel that we know of. A stroke of luck on their part. Your sister will have to do as queen instead, unless she fails."

Titus stared at his father, shaking his head. "If you know we can't kill the prince, why can't I kill Vivian now that we've broken the bond?"

His father grabbed his shoulder and squeezed. "Because, my boy, we'll never stop trying, and one day, we might succeed, and if we do, you'll be ready with that brat at your side."

Unbeknownst to Titus, Vivian had overheard their entire conversation. They'd kept her in the dark about who they were for a year. He knew she'd find out, but he'd hoped it would be after they achieved their goal.

In true Vivian fashion, she wasted no time confronting him. Tried to kill him, actually, but his skill outmatched hers by a landslide.

"Everyone adores Violet," Vivian spat. "Poor Violet can't defend herself. Sweet Violet always picking flowers with her head in the clouds. The gods chose me, yet everyone still thinks she's perfect. I saw the way boys watched her; how adults fawned over her like she was a precious gift, but not you." Her lip trembled, taking Titus by surprise. Never had the woman cried in the fifteen years he'd known her. "But it was all a fucking lie."

"You have no choice but to stay," Titus informed her. "You committed treason when you married me, and if you evade the crown, our faction will hunt you down to keep you quiet."

Always the strategist, Vivian countered, "What if I bring you

Violet? I'll tell her I threatened you somehow. We can work it out. She loves you. You can pass her off as me or tell the others I found out the plan and you killed me. I'll disappear."

Why would she rather leave than help them take the throne? She would no longer be considered a traitor by the crown if they defeated the royals. "Is being married to me that bad?"

Vivian's lip curled. "I refuse to stay with someone who wants her. I almost married a man just like you, pining after my sister like a love-sick fool. I won't do it. I'd rather fake my own death."

He couldn't force her to stay without chaining her in a cell. The idea appealed to him, but if the day came for them to take the throne, he'd need her cooperation. Looking into her hate-filled face, he knew she'd never be compliant.

"If you harm a hair on Violet's head, I will gut you myself."

Vivian looked fit to be tied, and he wondered if she would attack him again. "I'll deliver her to you safe and sound, and then you and your faction will leave me be."

The way she said faction, you'd think they were venomous snakes. Finding out your husband despised you and was a rebel in one day must be getting to her. She'd get over it.

"Fine, but if you try to renege on our deal, there isn't a place you can hide where we won't find you," he promised her.

He'd not seen her since.

Roman marrying Violet crumbled every plan they had. His father's back-up plan of uniting with the other Eden factions in an organized attack would fail spectacularly. Each faction had their own ideas of who should take the throne, some wanting to do away with the throne all together. Eliminating the royals would lead to civil war.

Titus had to find Violet and get her out of there because being Roman's mate put a target on her back, and he'd be damned if he let them touch her.

40

Instead of leading Violet to the bunker after the wedding festivities, Roman guided her toward the palace gates. "I have another wedding gift for you." *And for me*, he thought, his cock hardening.

She eyed him suspiciously. "Your last surprise was deranged. I don't think I can handle another."

He should have known Violet wouldn't want to torture someone, but she had been pissed enough at Marissa that he'd thought she'd make an exception. A misstep on his part.

"It's nothing like that," he promised. "You'll like this one."

Violet waved her hand for him to proceed. "Fine."

Guilt pricked his chest, but not from him. Stopping her, he snaked his arm around her waist and pulled her close. "What do you have to feel guilty about?"

Slight anxiety joined the guilt. "I didn't have time to get you anything as a wedding gift. I thought we were only celebrating our birthdays." Her lips twisted to the side. "How did you have time?"

"I'd planned on surprising you, regardless." He pecked her

on the forehead and steered them toward town. "This gift is also for me."

They approached the pleasure house, and Violet smiled excitedly. "You got us a room?"

Roman held the door open and ushered her inside. "Better." The large man who guarded the door bowed his head. "Your Grace. Everything is ready."

The man studiously avoided Violet. Smart man. Had he looked at Roman's wife, knowing what would soon happen, he'd have lost his ability to see. "Thank you, Rodney."

"I'll be outside. You can lock the door from the inside when I step out." The man exited quietly, and Roman lowered the lock.

The dim lights barely illuminating the red walls of the large pleasure house set an erotic scene, and Roman's cock tried to rip through his trousers.

Violet's eyes darted around the viewing room. "Where is everyone?"

Roman descended the stairs until he reached the front row. A pane of glass with holes in the top to allow sound through separated them from the stage. "I rented out the entire place for tonight."

His mate sat beside him on one of the plush couches, but he grabbed her hips and hauled her up to stand in front of him. "I thought you wanted me in a private box," she murmured. She'd worn a fitted bodice for their wedding with no breast band, and he could see her nipples straining against the fabric.

"The entire building is our private box tonight." Reaching up, he unlaced the front of her dress to reveal the gift underneath. Her breasts were heavy in his palms, the dark nipples eager to be seen. "Can I rip this?"

She slapped his hand away. "No. I want to keep it."

"Does that mean I get to see it on you again?" he asked. The thought of peeling this off her again and again seemed more appealing than ripping it from her beautiful body.

She smiled coyly. "I guess we'll see."

Roman shimmied the dress over her hips, spun her around, pulled down her underwear, and swatted her ass. "That smart mouth will get you in trouble, princess."

He soothed a hand over the red mark on her perfect-for-him ass. Violet glanced over her shoulder. "Good."

Seconds later, a man and a woman, both blindfolded, fumbled their way on stage until they reached the bed. "Why can't they see?" Violet mused and stepped closer to the glass.

Roman stood and undressed. "Because no one but me will see you like this."

He sat back down and grabbed her hips. "Have a seat, wife." Once seated firmly in his lap, Violet squirmed. The head of his cock wept. "This will be over before it starts if you don't sit still," he warned.

The woman on stage kissed down the man's body, her cunt on full display with her ass in the air. Roman averted his gaze to Violet. Watching her excited him more than watching the performers.

The peaks of Violet's nipples hardened further when Roman grazed them with his thumbs. "Is your cunt crying yet, wife?"

Glancing from the stage to him, she reached down, swiped her fingers across her pussy, and coated his lips with her sweetness. "I've been wet since we stepped inside."

Roman wrapped his tongue around her fingers, eager for a taste. "Lift up."

The shining dark flesh of her cunt taunted him, but he pressed his lips together to keep from shoving his tongue inside her. They would get to that later.

He leaned back and wrapped one hand around her hip and the other around his dick. "Seat yourself on my cock."

Looking between her legs, she eased down and paused when his swollen head rubbed against her entrance. "Prepare yourself," was her only warning before she impaled herself in one quick motion.

Roman jerked forward and grunted. "Fuck, princess, are you trying to kill me?" Violet giggled, and he moved her hair to nip at her neck. "Is that funny?"

"What's the matter, prince? Can't take it?" she taunted.

His lips brushed the side of her neck. "It's *King*."

The man on stage cried out, grabbing Violet and Roman's attention seconds before he jerked out of the woman's mouth and sprayed cum all over her face. Violet moaned and rocked her hips once. Roman hissed and covered both of her breasts with his hands.

"Do you want?" he asked low. "For me to shove my cock down your throat until I paint your face with my scent?" He pinched her nipples, and she jerked her hips again. "Or maybe you'd rather I coat your tits, so it smears between us when I fuck you."

"Rome," she breathed and circled her hips. If she moved any faster, he wouldn't last, so he ran his hands down her sides until he reached her waist to stop her.

"Don't move." One of his arms banded around her waist, and the other crept its way to her clit to rub light circles.

His mate whimpered and tried to move, but he held her steady. "I need to move," she protested with a curse.

Roman pinched her clit and she cried out. "You'll move when I allow it."

"Rub harder," she panted, straining against his arm, "and faster."

He continued the slow assault with the slightest pressure.

The bond allowed him to feel her pleasure building just enough to reach the edge, but not enough to tip her over. "Play with your nipples," he commanded.

"Godsdammit, faster," she pleaded, but he held fast.

The man on stage had the woman bent over with his head between her legs. As her moans and cries rose, Roman moved his fingers faster. "When she comes, you come."

Violet leaned her head back to rest on his shoulder. "You're trying to kill me."

The woman on stage's cries reached their peak, and Roman gave the queen what she wanted. With his free hand, he rocked her hips back and forth until she took over.

"Look how well you ride my dick." Her inner muscles pulsed around him, and he moved his free hand to her lower abdomen and pushed.

Violet screamed and bowed her back. The muscles in her body locked as liquid drenched his cock and thighs. This hadn't happened the other times they'd fucked. He moved his hand between them and ran it through her slick. "Fuck, baby, you soaked us both."

She sprang to her feet, and he hissed, his aching cock hating the loss of her. She assessed the wet spot on the cushion. "I don't know what happened."

He did. Slayton's brother had told him this could happen. Roman grinned and leaned forward to swipe his tongue up her thigh. "You squirted for me."

Using his hand to press her against the glass, he slid to his knees on the floor and hoisted one of her legs over his shoulder. "I want it again." His tongue ran across her swollen lips.

Violet bumped her head against the glass and moaned. "I don't think it's something I can do on command." Each husky word shot straight to his cock.

He hummed against her slick folds. "I don't care how you come, as long as it's somewhere on me."

The leg hooked over his shoulder tightened to bring him closer, and he chuckled against her. "That's my girl. Take what you want."

He fucked her with his tongue until her knee buckled beneath her and her orgasm shot through her. No squirting this time, but he didn't care. She tasted divine either way.

He stood and lowered his mouth to hers with a heated kiss. "Turn around and put your hands on the glass."

Violet spun around, pressed her hands to the glass, and slightly arched her back. "Like this?"

Roman groaned at the sight and slapped her ass. "Fuck yes." He slammed his cock into her pussy without warning and slapped a hand against the glass next to one of hers.

Violet yelled his name and braced herself to keep from hitting the glass. "Oh my gods."

His dick bottomed out with every thrust, needing to be as far inside her as possible. Curses and praise spilled from his lips, and he thought he might die from the pleasure.

"Roman," she begged, and he slid his hand from her hip to her clit.

His middle finger worked her clit, and his palm pressed on her lower stomach—a spot Slayton's brother swore made them come harder. "Bounce your ass against my dick, baby."

Their bodies slapped together, the performers on stage forgotten completely. Both emitted strangled sounds and moans every time he drove his cock into her slick cunt until she exploded around him, her walls milking his cock until his own release nearly brought him to his knees.

Separating from her left him cold, and he dragged her to the couch behind them until he sat down with her straddling his lap.

He threaded his fingers through her hair and brought her mouth to his and whispered, "Again."

The next morning, Violet and Roman walked hand-in-hand through downtown, glamoured invisible so as not to be bombarded by townspeople.

A commotion near the town square drew Violet's attention, and she tugged Roman along for a closer look. "What do you think is going on?" she asked.

The king looked proud, putting her on high alert. "Another surprise."

Violet stopped and turned to him fully. "What did you do?"

"Come and see." This time, he pulled her toward the open space, pushing his way through the crowd. Those he shouldered past jumped with bewilderment, wondering what invisible force had moved them.

There, in the middle of the crowd, Becks stood, chained to a wooden pole on a make-shift stage. "Roman," Violet gasped and hurried forward. "What have you done?"

Ares stood guard at the steps of the stage, smirking at the king and queen. Roman must have lifted their glamour because the crowd gasped and murmured. "Took you long enough," Ares drawled and held out a pair of shears to Roman, who in turn, handed them to Violet.

"She cut your hair shorter than you wanted on purpose." Roman's face darkened with every word. "You cried. I could not allow her to go unpunished."

Violet gaped at him. "So you chained her to a pole?" She held up the shears. "I'm not cutting off her body parts."

Roman snorted. "If I thought you would cut off her hands, I

would have requested something sharper. Those are for her hair."

Violet's horror ebbed, and she looked down at the shears. Did it make her a monster if she wanted to humiliate Becks for what she'd done? Afterall, it wasn't like the woman had chopped all of Violet's hair off.

No. She couldn't do that. It was too harsh.

However, everyone knew what Violet meant to Roman, who she would become once they married. Could she let the disrespect slide?

"It's too cruel," she whispered to her husband. "I can't."

Roman sighed and took the shears from her outstretched hand. He leaned down and kissed her lips. "I can."

Violet moved to stop him, but Ares blocked her path. "Let him do this. The townspeople need to know they cannot disrespect their queen. This is a mercy compared to what he wanted to do to her."

Violet stood next to the stage, and Roman addressed the crowd. "Violet Maekin is my true mate, making her your queen." Murmurs rose around them, some with disbelief, others with quiet outrage. "Let this be a lesson to anyone who thinks they can disrespect my wife." The noise grew louder.

Roman approached Becks. The woman pleaded and yanked on her chains, but he ignored her, motioning for Ares to hold her head still. Roman grabbed a piece of Beck's hair and cut it off at the scalp. Becks sobbed, begging him to stop, but he paid her no mind and lifted piece after piece. *Snip. Snip. Snip.*

Becks' hair looked choppy and uneven, some places hanging to her ears, others close to the scalp. Roman stepped back to admire his handy work. Satisfied, he revealed her to those present. "Were it up to me, her hair would still be intact, and her head would not; but your queen has a kind heart." Silence descended. Roman scanned the crowd, meeting everyone's gaze. "I do not, and you would do well to remember that."

Roman handed the shears to Ares, who passed them to Gunnar. The latter glanced at Violet with a satisfied smile and shot her a thumbs up. She couldn't help herself, she laughed.

Roman took her hand, kissing it. "Where to next, wife?"

Violet stared at him a moment before launching herself into his arms. "You're unethical and insane, but I love you."

His chuckle rumbled against her cheek. "I love you too."

41

Violet stood at the gate to the bunker with Dani, Kaylie, Khrista, and the rest of her staff. "Everyone remembers what to do?"

"You're sure he won't be mad, Your Grace?" one of the younger maids asked.

Violet waved her off. "Of course not. If he is, I'll handle him."

It'd been years since Violet had pulled off a prank, having left the childish antics in her youth, but the idea came to her as a passing thought that wouldn't go away. Roman wouldn't be upset; pulling pranks around the palace had been their thing, a secret only they knew.

She'd never pranked him before, but there was a first time for everything. With the threat of rebels and his new duties as king, Roman needed something fun.

War stood next to her, and she pointed at him. "Do not tell him." The tigon nodded, and she turned to the others. "Okay, everyone; to your places."

Roman nodded to Dani and Kaylie, who ignored him. His hand froze in his pocket. Never had either guard been rude to him before. "Is something wrong?"

The two women jumped, and Kaylie scanned the surrounding area. "Did you hear that?"

Dani nodded and peeked through the bars of the gate. "There's no one in the bunker courtyard. Maybe someone's conversation from the compound carried on the wind?"

Roman looked between the two. "I'm right here." He waved his hands in front of their faces.

"Shit," Kaylie hissed and drew her sword. "It's too close to have carried on the wind."

Dani nodded, drawing her sword, too. "*Show yourself*," she called out.

Had he glamoured himself? Focusing on making himself visible, he waved his arms again. "What is with you two?"

"Who are you?" Kaylie demanded, looking right through Roman.

"Are you to tell me you do not recognize your king?" he drawled.

Both women snapped to attention. "Forgive us, Your Grace. We did not realize it was you with your glamour."

Roman huffed. "I'm not glamoured."

The guards looked at one another. "We can't see you, Your Grace."

Dani stepped forward and reached out, yanking her hand back when it made contact with Roman's shoulder. "Your Grace, we cannot see you."

"What the fuck is going on?" Roman muttered to himself and pulled out his key to unlock the gate. "I'm going inside."

The women jerked and looked in his direction, having not

realized he'd moved. "Yes, Your Grace. We apologize for pulling our swords on you."

Locking the gate behind him, Roman stalked toward the house, throwing open the front door with a loud bang. "Roman?" Violet's sweet voice floated through the air. "Is that you?"

He rounded the corner to their sitting room and relaxed at the sight of his mate. A maid sat with her, holding a box of beads. "Hello, princess." The maid jumped with a squeak and looked around.

Not this again. "Khrista, can you see me?"

The woman searched the room. "N-no, Your Grace."

Violet looked directly at him and tilted her head to the side. "Why are you still glamoured?"

As a royal, she could see through royal glamour, but he wasn't glamouring himself. "I'm not," he all but growled with frustration. "Dani and Kaylie couldn't see me either."

Violet's brows drew together, and she set her sewing on the coffee table. "Then you must be glamoured." She twisted her lips to the side. "Do not play jokes on the staff. They might quit."

Roman threw his hands up. "I'm not!"

Standing slowly, Violet made her way to him. "Is something wrong with your magic?"

"Obviously," he snapped, then softened his voice. "Sorry. I'm not upset with you, but I don't understand what's happening."

"Call War. He's somewhere around the house."

"*Come to the sitting room,*" he said through the *familiar* bond. "*Something weird is happening.*"

"*On my way,*" the tigon replied immediately.

The beast trotted into the room. "*What's going on?*"

Roman waved his hand over his body. "Can you see me?"

War chuffed. "*As your* familiar, *I can see through your glamour.*"

"How do you know I'm glamoured?"

"Familiars *can see the shimmer of magic surrounding whatever royals' glamour.*"

Roman stabbed a hand through his hair. "What else can you do that I don't know about?" He shook his head. "It doesn't matter, because I'm not using my glamour right now."

War examined Roman from head to toe. "*Yes, you are.*"

"No. I'm. Not," Roman insisted through gritted teeth. "I think I would know if I'm using my own glamour."

War looked to Khrista, who seemed to understand his unspoken question. "I can't see him."

"*See,*" the beast shot down the bond. "*You should work on your humor. This isn't funny.*"

"I'm not glamoured!" Roman shouted.

Violet flicked him on the forehead. "Do not yell at them. It isn't our fault your magic is malfunctioning."

"Have you heard of a royal's magic doing this?" he asked War, who shook his head. "Fuck. Where is the rest of our staff?"

Violet crossed the room and pulled the bell pattern that called everyone to the sitting room. The others filed inside. "Is something wrong, Your Grace?" one of the men asked.

Violet pointed at Roman. "Can you see Roman?"

They turned their heads in the king's direction. Some shook their heads, others responded, "No."

"What the fuck?" Roman yelled again, making them jump. "Would everyone stop jumping every time I speak?"

"Our apologies, Your Grace," Khrista replied. "It's startling to hear your voice when we cannot see you."

Just then, Babs ran down the hall toward Roman, clucking up a storm. The hen wasn't a *familiar*, but if her skidding to a halt in front of him and flapping her wings was any indication, she saw him fine. He bent down and picked her up, tucking her into the crook of his arm.

"Babs can see me," he accused and lifted his gaze to the others, finding them all trying to contain their laughter.

"Who let Babs in?" Violet complained. "We had him going."

Roman kissed the top of Babs' head and set her down. "Is this a joke you've cooked up, dear wife?" Violet rolled her lips together to contain her smile. "You'll pay for that."

He made a grab at his mate. She squealed and took off running down the hall as the others laughed. Roman caught up to her with ease and scooped her into his arms. "Thought to trick me, did you?"

"We did trick you," she taunted with a bright smile to rival his own.

"I'm going to redden your ass for that." She squirmed in his arms to free herself, but he saw the desire in her eyes.

Inside their room, he kicked their door closed, sat on the bed, and turned her over across his lap. Lifting her skirt, he groaned at her bare ass. "No underwear?"

"Don't you dare spank me," she said with no heat.

His hand came down on her cheek with a loud slap. She yelped and struggled against his hold. "I'm sorry," she cried, but he heard the laughter in her voice. Bringing down his hand again, she tried to reach back, but he swatted her hand away. "I said I was sorry!"

Rubbing soothing circles over the red mark he left behind, he leaned down to her ear. "Show me how sorry you are."

He released her, and she scooted off the bed and to her knees before him. Reaching for the buttons of his pants, she made quick work of pulling out his aching cock. Without breaking eye contact, she scraped her nail across the small knot on the underside of his dick where the head met the shaft.

He hissed and jerked his hips. "Fuck, princess."

Grinning like a cat, she lowered her head and guided the head of his cock into her mouth, sucking on it like a hard candy. He moaned and shut his eyes. If he looked at her, he'd last all of five seconds.

Violet worked her tongue around him, licking the precum from his tip. His sounds were more animal than man, and he couldn't help but lift his hips. The wet heat around his dick disappeared and he opened his eyes.

His wife twisted her hair behind her head and tucked it into the collar of her dress. "It's in the way," she explained.

Leaning forward, he untucked her hair and twisted it around his fist. "Get back in place."

The flare of heat in her eyes encouraged him to guide her to his aching cock until he hit the back of her throat. She gagged. "That's my girl." Pulling back on her hair, he moaned at the feel of her lips dragging along his shaft. "I'm going to fuck your mouth. Don't forget to swallow."

Nodding, she lifted her gaze to his, and he was lost. He braced himself with one arm and moved her head with the other, thrusting his hips with every downward movement of her slick mouth.

Instead of gagging, she swallowed, taking him deeper with every thrust. Each stroke was pure ecstasy. His wife had the mouth of a goddess. "You're perfect," he grunted, moving her faster.

Tears leaked from the corners of her eyes and drool dribbled down her chin. Roman's balls tightened, and a shiver raced down his spine. Seconds later, he shot hot ropes of cum down his mate's throat, and like the good girl she was, she drank it all.

Their rhythm slowed, and when his cock softened, he withdrew from heaven and pulled her into his arms. "Apology accepted."

The next morning, Violet woke alone to the sound of Babs squawking outside of the bedroom door. Grumbling, she threw back the bedclothes and trudged to the door.

Throwing it open, she glared at Babs. The hen charged inside and flapped her wings at Violet's feet.

"It's a little early for you to be causing such a fuss." The hen pecked at her shin and Violet scooted back. "Bad chicken. That hurts." Babs ran forward and pecked her again but much softer. Violet snorted. "So, you do understand me."

Bending down, she scooped Babs into her arms. "What has you so wound up, pretty girl?"

Babs burrowed into Violet's chest. "You spoiled thing. I'm going to set you down." The hen bristled, and Violet tutted. "I have to get dressed."

Dressed and ready for the day, Violet carried Babs outside and let her loose in the courtyard. The hen trailed her to the gate, and Dani popped her head around to look through the gate. "It's pointless to put her in the coop," Violet explained. "She'll escape."

She unlocked the gate and Babs went nuts, running forward and flapping her wings. Violet closed the gate and looked down at the frantic hen. "What has gotten into you?" The hen clucked and ran in circles around her legs.

A growl sounded from outside the gate, and War stared at Babs. The latter charged the gate, sending the tigon scrambling backward. "Babs, stop teasing War. You can't come with us to the beach."

Babs flapped in protest, and Violet blew out a long breath. "Fine, but I'm putting you on a leash."

War snorted, and Dani whipped around. "Don't provoke her," she admonished the beast. The guards had a rapport with the tigon because he waited at the gate for Violet if he'd been out hunting and lazing around the jungle the night before.

Violet spun around and hurried toward the house. "I'll be right back."

42

"What do you mean she lost her?" Roman demanded.

His mother rubbed her forehead. "Tilly must eat. She stayed close, but somehow Vivian slipped away."

Roman slammed his fist down on his desk; a resounding crack splintered across the room.

"Do not throw a fit with me," Sarah scolded her son. "If you had brought her in from the start, we wouldn't be dealing with this now."

She was right, but had he brought her in, he couldn't have discovered her true intentions. He had a feeling Vivian had ties to the rebels, otherwise, she wouldn't have been there during the border attack.

If they'd captured her, they'd never know. Violet would never consent to the torture of her sister, and Roman refused to hide things from her.

"Send War out to find her," his father suggested. "He can track her."

"I'll not leave Violet unprotected, and I doubt she would willingly follow me around all day."

"Honey," his mother interjected. "Violet is a royal now. She can glamour herself invisible."

True, but he didn't like the idea of her being alone. "I'll skip our council meetings, and you can plan her coronation without me," he decided. "I'll stay with her and go wherever she wants."

His father's jaw hardened. "The council needs their king right now. Our spies think the rebel factions are working together. If they all attack at once, we need to be ready."

Roman rubbed his temples. *This is a fucking mess.* "She will *not* go unprotected until we find Vivian." Or ever.

Roman stepped out of the tree line onto the sandy shore. War sat not far away, watching Violet... and Babs? Violet squatted in the sand and dug out a shell with Babs happily at her side, a rope going from Violet's wrist to a make-shift harness wrapped around Babs' chest.

"*The hen is a nuisance,*" War grumbled down the bond. "*She should be at the palace farm with the rest of the vermin.*"

Roman chuckled. "You're big enough to eat her, yet she frightens you."

"*I cannot eat her because of you. She has free rein to attack me with no repercussions, and she knows it,*" the beast grumbled.

"*I need you to find Vivian,*" Roman communicated down the bond, not wanting Violet to overhear. She looked happy, and he'd not ruin that; he'd tell her tonight. "*She has slipped from Tilly's detail, and we need to find her.*"

"*I'll find her,*" War promised and disappeared into the trees.

Roman took off his socks and boots. "Need help?"

Violet twisted around and beamed at him. "I thought you were meeting with the council?"

Plopping down in the sand, he grabbed the bucket and held it out for her to drop her treasures in. "I left early to find you."

She leaned forward and kissed him. "I'll take any time with you I can. You've been busy lately."

"We think the rebel factions are working together to plan a large-scale attack." He hadn't wanted to ruin their time here, but neither did he want her to think he'd willingly stayed away during the day.

"Are they going to spread out and attack the entire kingdom at once or will they all attack the capital?" she mused and dropped another shell in the bucket.

"We don't know," he admitted. "We have to be ready for both."

She nodded and brushed sand from another shell. "What can I do to help?"

Roman's heart beat hard. "If there is an attack, stay in the bunker. It's the safest place."

"And leave everyone else out to dry?" she asked incredulously. "Tell those living in the warrior compound to bring the children to the bunker. I'll keep them inside with me."

His heart tried to jump from his chest to attach itself to hers. Gods, he loved her. "You are a great queen."

Pink stained her cheeks. "I am only doing what any other person would do."

They moved on to other things, talking and laughing the afternoon away while Babs demanded their attention.

He'd always wanted to be the one to hold her bucket.

And now he was.

Violet and Roman sat around their dining table with their friends before heading to the coronation festival downtown. The coronation wasn't for another two days, but they held a festival beforehand. Normally people travelled from all over the kingdom to attend, but with the last-minute change in plans, they didn't expect as big of a turnout this time.

However, the warriors and guards were on high alert, and Roman's parents were already at the festival to glamour the townspeople if needed.

A celebration provided a perfect target for a rebel attack on the capital, but it also made it easier for the royals to protect their people since they were all in one spot. War had been gone a lot recently, leaving Griff, Slayton, and Ares to stay with Violet, but he'd returned tonight in case they needed aid.

Violet thought the coronation would be a better target for the rebels, but the council wanted to take precautions with the festival too.

Dinner with friends helped them forget their woes, if only for an hour or two.

Violet laughed loudly. "I thought he would cry."

"It's not that funny," Roman muttered and sawed into his steak.

Violet tried not to laugh again, but she couldn't help it. "It really was."

Slayton pointed his fork at Violet. "Next time you decide to trick your husband, I want in on the action."

Roman reached across the table, snatched Slayton's fork, and pointed it at him. "Don't point a sharp object at my wife."

Slayton snorted and picked up his steak with his hands. "I'm more scared of her than you."

Roman muttered something under his breath and Slayton chuckled, tearing into his steak with his teeth.

War darted through the dining room, followed by Babs flapping after him.

Griff coughed and beat his chest. "Was that a chicken in a skirt?"

"Babs," Violet, Roman, and Slayton said in unison.

Ares smirked at Violet. "You sewed her an entire wardrobe, didn't you?"

"She loves it," Violet said defensively. "If she insists on coming with me, she needs pretty dresses."

"Do her leashes match her skirts?" Griff teased.

Violet sniffed and said primly, "Roman said she looks nice."

Slayton, Griff, and Ares slid their gazes to Roman. He stared back and set his silverware down. "I think the outfits are cute."

Seconds ticked by before the table erupted with laughter.

The street lamps burned bright around the town square to illuminate the carts and dancers giving life to the coronation festival. Violet held Roman's hand and marveled at the trans-formation. It was ten times grander than the small festival she and Roman had attended before she left to travel. A shudder ran through her at the tainted memory.

Roman squeezed her hand. "What's wrong?" He tapped his chest. "I can feel you."

"I was thinking how much better this is than the last festival we attended," she rasped.

Roman stopped them and gently grabbed her nape. "No one will hurt you again. Not only do you have the loyalty of every guard and warrior in this kingdom, but you also have the power of royal glamour. Assuming I don't kill them first."

Violet nodded. "I know, but that doesn't make the memory any better."

Kissing her forehead, he dropped his hand to the small of her back and led her onward. "We will make new memories."

They passed a food cart and the man at the front huffed. "What do you mean you can't serve mayonnaise?"

"The crown made it illegal to serve mayonnaise, sir. We don't have any." The poor vendor couldn't be any older than eighteen, and appeared scared to death of the ranting man.

Violet gasped and looked at Roman, who dutifully avoided her gaze. "Did you outlaw mayonnaise?"

His scratched his jaw and peered down at her. "That depends. If I say yes, would you be upset?"

She popped his arm lightly. "You can't outlaw something because I don't like it."

His lips quirked into a cocky smile, and she wanted to both kiss him and smack him at the same time. "Yes. I can."

"You're incorrigible," she muttered, but deep down, she loved it. Loved *him*.

Together they made their rounds and danced the night away, replacing the bad memories with the good.

43

Griff glared at Babs, who adorned a pink fluffy shirt with a matching bow attached to the top of her head. "Why did you bring the chicken?"

Violet smiled down at the hen strutting beside her as they walked through the thick jungle, thoroughly enjoying herself. "She gets upset if I leave her."

"And a chicken being upset matters why?" Griff asked, drawing out the last word. Babs pecked at his leg with an indignant flutter of her wings, and he moved quickly to Violet's other side.

Ares brought up the rear of their group and snorted at Babs' antics. "Can she understand you?"

"I like to think so." Violet looked pointedly at Griff. "She understood him insulting her."

Griff grumbled under his breath and whacked at a low-hanging branch. They'd ventured far into the jungle looking for a rare flower Violet had heard about. The petals bloomed out flat like a star, but what had piqued her interest was the color.

The entire flower, from root to petals, was bright pink. Most flowers and plants had a different color stem, but not this one.

"How much longer until you give up?" Griff griped. "It will be dark soon."

War appeared before them, halting their movement. "What are you doing here?" Violet asked the beast and then mentally kicked herself. She reworded her question so he could answer. "Have you been hunting?"

War nodded once, but he scanned the area around them. His quill sheaths raised, and Violet hurried toward him. "What's wrong?" *Dammit.* "Is something out here?"

The tigon contemplated for a moment before nodding again.

Ares appeared at Violet's side. "If something is out there, we need to leave. We'll find your plant later."

"Flower," Violet corrected on instinct while bending down to scoop Babs into her arms. "War, are you coming with us?" The tigon shook his head.

"Violet." Vivian stepped out from behind a tree.

Griff and Ares drew their swords, and War jumped in front of Violet with a warning growl.

Vivian held her hands up. "I'm not going to hurt her. I just need to speak with her."

"You two can speak once we're at the palace with Roman," Ares told her coldly. "Remove your weapons or I'll remove them for you."

Vivian's lips pressed into a thin line. "I'm not going to hurt her," she repeated and focused on Violet. "Vi, I just want to talk." She looked pointedly at the two men flanking Violet. "Alone."

Griff barked out a laugh. "You're fucking delusional if you think we'll let you anywhere near her."

Vivian's hands clenched at her sides. "She is a grown woman who can speak for herself."

"And Roman is a grown man who will separate your head from your body without hesitation for endangering his mate," Ares countered.

Vivian's eyes flared. "I'm his mate. She's nothing but his girlfriend."

Violet's shock quickly turned to anger. Babs, sensing her emotions, screeched loudly. "You lost that privilege when you married my ex-boyfriend," Violet spat. "On our twenty-fifth birthday, the gods bonded Roman and me, and hours later, we married. You should be on your fucking knees before me, begging for your life." Violet's venomous words surprised her, but she'd meant them. Violet didn't want her sister to die, but she'd not have this bitch thinking she had any claim to Roman. "Say what you need to say and leave before I let War rip your throat out."

Vivian's lip curled. "You can lie about being Roman's mate all you want, but the truth is, the gods chose *me*, not you." She moved her eyes from Violet to War and back again. "War is a *familiar*. He wouldn't hurt me unless I tried to kill an innocent."

War roared and lunged forward, snapping at Vivian. She screamed and stumbled backward.

Violet's arms tensed too tightly around Babs, and the hen pecked at her arm. Violet set the bird down and removed her leash. Straightening, she crossed her arms and stared at her sister. "Think what you want, but I am Roman's mate. You had your chance, and you threw it away." She stepped forward, her two guards moving with her. "Your hatred for me drove you to lose the best thing that ever happened to you, all because you couldn't stand my happiness."

"Titus was *mine*," Vivian ground out, clenching her teeth

hard enough to crack bone. "He said he loved *me*, and you stole him. Perfect little Violet, always needing someone to protect her. Always getting whatever she wants by playing the victim."

Violet reared back. "What are you talking about? You had everything, Viv. Dad spent all his time with you. The gods bonded you to Roman first. Boys fawned all over you. Titus fucking chose you over me. Stop looking for reasons to hate me that don't exist."

The bitterness in Vivian's laugh crawled across Violet's skin like a battalion of ants. "Playing the victim again. The gods may have bonded me to Roman, but it was you he wanted. Dad only trained me because he didn't want his daughter to be an embarrassment amongst his warriors. The boys chased me because Roman wouldn't let them have you." A tear rolled down Vivian's cheek, and Violet had the stupid urge to hug her. She hadn't thought her sister possessed the ability to cry. "And it was you Titus wanted all along. His father leads the southern rebel faction. I was a pawn, but you were his obsession."

Vivian couldn't have shocked Violet more if she'd grown a tail.

"Were you in the rebel camp?" Ares demanded as Griff said, "You need to come with us now."

"Viv," Violet began.

"Just shut up," Vivian snapped.

Violet drifted toward her sister, stopping next to War. "No. This is ridiculous. It's clear we both had misconceptions about the other." She shook her head sadly. "Even if what you said was true, how is that my fault? I never blamed you for anything, and all I wanted was for us to be how we used to be as kids." She swiped at her own tear. "We felt the same, but you unfairly twisted your feelings into hate."

"I don't hate you," Vivian corrected her, "and believe it or not, I'm trying to save you. If I wanted to hurt you, I would have done it at the border."

Griff moved between Violet and Vivian. "What do you mean save her?"

"You need to come to the southeastern forest," War practically shouted down the bond. *"I tracked Vivian to Violet and her guards. Something else is amiss, I can feel it."*

Roman knocked over his chair at the council table in his haste to leave.

His father stood as well, poised to fight. "What's happened?"

"I don't know," Roman said, throwing open the door. "Vivian approached Violet in the jungle, and War said something is wrong." He took out his key to the bunker and handed it to his mother. "Get those in the compound who can't fight to the bunker and send someone to alert the townspeople to find safety."

Throwing open the council chamber doors, Roman sprinted through the halls, across the courtyard, and into the dense trees, praying he reached his wife in time.

All the hours of studying and training Roman's father had forced him to do as a child served him well because he knew every inch of his kingdom like the back of his hand. Branches scraped against his exposed skin as he ran, but he didn't care. Nothing mattered more than getting to Violet.

Somewhere a woman yelled, and the closer he got, he realized the voice belonged to Vivian.

"What do you mean save her?" Griff demanded seconds before the world around them erupted in chaos.

The sounds of shouting and footsteps trampling the

brush surrounded them, and to Roman's horror, rebels, dozens of them, maybe more, burst into sight. *"Violet,"* he yelled. She ran toward him with terror written all over her face. "Use your glamour and run northeast toward the palace," he yelled to her, pointing toward the capital. "I'll find you."

His mate nodded and switched course. The rebels descended upon them, and glamouring himself, he ran to Ares and Griff, cloaking them too. "I glamoured you two. Find my parents and warn them." The two men spun around and crashed into one another. They couldn't see through the glamour. "Ares stay to the left and Griff stay to the right," Roman instructed.

Roman looked around for War. *"Meet us back at the palace."*

"We won't let them get to the capital," War promised. *"We're coming."*

Roman tried to make sense of the statement but failed. *"We?"*

Everything happened in slow motion. Fae beasts of every kind appeared behind the rebels with War leading the charge. The ferocious roars were deafening as they attacked the rebels, ripping them to shreds. The fighters never stood a chance.

Roman stared slack jawed at the blood bath and took off running to find Violet.

Vivian watched Roman call out to her sister. "Violet!" Violet ran toward him. "Use your glamour and run northeast toward the palace," he instructed, his voice betraying his worry. Vivian noted the direction and watched her sister flicker out of existence.

Dammit. Vivian stood off to the side, having been forgotten

by the king, and waited for him to turn away before she ran after her sister.

She strained to hear her sister's clumsy footsteps and loud breaths and slowed herself as she neared. Violet screamed and appeared on the ground; her head covered in blood. She must have tripped and hit her head.

Vivian dropped beside her sister and assessed the damage. The fighting behind them grew louder as the rebels closed in. "Can you stand?"

"I think so," her sister replied in a daze and grabbed Vivian's hand to stand. "Where's Roman?"

"I don't know, but we need to get to the palace where it's safe," Vivian said, throwing her prior plans of handing Violet over to Titus out the window.

Vivian wanted her rightful place on the throne that she'd allowed her jealousy and stupidity to throw away, but that dream died amongst the trees today. She hadn't believed Violet's claim of being Roman's bonded mate until Violet's glamour hid her from the other fae. The bond didn't make a royal love their mate, but Roman never needed a bond for that. He'd loved Violet since they were children, Vivian had seen it written on his face every day.

Nothing in this world would stop him from getting to Violet, not even death. Roman would send himself to the gods and claw his way back with Violet in his arms.

Jealousy stabbed at Vivian, but she shoved it down. It had done her no favors in the past, and it would do her no favors now. Her sister hadn't ruined her life. That crime belonged to her hatred for Violet, and it was time to let it go.

Vivian stood with Violet and steadied her wobbly steps until someone yanked her back by the hair and threw her to the ground. "What did you do to her?" Titus snarled at Vivian.

Violet gasped and stumbled, stealing Titus' attention, and

he lunged forward to catch her. "You're safe now," he cooed, gingerly touching the gash on Violet's head.

She tried to free herself from his hold. "Let me go." Violet shoved him to no avail. "You lost the right to touch me."

"It wasn't like that," Titus insisted and cradled one side of her face. Vivian almost laughed when Violet tried to bite him. "You're all I want, but it had to be her, but not anymore."

Violet struggled in his hold, his arm tightening around her. "You're a rebel and a liar and married to my sister! Had I known she loved you, I wouldn't have given you the time of day."

Vivian blinked at her sister. She wasn't oblivious to Violet's feelings for Roman when they were younger, nor did Violet's efforts to distance herself from the prince go unnoticed. Would she have turned away Titus too?

Vivian scrambled to her feet and yanked Titus back. "Unhand her, you asshole."

Titus whipped around and shoved Vivian. "You were supposed to bring her to me in exchange for your freedom, yet you tell me to release her?"

Violet gasped and the betrayal on her face hit Vivian in the chest. "I thought you would keep her safe, but not even you could save her now that she's bonded and married to the king."

"Step back," Titus growled at Violet and withdrew his sword. Fuck. He was a better fighter than Vivian, but she couldn't let him take her sister.

In her peripheral vision, Vivian watched Violet, waiting for her to move far enough from Titus that Vivian could stand between them and fight him off without hurting her sister.

"Put your sword away, Titus," she said with a steadiness she didn't feel. "You've lost her. Roman will never let her go.

He'll search for her until he finds you, and when he does, he'll gut you like the pig you are."

Titus sized her up and scoffed. "You're not worth the blood on my sword. Walk away now and I won't hurt you. Consider our deal done."

Violet crept far enough away and poised to run. Poor girl wouldn't make it three steps before Titus grabbed her again, and Vivian knew she had to make her move. One thing she had that Titus didn't was speed, and she darted between him and her sister. "Violet, *run!*"

Titus roared and charged forward, the metal of his sword colliding with her own. "I was going to let you go," he grunted and swung his sword, narrowly missing Vivian's arm.

"Fuck you," she sneered and sliced the side of his leg.

He cursed, but Violet's retreat caught his eye and he made to follow her. Vivian rammed him with the side of her shoulder. They both went sprawling to the ground, their swords hitting the earth beside them.

If she could reach the dagger in her boot, she could take him out.

But she'd never get the chance because Titus drew his first.

"Titus, help!" Violet screamed, not knowing what else to do. He snapped his gaze to hers, and she glamoured Vivian invisible, hating herself for not thinking of it sooner.

Vivian shoved Titus hard enough to roll out from under him. "You're glamoured, Viv, run," Violet cried, glamoured herself, and ran in her sister's direction.

Titus cursed and followed in their direction. "Violet don't do this," he pleaded. "I can keep you safe. You belong with me. I love you."

A condescending tsking sound followed his declaration, accompanied by Roman's deep voice. "I thought the men in this kingdom would have learned by now that loving my wife is as dangerous as harming her."

Violet stopped cold and twisted around in time to see Roman fist Titus' hair and rip his head from his body.

Violet thought she heard the faint sound of clucking before her world went black.

44

Roman lay under his and Violet's bed with his wife tucked safely in his arms. "I don't need to hide under here," she insisted with care, as if dealing with a feral beast. "I'm okay."

The day's events played in a loop in his head, fueling his scattered emotions. He could feel that Violet told the truth, her emotions twisted up but not overwhelming like his.

He'd lifted Violet's limp body off the ground and taken her to a healer. They'd cleaned up her head wound and waved something under her nose to wake her up. After they'd assured Roman at least ten times she'd be fine with plenty of rest, he'd carried her home and slipped them both under the bed.

"*Open the bedroom door,*" War rumbled.

"*How did you get inside the bunker?*"

"*Your mother let me in. Open the door.*" *A moment passed, then,* "*Let me in or I'll break in,*" the beast warned.

Roman sighed. "War's here. I need to let him in or he'll—" No sooner had the words left his mouth than the tigon barreled through the bedroom door, splintering the wood. "Break the door down."

War growled and padded across the room, and Violet laughed. The bed skirt ruffled, and War's paws and nose appeared under the edge of the bed.

"I need to see her," the beast insisted. *"You should have made the beds higher."*

Roman kissed Violet on the forehead. "If he doesn't see you in the next five seconds, he might rip the bed apart."

Violet giggled and scooted out from under the bed. By the time Roman had joined her, she had her arms wrapped around War's neck. "I'm okay." She pulled back and kissed his cheek. The tigon purred and nudged her cheek with his nose.

Never had Roman seen a creature jump higher than War did when Babs came racing into the room. The tigon abandoned Violet, bounding onto the bed with a biting growl. The vicious little hen waddled as fast as her stick legs could carry her into Roman's arms.

He picked her up and pet the top of her head, smiling as she burrowed into his chest.

Violet tilted her head back to stare up at War from her position on the floor. "Don't worry, big guy. I'll protect you."

"The only thing you're doing is climbing into bed," Roman interjected.

Violet used the bed to stand and pointed at him. "You're covered in blood, and I'm covered in dirt. We both need to bathe and eat before you tie me to this bed."

He lifted a brow and grinned as a pretty blush spread across her face.

"I'm leaving," War grumbled and jumped off the bed. He nudged Violet once more, then disappeared through the broken doorway.

Violet bid him goodbye and held out her arms for Babs. "You need to rest too. You've had enough excitement for the day." Roman had examined the hen for injuries earlier. Other than her ripped skirt and missing bow, she was fine. He trailed after Violet to Babs' coop and helped her lock the escape artist inside.

Roman held Violet's hand as they stepped into her parents' cottage in the warrior compound. Meri and Edgar sat on either side of Vivian on the settee in their front room, speaking about something Roman couldn't make out.

Roman's father, who led interrogations, had released Vivian earlier after gathering all the information she had on the rebels and their base. She'd claimed Titus had moved them to a remote village she'd never heard of on the southwestern side of the kingdom where his parents lived.

Unbeknownst to her, it wasn't a village at all, but a rebel camp with small cottages and a training ground. Everyone knew to keep quiet around her and had hidden anything identifying them as rebels.

For over a year they'd fooled her, and when Titus had started to pull away from her, she'd followed him to see if another woman held his affections. Instead, she'd overheard him with his father and confronted him.

She had no information on the other rebel factions, and the beasts War brought had left no survivors to ask, but it was safe to assume the beasts had taken out a large chunk of the rebels from different areas of the kingdom. They'd succeeded in coming together for an attack but hadn't counted on the beasts turning on them.

Roman's men would head out for the rebel compound tomorrow. With luck, Marissa would be there, too. At Violet's insistence, the woman had disappeared. Until they located her, they'd put a warrant out in every village in the kingdom.

Meri's tear-stained face raised to Roman and Violet. "Thank you," she whispered. "For sparing her. We know you were within your rights to execute her." Her throat bobbed.

Vivian's jaw flexed, her eyes downcast.

Roman tipped his head toward Violet. "Thank her. Had it been up to me, her head would be on a spike."

Everyone in the room stared at him, Meri crying out, and Violet gasping. "Stop that," his wife chided. "He's joking."

No, he wasn't, but he'd let her believe what she wished.

Edgar tracked Roman's movements across the room as he and Violet sat down. The general knew Roman well, having trained him since childhood. Roman recognized the man's knowing look.

Violet pulled her shoulders back and straightened her spine, looking every bit the queen she was. "We came to discuss Vivian's fate." Vivian stiffened, and her parents exchanged a look, but no one dared interrupt the queen. "You will leave the Tropical Kingdom indefinitely."

Vivian stared down her sister. Roman expected hatred or anger but found resignation.

"You may visit, but only with written consent. When you wish to visit, you will send in a written request. We will not deny you, Viv, but you will need permission so we can send you an escort."

Vivian remained silent, and Roman sensed his mate's trepidation. Having authority over people did not come easy to her yet.

"This is not to punish you, Viv," she said softly. "It is for your safety. Residents of a small village attacked me because they thought I was you."

Vivian shot to her feet. "What?"

Roman stood and moved in front of Violet. "Sit down."

Vivian glared at him and lowered herself into her seat. "I

wouldn't hurt her, I just—I didn't know." She swallowed and looked at Violet. "I'm sorry. For everything."

Roman sat down and snaked an arm around his wife's waist. Violet leaned into his side for comfort. "I know, and I wish things could have been different between us."

Vivian leaned back and rested her head against the back of the settee to stare at the ceiling. She whispered, "I wish the gods had bonded him to you first. What was the point?"

"The gods know what they're doing," Meri said with unwavering certainty. "Fate cannot be questioned or fought."

Vivian let out a hollow laugh. "That's easy for you to say. You weren't duped. Your heart wasn't shattered into a thousand pieces."

"I was," Violet snapped. "My heart was broken, but not only by Titus, by you, too." Roman fought the urge to wash her mouth out with soap for reminding him she'd once loved another. "Fate doesn't force you to act a certain way. That was your choice, and now you must deal with the consequences."

Silence.

Violet stood. "I would like to have dinner with you all before your departure," she informed her sister. "We are not close, and have not been for well over a decade, so I'll not pretend to be now. But I do love you, and I only wish you the best."

Vivian's eyes searched Violet's before she nodded slightly. "I love you, too."

War and Roman strolled leisurely behind Violet and Slayton as Roman dismally watched Slayton help the queen gather flowers. It should be him holding her basket, but she'd complained that she'd had no time with Slayton since her return.

"You cannot kill him," War informed him unhelpfully.

Roman glared at his *familiar.* "For now."

Violet and Slayton stopped to pick another bundle, and War plopped down on his hind quarters. *"Everyone knows you like the man. Why do you deny it?"*

Slayton sniffed a flower Violet held out for him and sneezed. Roman grinned. "Where's the fun in that?" He considered the tigon at his side. "The beasts from the forest, the ones who fought for us. How is that possible?"

War cocked his head to the side, piercing Roman with his unusual eyes. *"Why do you think the gods gave royals* familiars?"

Roman's brows drew together. "Companionship and protection."

War made a snorting sound, and Roman scowled. *"You think the gods sent us to be your friend?"* He had. *"We are protectors of the kingdoms, just as royals are. In times of need, we can connect with every animal in our kingdoms and call on them for help."*

Roman scratched his jaw. That couldn't be right. "Not every *familiar* is derived from the fae lands. The Mountain King has an owl."

If tigons could roll their eyes, War would have. *"The gods give every royal a* familiar *they need. For whatever reason, the Mountain King needed an owl. You needed me."*

"To protect Violet," Roman said more to himself than War. "Only a beast of your caliber could have saved her from the rebel attacks."

Roman swore War puffed out his chest. *"You are correct."*

"Why don't *familiars* tell the beasts not to attack normal people? And why didn't the rebels just glamour themselves and run?" Roman mused. He had a million questions.

"Animals are wild. We do not disrupt their nature unless abso-

lutely needed," War explained. *"When called upon to protect, they can see through their enemies' glamour."*

"Roman!" Violet shrieked. Had he not felt her excitement through the bond, he would have thought something bad happened and killed Slayton on reflex.

He and War started toward the other two. "What is it, princess?"

She waved a solid pink flower proudly in the air. "I found one."

He had no idea what she was talking about but smiled anyway. "It's beautiful." Slayton held out the basket, but Roman plucked the flower from his wife's hand. "I'll carry it."

45

A cold sweat marred Violet's forehead and she shook out her arms. "What if they throw things at me and boo me?"

"Then they will die," Roman said as if he hadn't threatened to murder people for a minor infraction.

She knew he wasn't joking, but said, "That's not funny," anyway.

The corner of his mouth tipped up. It was a game they played now—him threatening people and Violet pretending to not take him seriously. No casualties so far, but Violet stayed at the ready to intervene if things went sideways. She loved his protectiveness, but she also couldn't allow him to turn the kingdom against them.

Both of their parents met them at the bunker gate, and Sarah pulled Violet into a tight hug. "I remember our coronation day." She stepped away and Felix reached for his wife's hand.

"Believe it or not, this one almost puked," he said, smiling down at her.

Sarah glared at him, and he grinned wide. "I did not. Don't scare the girl."

Their familiar teasing loosened the knot in Violet's chest. *Every mate since the beginning of time went through this*, she reminded herself.

They were also bonded to their mate from the beginning. There were those in the kingdom who did not believe she and Roman were bonded mates, and they had no real way to prove it. Roman didn't care. Violet did. Slipping her arm through Roman's, she breathed out a calming breath. "I'm ready."

Everyone in the capital and many others from around the kingdom showed up for the coronation. The lore of Roman's first mate breaking his bond and him marrying the sister had spread to all corners of Eden. A situation like theirs had never happened before.

They'd not invited the royals from other kingdoms on such short notice, but word had spread throughout the Tropical Kingdom like wildfire. A dais stood tall in front of the palace; the courtyard packed to the brim. Violet stood at Roman's side in the middle of the platform with War sitting patiently on Violet's other side.

Sarah stood with her husband, amplifying cone in hand, and announced Violet for all to hear. In normal circumstances, the current king and queen crowned the new king and queen, but Sarah and Felix no longer ruled the kingdom, Roman did. Therefore, he'd be crowning his own queen.

He stepped forward and took the crown from his father's hands and turned to the crowd, refusing the amplifying cone. His booming voice carried far enough to count. "There is no better woman to be my soulmate, wife, and queen than Violet

Maekin Covington. I have known this since I was twelve years old." He paused to survey the crowd, daring them to object. "When the rebels attacked, it was Violet who insisted those who cannot fight be sheltered in our home. When the townspeople of a nearby village stood by while men beat my wife, it was she who insisted the children be led away. It was she who saved the life of two of the people responsible for her attack."

Cheers rippled through the crowd, and Violet's throat tightened with gratitude that was squashed by an angry shout. "*Marrying her is an abomination.*"

War growled, and Violet clutched at her chest as Roman's fury ripped through her—a feeling so strong, it stole her ability to speak. Regardless of her mate's white hot rage singeing Violet from the inside out, Roman's face remained impassive. Violet tried to soothe his anger through the bond, but nothing changed.

He clasped his hands behind his back and said diplomatically, "If anyone has grievances with the crowning of my wife, please bring them to the front and I will hear your reasoning."

Violet moved to the other side of the dais toward Sarah and Felix. "You have to do something."

Felix looked worried, but Sarah looked proud. "You don't understand," Violet insisted. "His emotions are scorching me from the inside out."

Sarah reached over and patted her arm. "Let him protect you in the only way he knows how."

Violet balked. "The only way he knows how is murder."

Sarah lifted a shoulder. "So be it."

"It's no use," Felix explained on a sigh. "They're just alike."

The blood drained from Violet's face at the realization no one would, or could, stop him. "Oh shit."

Only the objector and his friend pushed their way to the

front. Violet knew more people agreed with them, but they must not be suicidal.

Roman motioned for the men to stand on the dais. Once satisfied, he walked to Violet. "I need you to stand with War."

She glanced between Roman and the men. "You can't kill them."

Roman's lips quirked. "I'm not going to." He pressed a hand to his heart. "I promise." He'd never lied to her, but his rage still burned bright.

Pursing her lips, she moved back to the middle of the dais next to War. Roman might not kill the men, but he would hurt them, of that, she was sure.

The men looked around, one of them having the good sense to be nervous, while the other remained unaware that the unhinged king had lured him into a trap.

"If you have an issue with my wife being your queen, you will state your reasoning," Roman announced loud enough for everyone up front to hear.

The first man rambled about the sanctity of the mate bond, the dangers of diluting the royal bloodline, and how Roman should find his original mate and force her to marry him. With every word, Roman's internal inferno grew, as did War's growls, and Violet almost told the man to shut up to ease the ache in her chest.

"And you?" Roman asked the other man, who paled.

"I, uh, I agree," he stammered.

Roman smiled without warmth. "Please turn to my wife so that you may look her in the eye as you denounce her."

The first man spun around, and the sneer on his face had Violet stepping back. The other man turned but kept his eyes on the ground. Roman placed himself in front of the men and turned to address the audience. "Their complaints have been heard." He withdrew his sword. "And denied." Faster than

Violet could track, Roman cut the tendons above their knees in one fell swoop. They both cried out and crumpled to the ground with rivulets of blood running down their legs.

Violet screamed and covered her mouth. She'd known he would hurt them, yet it shocked her all the same. Searching the sea of faces around her, she spotted Slayton and called his name. "Fetch a healer. Hurry." Her friend saluted her with a wink and disappeared into the crowd.

Why does everyone act like Roman's actions aren't disturbing?

He grabbed both men by their collars and dragged them down the steps of the dais, throwing them to the ground.

The king re-ascended the steps, took the crown from his mother, and zeroed in on Violet. Closing the distance between them, he placed the crown on her head and projected his voice to the stunned crowd. "If you refuse to accept your queen, you will forever kneel before her."

His gaze held Violet hostage as he dropped to one knee and bowed his head. The crowd followed suit, lowering to the ground like a wave rolling toward the shore. Even War laid on his belly at her feet. Violet's heart nearly beat out of her chest, and when Roman lifted his head, that blasted organ jumped right into her throat.

He reached for her hand and pressed it to his chest. "I will spend the rest of my life on my knees for you, Your Grace."

Fighting against the stinging in her eyes and nose, she lowered herself to the ground. "And I, you, but I'm not calling you Your Grace."

Laughter burst out of him, and he yanked her into a deep kiss. She knew her love flowed down the bond to him, just as his filled every part of her.

A throat cleared behind them, jerking them from their little bubble. "It's time to present the people with their queen," Sarah said fondly and rejoined her husband.

Together, Roman and Violet stood and walked to the edge of the dais. Roman held up their joined hands and boomed, "Long live Queen Violet!"

The crowd erupted with cheers and clapping, and to Violet's surprise, she saw genuine happiness on the faces of their people.

"No one is to enter the throne room," Roman instructed the man and woman guarding the throne room doors. He dug into his pocket and pulled out balls of cotton. "And put these in your ears."

The guards hesitantly took the cotton from his open palm, dutifully stuck it in their ears, and promised to guard the doors with their lives.

"Was that really necessary?" Violet asked Roman once he'd closed the doors. "I don't think visiting the throne room requires an infantry on high alert. Why are we here anyway?"

Roman said nothing as he led her to their thrones. Two oversized high-back chairs made of solid gold with purple velvet cushions covering the back and seat. He positioned himself behind her and kissed her neck. "We need to bless our thrones."

She laughed and reached back to hook her hand around the back of his neck. "And how do we do that, *prince*?"

Smoothing his hand across her silky skin, he dipped one hand into the front of her dress and cupped her breast. "By coating them with the queen's cum."

Lust overcame her, and she covered his hand with hers and squeezed. "And yours."

He hummed against her neck and straightened, removing

his hands from her body. "My cum belongs inside of you, and nowhere else."

Violet hesitated because now that they were married, they needed an heir. "I need to tell you something." Roman froze and she twisted to look at him. "It's nothing bad," she rushed, "and I should have told you sooner, but I didn't think about it. I'm on a tonic to prevent pregnancy."

Roman's eyes danced, and he moved closer, pressing his hard cock against her. "Is that all?"

She chewed the inside of her cheek, trying to figure him out. "Well, yes. I know we have to have an heir, but I'm not ready for children yet, and I've been on it since I started dating Dom—"

"Do not say his fucking name, or I'll redden your ass," Roman warned in a growly voice that made her clit throb. "I've been on a tonic from the first time I thought about fucking you."

Violet's mouth popped open with surprise, and Roman slipped two fingers inside. She instinctually closed her lips and sucked. "I knew once I had you, I wouldn't want to share you for a very long time." Removing his fingers from her mouth, he used his other hand to gather her skirt while he slipped his fingers between her thighs. "You can stop taking yours. We're safe."

Violet took her skirt from him, held it at her waist, and lifted her leg to hike around his waist. He wrapped his free arm around her to hold her steady and continued to slowly run his slick fingers between her folds. He had a habit of teasing her with the lightest touches, and she both loved and hated it at the same time.

"Please," she begged, canting her hips forward.

Roman dipped his head to capture her lips and ghosted the tips of his fingers across her entrance. She reached between them and wrapped her hand around his arm, pushing it against her.

"Needy tonight, aren't we?" he teased, refusing to give her what she wanted. "You're not wet enough."

Bullshit. She bit into the tattooed flesh of his neck, careful to avoid his healing brand. For whatever reason, Roman loved biting, and she knew he would lose control if she marked him.

Roman groaned, and the ground disappeared from beneath her, his fingers plunging into her pussy. She threw her head back with a long moan and tried to press herself against his hand.

"You're impatient tonight, wife." He withdrew his fingers and set her on one of the thrones. "I need to teach you a lesson in patience."

He lowered to his knees in front of the throne and licked a line from her inner thigh to the juncture of her thighs, stopping just before her pussy.

She wrapped her thighs around his head to prevent him from pulling back. "Do not tease me."

His large hands wrapped around her thighs and pried them open. He nipped at the inside of her thigh, then leaned forward, running his warm tongue the length of her cunt. Violet clutched the arms of the throne.

The man teased her for an unnecessary amount of time, dipping his tongue in every valley, skimming over her sensitive skin with torturous care. He'd tease her clit with the lightest flicks of his tongue, and when she neared her climax, he'd lightly suck, stopping just short of her release.

"Roman, please," she begged, and the asshole smiled against her.

"Patience," he chided playfully. "Your cunt missed me and needs attention."

"We fucked this morning," Violet protested, moving her hips the best she could.

He pulled back and stuck out his bottom lip. "Are you saying she doesn't miss me?" He looked down and ran his thumb across her clit and sighed. "We can stop."

Violet grabbed a handful of Roman's hair and shoved his head back between her legs. "I will fucking kill you."

He laughed hard enough to tickle her pussy, and she squirmed at the feeling. Finally, he pushed his tongue into her entrance, fucking her with his mouth in earnest. Running a hot trail to her clit, he sucked it into his mouth and pushed two thick fingers inside her.

A violent orgasm ripped through her, seizing her muscles and forcing her back to arch. He didn't relent, and she thought she might, alternating between wanting him to keep going and needing him to stop. Too much. It was too much.

His movements slowed, and her body twitched, her legs still drawn up, until he finally released her. The shit-eating grin on his face said he knew the pleasurable pain he'd put her through.

Standing, he reached around her and tugged her skirt out from under her, hooked his hands under arms, and pushed her to the back of the throne in an upright position.

"What are you doing?"

He grasped her hips and dragged her forward, the soft velvet assaulting her too-sensitive skin. "Blessing the throne."

Violet climbed off the large chair and heated at the sight of the damp streak down the middle of the seat. "I thought you were kidding."

Roman moved her like a doll to stand in front of the other throne and slowly removed her dress. "One more to go."

"Isn't this your throne?" she asked with a coy smile.

He caressed her backside and squeezed. "It is. Think you can soak me again?"

She'd never admit it to him, but she'd asked her friends about squirting to see if she could do it again on command. Slayton had jumped up and asked if she wanted Roman to murder him. Apparently, sex talk with Slayton was off limits.

Griff wouldn't know, so she asked her two new friends, Dani and Kaylie. Kaylie was oddly obsessed with body fluids, especially cum and spit, and immediately launched into an explanation on squirting.

Nothing guaranteed Violet could do it again, but she'd try. A sharp sting yanked her from her thoughts. Roman chuckled and licked the new bite mark on her ass. "Get on your back."

Violet's nipples stood erect at his commanding tone, but instead of obeying, she flipped around and lifted her chin. "I want to be on top."

He dropped his shirt to the ground and stepped out of his pants. "I need you on bottom to get as much cum on my seat as possible."

"You're really serious about the cum seats," she mumbled. Pushing her hair behind her ear, she prayed her cheeks weren't blistering red. "It's easier to squirt if I'm on top."

Roman's movements ceased, even his breathing. The silence stretched on for too long, and Violet lost her nerve. "Never mind." She started to climb onto the throne, but a large hand stopped her.

Roman cleared his throat, his voice gravelly. "If you say shit like that, I'll come before I'm inside you."

She snapped her gaze to his. "You'd like that?"

Roman closed his eyes and groaned. "Baby, I want to coat every inch of my body with it." Moving her aside, he sat on the throne and lounged back. "Drop that pretty cunt on my cock and ride me like a good girl."

Once she'd positioned herself over his swollen head, she looked him in the eye and impaled herself to the hilt. Roman hissed and latched onto her hips. "Fuck."

As always, she gave herself a moment to adjust, then rolled her hips. She needed to hit her spot inside and her clit at the same time. It didn't take long to find her rhythm, and if she leaned back and pressed on her lower stomach, she hit them both.

Roman leaned forward and latched onto her neck, sucking hard enough to leave a bruise and whispering words of encouragement.

You're doing good, baby.

Just like that.

Fuck, you're perfect.

Ride me harder. Yeah, like that.

She rose higher and higher, her cunt pulsing tighter and tighter. Bearing down, she felt the release of fluid as she exploded and cried out. Roman took control, slamming her on his dick faster until he stood quickly and shouted her name, filling her completely.

He slowed his movements until she'd milked every last drop from his cock. "Damn, princess."

Violet giggled into his neck and lifted her head to kiss lips. "Why did you stand up?"

"Didn't want it to mix with yours on my seat." He turned toward the throne and unseated himself to place her on the ground. "Look what you did," he said with pride.

She flipped around and gaped at the huge wet spot darkening the purple cushion. Looking from one throne to the other, she noticed the consistency wasn't the same. "I don't think that's cum. It's too watery." She gasped and flipped around. "Oh my gods, did I pee all over you?"

Roman moved her out of the way, leaned down, and licked

the wet spot. "Nope, that's all you." He licked it again and straightened. "Tastes like you, not piss, but you're right, it's thinner."

"I can't believe you licked that." She wrinkled her nose. "How do you know what pee tastes like?"

Without answering her, he scooped up his pants and pulled them on. "We need to get home."

Violet looked around and picked up her dress. "Why? What's wrong?"

Tugging on his shirt, he shot her a devilish grin. "We need to bless every piece of furniture in our house."

EPILOGUE
TEN YEARS LATER

Babs strutted around Violet's feet, tangling the leash around her legs. The old girl was getting up in age, not moving as fast as she used to, and ornerier than ever. Today she wore a black and white skirt with a matching bow to match Roman's legendary mask, even though he no longer wore it.

"Can you untangle me?" Violet asked Slayton, who held a four-year-old little girl with fair, freckled skin, almost a spitting image of Violet's mother, save for her light brown eyes and sandy blonde hair.

Slayton handed Diana to Violet and worked on untangling Babs' leash. "Is Reyna coming?" Violet asked after Slayton's wife. They had no kids because Reyna claimed children derived straight from Orcus himself, and Slayton said Di was more than enough.

"She'll be here, but she's running late."

Reyna had become a close friend of Violet's after she and Slayton started seeing each other eight years ago. She was a hyper little thing with dark, hooded eyes, sleek black hair, and light brown skin. She practically bounced around everywhere and talked non-stop, the exact opposite of Slayton. She fit in with their group perfectly.

Ares and Griff stood not far behind with their wives. Violet wasn't as close with them as she was Reyna, but she still considered them friends.

"Is he nervous?" Amos, the Desert King, asked Violet from behind. He'd shown up that morning to surprise Roman for his big competition. Amos and Clover had visited the Tropical Kingdom a week after Violet's coronation and stayed a couple of weeks. In that time, Roman and Amos became close, often travelling to see the other a few times a year.

"I think so, but he won't admit it," Violet answered honestly and pointed at a young man of about twenty sitting a few rows in front of Roman. "That guy won the last three competitions, beating both Roman and Kelty. They hate him."

Amos moved to stand beside her and glared at the poor kid. "I could scare him."

Violet laughed. "Don't you dare." Diana reached for Amos, calling his name in her half-baked toddler speech, and his eyes twinkled as he scooped her into his arms. "How's Rose?" Violet asked. Rose was Amos and Clover's seven-year-old daughter.

"She has an attitude," he grumbled. "Like her mother."

Violet huffed out a laugh. "You're one to talk, *Brutal King*." Amos shrugged and bopped Diana on the nose.

"I'm not holding this chicken all day," Slayton said from Violet's other side. Babs pecked him on the leg, and he glared at her.

Reyna appeared next to him and held out her hand. "I'll take her, you big baby."

Slayton gladly passed the hen off and gave Reyna a quick kiss. "How was work?"

Reyna launched into an animated monologue about the

staff gossip she'd heard that week at the palace, where she worked as a healer.

The announcer lifted his amplifying cone and announced the beginning of the tournament, and a hush fell over the crowd. Since seeing Roman in his first competition a decade ago, Violet preferred to stand in front of the stands instead of the box with their parents.

She no longer had to glamour herself because the people who ran the competition insisted they give her and her guests her own area on the arena floor. At first Violet had refused because Roman wanted to be like every other contestant, but he insisted she accept the offer so he could see her better.

She'd agreed, and now the royals had two boxes; one at the top and one on the floor in front of the stands.

The announcer introduced each contestant, and of course when they announced Roman, everyone went crazy. He hated it, but what did he expect? He's their king, and they adored him. They're also terrified of him, and that might have had more to do with it, but Violet wouldn't tell him that.

War padded over to Violet, and Diana squealed, wiggling until Amos let her down so she could run to her best friend. From the moment Violet found out she was pregnant, War had refused to be apart from the baby longer than necessary.

Diana tried to hug the tigon's neck, but her little arms weren't near long enough. War laid down on his stomach until Diana climbed on his back, then stood.

"*Begin*," the announcer bellowed, his words ricocheting around the arena.

Violet's eyes ticked between Roman, Kelty, and the new kid. They'd not announced it, but this would be the king's last competition, and she knew winning meant a lot to him. He'd stayed up all hours of the night practicing over the last month.

"Go, Daddy!" Diana yelled and clapped her little hands.

The minutes passed and then it happened. Roman moved on to his last puzzle before anyone else, his elation and hope flowing freely down their bond.

"He's going to do it," Slayton whispered to himself, but Violet heard him. He knew how much this meant to Roman, too, and despite what Roman claimed, the two were like brothers. "Come on, Rome."

Diana tapped the top of War's head, and he lowered to the ground to let her off. Before Violet could stop her, she took off running toward Roman. Violet and War shot after her just as screams went up around the arena. Roman pumped his fists in the air with a victory yell and spun around toward his family.

His eyes brightened when he saw bouncing blonde curls hurdling toward him, and he ran full speed, snatching Diana into his arms mid run. Violet readied herself and wrapped her legs around him when he picked her up too, careful not to smoosh their daughter.

Diana covered her ears but smiled wide, showing her tiny teeth to her father. "Daddy won."

"That's right, tiger," he said, kissing her forehead. "Daddy won."

Please consider leaving a review on Amazon by scanning the QR code below! If not, I get it. Reviews are tedious.

Fae Kings of Eden (Interconnected Standalones)

Viciously Yours (Rennick & Amelia) January 2024
Obsessively Yours (Roman & Violet) April 2025
Tragically Yours (Dean & Fawn) September 2025
Brutally Yours (Amos & Clover) March 2026

OTHER WORKS BY JAMIE APPLEGATE HUNTER:

Vincula Realm (Duology)

The Umbra King (Rory & Caius part 1) September 2022
Aeternum (Rory & Caius part 2) March 2023

ABOUT THE AUTHOR

*"I do the bare minimum, but I don't do less than
that."*

-Garrett McNeill

LET'S CONNECT!

Scan the QR code below for links to my website, newsletter signup, social media, and more! Or visit beacons.ai/jamieapplegatehunter

ACKNOWLEDGMENTS

Thank you to everyone who supported me in my personal and professional life. I appreciate you more than you could ever know. Without you, this book would not be possible.

I am not going to name anyone because my goldfish brain will forget someone and then I will think about it for the rest of my life. I already have too many embarrassing moments to rehash. I don't need another.

CONTENT WARNINGS

Graphic violence and death, gore, morally black actions by a main character, stalking, voyeurism, sexually explicit scenes, and mature/obscene language, injured animals, war/battle scenes